The Healer's Magic

The Healer's Magic

BOOK 3 OF BEADS OF BONE

C.J. Hosack

Copyright © 2026 by C.J. Hosack

All rights reserved. No part of this publication may be reproduced, distributed or transmitted in any form or by any means, without prior written permission. No part of this publication may be used in any manner for the purpose of training artificial intelligence technologies to generate text, including without limitation, technologies capable of generating works in the same style or genre as the publication.

Space Wizard Science Fantasy
Raleigh, NC
www.spacewizardsciencefantasy.com

Publisher's Note: This is a work of fiction. Names, characters, places, and incidents are a product of the author's imagination. Locales and public names are sometimes used for atmospheric purposes. Any resemblance to actual people, living or dead, or to businesses, companies, events, institutions, or locales is completely coincidental.

Cover art by Katie Cordy
Editing by Courtney Brooks
Book Layout © 2015 BookDesignTemplates.com
"Gesta Praediana" by Lehonti A. Pérez Ovalle
Luc's Poem by Praedo's Scribe by Emily Gearheart Lim

The Healer's Magic/C.J. Hosack.— 1st ed.
ISBN 978-1-960247-54-4

Author's website: https://cjhosack.com/

To Cynthia and Robert
Thank you for welcoming me with open arms into your hearts

CONTENTS

Chapter One — 5
Chapter Two — 12
Chapter Three — 20
Chapter Four — 32
Chapter Five — 42
Chapter Six — 51
Chapter Seven — 55
Chapter Eight — 68
Chapter Nine — 73
Chapter Ten — 85
Chapter Eleven — 92
Chapter Twelve — 106
Chapter Thirteen — 115
Chapter Fourteen — 126
Chapter Fifteen — 136
Chapter Sixteen — 145
Chapter Seventeen — 153
Chapter Eighteen — 159
Chapter Nineteen — 167
Chapter Twenty — 177
Chapter Twenty-One — 187
Chapter Twenty-Two — 198
Chapter Twenty-Three — 211
Chapter Twenty-Four — 221
Chapter Twenty-Five — 232
Chapter Twenty-Six — 240
Chapter Twenty-Seven — 251
Chapter Twenty-Eight — 258
Chapter Twenty-Nine — 272
Chapter Thirty — 287
Chapter Thirty-One — 297
Chapter Thirty-Two — 304
Epilogue — 314
Appendix I: The Ancestral Houses — 330
Appendix II: Luc's Poem as recorded in *On the Legend of Luc, Praedo's Scribe* — 331
Appendix III: Gesta Praediana — 333

Chapter One

Follow these verses to where they shall end,
Where both our stories shall join and resign,
And may his old bones your strength now refine,
When the dragon rises to battle again.

Gesta Praediana—Luc's Epic Poem

Ryn looked up at the heavy wood door of the Library Curator's office. Clayr had sent a note late last night for Ryn to come before first bell. Clayr was Ryn's second mom growing up, it was normal to get notes from her, but this was an official summons sent in the middle of the night. Ryn took a deep breath.

She was sure it was about her supervisor, Sandy. She had caught Ryn searching birth records from the villages around the orphanage where the white-hair youth had left her.

Ryn lifted a shaking hand, knocked, then pressed the latch on the office door.

"Oh good. Come in and have a seat." Clayr set aside some documents she was reading and indicated the chair in front of her enormous desk.

Ryn sat, back straight, feet crossed under the seat, the tip of her toes touching the floor. She clasped her hands, running her thumb over her white knuckles.

Clayr pulled a book from her drawer. It was Ryn's orphanage book. The record Ryn had returned to the Library, having finally found the correct orphanage to which it belonged. Unfortunately, it hadn't brought her any closer to finding her birth parents. At least she was able to return it to Walt, the Master Restorer, with the book's correct provenance, and it was properly referenced in the Library for someone else to use.

"I've been looking over this orphanage book. The work you did to restore it is quite impressive," Clayr said.

Ryn's heart lifted.

"Yll told me how much leg work went into tracking it down. I must say, this was quite the task you took on, and you performed beautifully."

Ryn blushed, relieved she wasn't in trouble. "Thank you."

"I was wondering if you would like to take your mother's job while she's away. It can be quite lucrative. The more documents you track down and bring in, the better the pay. It would be a promotion for you. Greater than normal for someone your age." Clayr leaned forward, hands folded on her desk.

Ryn's heart sank. Taking her mother's job of document collection meant she would work for the Library, but would be on the road most of the time, away from the Library. She had lost count with the number of times the powers that be had tried to take her out of the Library. She fought hard to stay. Maybe life was telling her there was someplace else she needed to be. She shook her head at the thought.

"That's very kind that you think I can handle Mother's job, but I really don't want to be away from the Library. Not now," Ryn said.

It had been a difficult couple of moons since the Winter Solstice Ball. Her mother Ryette, her uncle Mik, and Zo's father, Lar, still hadn't returned from chasing that Zmej man who had tried to destroy the tree that was at the heart of the Library. Ryn and her stepbrother to be, Zo, had almost been roasted by Zmej's strange blue fire magic. Then there was the trip to the orphanage, which brought her tantalizingly closer to finding her birth family, but had revealed there was something wrong with Zo's Healing magic. Ryn was worried about him. These days he was always pale, with a distant look in his eyes, like his mind wasn't completely present. She would walk with him to the physician's office, or have meals with him in the mess hall at the Library, but he didn't say much. Iden, Zo's boyfriend, was concerned as well. Ryn did not want to leave Zo. She felt helpless to do anything, but she wanted to be there for him.

Clayr frowned, running her hand across the tree calf binding of the orphanage book.

"I know you have grown a special bond with the Library, but I think you would do well in materials collection."

Ryn folded her arms across her chest. "I'm quite happy with my assistant researcher position." Every birth record from the peninsula was one step closer to finding her record.

Clayr's eyes drifted out the window where the sun was shining on the damp Library grounds, making the grass a vibrant green. She sighed.

"I'll be truthful with you Ryn, Sandy has been in my office daily complaining about you. I would move you to another supervisor, but the leadership is fracturing—dividing into camps. I'm sure you've noticed."

Ryn nodded. She just wanted to crawl under a rock somewhere. There was more than the usual whispering and huddling in small groups. Yesterday Ryn approached a docent about a missing reference book, and the docent backed away, making some excuse about her supervisor needing her help. What happened with the Heart Tree was the talk of the Library. Some people didn't believe it happened. Some people whispered she needed to see a mind Healer—just loud enough for her to overhear. Library Regent Jeris, and by extension his daughter Prym, who had always hated Ryn, blamed Ryn for the decision not to move the Library to the new facility on Viatoro—the ancestral island of Travel magic island. The revelation that the Library materials and the Library building had become entangled over the years infuriated Jeris. All of the Board members and Library workers who had backed the move were sulky at best, but generally downright rude to Ryn.

Her gaze took in Clayr's office, landing on a book on the bookcase which was actually a box Ryn had opened with one of Clayr's keys on her keyring. She remembered the necklace that had a glass pendant with a red liquid inside. Clayr's desk was full of all sorts of hidden drawers and mysteries. On the opposite wall was the painting of Waatch before the Library was built, which had a cupboard behind it. Ryn's eyes drifted out over the Library grounds. There was so much she knew about the Library, and so much that was still a mystery.

"So, you're telling me I have to leave," Ryn responded at last.

Clayr rubbed her forehead. "The Library has a contract with you. You haven't broken it, in fact your service to the Library has been above and beyond expectation. I personally appealed to the Board to give you a commendation for your bravery, and for saving the Library."

"But the Ancestor descendants don't see it that way," Ryn said it for her.

Clayr stood and paced to the windows. "It's not just you. Even though we found the saboteur and saved the Library, the Board is still not pleased with my performance."

Ryn swallowed. If the Library Board of Regents made a unanimous vote of no confidence in Clayr, the one advocate for Ordinary, non-magic workers in the Library, they could all lose their jobs.

"It's not fair. We found Zmej. We fought him and the wolves. We saved the Library." Ryn's voice surprised her. The whine in it sounded like when she was five and throwing a tantrum.

Clayr heaved a huge sigh, then returned to her desk, pulling out a piece of paper. "If you won't take the promotion to document collector, I have only one other option, and it is a demotion."

Clayr pushed the paper across the desk to Ryn, who picked it up, heart racing and hands trembling. She didn't want to give up her tenuous hold on her assistant researcher position.

The paper read: *Docent scribe for...*

"Docent?" Ryn's voice was flat as she tried to keep it even and not dip into tears.

Clayr picked up her pen, twisting it in her hands. "The position is a demotion, but it will get you out of the sight of the majority of the Library workers. It's a scribe position for a special project, in a secure section of the Library that has its own entrance. I'm afraid you're going to have to either accept the document collector position or the docent scribe position, or I will be forced to release you from your contract with the Library."

Ryn fought the tears. She couldn't believe what she was hearing. Either she left the Library or hid in the Library, or she would be cut off. None of it was appealing. She considered the document collector job. It had been thrilling to hunt down the providence of the orphanage book. Her gaze drifted out the window to the Boiler building where Zo worked. She couldn't leave. She didn't want to leave. The memory of the touch of the bark of the tree at the heart of the Library came strong to her mind. Exploring another hidden part of the Library was intriguing.

"I'll take the docent position." Ryn's head bowed, as she tried to hide the tear that escaped the corner of her eye.

Clayr came around her desk and put her arms around Ryn's shoulders. "I'm sorry. This is not how a hero of the Library should be treated. Once your mother returns, and I can get the Board of Regents off my back, I will make sure you get that real promotion you deserve."

Ryn nodded.

"The instructions for where to report are on that paper. You can start today, or tomorrow if you'd like a day to adjust, but I can tell you that they're in desperate need of your help, so if you decide to go today, it would be much appreciated."

Ryn held the paper up, but the writing was blurry because of her tears. Despite how connected she felt she wondered why she kept fighting to stay with the Library. After all she'd done, in the end it was an Ancestor-run institution. Her encounter with the Bead Ceremony at House Viator made her fear she wasn't of Ancestor blood. Clayr was head of the Library now, but how long would that last? The day was sure to come when Ordinaries would be kicked out of the Library. Ryn was sure of it.

"Before you go, I have news of your mother. She sent a letter..." Clayr rounded her desk, pulled out a stack of papers from a drawer, and shuffled through them. "Here it is."

Clayr handed a page of a letter to Ryn. It was clearly missing the back page, but one glance at Clayr's face told Ryn not to ask about it. It read:

> *Dearest Clayr,*
> *We've chased Zmej across nearly every island and still can't figure out exactly what he is up to. He is clearly preparing for something. I wish I had paid more attention to him as I was growing up. Maybe I'd have a better idea of his plan. Everywhere we go the Ancestral House leadership seems to respect and take counsel from him. I don't like it. I have evidence that Zmej is the one who seeded the feud between House Pentral and House Viator. I think he may have had a hand in whatever happened to my father.*
> *Our last stop was to Viatoro. My mother got a message to Mik that Zmej had requested a meeting with her. We hoped to trap him there, but the meeting looked to be a set up to get to me. Unfortunately, during the confrontation Moult's location was disclosed. We are on our way...*

That's where the page ended.

"What?" Ryn flipped the letter over to make sure she hadn't missed something. "Where's the rest? Is Mother on her way to see Dad?"

Clayr opened her mouth to respond when the door to her office burst open.

Errol, captain of the Library guard strode in, out of breath. Sudden movement outside Clayr's office window drew Ryn's attention. Guards were running to and from the guard house.

"What's happened?" Clayr demanded.

"We found Assistant Researcher Tammy's body at the bottom of the front steps."

Ryn and Clayr both gasped. The day of Prym's debut party came back to Ryn's mind. Tammy had used her illusion magic to scare Ryn and make her fall in the dirt. She had been one of those whispering rumors about Ryn in the Library. Ryn didn't like her, but she didn't wish her dead.

Ryn swallowed a Zo-like swear word.

Prym ran into the office, tugging on Errol's arm. "Help! You've got to help her."

Chapter Two

Follow the call of the owl at night,
To a secret passage where ye will find light.

This passage is attributed to Luc in On The Legend of Luc, Praedo's Scribe. Given that it comes to us through a secondary source, I am not sure of its validity. The voice is certainly different from Gesta Praediana. Still, it is an old source and not to be discounted.

- From the journals of Moult de Dico

Zo entered his dorm room ready to collapse into bed. He had picked up extra Library temperature taking shifts. Nix was still unable to find someone to do second shift, so Zo was working back-to-back shifts. The extra work took the place of his Healing lessons, which he could no longer perform. He'd avoided the Waatch Healing house ever since he had killed the wolf with his Healing magic.

Zo's fingers went to his bead necklace. There was only one bead there, his fire magic. The Healing bead had crumbled and disappeared some days after he killed the wolf. The good news was, that old hag Madame Sano, his ghostly Ancestor teacher, was gone. The bad news—so was his Healing magic. He had seen the looks Iden had given him when Zo had his shirt off. Iden knew something was wrong. When Ryn got hit by the wagon outside the orphanage he wasn't able to heal her, so she knew. He suspected Wilmar knew something. Wilmar always knew when something was off. That ability was why Wilmar was a great physician. No one else knew. Zo worked hard to keep his inability to Heal secret. He hadn't even told his brother Regg. Zo couldn't believe that his Healing magic was gone. Part of him held out hope that there was a way to fix it. Maybe there was some hidden magic out there that could reverse the damage.

Jinx, his adolescent kitten, was curled up in the middle of Zo's bed. He picked up the cat, then crawled into bed, curling himself around Jinx, who squirmed until Zo let him go. Shaking its head, it proceeded to walk across Zo's face to settle on the other side of the bed.

"And good morning to you too," he said, as he drifted off to sleep.

* * *

Zo walked the familiar path between Wilmar's—the Waatch physician's—office, and the Library. It was late, and dark. Rain blotted out any light from the sky, and most of the street's windows were dark. He passed the homes of those who worked for the Library, or who worked to support the Library. They showed the workers were fairly well-off, clean, neat—with spring flowers growing in the gardens. Tonight, all was shadowed in the darkness, a darkness that reflected his mood.

He turned the corner and bumped into someone on the street.

"Sorry." Zo said.

The person turned and glared at him. Recognition spread across Jett's face as he turned up his collar and hurried away.

Zo shook his head and continued on. A shadow was following him, he could feel its presence hanging behind him, just out of reach. It was similar to when the Protector of the Library had first followed him and Ryn in the underbelly of the Library. Now Zo wondered if Jett had felt the shadow too.

A mouse ran out from a crack in a building. It stopped in front of him and stared into his eyes, panting as if it was being chased. The looming shadow from behind pressed down on Zo. He scooped up the mouse.

"Do it," a dark voice whispered in his ear.

Zo reached out a finger. The mouse's eyes glowed red, its grin turned malicious as the mouse began to grow. Zo jerked his hand out from under the mouse. It didn't drop far—it was nearly as big as he was now. Dodging to the side, Zo ran across the street and then took off toward the Library. There would be guards there, people who could help, a place to hide. The shadow pressed down on him as the mouse continued to grow large enough to tower over the homes. The mouse was gaining on him. One step for the giant mouse was several for Zo.

The shadow slid in front of him. He pulled up short.

"Naughty. You should have killed it." The formless dark shade shook its finger at him.

The mouse screeched. It was a mousy squeak, amplified to echo through the caverns of the street. A mouse hand knocked him over, long teeth went for his neck...

Zo fell backward. His fall seemed to go on for too long. He found himself on his bed, sweat dripping down his back, he threw off the covers. The kitten Jinx's tail smacked him in the face. He pushed the tail aside and sat up. His childhood cat, Beardslee, was sitting next to his bowl looking at Zo expectantly. Zo crossed to the cupboard, pulling the door open.

"Sorry Beards, the crock is empty. I'll go see if Norm has any."

Zo opened his door, but the cold spring air on his sweaty shirt made him shiver. He pulled on his coat and stepped outside. Hunched over, he crossed the Library grounds on his way to the guard house. A bluebird sang in the budding cherry tree next to the walkway. Dark clouds passed overhead briefly muting the bright spring colors that had begun to appear. A girl walked along the sidewalk beside him. He recognized her. She was the Library worker he had met at that abominable party for Prym. The one who had been all decked out in yellow bows and had flirted with Iden. She had knocked Ryn off her feet with her magic. Recently, he had caught her making fun of Ryn's experience defending the Library from Zmej. Zo's heart raced and his blood pounded in his ears. She was dressed in researcher black, but all Zo saw was that yellow bow nightmare she had worn when he first met her.

She glanced at him, her face turning pale. Her steps quickened as she hurried past him, but he was quicker. He reached out and grabbed her arm. Rage flowed from his heart out into her body. It dove straight for her heart, exploding it into hundreds of tiny pieces...

* * *

Zo jerked awake at the sound of feet pounding on the cobblestone outside and voices shouting. The room was spinning, and his limbs were heavy. His mouth was dry, and he worked moisture back into it. He felt terrible, like he was ill. He swayed as he sat up, then stumbled to a water pitcher and poured himself a glass. The water helped a little, but he was still disoriented. The cats both lay on the table staring at him. He grimaced and drank another glass.

Someone pounded on his door.

Zo stumbled over and opened it to a panting and pale Fergus, a friend and Library guard. Zo squinted at him in the light of the day.

"Zo, Master Nix is calling for you. An assistant researcher has been found collapsed on Library grounds. Nix wants you to come examine her. You're closer than Wilmar."

Zo's head spun. The dreams he just woke from flashed through his mind.

"Who was it?" Zo whispered.

Fergus rubbed his forehead. "I don't know her name. She's one of those girls always hanging out with Prym."

Zo's legs became limp as seaweed. He grabbed the doorframe as they tried to buckle beneath him. It had been a dream. He had only dreamt that Tammy was killed. Right?

Fergus reached out and grabbed Zo's arm. "You alright?" he asked, brow furrowed.

Zo rested his forehead on the coolness of the frame. After taking a few long, deep breaths, he straightened, nodding.

The look of concern on Fergus's face irritated Zo. He used that irritation to propel him out the door and toward the Library.

As they walked, Fergus hovered over Zo like he thought he might collapse at any moment. Zo had seen himself in the mirror lately, but had tried to ignore what was there—pale skin, sunken eyes, with dark circles around them. Everyone's face lately looked like Fergus' did right now. Zo hated it. They all asked if he was feeling well. Wilmar had insisted on checking him over from head to foot, but he couldn't find anything wrong. That was because Zo was slowly being eaten away inside by the horror that he had killed a living thing with his Healing magic. A wolf, a mythological creature that apparently wasn't so mythical. Now his Healing magic was gone.

The walk across the Library grounds began to feel like he'd done it before. The same bluebird sang in the cherry tree. He couldn't shake the sense.

When they got to the steps to the Library main entrance, Errol, captain of the Library guard, was there along with Library guards Norm, Ed, and Bart, who was keeping a group of Library workers at the top of the stairs. Nix was talking with Errol. Nix's face was red. Not from the heat of the Boiler Room this time, but from anger. Zo knew that look. It meant Nix had been arguing with someone. Nix turned in time to see Zo and Fergus approach.

"There you are! Will you check this poor young lady? We need to know what happened. If it's some kind of plague we need to alert the Waatch authorities immediately," Nix said.

Zo looked down at Tammy on the ground. He knew she wasn't ill, or injured. This was the exact spot he saw in his dream. Was it a dream? Could he have been here and done this?

He knelt beside her and examined her body. Zo reached out his hand and put it on her throat. It was still warm, but cooling. There was no pulse.

"She's dead." Zo choked on the word.

"Did she fall and hit her head?" Fergus asked.

Zo lifted her head, then made a show of searching for an injury he knew he wouldn't find. She had been killed by magic—and he was terrified he'd done it.

Zo frowned. "No sign of injury, or disease," Zo said in a shakier voice than he wished.

Nix put his large, warm hand on Zo's shoulder. His eyes held Zo's, like he was trying to see into Zo's mind. Zo swallowed. He had worked really hard to hide the absence of his Healing magic, but Nix was hard to hide from.

Nix nodded. "That's fine, son. You don't look well. You go get some more rest, we'll take care of things here."

Zo nodded and stood, but instead of returning to his dorm room he watched them bring in a cart for the body.

Clayr, Madame Curator, came rushing down the stairs with Ryn and Prym on her heels. Zo groaned inwardly. This was not something he wanted Ryn to see.

"What happened?" Clayr demanded.

Errol began to tell her Tammy was dead.

Pym screamed and ran down the stairs, throwing herself over Tammy's body. "You did this!" She screamed at Zo.

Zo flinched back from her, his heart racing.

Jeris stormed up, cloak flapping behind him. "What has happened here? Clayr, I swear you are on thin ice with the Board."

"I don't condone killing under *my* leadership." Clayr tone cut like a knife.

Jeris grumbled something under his breath.

Prym howled.

Ryn tugged on Zo's jacket. "Hey, you alright?"

Zo looked down at her, and irritation bubbled up inside of him. The last thing he wanted was Ryn discovering he could have done this. She and Iden had been especially annoying with their concern lately. He closed his eyes and took a deep breath. Snapping at her wasn't going to be good.

"Fine," he said, but there was still a growl in his voice.

He opened his eyes to see tears in hers. He wanted to punch something. He was so angry at himself. Ryn and Iden were the two people he really didn't want to snap at.

"What's going on?" she asked.

"I can't talk about it right now," Zo said as he watched Jeris pull Prym off Tammy, and Clayr examine the body, then cover her up.

"Um, alright." Ryn seemed to shrink from him, which made him even more frustrated.

Nix crossed the scene to them.

"I want you to take your next shift off and go see Wilmar," Nix said.

"Wilmar's already examined me. I'm fine," Zo said.

"Clearly, he's missed something. I'll take you to the Healing house."

"No!" Zo barked. "I'm fine. I don't need a bunch of Healers poking around in me."

"Fine, but I'm still giving you tomorrow off. You've been driving yourself too hard, you need some rest."

Zo frowned. That was the last thing he needed. The thought of being alone, by himself in his room, terrified him.

"I'll come with you," Ryn said, with that look on her face she got when she had something she really needed to talk to him about.

He almost said no, but her eyes told him it was important, so he turned to trace his steps back to his dorm room. The sound of the cart moving away with Tammy's body, made Zo turn and vomit into the bushes.

Ryn put a light hand on his back and a cool hand on his arm. "You're sick. I'll get Fergus to loan us a wagon to take you to Wilmar."

Zo spit stomach acid into the bushes. "No. I'm fine. I just need to lie down."

His nose burned and his eyes watered.

Ryn slid her hand around his waist and wrapped his arm around her shoulders. He almost chuckled. She was far too small to help him walk, but the gesture warmed him and gave him strength.

At his dorm room Ryn settled him into his bed, then found his small mop bucket and put it on the floor next to him. Jinx and Beardslee were meowing and rubbing against Ryn's legs. She took Zo's crock from the cupboard and fed the cats.

It couldn't be real, Zo thought. *In my dream the crock was empty and I went looking for Norm so I could get more fish for them. I couldn't have killed her. I would never.*

Once the cats were happily eating, Ryn pulled a chair over to sit next to Zo's bed. She folded her arms and raised an eyebrow at him. That was her signal she wanted him to spill it. He opened his mouth, but the thought of even saying that he might have killed Tammy in his dream wouldn't come out. In fact, having his mouth open made him want to vomit again. He laid his head down on his pillow.

Ryn sighed, and smoothed his hair away from his forehead. He knew she was covertly trying to see if he was running a fever. He wasn't. He didn't feel feverish. Ryn settled back into her chair, hands in her lap, her head bowed.

"What's up, parva soror?" he asked.

"They're demoting me at work. I'm to be a docent now helping as someone's scribe for a translation." Ryn rubbed at her eye, he knew she was covering a tear.

"Why would they do that?" Zo's head came off the pillow.

"I'm a problem and they want to get rid of me." Ryn's voice was gravely from fighting tears.

"Nonsense. They're just jealous you have such a deep connection with the Library."

Zo lowered his head back to his pillow. He yawned.

Ryn stood and pulled his blanket up to his chin. "Sleep now. Tomorrow's your birthday. Maybe everything will right itself."

Zo swore, then he groaned. He had tried to forget that his birthday was coming. The last day he could be visited by his Ancestors. The day they were supposed to give him his final lesson, and he would officially be an adult with full use of his magic. Except his Healing bead was gone, and so was his Healing Ancestor Madame Sano. He was terrified there would be no final lesson, because he could no longer access his Healing magic. He never wished so hard to hear her crone voice again. He had spent most of his life avoiding his Healing magic. Now he would give his life to the study of Healing if he could only have it back.

Chapter Three

And now, I've grown old, in a cavern I stay,
And search with my lyre for perfect refrain,
Till under the echoes of earth's arcane,
A deep song of bones calls my heart to play.

This excerpt from the GP (Gesta Praediana) was the clue that led me to these caves. The peninsula is notoriously full of them, and it has taken me years of exploration to find what I feel is the right series of caves.

- From the journals of Moult de Dico

Ryn was in a strange state where she knew she had to be dreaming, but everything felt so real. She was standing in the Library Heart next to the tree. The leaves rustled as if in the wind. They seemed to be saying something, but Ryn couldn't make it out. It was just barely beyond her grasp.

"I don't understand," she said to the tree.

The branches moved to reveal the stump where a branch was missing.

Ryn approached the stump reverently, on her tip toes. She reached her fingers to the sap that dripped like tears.

"How did you lose a branch? Who cut it off?"

The tree went still.

"I wish I could do something to help," Ryn said, cupping the tear sap in her hands.

Everything misted over, and the air became heavy and damp. Ryn stood on a glass surface that rippled like water.

"You can help." came a sweet voice that dripped like rainwater into a puddle.

Ryn squinted into the mist but could see no one. She cupped the tear to her.

"Who's there?" Ryn asked the mist.

The water beneath her feet rippled and rose up to take the form of a woman made of water.

"The magic is there for the taking, but you must forsake this world, and be restored to your rightful one. We made a grave error in letting you go. Please come back."

Ryn stared into the watery figure's eyes, but as she did the eyes, face, then body became mist.

"Wait! What do you mean the magic is there for the taking? Who am I? I can't have magic if I don't know who I am!"

The mist faded to darkness. The tear Ryn clutched to her glowed brightly then disappeared.

"Don't go," Ryn sobbed into her empty hands.

* * *

A knock at the door startled Ryn from her sleep. Her neck had a crick in it from falling asleep in the chair next to Zo's bed. Something heavy weighed in her chest. She was trying to catch the last threads of her dream, but they fled from her. Zo didn't stir. He looked more peaceful than when he was awake. She got up slowly, her muscles stiff and cramped, and answered the door. It was Iden.

"I just got off my research shift, and Fergus said Zo is looking worse," Iden said.

Ryn tried to nod, but her neck protested as she moved aside to let Iden in.

Iden went to Zo and knelt beside the bed, placing his hand on his forehead.

"I don't think he's sick. Something happened when that wolf bit him in the neck. Do you think maybe it took his Healing magic?" Ryn whispered.

Iden shook his head. "How could it do that? It's just an animal."

"Just a mythical animal that's not supposed to exist. Who knows what it can do? All I know is that ever since that night, Zo's Healing magic seems to be gone and he keeps looking worse every day."

Iden kissed Zo's temple and stood. "Maybe it was when he was in the Heart of the Library fighting fire with fire."

"Why would his Fire magic take away his Healing?"

"Anger used to block his Healing. Or maybe something that Zmej guy did?" Iden rubbed his forehead with his fingers. "What if he can't finish his Healing lessons?"

Ryn's stomach flipped at the thought. She crossed the room to put a nervous hand on Iden's arm. His good looks always flustered her, but she told herself that was a good cover for her shakiness. "There's nothing we can do. He won't tell us what happened. We'll just have to do what we can."

Iden nodded slowly. "I wish he would just let us in so we could help. I've been shut out of his mind since the Solstice ball." Then he turned to Ryn. "I'll stay with him. You can go back to your shift, or go get some rest."

Ryn stretched, then rolled her neck out. "Alright, but if anything changes, please send someone to get me."

Iden gave that lopsided smile Ryn had always found endearing. "Of course."

* * *

Ryn left Zo's room and started in the direction of her and Brynd's dorm, but found herself wandering the gardens. She remembered the gardens of the new facility where her grandmother tried to move the Library on Viatoro. Even in the middle of winter it was beautiful there, perhaps more beautiful than these gardens. She occasionally felt guilty for wishing the Library could be more like that building. It was perfect, soaring glass windows around the outside for study, dark interior core to protect the materials. Ryn gazed over her shoulder at the Library. Her Library, as she found herself thinking ever since she'd touched the tree at the Library's Heart. It may be bursting at the seams, have a difficult shelving system to navigate, and be riddled with hidden rooms and staircases, but that's what made it a part of her. She couldn't imagine it any other way, even if the new shelving system would make research go faster.

A break in the garden path opened to a circular court with a fountain at the center. Water bubbled up and out of stone lotus flowers, the symbol of knowledge and wisdom. Ryn sat on a bench and watched the water bubble. Zo always had a lot of wisdom for her. She wished he was his old self again so she could talk to him, and he could help her sort through the mess of swirling thoughts in her head. She wasn't sure if taking the demotion was the best choice. Maybe she shouldn't be afraid to live beyond the walls of the Library and Waatch. She really hadn't been far. The island of Viatoro was the furthest she'd traveled from home. It would be good to see more of the world. She felt the Library's presence at her back without turning to look at it. It was comfort. It was home.

She sighed.

And then there was the prospect of leaving the Library and her only source of finding her birth family. The orphanage had been a dead end. Another dead end in a very long line of dead ends. She had verified that a young man, with snow white hair, had dropped her off at that orphanage as a tiny baby, just as she had seen in a dream, but the orphanage had no record of who he was, and there were no records she could find to identify him. She had to keep looking. There had to be birth records still out there. Somewhere was the record she needed. There was also the mystery book that Yvette, the head of the orphanage, had mentioned. It could be hiding in the Library somewhere as well. It may have been accessioned when her orphanage record came in. Where else would it have gone?

The water gurgling up through the stone flowers seemed to be whispering to her, telling her something...something important.

She needed to stay. She needed the Library, and she knew it still held the answers she was seeking. She stood and turned to the path that led back. She was going to take the translator job, and she was going to use her off time to find that book and the records she needed. She had come this far; she wasn't going to quit just because descendants of the

Ancestors wanted her gone. She fished the instructions Clayr had given her for her new job out of her pocket. She wasn't familiar with the manager it said to report to, but she was sure Brynd would know who it was.

Ryn found Brynd and Yll chatting at the reception desk in the grand foyer. Yll had been Ryn's best friend since they were toddlers, but this past year seemed like they had been through the roughest times together. From trying to fit in with the Library, to Yll's betrayal, to attempted kidnapping, and the near destruction of the Library, they had seen quite a bit since last summer. Ryn had met Brynd here, and she had been Ryn's even tempered solid brick—which Ryn had needed so much over the past few moons.

Once they saw Ryn, Yll wrapped her arms around her and gave her a hug. "I'm so sorry, momma told me about the demotion."

Ryn leaned into her embrace. "Yeah."

Brynd leaned in and whispered, "I heard you were with Madame Curator outside on the steps. Was it really Tammy?"

Ryn shuddered. "I guess so, I didn't actually look."

"She's our age. How does something like that happen?" Brynd asked.

Yll's eyes seemed to focus on some distant place. "It seems like I was just hanging out with her, even though it was last summer."

Ryn frowned. She didn't like Tammy.

"Do you think someone killed her?" Brynd's voice was barely audible.

Ryn started. "Who would do that? Why? And how? There didn't seem to be anything wrong."

"I mean—how else does a young healthy person just drop dead?" Yll asked.

Ryn shook her head. "I don't know, but she's clearly in Prym and her father's camp of Ancestor dominance of the Library, so who would have a motivation to kill her?"

Yll shrugged her shoulders. "Someone who's against the Ancestor dominance of the Library?"

Brynd furrowed her brow and raised an eyebrow. "Like an Ordinary? An Ordinary with no magic could kill someone without leaving a mark?"

"I don't know." Yll threw up her hands. "Maybe it was something she was researching. Anyone know what materials she was pulling?"

Brynd tapped a finger to her lips. "I don't know, but I could find out."

Yll nodded slowly. "That would be great."

"I think you two have been listening to too much Library gossip. Probably she had some disorder that we didn't know about. The Healers at the Waatch Healing house will examine her and we'll know what happened. In the meantime—" Ryn turned to Brynd. "Do you know where I can find a research manager named Kay?" Ryn pulled out the instructions Clayr had given her. "I'm supposed to report to her."

Brynd took the paper and read it, eyes growing wide. "They really did demote you. I'm so sorry Ryn."

Ryn shifted from one leg to another, trying not to look around and see who might be close enough to have heard Brynd. "Do you know who she is?" Ryn asked again.

Brynd handed back the paper. "Sure. Her office is on the third floor around the corner from the restricted section materials desk."

"Thanks. Clayr gave me till tomorrow to start, but there's too much going on for me to sit in our dorm room. I'm going to at least find out what this new job is about before the closing bell rings," Ryn said.

"Good luck." Yll gave her another quick hug.

* * *

Ryn was out of breath by the time she reached the top of the main staircase on the third floor. The darkening of the light through the windows told her the closing bell was closer than she thought. She needed to hurry to catch Kay before she left for the day. One of the assistant researchers at the restricted materials desk smiled and waved at Ryn. She and Ryn had worked together on some reshelving projects.

Around the corner she found the door she hoped was to Kay's office. She knocked.

"Come."

Ryn opened the door. An elderly woman with grey hair in a black researcher's dress sat behind a desk buried in books and documents.

"Can I help you?" she asked.

"Are you Kay?" Ryn asked.

"Last time I checked," the woman said, her gaze still fixed on the document in her hand.

Ryn stepped forward pulling out her job instructions and handing them to Kay. "I was told to report to you."

Kay glanced up at the dim light coming from a high set window. "A little late, aren't you?"

"Sorry, with all the excitement today, I got a bit delayed, but Madame Curator said I could come today or tomorrow."

Kay stood and pulled out a ring of keys from her drawer. "Well, I was finishing up so I could leave, but I can take you now. She might have left already, but we'll see."

"Who?" Ryn asked, but Kay ignored her and grabbed the gilded frame of a painting on the wall. It was a scene of a man sitting on the side of the road writing in a journal. Ryn thought it must be a painting of Luc. The painting swung open revealing a large keyhole. Kay took her key ring and inserted a key. A door swung open to reveal yet another secret staircase. There were many hidden passageways inside the Library, but this one made Ryn's eyes widen.

"I thought there were only three floors to the Library," Ryn said.

Kay chuckled, grabbed a lamp from her desk, and began to climb the stairs.

At the top was another door. Kay knocked on it. To Ryn's astonishment someone said, "Enter."

The door opened and Kay ushered Ryn into a room about half the size of the researcher's room downstairs, filled floor to ceiling with shelves of books. There was a comfortable looking couch with a low table in front of it, and seated at a lone desk was a girl in a black researcher's dress using some sort of metal press on a piece of paper.

"Lyssa," Kay said.

The girl finished what she was doing then turned toward them. Her eyes looked in their direction, but did not meet theirs.

"What do you want? I'm really busy, everything is so slow without an assistant." She made a cutting gesture toward the work on her desk, but her hand hit the edge of it instead. She swore, shaking out her hand. "Which you've been promising me for moons now."

Kay grimaced. "It's only been a few days. Anyway, Lyssa, this is—what's your name girl?"

"Ryn."

"Your new translation assistant."

"Finally!" Lyssa said.

"This is Lyssa, our resident finger reader, and translator for the blind." Kay waved at Lyssa.

Lyssa held out her hand, not quite toward Ryn, but close. Ryn crossed the room to take Lyssa's soft, warm hand and shake it.

"Charmed, I'm sure." Lyssa sighed. "Let's get to work. I'm so behind after my last assistant went running for the hills."

"Lyssa, you can't afford to run off another assistant. Be nice."

"What are you talking about? I'm always nice." Lyssa gave Kay a toothy grin that gave Ryn chills.

Kay answered her with a look, but Lyssa's eyes were focused slightly above Kay's face.

"I will leave you to instruct your new assistant," Kay said. She turned to Ryn. "I'm leaving for the day, you won't be able to exit the way we came, that way will be locked. Lyssa will show you the way out. Tomorrow you will enter through that back entrance."

"Sure. Thank you." Ryn gave a small curtsy as Kay's eyes narrowed like she was silently praying to the Ancestors that this was going to work.

After Kay shut the door behind her, Lyssa turned back to the paper on her desk. "Well, let's get to work."

Ryn examined the paper. She was surprised to find it blank. She bent down so the light shone on the paper at a different angle. It had raised bumps on it.

"What are you working on?" Ryn asked.

Lyssa's eyes rolled. "Translating—duh."

Ryn shook her head, confused. "Translating what?"

"Look, all you have to do is sit right there"—Lyssa gestured toward a chair next to the desk—"and read from this book."

Her hand drifted over her desk, passing over some strange pressing tools that looked like they made dots instead of letters or designs. Ryn was so absorbed in figuring out what the tools were for that it took her a moment to follow Lyssa to one of the books. Lyssa felt along its cover with her fingers till she found a paper that was stuck in the book. It had no writing on it, but Lyssa ran her fingers over the top of it then nodded. "Yes, this one." She pushed the book toward Ryn, upsetting a few papers on her desk.

Ryn took up the book, resetting the papers that had been disturbed.

"Sit, read out loud. That's all you need to do. Won't tax that pretty little head of yours."

"How do you know I'm pretty?" Ryn asked.

Lyssa glared daggers at her. "All my assistants are empty-headed pretty little docents who failed at pulling materials. This is the last-ditch assignment Clayr gives before dismissing someone. Last chance, pretty face, start reading."

Great, I have to spend who knows how long with this grumpy girl who likes to judge people before she even knows them. Ryn couldn't help it. Lyssa probably had reasons for being grumpy. Not being able to see would make Ryn grumpy for sure, but why did Ryn have to deal with this now? Right when she had so many things already making her anxious.

Ryn cleared her throat. Maybe she was on her way out after all. With shaking fingers she opened the cover, turned the endpaper, then froze. It was a history of House Viatoro. Could she never escape that House?

Lyssa pulled a fresh piece of paper from a neat stack. "Start with the title page, don't leave anything out, and I mean nothing. This needs to be a faithful translation."

Ryn nodded, then realized how dumb that was.

Lyssa felt each pressing tool then arranged them in front of her. "Begin."

Ryn would read, then stop while Lyssa carefully pressed bumps into the paper. The process was slow and painstaking. Ryn wondered if there was a way to speed the process up a bit.

"Are those dots words?" Ryn asked.

Lyssa's eyes drifted toward Ryn, they were half narrowed like she was either annoyed or half asleep. "Both. The dots are on a grid that make letters, letters make words."

"Can I see?"

"You can see all you like," Lyssa growled.

"I mean, can you show me?" Ryn's words tumbled out.

Lyssa sat back, eyes wide. "Sure."

Lyssa handed Ryn the page she'd been working on. Ryn ran her fingers over the bumps. It made no sense to her.

Lyssa dug around the pile of papers on her desk. "If it helps, here's the letters and the pattern corresponding dots."

Ryn ran her fingers over each letter. "This seems really hard."

"It's certainly not easy, but I have a secret."

Lyssa got up from her desk and went to the shelves of books. Her fingers felt along the spines till she got to one small, worn, leather bound book. She pulled it off the shelf and brought it back to her desk.

"This here is the original copy of Luc's journal," Lyssa said.

Ryn shook her head, then stopped herself. "It can't be. I've seen Luc's journals, they're in the restricted archives."

"Ha! They think it is, but I have proof that those are copies."

Lyssa opened the book and turned it toward Ryn.

"Read," Lyssa said.

Ryn picked up the book and opened to the title page. "*Gesta Praediana*, yes, I've seen this before."

"Don't read with your eyes," Lyssa said.

Ryn brought the title page closer, turning it sideways. There were raised bumps below the title. She ran her fingers across it.

"What does it say?" Ryn asked.

"You tell me."

Ryn used the key for the letters and bumps. It took a long time to figure it out.

"The branch is the key. That's a strange subtitle." Ryn's thoughts wandered to the protector of the Library and his mentioning the branch, the stone, and the sword. She knew the stone, and thought she knew the sword, but the branch was still a mystery.

"Isn't it though? That's how I know this it's the real journal."

"How's that?" Ryn ran her fingers over the bumps again, memorizing every letter.

"Because Luc invented finger reading and the bumps. He was losing his eyesight at the end of his life."

Ryn's hand drifted down the page and found more dots she hadn't noticed.

"TLTRP—What is that supposed to mean?" Ryn asked.

Lyssa's hand drifted toward the book. Ryn put it under her hand.

"There." Ryn put her finger on the letters. "I mean, at least I think that's what it says."

"Hmmmmm—Yes, that's what it says, and I have no idea, I've never noticed those before." Lyssa's fingers slid across the letters.

* * *

At the sound of the closing bell, Ryn set the History of Viator down. Her throat was dry from reading, and re-reading. Lyssa seemed fast with the pressing tools, but it was still tedious.

"I guess it's closing time," Lyssa said, her hand drifting around the top of her desk till she found a box, and began loading the dot presses into it.

Ryn stood and stretched. They'd only been at it for a short time, but she was somehow stiff from sitting. She roamed the shelves while Lyssa put her things away.

To the left of Lyssa's desk, behind the couch, were shelves that contained a few books with an unbound book next to it made up of pages of dots. Apparently, these were all of Lyssa's finished projects. There were only a few.

Wild Magic Truth and Tales, The Real History of the Library, The Truth of Sprites and Where to Find Them...

"*How to Kill a Dragon?*" Ryn read the spine of the last book on the shelf.

"Oooo—that's a good one! I enjoyed translating it, but the docent who read it left because it was too gruesome. Did you know dragons lay eggs? Or at least that's what the author of the book says. One of his 'ways' to kill a dragon is to destroy it as an egg. He claims someone named Eladorys destroyed an egg once. You ever heard of such a thing?" Lyssa asked, standing from her chair, anchoring herself with a hand on the desk.

Ryn shook her head. She'd studied as much as she could find about Luc, the dragon, and the early days of the Library and had never heard of such a thing.

Ryn turned back to the shelf. "I'd like to pick your brain sometime. These are all books on subjects for which I have a lot of questions."

Lyssa's smile was lopsided, her face tilted up. "Tomorrow, right now, it's time to get something to eat."

Ryn's stomach growled.

Lyssa laughed.

Chapter Four

I've been in this cave for a year or so...I think. Time passes differently in the dark. Exploration of the caves and passageways has been slow. The lantern fuel only lasts so long. I've resorted to taking multiple lanterns with me, but now I'm straying too far from the entrance cave I've made my home. I'm afraid I'm going to get lost down here and some far off generation will find my bones.

- From the journals of Moult de Dico

Zo jerked awake. It felt like he'd slept for days. The light coming through the bottom of the curtain said it was morning, or maybe evening. It was difficult to tell. Beardslee was lying on his feet. Jinx was next to his head, and Iden's arm was wrapped around his midsection. Zo snuggled deeper into Iden's warmth. They didn't fit well together on Zo's bed, but Zo was grateful he was there to press closer. The comfortable familiarity of Iden made Zo sigh. If it was morning, and Zo had slept away yesterday, it was because Iden's presence soothed Zo's hurts. Iden stirred and tightened his arm around Zo's middle, as if he was holding on to something he was afraid to lose.

"Good morning," Zo mumbled with a smile as he felt Iden's body come awake.

Iden pulled Zo even closer.

"Happy birthday," Iden whispered into Zo's ear, then began nibbling on his earlobe.

Fire raced through Zo's body. He turned to Iden and kissed him with as much want and need as he could put into it. Iden pulled back gasping, and Zo caught the tightness around his eyes and the slight furrow to his brow. Zo figured he must still look sick, even after sleeping for over twelve hours. He didn't care. He wasn't glass that was going to break. He went back in for another kiss and Iden surrendered himself to their passion.

* * *

When Zo finally rolled out of bed, Iden grabbed his hand and kissed it. Zo felt a warmth inside he hadn't felt in a while, but he was still bone weary, and worried. It seemed no amount of sleep was going to cure that. He didn't want to think about his final lessons. His muscles were protesting having laid in bed so long. He stretched his arm over his head and bent to the side. There was a cramp forming there. Iden made a contented squeaking noise as he stretched himself and rose out of bed. He looked so good to Zo: bed head blond hair, sleepy blue eyes, and a torso full of muscles that didn't come from his collections management job in the Library. Zo knew he couldn't compare to Iden. Zo had lost a lot of weight this past moon and the winter rains made him pale. He didn't know how Iden stayed in shape. He needed to ask him what his secret was.

Iden brushed the back of his fingers on Zo's cheek. "It's your birthday, we could stay in bed all day."

Zo smiled at the idea. "Naw, I think I've spent too much time there. Let's get breakfast."

Iden's eyes lit up at that idea. "Yes! But not the mess hall, let's go to our breakfast place."

"Of course," Zo smiled, slipping his arm around Iden.

Iden's gaze was penetrating and hungry. "We could go for a late breakfast."

Zo chuckled.

* * *

After devouring their favorite breakfast of tiny pasta and cheese patties with eggs on top, smoked salmon, and gravy with lots of extra bacon on the side, Zo and Iden walked the streets of Waatch on the way to the north gate of the city. Iden hung his arm on Zo's shoulders, and Zo didn't care—even though they were passing through the Library manager's neighborhood. Ever since the winter solstice ball and the destruction of Zo's Healing magic, he no longer cared who knew Iden was his boyfriend. Ancestor descendants loved to ostracize those who were attracted to the same sex. They sent those caught to the isle of Exile—or worse. House Sano, the Healing house, was one of those with zero tolerance for such relationships. They valued passing on their power, Healing magic, to their children and grandchildren above anything else. For many years, Zo had been terrified of revealing how he felt about men. His parents certainly wanted him married to a girl and producing heirs. Zo was no longer afraid to disappoint them. Iden showed him there was no reason to fear these people, and Zo's dad, Lar, seemed to at last be accepting of it.

The sun on Zo's face warmed him and he relaxed into Iden's side.

"Are you prepared for your final lessons?" Iden asked.

Zo's stomach tightened. "Yeah."

"It's part of turning eighteen, that final lesson. It's why I'm taking you to the beach—I'm sure that final fire lesson will require some space where you won't burn the Library down." Iden laughed.

"You're right. My mind's been too preoccupied to consider that."

The truth was Zo hadn't had a lesson in a while. His Healing lessons ended the moment he killed the wolf, and he'd maybe had one fire lesson since. His brain had been so focused on dealing with the loss of his Healing, he hadn't been able to think about much else. It was like half of him was missing. Like a huge hole had opened inside of him and sucked away half of who he was. Nothing eased that ache. He rubbed his sternum, trying to ease the tightness there.

Iden cleared his throat. When he spoke his voice sounded shaky. Zo had never heard him sound so nervous. "Um—what about your Healing magic. Is everything going to be alright there?"

"I...I wish I knew."

"Well, I'm here for you. Whatever happens." Iden kissed him on the temple.

Iden grinned. "I'm looking forward to a spectacular fire show."

Zo grunted. Lately Regg, his brother, had been showing better proficiency with Fire and Healing. Zo had always outperformed his brother in the past. There was a pulling sensation in his gut as he thought about it. He wanted to be the best again, at everything.

* * *

When they got to the beach, Iden spread his coat on a log so they could sit. Despite it still being chilly, Zo pulled off his shoes and socks and stuck his toes in the cool sand. He was fortunate he wasn't having his final lesson in the heat of summer. Iden pulled out a couple water skins he'd been hiding under his coat and handed them to Zo. Heat rose to Zo's cheeks as he accepted them and slung them across his body. Of course, Iden had thought of keeping Zo hydrated during what was certain to be the most grueling Fire lesson of Zo's life, and of course Zo had forgotten. He rubbed his forehead, wishing he could bring his brain back to the practical things in life that would keep him alive. At least he had Iden to do that for him. It's good that he did, otherwise he might end up a burnt crisp.

Zo's fire bead started to grow warm, signaling the oncoming lesson. Zo stood, and Iden grabbed his hand and kissed it.

"Good luck," Iden said.

Zo nodded, not trusting his mouth to open. He recalled the moment, not too long ago, when Master Ingis and Madame Sano had visited him at the same time. He fingered his lone bead at his neck.

He walked closer to the water and sat on the cool sand, legs crossed, palms resting gently on his knees. He closed his eyes and breathed in a long inhale and a slow exhale. He continued that pattern till he felt Master Ignis in his mind. He opened his eyes.

Master Ingis stood before him, arms folded, with a frown on his face.

"You finally managed to get rid of Sano, I see," he said.

Zo's calm vanished in a flash of heat, fire flaring around his fingertips.

"Not by choice," Zo shot back.

"Everything is a choice, child. The consequences for that one action will be severe. Makes this lesson almost useless, but I'm obligated to finish, so let's get to it." Master Ingis raised his hands, and fire engulfed them as he began to spin it into a huge flaming ball.

Zo jumped to his feet, hands forming his own ball of fire. "What do you mean, severe?"

Master Ingis made a lopsided grin that resembled a grimace, and shot his ball of fire straight at Zo's chest. Zo dove sideways into the sand while launching his fireball at Master Ingis. The fireball dissipated as it grew close to Master Ingis. Zo's mouth hung open, letting sand in. He spit it out.

"How?" Zo asked.

"Your final lesson, the reverse of Fire magic—extinguish the fire—but be careful, absorbing too much can make you crispy."

"I can extinguish a fire as well as start one?" Zo had never realized this.

Master Ignis gave a tight smile. "Yes, however the heat still has to be dissipated, usually through your body. If you extinguish a house fire there will be nothing left of you but a pile of ash."

Zo paled. "How big of a fire is safe to extinguish?"

"Depends upon the person. Matt, seventeenth generation of House Ignis, put out a burning bush once... cooked all his insides." Master Ingis chuckled.

Zo swallowed hard. Master Ingis sent another fireball straight at Zo, who was scrambling back to his feet.

"Hands out, disperse the heat," Master Ingis said.

Zo thrust his hands out, thinking of extinguishing the fire instead of lighting it. The fireball hit his hands. Zo yelped as he shook them out. They burned like he'd touched a boiling pot.

"Hmmm, maybe I'll take care of House Sano's problem for them," Master Ingis said as he sent another fireball directly at Zo.

Zo dodged again, waving one hand at the fireball as he tripped over a piece of driftwood in the sand. The flames grazed Zo's side, singing his jacket and sending a wave of heat through his chest.

Zo swore. *He really is trying to kill me! Can a ghost of an Ancestor kill me?*

"Take it in!" Ingis yelled, launching his next fireball attack.

Zo, still on his side, threw up a handful of sand in an effort to put it out, but the fireball came straight for him. Zo flung his arms in front of his face, thinking of the cooling sand and extinguishing the fire. His hands sucked in the fire, heat raced down his arms and through his body, finally shooting out through his feet. He lay on the ground, gasping. His insides did feel cooked. He felt like the bacon he'd had for breakfast—crispy everywhere.

"Drink," Master Ingis commanded.

Zo was staring at his red burned hands, marveling that there was a reverse to Fire magic as well as Healing magic.

"Is there a reverse to every magic?" Zo asked.

"Those are all House secrets, but I imagine it to be so. Drink, or you'll dry out like dust."

"But if the reverse of Healing is killing, and that is forbidden, then what is the final Healing lesson?" Zo doubted Ingis would answer that question.

Master Ingis shook his head. "Not my House to tell you, but since Sano is through with you I will. The final Healing lesson is an oath to NOT use magic to kill. Too late for you."

Zo opened one of the water skins and drank from it. It was warm, but his throat greedily took it in. He drank the skin dry.

"Now you will kneel." Master Ingis said.

Zo looked around the beach then back at the Fire Ancestor. "That's it? Aren't we going to work to perfect the lesson?"

Master Ingis chuckled. "If you happen to survive breaking House Sano's oath, you can practice more. Kneel."

"But I didn't make..."

Ingis glared at him.

Zo knelt in the cooling sand.

Master Ingis placed his hands upon Zo's head. Even though the ancestor was just a ghost of a spirit, Zo could feel the weight of his hands.

"Covenant with Praedo, me, and all the ancestors, that you will use your power of fire to help and not harm, to build and not destroy."

"I so swear." Zo said.

Master Ingis made a choking noise in the back of his throat, like he didn't believe Zo's promise.

"By the power that was bestowed upon me by the Dragon Slayer, my greatest friend whom I loved dearly and lost, Praedo, I now bestow that power upon you, Zo of House Ignis."

Master Ingis began to glow bright white. Warmth spread from his hands onto Zo's head and down through his body. Zo's fire bead flared coal hot and burning. Zo screamed at the pain on his collar bone. It felt as if the bead was boring into his bone, into his chest. Heat consumed his entire body and he thought for sure he was about to become that crispy burnt shell Master Ingis had mentioned. Then it all left, and Master Ingis and his bead were gone. What was left was a circle with the symbol for fire burned into his skin.

* * *

"That was the oddest thing, watching fireballs shooting at you out of nowhere," Iden said on the walk back to town.

Zo rubbed at his chest. After the fire lesson he had sat on the sand long in meditation, hoping that maybe the old crone Madame Sano would come. What he wouldn't do to hear her cackle right now. He just couldn't admit his Healing was gone and that he was broken. Fear that Iden would leave him raced through his heart and mind. This was Zo's birthday. His opportunity to gain his Healing magic was past. It was gone forever and he was forever half of a whole—someone with only one magic. He pulled his collar up higher so no one could see he only had one beadscar. Zo didn't think Iden deserved a broken boyfriend.

"I'm sure the fight looked strange," Zo agreed, his voice sounding distant even to himself.

He still didn't understand what Master Ingis was talking about when he said Zo wasn't "worth the time because of House Sano." Butterflies fluttered around inside Zo's stomach. He would need to avoid the Waatch Healing House at all costs. He didn't know what Ingis meant, and he didn't want to find out.

"So—did the old crone come?" Iden's words were playful, but his voice was a nervous whisper.

"No," was all Zo could get out.

Iden stopped Zo. "I'm so sorry, Wildfire. I wish I could do something for you. I should be able to sense it from your mind. We are close enough for my Mind magic to allow us to communicate, but ever since the wolf attack our connection hasn't progressed."

Zo faced Iden, standing there in the sunshine, his shoulders filling out his coat in a way that brought back memories of their morning together, his face glowing with a touch of the sun after the long, dark winter. He was everything Zo could ever hope for, and everything he had to lose. Zo opened his mouth to say everything was fine. Iden's eyebrows shot up like he knew Zo was about to be untruthful. Zo swallowed.

"I'm worried." Zo's hand cracked his knuckles against his thigh. "I don't know what is wrong with me, and I'm scared."

It was a half-truth. Zo knew his broken Healing magic was the problem, but he couldn't bring himself to say the words, not even to Iden.

Iden nodded, wrapping his arms around Zo and cradling his head to his shoulder. Zo breathed in deep the smell of salt air on Iden. He stifled the sob he wanted to let out into Iden's shoulder, but couldn't keep a tear from sliding down his cheek. Iden held him like that for a good long while, then they turned and entered the gates of Waatch.

* * *

Iden dropped Zo off at his dorm room with a suggestive wink that Zo should wear the outfit Thax had made for him for the Winter Solstice Ball. Zo complained that it was too formal for dinner at Wilmar's and Iden better not be planning to surprise him. Zo really hated surprises. Iden's grin grew and he told him he'd see him later for dinner. Then he hugged Zo so long he almost suggested Iden stay for the rest of the afternoon. With a quick kiss he was gone.

Zo collapsed onto his bed. A wave of exhaustion washed over him. The fire battle with Master Ignis had drained him. If he was being honest with himself, he would have to admit that waiting for a Healing lesson with Madame Sano was necessary, because he was too worn out from the Fire lesson to walk back. He had needed that time to recover.

Jinx jumped up on the bed, and Zo wrapped his arm around the cat pulling him close, then he drifted off to sleep.

* * *

Zo was walking the halls of the Board of Regents building. He passed the room where he had been present while the Library guards had interrogated Jak and Dan about their attempted break in at the Library's Heart. Jak and Dan had been able to convince Clayr to let them help her find the Library saboteur. Zo turned the corner and started up a grand staircase in the middle of the building. The stairs spanned the length of a high-ceilinged foyer. The wood steps made a sharp sound as he took the stairs two at a time. He was in a hurry, and his legs were carrying him up to the next floor quickly. Once at the top, Zo turned to the right and headed down a hallway lined with extra wide office doors on each side. His steps slowed as he shifted his weight to the balls of his feet to keep his footfalls silent. The thick carpeting helped. When he came to the second door to the last at the end of the hall, he stopped. There was a light shining on the carpet from under the door. Someone was still in the office. Zo opened the door and stepped inside. A large desk occupied the majority of the room, but off to the right was a fireplace and two large wingback chairs. Someone occupied one of the chairs next to the fire.

"Just leave the teapot on the desk, I'm in the middle of something here," a deep male voice came from the folds of the chair.

Zo crept silently forward. This time there was no anger. Zo felt nothing as the grey-haired man turned to him, eyes going wide. He opened his mouth to say something, but Zo's hand shot out around his neck. Zo watched the life in the man's eyes go out, as his body slumped forward.

Chapter Five

In the Canticum Animationus it reads:

Spears, helms, and armor obeyed his call,
Each metal heart by spirit ignited;
Their clangor rose, in glory united,
Awaiting command from one and all.

Ancestor magic today is a pale imitation of Praedo's power of old. No wonder so many seek to restore it. Imagine animating an army of spears and armor!

- From the journals of Moult de Dico

Ryn stood outside Zo's room and knocked. A chill breeze blew her skirts. She shivered. It had been a nice sunny day, but the sun was setting and the temperature was dropping. A firm reminder that they were still closer to winter than summer. Zo didn't answer. His window was dark. Ryn began to worry. Maybe Zo had already left for Wilmar's? That would be bad. Nix had barely left to help Wilmar prepare for the party they were throwing for Zo, and Iden had gone to pick up the cake from the bakery before they closed for the evening. If Zo got there before everything was ready, the surprise would be ruined.

Ryn pounded on the door again, frustrated she hadn't gotten there sooner.

The door opened slowly to a pale and disheveled Zo.

Ryn gasped. "Did you just wake up?"

He squinted at her with one eye open.

She pushed past him into his room, scooping up Jinx who was making a break for the door. It was dark in his room. She went to his desk to light the lantern, but there wasn't any way to light it.

"Do you mind?" she pointed to the lamp.

Zo rubbed his forehead, then shuffled over to the desk and lit the lamp with a snap of his fingers. He covered his eyes while Ryn adjusted the light to make it brighter.

She turned to him. "Well, this won't do."

His wardrobe door was open, so she started sifting through his shirts and coats looking for the one he wore the night of the Winter Solstice Ball, trying to ignore the bile rising from her stomach at the sight of her brother in this state. She managed to find the waistcoat, jacket and pants and hand them to him. He stared at them in his hands. She stepped back when the lamplight reflected off a tear that trickled down his cheek. She looked away at Jinx playing with a bug in the corner. She closed her eyes and breathed deep, then took the clothes from his hands and pulled him over to sit on his bed.

She grabbed his cold hands. "I haven't asked what's going on since the day outside the orphanage when you said you couldn't heal my cut. I know it's personal. I want you to know I'm here for you. Whatever you need. You are important and you matter."

Zo nodded, rubbing his eye. He took a deep breath, then let it out slow.

"I think I'm a killer."

Ryn's queasy stomach turned to stone. "No you're not, don't be silly."

Zo cracked his knuckles on his leg. "I killed that wolf with Healing magic. I used my power to explode its heart."

Even though they had speculated what happened, Ryn still found herself gasping. "Oh no."

Zo put his head in his hands. "I didn't know what else to do. The wolf was seconds away from tearing out my throat and then coming after you. Fergus tried to stab it, which did nothing. It happened before I could even think about it. I just reached out and the wolf was dead."

Ryn lowered her hand covering her mouth. "Was that why you had the convulsions after you threw off the wolf?"

Zo nodded again. "There's this power that flows into you when you kill something. It can be intoxicating." Sweat beaded on his forehead.

"What can we do? There has to be a way to heal you, to get your magic back. Didn't Madame Sano give you your last lesson today? Surely she fixed it."

Zo ran a hand down his face. "My Healing bead crumbled to ash and disappeared. So did my lessons." He pulled down the Ordinary type shirt collar he had taken to wearing. There was only one beadscar there. "Today was the final day to take them. I was hoping that given it was my final lesson that Madame Sano would at least show up to gloat, but she didn't come."

The beadscar transfixed Ryn. It was her first time seeing a fresh scar. It looked red and raw.

She put out her hand toward his collar. "Does it hurt?"

Zo gave a bitter sounding chuckle. "Everything hurts right now."

"Well, defending your life, and everyone else at the ball from that monster doesn't make you a killer," Ryn said.

Zo pounded his knuckles against his thigh a few times. "I've been...I don't know...dreaming? But it's real. I was following Tammy and I reached out and touched her and killed her, then I woke up like I was dreaming, but Fergus came and told me Tammy had collapsed. How could that be? How could I be dreaming, but seeing something happening in real time?"

Ryn rocked back. "Well, I've been dreaming about my father lately and I'm pretty sure they are more than dreams. I think I'm actually talking to him. He has Mind magic, so maybe you're seeing through Mind magic?"

"But you have to know someone really well to communicate with Mind magic. The only person from House Dico I'm close to is Iden, and he doesn't have a magic that could kill someone like that."

Ryn rubbed at her temple. "Anyone else you know with Mind magic and Healing magic?"

"Just my friend Ayn who is a mind Healing student I know, but I wouldn't say we were close."

Zo stood slowly, walked to his dresser, poured himself a glass of water, but just stared into it. "I just had a dream, before you woke me. I was in the House of Regents. I think I killed a Regent."

Ryn swallowed hard, heart racing. She took a deep breath. "But if a Regent was dead the news would be all over the Library grounds. I'm sure it was just a dream."

Zo took a gulp of water, then stared at himself in the mirror. He paused so long Ryn was worried he wouldn't move forward.

"I hope you're right," he finally said.

Ryn didn't know what to do. She fought the impulse to run outside and burst into tears. To rage against the stars and the Ancestors. She hated the fact that she didn't have magic, but seeing Zo lose his magic in this horrible way was so much worse. If only she could do something to fix it. To fix everything. She just wanted everyone to be happy. She took a deep breath to keep the tears away.

"Let's get you out of this room and away from the Library and all the Ancestor garbage." Ryn held up his clothes.

Zo sighed. He stared at the clothes in her hands for a long minute.

"Sure." He finally said. He pulled off his shirt and started to undo his pants.

Ryn squeaked and jumped up. "I'll just wait outside while you change."

Zo gave slow nod, like he wasn't even thinking about her being in the room. That wasn't like him. Normally he would have cracked some off-color, cheek-blushing joke. Ryn leaned against his door outside trying to sort through everything he'd told her. She had suspected something bad happened with the wolf. She also suspected Zo's "friend" Keir was the one who had taught Zo about killing with magic. Keir gave her the creeps, and he seemed to have little care for the people around him. She had been relieved when Zo lost interest in him, but it looked like it came too late. The damage was done. A tear leaked out of her eye and coursed down her cheek. This was not what she wanted for him. Wilmar, Nix, Iden, and Ryn had worked hard to get Zo to finally embrace his Healing magic, and now...she couldn't even think about it. The thought that he was only going to have half of his magic for the rest of his life, along with the fact that he was so incredibly gifted and talented in Healing. She could see how much he enjoyed it. Her heart felt like someone had reached inside her chest and squeezed it.

"I'm dressed." Zo's voice was faint through the door.

Ryn took a deep breath. She didn't want him to see her worry. This was his birthday. Everything had to be alright.

* * *

The walk across Waatch to Wilmar's was awkward. Despite what Ryn had said about getting away from Library grounds and Zo's worries, she found herself thinking about everything he'd said. It was on her mind, so it was all she wanted to talk about, but she knew he didn't want to talk about it, so she couldn't think of anything to say. Zo was unusually quiet.

When they were almost to Wilmar's, Zo shook himself like he was waking up from a daydream. "What decision did you make? Are you staying with the Library?"

Ryn looked up into his eyes to see he was there, fully present, and looking genuinely concerned about her. She fought down tears of relief to see him coming back to himself.

"I decided to stay. The job seems boring. All I'm doing is reading to someone so they can translate it into this bumpy language. No research at all, but it's way up on the *fourth* floor so at least no one will bother me," she said.

Zo nodded, completely unfazed by the mention of the fourth floor. Was it something he knew about that she didn't? Or was he still somewhat distracted? It was hard to tell.

When they reached the street Wilmar's office and the Waatch Healing House were on, Ryn watched Zo's gaze drift to the Healing House, then he shook again. She grabbed his arm, and pulled him to Wilmar's door, silently hoping Iden and everyone were ready inside. She and Zo had delayed long enough for everyone to be waiting for them by now. She knocked on the door.

Right as she knocked Zo turned to her and said, "I hope Wilmar and Iden aren't trying to surprise me with a party."

Ryn gulped as Wilmar opened the door and Ryn and Zo entered to Iden, Nix, Yll, and Regg yelling "Surprise!"

Zo glared at Ryn, who gave him an ear to ear cheesy, guilty grin.

Regg came forward and slapped his brother on the back. "Officially free of magic lessons. Congratulations!"

Ryn tried not to wince at Regg's comment. She just broadened her smile.

Iden embraced Zo with a mischievous grin that said he knew full well he was in trouble for organizing a surprise for Zo. Then Nix took Zo and engulfed him in a hug. Ryn wasn't sure how Zo was breathing, and was relieved when Nix finally let him go and Zo was still conscious.

Wilmar was next for a hug. When he pulled away, he was wiping his eyes on his sleeve. "Come everyone, the food is ready." Wilmar lifted his arms and herded everyone out of his exam room and into his living space.

"You love me, you know you love me." Iden slipped his arm around Zo's waist and kissed him on the cheek.

Zo gave him what looked like a forced, fake grin, then he relented and melted into Iden.

Wilmar had squeezed two tables together into his small kitchen, and everyone took a chair around the tables laden with fish, tender spring leafy vegetables, and mashed squash. Ryn found herself seated next to Regg and Yll. Zo was at the other end of the table next to Iden and Wilmar, so Ryn leaned over to Regg.

"What did the Healers find out about Tammy's death?" she whispered to him, eyes on Zo, who was in deep conversation with Wilmar. She hoped he wouldn't hear her.

Regg glanced at the others across the table. He might have been confused about why she was whispering, but he responded with his voice lowered. "I don't know. The Healing Masters won't talk about it, but it's serious, I've never seen Master Don that pale before."

Despite everything that had happened with Zo and Regg's mom, Regg had been back at the Waatch Healing House to continue his studies since her departure back to the Healing island, Eileansano.

Yll leaned in to join the conversation. "Maybe the Healing Headmaster gave my mother a report. We should go see her at the cottage later."

Since Yll had started working at the Library, Clayr and Yll had moved to the small curator's cottage on the Library grounds. Clayr loved her home in Sooke, but these days she didn't dare leave the Library grounds for long. There were still too many who opposed her in the Library, and on the Board of Regents.

Wilmar tapped his fork on the side of his glass to get everyone's attention. "Thank you all for coming to celebrate the best apprentice I've ever had."

Nix grunted. "He's the only apprentice you've had."

Wilmar glared at him. "Hush now." Wilmar turned to Zo. "I know the past moons have been rough ones, but I'm so proud of the work you've done and the difficulties you've overcome. I'm amazed at how good you are with the patients. You've been a blessing from the Ancestors to me."

"He's a hard worker too—even if he's a weakling grunt who can't handle the heat of the Boiler room," Nix added.

"Hey..." Zo started.

"To Zo." Wilmar lifted his glass. "The first Healer physician!"

"Harrah!" Ryn lifted her glass to her brother, forestalling anyone else's comments.

Iden put his arm around Zo's shoulders. "To Zo." He lifted his glass and drank. Then he stood. "I have a gift for you."

Iden went down on his knees next to Zo's chair.

Zo's eyes widened in surprise.

"I wanted to do this at the ball, but things happened. So I waited for this night. The night we celebrate you. I remember that first evening I saw you at that silly debut party. I couldn't take my eyes off you. Ever since then I've come to know the truly caring person you are."

Zo opened his mouth like he was going to object, but Iden held up his hand to forestall any argument. "I know you think you've been terrible, but the fact that you overcame your fears and stood up to everyone for me. The fact that you chose me." Iden's voice cracked. "It means everything."

Iden pulled a long box out from inside of his coat. When he opened it there were two necklaces resting on a velvet cushion inside. Ryn gasped.

"So here I am in front of your family...our family...those who matter, asking you if you would promise yourself to me." Iden picked one of the necklaces out of the box and held it up.

Zo sucked in his breath. Ryn watched his face go from dazed look to tears welling up in his eyes.

"Yes, of course." Zo's voice was hoarse and breathless.

Iden grinned and with shaking hands he undid the clasp and helped Zo put it around his neck. Then he took the second necklace from the box and Zo's unsteady hands hung the second necklace around Iden's neck.

Iden kissed Zo to the sound of much cheering. "Not that we need another magical connection with the necklaces. Our bond through my Mind magic makes me happy." He laughed.

There was a knock at the door. Wilmar frowned, then rose to answer it, muttering about having hung out the do not disturb sign, and how everyone always ignored it.

Ryn heard a woman's voice ask Wilmar for a crock of a sleeping something she didn't quite make out, then Zo's friend from the Healing House entered the room.

"Ayn, it's good to see you. How's the Healing House?" Zo rose to give her a brief hug.

Ayn pulled away from Zo. "It's good to see you too. I've missed your sass." She looked around at everyone gathered around the table. "What's the occasion?"

"Zo's birthday," Regg answered.

"Oh!" A shadow seemed to pass across her face, like she was calculating how he hadn't been taking Healing lessons lately and what that might mean. "Happy Birthday. I'm afraid I bring horrible news."

Ryn's stomach clenched.

"Regent Jordan de Mare has been found dead in his office in the Library House of Regents," Ayn said.

Ryn's gaze shot to Zo's face. What little color he had left there drained from it completely. He looked like a ghost.

"Are you sure?" Yll asked.

Ayn shifted her gaze to Yll. "His body has been brought to the Healing House to determine the cause of death. The Healing Masters sent me to get some of Wilmar's potions."

"They're Healers who heal with magic, why would they need..." Ryn started.

Wilmar came from his exam room with several jars and crocks.

"I'll help you carry those over." Zo took a few of the bottles from Wilmar.

"I can do it," Wilmar said. "You stay and enjoy the party."

Zo's gaze finally met Ryn's. "No, I need to go. I won't be long."

Iden stood and kissed Zo on the cheek, pressing his forehead against Zo's. "We'll wait for you."

Zo nodded, then said, "If it gets late go on home. I'll catch up with you later."

As Zo passed Ryn, she grabbed his arm and squeezed it. He gave her a sad, lopsided grin, then he was gone.

Chapter Six

And this passage in the Canticum Spiritus—I've never seen anyone with Spirit magic call forth the dead:

Praedo then raised his hand to call—
And under the moon, in spectral gleam,
Ten thousand spirits began to stream,
Arrayed for battle beside the wall.

- From the journals of Moult de Dico

Zo followed Ayn across the road to the Healing House, dread pounding in his heart with every footstep. The Healing House was the last place he wanted to be, especially after what Master Ingis said earlier that day—but he had to know. He had to see if the body lying in the Healing House was the same man he'd seen in his dream. Somewhere deep inside he knew it would be, but he hoped, oh, he hoped it wouldn't be.

Healing students were on the stairs of the grand porch, clustered in groups and talking in low whispers. Many of them turned to glare at him with furrowed brows and pursed lips. Some gasped, hands going to their mouths. Zo wasn't sure if it was in response to news, or to him. He wove his way through the entirety of the student body who were milling about the front entrance. Once they entered the receiving hall, Zo understood why—the hall was filled with Library administrators and guards, as well as Waatch bureaucrats. He waded through the crowd by following close on Ayn's heels. They passed an open exam room with people standing in the hall looking in. Zo stretched up on his toes and was able to see the body on the table inside. The body was marble white, and drained of color, but it was definitely the man he'd killed in his dream. Zo's knees went shaky and weak. Somehow, he managed to follow Ayn down the hall to another exam room where a few of the Healing Masters, plus the headmaster were in conference with each other. Their conversation ended when Zo and Ayn entered the room. They all turned to look at Zo as one, and he knew instantly that coming here had been a huge mistake. He set the potion bottles down on a table and turned to leave as quickly as he could.

"Zo," the headmaster said.

Zo kept going, making his way past Ayn and out into the hall before the headmaster's hand came down on his shoulder and pulled him to a stop.

"Slow down, I just need a brief chat with you," the headmaster said.

"I really need to get back to Wilmar's," Zo said, trying to shrug off the headmaster's hand.

"I just need a moment."

Two of the headmaster's burley orderlies appeared in the hall blocking Zo's exit. His heart began to pound. He didn't like this, not at all. He didn't know what having his Healing magic disappear meant and he didn't want to find out.

The Healing headmaster pulled at Zo's elbow and gestured to the exam room next to the one where the Healing Masters were gathered.

Zo swallowed hard, his feet shuffling toward the exam room. He had fought off Zmej and the man's blue fire, but now each step felt closer to doom.

Once inside, the headmaster closed the door, and gestured for Zo to sit up on the exam table.

"I haven't seen you in a couple moons. You don't look well." The headmaster folded his arms, eyes narrowing as he examined Zo from head to toe.

Zo shrugged. "I work a lot. There's not much time for taking care of myself."

It was true—Zo didn't have time to take care of himself. He also didn't have Healing magic to heal himself. Zo's heartbeat quickened.

"What have you been up to?" the headmaster asked.

"We are short staffed in the Boiler Room, I've been taking double shifts there."

"I thought we agreed you would study here at the Healing House, but you've not taken your studies since before the winter solstice," the headmaster said.

"I'm avoiding my mother; she's trying to kidnap me."

"But she's been gone for nearly a moon."

Zo just stared at the headmaster. He wasn't going to offer any explanation that could incriminate him.

The headmaster began a slow walk around the exam table, eyes fixed on Zo. "I hear while you were studying, you became friends with a student named Keir de Sano. Is that true?"

Zo began to sweat, he hoped it wasn't visible to the headmaster. "I met him once or twice."

The headmaster stopped his slow pacing and glared at Zo. "We've heard it said that Keir held meetings to discuss forbidden Healing arts with other students. Did you attend any of these meetings?"

Zo took a deep breath to keep from swallowing again. "Look, I met him at the Ghost Festival and a few times here in the halls. What's this about? I came here to see if the rumors are true—did the Regent die the same way as Tammy?"

"It looks that way."

"And what way is that?" Zo rolled his neck and glared at the headmaster.

"I think you know."

Zo flushed hot. "No, I don't know. There's something going on here that you are hiding from your students, and repression breeds experimentation. Tell us what happened."

"Tell me first—what is the last Healing lesson? What is the oath you make to Madame Sano?" The headmaster came to stand right in front of Zo.

Zo shifted on the table, cracking his knuckles against his thighs.

The headmaster's hand shot out so fast Zo didn't have time to react. He pulled aside Zo's high, open collar to reveal the one beadscar for fire. Zo slapped away his hand. The headmaster breathed a heavy sigh. Tears welled up in his eyes as he bowed his head and turned away. He paused with his hand on the exam room latch.

"Stay here, I'll be right back," he murmured, his back to Zo and his head still low in defeat.

Once the headmaster left the room, Zo slid down from the table. There was one window in the room, but it was high up on the wall. He'd just have to fight his way out. He made his hands hot, not wanting to burn the place down with fire, and potentially hurt patients and students. As he lifted the latch, the door burst open, flinging him backward. The room filled with muscled orderlies and Healing Masters. The orderlies had thick gloves on, one had a white rag balled up in his gloved hand. Zo caught a whiff of a familiar smell, he had crushed the ingredients for it. It was the medicine Wilmar had patients breathe in to put them to sleep for surgery.

Zo shoved the exam table under the window and leapt on top of it. The window was his only chance for escape. He jumped for the windowsill. His fingers grazed it as gloved hands grabbed his ankles. He fell, his chest hitting the exam table hard enough to knock the wind out of him. As he struggled to breathe, he was pressed down into the table. His arms yanked behind his back. Someone held the cloth over his nose and mouth.

"Breathe in." The headmaster's voice came calm and soothing. "Everything is going to be alright, just breathe."

Zo fought. He struggled, thrashing and kicking. He wasn't going to breathe. They weren't going to have him.

His lungs burned until he gasped. The sickly sweet smell of the sleeping draft entered his mouth and lungs. He couldn't believe he had brought his own doom with him across the street. He felt dizzy.

"That's it." A gloved hand smoothed Zo's hair out of his eyes. "Take another deep breath."

Zo struggled to hold his breath again, but he lost. The sleeping drought entered him, and his eyelids plunged him into darkness.

Chapter Seven

I think the isolation is getting to me. I used my Mind magic to send a dream to Ryn. I haven't seen her in so long. She has grown into a lovely young woman. I wish I could be there for her Debut party. I sent her clues about the orphanage where I got her. Ryette will be angry if she finds out.

- From the journals of Moult de Dico

  They all waited until it was long past dinner time for Zo to return. Ryn sat at Wilmar's window and watched the students, as well as important people, coming and going from the Healing House. Zo's familiar figure didn't appear. Her foot wouldn't stop bouncing. What if they thought Zo had something to do with the deaths? She was shocked when he told her he had killed the wolf. Zo was the type of person to scoop up a spider and put it outside rather than killing it. She was certain if it had only been him in the room, he would have let the wolf rip his throat out. Ryn's chest tightened at the thought that Zo had lost his magic because of her. That he had worried the wolf would attack her if he let it kill him, so he had killed the wolf. All the sickness and suffering he'd endured the past moons was her fault. And now, he was across the street facing who knew what.
  Everyone else finished Wilmar's dinner, but Ryn couldn't eat. She was the only one who knew that Zo could potentially be in big trouble.
  Ryn watched as Library Regent Jeris, Prym's father, entered the Healing House with a full Library entourage. Her stomach twisted.
  Iden's hand came down on her shoulder, startling her from the view out the window. "He'll be alright. Your brother is smart and resourceful. He'll be fine."
  Ryn looked Iden in the eyes and fought back tears. She nodded, forcing herself to smile.

Regg took his coat from the coat rack. "I'll go see what's going on."

"Let us know right away," Yll said.

Regg nodded, pulling her into a hug and kissing the top of her head.

When Regg had left, Wilmar and Nix exchanged a dark look that Ryn didn't like.

"You three go on home," Nix said.

Ryn and Iden opened their mouths to protest.

Wilmar gave her his best reassuring physician's smile. "We'll let you know as soon as we hear something."

Wilmar put Ryn's cloak around her and squeezed her shoulders.

Nix hustled the three of them out the door, then walked them down the street and made sure they headed for home.

"Rude," Yll said as they left Nix behind at the corner.

"We should go around the block and sneak into the Healing House," Ryn said, looking over her shoulder back the way they'd come.

"That place is swarming with authorities," Yll said.

"All the better to hide in the crowd," Ryn argued.

Ryn looked up at Iden. He had always been one to buck authority, just like Zo, but Iden's eyes were fixed, lost in his own thoughts. He spread his arms and put one arm around each girl.

"Let's get you home. I'm sure Zo will be home as soon as things die down a little," Iden said, hurrying them along.

Ryn almost wondered if Iden was going to return to insert himself into the crowd without them. She nearly accused him of the thought and demanded he bring her along, but his shadowed eyes and pursed lips made her think twice about it.

Ryn wanted to stay at Zo's place till he got home, but Iden insisted she go home to her dorm room to wait. Clayr wasn't at the Curator's cottage, so Yll decided to stay with Ryn in her room. They found Brynd reading by the fire, baking apples. The room smelled of sweet tartness and spices. Ryn's stomach grumbled and reminded her she hadn't eaten much of Wilmar's dinner.

Iden said he would stay at Zo's and take care of the cats. He promised to let them know the minute Zo returned.

Brynd had heard about Regent Jordan's death, of course. Yll filled her in on how Zo had gone to find out what happened and hadn't returned. Brynd poured some mugs of chamomile tea and pulled the apples off the fire.

Abby, her cat, jumped into Ryn's lap when she sat. Ryn petted her with long strokes all the way down her tail. With each stroke she tried to empty her mind of her worries, but all she could think of was the last sickly look Zo had given her before he walked out Wilmar's door.

"I'm sure everything is fine," Brynd said.

The warm apples, the chamomile, and Brynd's calming presence managed to warm Ryn all over and make her sleepy.

"I'm just going to lay down for a while. Wake me if there's word," Ryn said.

* * *

The next thing Ryn knew she was startled awake by the sun peeking through the bottom of the curtains. Yll and Brynd were both gone. Ryn hadn't changed into her night clothes as she was thinking she'd only nap for a bit, but she had slept the whole night. She was late for her shift at the Library, so she quickly cleaned up and dressed in her researcher's dress. She fed Abby, then rushed out the door.

She couldn't resist stopping by Zo's room, even though she was already late. She pounded on the door, but no one answered. She was tempted to go inside and make a thorough search of his room. Maybe he was just asleep like he had been before the party. The morning bells in the bell tower began to chime, and Ryn abandoned Zo's doorstep hurrying down the path toward the secret entrance Lyssa had shown her.

On her way around the back of the Library, she ran into Fergus.

"Morning Fergus! You wouldn't have happened to see Zo anywhere last night or this morning. would you?"

Fergus stopped and rubbed at his eyebrow. "I'm pretty sure I saw him earlier entering the Boiler Room. He must have been starting the morning shift."

Relief flooded through Ryn. She ran up to Fergus and threw her arms around him. He smelled pleasantly of soap and the clean wool his uniform was made of. His hands came up around her and held her there, flooding her with reassurance and warmth.

"Thank you." Ryn's voice sank low with emotion.

Fergus chuckled. "Of course."

Ryn found herself releasing Fergus somewhat reluctantly, then she rushed off up the back Library steps before he could see her blushing. She was already chiding herself for being so impulsive. What would Fergus think of her?

At the far end of the porch away from the Library back door there was a recessed nook with a stone statue of Luc, the dragon slayer's scribe and one of the founders of the Library. Ryn pushed a stone behind his head, and the stone wall opened inward just enough for her to slip inside, then it closed again. It took a moment for her eyes to adjust to the dim light. A low burning lantern illuminated the staircase. Ryn took a deep breath and tackled the staircase that went four flights up.

* * *

"You're late," Lyssa said without raising her head from the bumpy pages she was running her fingers over.

"Sorry, I had a rough night." Ryn slipped her cloak off and hung it on the rack by the door.

Lyssa grunted. "Don't we all."

Ryn took her seat beside the desk, suddenly panicking that she couldn't remember which book she had been reading the day before. Her time here with Lyssa seemed so far away.

Lyssa sighed. "So useless. It's this one." Her hands moving to a book on the corner of the desk, and holding it out to Ryn.

Ryn accepted the book. "Of course."

Lyssa shuffled some papers around on her desk, reading the bumps with her fingers till she had them all stacked and organized. She gave a satisfied nod, picked up her metal tools.

"Let's get the day started," Lyssa said.

Ryn eyed Luc's journal still on the desk. "Before we start, do you mind if I have another look at that?" Ryn pointed to the journal.

"At what?" Lyssa frowned.

Ryn wanted to hit herself over the head. "Sorry! The Gesta Praediana."

"Sure."

This time Ryn looked the book over, from cover to cover, flipping through the familiar pages of the story, but the only place she found the embossed bumps was on the title page. She set the book back on Lyssa's desk.

"Satisfied? Can we get to work now?" Lyssa asked.

"Yes, sorry."

Ryn turned to the page of Viator's history she remembered bookmarking the day before and began to read.

***

By midday Ryn was starting to see why no one stayed long in this assignment. The work was tedious and slow. Ryn read a line from the history book and Lyssa felt for the right presses, pressing them onto the page backward so that it could be read left to right when the page was finished. It took re-reading a passage several times to make sure the raised bumps were pressed in the right order. One page took most of the morning, but when Lyssa turned it over and ran her hands across the bumps reading back what she had written Ryn couldn't help but be impressed. She looked down at the book on her lap and shuddered. How long would it take to translate the whole book?

A bookcase opened and a researcher appeared with a tray.

"Lunch time," she said, placing the tray of food on the low table in front of the couch.

"Good, I'm starved." Lyssa stood, one hand on the corner of the desk. Stepping carefully out from behind her desk, she made her way over to the couch and sat. The researcher put some cut up sandwich pieces on a plate and put it in Lyssa's lap.

"Did they cut it like I wanted them to?" Lyssa asked, her hand feeling for the sandwiches.

"Yes, of course," the researcher said.

Lyssa frowned. "There's still crust on this bread. How many times do I have to tell them I don't want crust on my bread?"

The researcher poured a glass of water. Placing it on the low tea table she guided Lyssa's hand to it.

"There's your water. I'll be off now, pull the cord if you need anything." She dropped a curtsey and turned to leave.

"Water? What does a girl have to do to get some juice around here?" Lyssa said.

"Spilled juice is sticky and messy." The researcher gave Ryn a sympathetic look then closed the bookcase shelf behind her.

"The help is useless," Lyssa said, nibbling on her sandwich.

Ryn stood awkwardly by the couch uncertain what she was supposed to do. Was she supposed to help Lyssa eat? Were they allowed to eat? They were still inside the Library where food was forbidden. She was sure Lyssa needed to eat here, but she was uncertain if she should.

Lyssa gestured with her hand. "Sit, eat."

Ryn took a piece of sandwich and sat on the farthest end of the couch away from Lyssa.

"So," Lyssa said between bites. "Where are you from? What Houses do you belong to?"

"I'm from Sooke," Ryn said, biting into the sandwich. "I'm adopted, I don't have a House."

Lyssa turned her eyes toward Ryn, but they didn't focus on her. "Another of Clayr's misfits—eh?"

Ryn swallowed. "I suppose so."

Lyssa's head dropped. "Why are you here?" She fingered another sandwich but didn't pick it up. "I mean, why up here?" She gestured to the room around them.

Ryn's mouth went dry and she poured a glass of water for herself. "I helped save the Library from a plot to destroy it." She looked down at the sandwich in her hand, not wanting to discuss the whole story. "So of course everyone hates me."

Lyssa starred in her direction. "Everyone hates me too," she whispered.

Ryn was thinking, *Can't imagine why*, but held her tongue.

"I wasn't born this way," Lyssa said. "A tumor grew at the base of my brain and pushed it against the back of my eyes. Healers have tried to remove the tumor. When they do, my eyesight gets better, but the tumor always grows back." Lyssa fingered a sandwich on her plate. "Mother's Matriarch of House Pentral. Father is Patriarch of House Flumen. Mother begged Clayr to hide me here. They are ashamed of their deficient daughter."

Matriarch of House Pentral? That meant Lyssa was related to Ryn's mother. Perhaps even a cousin. Ryette's father had been from House Pentral. Ryn swallowed. Ryette's father had been killed, and her husband had disappeared. She decided to keep that Ryette was related to herself.

"Wait, you have spirit magic and *lightning*? Is that even safe in the Library?" Ryn asked.

Ryn's eyes dropped to Lyssa's open collar. Two beads still hung on a cord. Lyssa looked older than Ryn and definitely too old to still have beads around her neck. She should be done training by now.

Lyssa's expression soured. "Don't worry, the Ancestors refuse to teach me the magic. I'm no threat to the Library."

The Ancestors refuse... Ryn was trying to process this information. "The Ancestors can refuse to teach you? You mean, you can have all the bloodlines, and be given your beads, but the Ancestors could decide not to teach you how to use it?" Ryn's eyes fell on Lyssa's beads again. "That's not fair."

Lyssa's hand drifted to her beads. "I keep hoping."

But if she's too old, it's too late. Ryn thought, but bit her tongue against saying it out loud.

Ryn looked at Lyssa and couldn't help but have compassion for her. Suddenly the gruff, grumpy exterior made sense. Not that Ryn agreed with it, but she realized there were occasions Ryn could think of when her behavior very much resembled Lyssa's. She felt shame creep through her.

"I'm sorry," Ryn said.

Lyssa's hand dropped from her beads. "It's not your fault."

"No, I'm sorry for judging you when I met you. That was wrong."

Lyssa picked up another sandwich. "It's alright, most people do. Looks like we're both cast off, wanna-be magic users."

They were, and somehow it comforted Ryn to have someone who really understood.

"Eat up," Lyssa said. "We still have a few million more pages to go." She gestured to the room around them filled with shelves and books.

Ryn swallowed hard. She wasn't sure she'd ever leave this room, there was too much to be done.

"Why are we doing these translations anyway?" Ryn asked.

Lyssa frowned around her sandwich. "The Library is dedicated to having all important resources available in every format a patron might require. Well, that's the official reason. The real reason is someone is hoping I can unlock the secrets Luc left with his bumpy finger reading process."

Ryn's brow furrowed thinking of Jeris and how he wouldn't care if someone without eyesight could read the

Ancestor's histories, but he absolutely did care about what Luc had to say.

"It's Clayr. I mean, Madame Curator, she is the one who wants it translated for others who need it." Ryn's eyes roamed the shelves. "Are there really so many people with limited eyesight who would need access to this information? Who would want to do that if the Ancestors are just going to deny teaching you?"

"Maybe the Ancestors don't deny everyone, just me." Lyssa slumped.

"I suppose a parent could also do research to help their child."

"Yeah, something like that." Lyssa sat forward feeling for the edge of the table. When she found it, she slid her plate onto it. "Or Clayr's just taking pity on me and giving me a job. Let's get back to work."

Ryn grunted. She supposed if their work helped at least one person find out who they are and where they came from it would be worth it. She knew all too well how important information was to her. If along the way she found something useful about Luc and his beads, that could be information people would kill for.

She watched Lyssa find her way back to her desk. It was going to be a long and tedious assignment, but it now seemed like a worthwhile endeavor.

"Tell me, adopted Ryn, you still have time before you're eighteen—are you looking for your Ancestors?" Lyssa asked as she felt around her desk for her tools.

Sadness and frustration swelled up from deep inside Ryn. She fought to keep it from her voice, but failed. "I have been looking. I found the orphanage where my parents adopted me, but the orphanage had no idea who my birth parents were. Some young man with white hair dropped me at their door and was never seen again."

Lyssa's hand stopped. "Interesting. I recall a myth about a white-haired boy. It was in that book on sprites I translated."

Ryn sat forward. "Really? But if it's a myth, it couldn't be my father, they'd have lived a long time ago."

"Yes, but maybe it's related. I'll do some digging." Lyssa waved her hand at the room around her full of books.

"That would be great!" Ryn tried not to let herself hope Lyssa would find answers.

"Sprites are fascinating. Did you know it's said they get their magic from the earth? Seems ridiculous to me," Lyssa said, but Ryn was distracted by something else on Lyssa's shelves.

"You have other books you've worked on. Do you remember everything you translate?"

Lyssa gestured to the pressing tools. "You've seen the process. We read the material over several times to get it right, I remember most of it."

"There's a book about the history of the Library, did you find anything unusual in the book?"

Lyssa face turned to Ryn, but her eyes were focused down. "I haven't read too many books on the history of the Library, but it seemed like a dry boring list of curators, and Library expansion. Blah, blah, blah."

"It didn't happen to mention anything about the foundation the Library was built on or a tree, did it?" Ryn asked. She had done lots of research on the Library already, but the book on Lyssa's shelf was one she'd never seen before.

Lyssa's face scrunched up. "Maybe, I really didn't pay a huge amount of attention, but I do recall something interesting about a sword."

Ryn sat up tall, her mind going back to the Protector of the Library and his showing Zo the Sword, the branch, and the stone. They have found the stone, but not the sword or the branch.

"Interesting! Can I look at it?" Ryn shifted to stand.

Lyssa reached her hand toward Ryn like she wanted to keep her seated. "Perhaps later, but for now—back to Viator history."

Ryn sighed. The story of her life these days—find a hint at a potential clue then back to work.

* * *

When the bell tower signaled the end of the workday, Ryn stood and stretched. Her eyes falling on the bookshelf where the finished translations were.

"If you don't mind, I'm just going to look through that history book," Ryn started.

"I do mind. It's a long way down. We'll look tomorrow."

Ryn clenched her teeth, but didn't argue.

Lyssa's fingers found a stick propped against the bookshelf by the door, then she held out her hand.

"What?" Ryn asked.

"Lead me, it's faster that way."

"How?"

"Let me take your arm, then we'll take the stairs together."

Ryn eyed the staircase. There was scarcely enough room for the two of them to go down side by side.

"Trust me."

Ryn stepped up next to Lyssa and let her take her arm. She had let herself be led by the arm, but this was the first time someone took hers. When she stepped forward Lyssa let the stick drift back and forth in front of her.

"Just tell me when to step," Lyssa said when they reached the first stair.

It was slow going at first, but with four stories of stairs they started to get a rhythm going. It still took an inordinate amount of time to descend the stairs, and by the time they exited the door leading outside, Ryn became increasingly unsettled wondering how Zo was doing.

They pushed their way out of the statue doorway and onto the porch. Her eyes were on the ground looking for obstacles to warn Lyssa about.

The real back door opened…and Lar exited. His hair was dirty looking, and sticking up in strange directions like he'd been running his hands through it in frustration.

"Lar," Ryn called to him.

He startled, not having seen her, then frowned.

"How are you here? Is Mother with you?" Ryn glanced around the back drive, expecting to see a carriage with her mother in it, but there was nothing. "What's going on?"

"Zo..." Lar choked. He turned whiter than the dead bodies Ryn had recently seen.

His hand grasped her arm. "Have you seen Zo? Where was he the last time you saw him? I need to find him right away."

"I..." Ryn stammered. She'd never seen Lar looking so pale, and his lips were trembling.

He glanced down at his hand on her arm and released her.

She took a deep breath. "I haven't seen him since last night. We were celebrating and then he went across the street to the Healing house."

Lar's gaze shifted to the gates of the Library that led to the west side of town and the Healing house.

"I need to go," he said, then hurried down the Library steps.

"Wait! Let me come with you!" Ryn yelled after him.

He paused on the steps and turned toward her, fidgeting like Zo would.

The door to the guardhouse opened and Norm started across the drive. Ryn waved him down. He nodded then bounded up the steps to her.

"I'm so sorry Norm, but could you see Lyssa home? Something urgent has come up." Ryn put as much pleading into her eyes as her frantic brain would allow.

Norm glanced in the direction he had been travelling, like he was needed somewhere else.

"Please Norm?" Ryn pleaded.

He sighed. "Sure, I'll find someone else to guard the east gate."

The words were barely out of his mouth and Ryn was flying down the stairs, calling to him as she went, "Thank you so much, I owe you! Sorry Lyssa!"

She ran down the steps. As soon as she was level with Lar, he was off toward the west gate. She had to know where he was going, and if he knew something about Zo. She had to keep up with him, and make sure he didn't absentmindedly leave her behind and disappear into the streets. She couldn't afford to lose him in the evening crowd. The thought made her break into a run.

Chapter Eight

Praedo's great power lay not in the blade,
Nor armor, nor magic, nor bone's sacred thread,
His strength was the truth that his spirit spread,
The faith and conviction he always displayed.

I'm still trying to discern what truth Praedo left behind. If it wasn't his sword, or his magic—what truth was Luc hinting at? Was it something that was common knowledge in Luc's day, or is it something that we have integrated into our society so that we don't know it came from him? I must send to Clayr for more sources.

- From the journals of Moult de Dico

Ryn jogged to keep up with Lar, but she was still three steps behind him. He never glanced back at her, only looking down at her when he paused to cross a street and she briefly caught up to him. Lar had always been quiet, but this was too quiet, and Ryn was too out of breath to ask any questions. She put her focus into following him and keeping up as best she could.

When they were almost to the Healer's street, her stomach did a flip flop. The confirmation of where they were headed made her heart sink. Had they found out about Zo and his dreams? About how the wolf died? Her legs and lungs already ached, but she picked up the pace. She should have known they would figure it out. She should have never let Zo cross the street to the Healing House. She should have made him stay and enjoy his party.

"Where's Mother?" she panted, trying to get Lar to slow down.

"She's with your uncle Mik. We've chased after Zmej from mainland to islands and back again. We're always one step behind him." Lar's voice sounded distracted.

Ryn tried again to walk fast enough to be next to him. She was still a couple steps behind. "Did you see a small boy with

Zmej? Brown hair with a messenger cap?" Ryn sucked in air, gasping. She didn't really owe it to Jak and Dan to find Maus, but the thought of Maus still trapped with Zmej made her heart hurt.

Lar glanced back at her. "No, but there is a little girl he has with him."

Ryn stumbled on a cobblestone. *A girl—What?* Maus wasn't a girl. Where was Maus? Ryn ran to catch up.

They turned down the Healer's street, and the Healing House came into view, her legs trembled. A hand came down on her shoulder and pulled her to a stop. Lar shook his head at her.

"Slow down, it will make us look anxious," he said.

"I am anxious!" Ryn squeaked.

"Take a deep breath. We need our wits about us."

Ryn tried, but her breaths wouldn't come as anything but short and shallow.

She followed him down the street and up the stairs to the Healing House. It was crammed with too many people. Students grouped in corners whispering, Waatch guards and officials coming and going. The air inside crackled with energy.

They passed a room with an open door. Ryn went cold inside when she realized there was a dead body lying on a table inside.

"They can't close the door?" Ryn said. Nobody answered.

Lar stopped in front of a guarded door.

"I need to see Paxon," Lar told the guard.

"The headmaster's in council with the Waatch magistrate," the guard said.

"I am Zo of Igis's father, I don't care if he's talking to Praedo himself, I demand to see the headmaster now!"

The guard's eyes darkened, but he knocked on the door and entered, closing the door behind him. When the door opened again, the guard held it for them. When the guard exited, the door shut softly, but to Ryn's heart it sounded like their doom.

"Lar de Ingis." The headmaster stood. "Have a seat." He gestured to the remaining seat in front of his desk.

Lar stayed standing.

The second seat was occupied by the Waatch magistrate. Ryn took up a position leaning against the wall behind Lar.

"What have you done with my son?" Lar demanded.

The headmaster moved to the side to get a good look at Ryn. "Who is she?"

"My betrothed's daughter, and a friend of Zo."

Friend? Ryn's shoulders drooped and her heart sank. *Am I not family? Of course, I'm never family, I'm always the friend. House Viator proved that.*

The headmaster again pointed to the seat in front of his desk. "Please sit, we have much to discuss."

Lar finally sat, followed by the headmaster taking his seat.

"I got your message. Where is my son?" Lar asked again.

The headmaster glanced at the magistrate then down at his thumbs he was rubbing together. "In the past two days there have been two Library deaths, one, a mere assistant, and the other, a Library Regent. Neither of the deaths was from natural causes."

"And besides my son working in the Boiler Room at the Library, how does he have anything to do with these deaths?" Lar asked.

"There were signs."

"What signs would say my son was involved? My son, who, as a boy, was upset when I killed a bee that had gotten into his room?" Lar folded his arms.

The headmaster exchanged a look with the magistrate again. "Both of the victims were killed with magic."

"What kind of magic?" Lar asked.

The headmaster shifted side to side in his seat. "There are no marks on the victims. They seemingly just dropped dead." The headmaster avoided the question.

"So they were killed with Spirit magic. Bring me my son and I'll be on my way."

"Unfortunately, it was discovered that Zo has used his Healing magic in an inappropriate way. One that has severe consequences," the headmaster said.

Lar sat up straight. "What do you mean? How do you know that he has done something inappropriate?"

The headmaster sighed. "It is forbidden for Healers to speak of it."

Ryn shifted her stance and could see Lar's mouth working, like he couldn't decide what words would explode out of him.

The magistrate turned to Lar. "The Healers cannot speak of it, but I can. I have studied Waatch law enforcement all my life and this is what is known—there is a reverse to Healing magic."

"Myths and legends. Why would a Healer use their magic to kill?" Lar waved his hand at the thought.

"There is a documented sign for Healers who have killed—their bead scar sluffs off, or as in the case with underage Healers, their Healing bead crumbles and disappears. This is a sign that has been documented in the legal history of Waatch as evidence to find potential killers," the magistrate said.

Ryn felt her insides turn cold. She wrapped her arms around herself in an effort not to shiver.

"There are a handful of Healing students missing their beads—your son is one of them," The headmaster's voice was barely above a whisper.

The magistrate continued, "Once a Healer has killed, their Healing magic is altered so that all it wants is to kill. In fact, it has been reported in ages past that it becomes like an addiction, often with the killer escalating from killing small animals to killing humans. There's some kind of rush apparently."

"Wait, that can't be true, Zo told me he had gone on Healing calls with Keir, and they Healed patients," Ryn piped up from the back.

The headmaster's eyes found Ryn's. "How did you know about Keir?"

Ryn's face flushed. She probably shouldn't have given away how much she knew.

"The effect can be different, it's more of a spectrum at first, but the more killing a Healer does, the worse they become," the magistrate said.

The headmaster rocked back and forth. "Keir is a special case, he has double Healing magic, from his mother and his father. His magic would be difficult to break."

"Paxon." Lar left off the headmaster's title. "I'm only going to ask this one more time before I burn this Healing House to the ground—*Where is my son?*"

Ryn shrank back from Lar's vehemence. Lar was always so quiet and mild, she had assumed Zo's fiery defiance came from his mother. Maybe Ryn was wrong.

The headmaster looked up at the ceiling as if pleading for help from the Ancestors. "Zo and the others have been sent to House Sano and the Healing Council to stand trial for their transgression."

"And what is the penalty for this *transgression*?" Lar snarled.

The Healing Master's pleading eyes found Lar's. "You have to understand, Zo is already sickly, pale, dark circles around his eyes—it's only a matter of time."

"No, he's fine. He's a little tired, but there's nothing wrong with him," Ryn's shaking voice piped up from the back.

"The penalty!" Lar shouted.

"You have to understand—the mind sickness that comes with…"

"Death," the magistrate said.

Chapter Nine

I can't be sure, but I think someone, or something followed me home from fishing last night. Shadows moved in the dark, and the hairs stood up on my arms. There was some kind of growl that was not from a bear, or a cougar. I shape shifted into a bat, but could not detect what was following me. Being a bat did give me an idea for how to delve deeper into the cave...

- From the journals of Moult de Dico

"What?" Lar and Ryn said at the same time.

"I am terribly sorry, you see..." The headmaster continued on, but Ryn's heart was beating in her throat, her head rushing with blood and swimming.

The office was suddenly too hot and too closed in. She needed to run...somewhere—anywhere. There had to be a way to escape this. If she could run fast enough and far enough this wouldn't be happening.

The headmaster stood. "There was nothing else I could do. The Healing law is clear, if anyone exhibits certain signs they must be sent to the Healing Council straightaway for examination. I sent you the message immediately so you could be informed. I will message the Council and request permission for you to address them. If you hire a Viator Traveler now you could plead his case to the Council before the boat with the prisoners arrives on Eileansano." The headmaster's hands twisted. "I am sorry. Zo was an incredibly talented Healer, and though he liked to be difficult, his heart was genuine. I will miss him."

The headmaster stuck out his hand for Lar to shake. Lar stood, glared down at the outstretched hand, then turned and left the office. Ryn followed, still trying to figure out how to crawl out of her skin and become someone else. They passed Ayn, standing in the hallway, tears streaming down her face as she watched them leave. Ayn was a mind healer. Maybe if Ryn swapped lives with Ayn she could heal her own mind, because right now, it was screaming to be taken from her body.

* * *

When they were some streets away from the Healing House—Ryn couldn't tell where they were—Lar peppered her numbed brain with questions.

"What happened? Did Zo tell you what happened? How did this happen?"

Dazed, Ryn looked at Lar trying to process what he was asking. Her jaw was working, no sound was coming out. Lar stopped and took her by the arms.

"Did he tell you anything that could help me save him?" His eyes were fire in the darkness.

Ryn finally found her voice. "He killed the wolf...the one who attacked during the ball...it was ripping out his throat, so he killed it with his Healing magic. Ever since then he hasn't been able to Heal. He's been sick, and looking worse every day."

Lar let his hands drop. He turned to resume their trip across town. "That's good. That's good—self-defense right? They can't have expected him to let the wolf kill him. I could use that."

Ryn rushed forward and grabbed Lar's arm. "Um—there's something else you should know. Zo was sleeping a lot...he had bad dreams."

"And?"

"At the exact time Tammy and the Regent were killed, Zo dreamed that he killed them."

Lar ran a shaking hand through his hair. He was quiet for a long time, then he let out a long breath. "It was a dream. That's all. Whoever killed them must have mind magic to send those images to Zo. I can see him killing that wolf, everyone's lives at the ball were at stake, but there's no way he dream walked and killed someone he didn't know."

Hearing Lar say it out loud, Ryn knew it was true. She was ashamed her mind had doubted, even for a minute. He killed a wolf to protect everyone, but he hadn't murdered anyone.

"Right," Ryn affirmed.

"Where's Regg? I need to see him," Lar asked.

"I didn't see him at the Healing House, but we only went to the headmaster's office. There're too many people at the Healing house though, I'm guessing he's with Yll."

Lar nodded and set off down the street, and Ryn was back to jogging to keep up.

*　*　*

They found Regg with Yll and Clayr at the Curator's cottage on the Library grounds. It was clear by the look on everyone's faces that they'd already heard the news. Clayr was certainly in the know about suspects in the murder of a Library worker and Regent. At the sight of Clayr, Ryn burst into tears. Clayr embraced her and held her tight.

"You can do something right?" Ryn sobbed into Clayr's shoulder. "You're the Curator of the Library, one of the most powerful people in the world. He's important to the Library. You've told them before to leave him alone, you could do it again."

Clayr hugged her tighter, then pulled back and wiped Ryn's tears with her thumbs. She kissed Ryn on the forehead, then hugged her again. "If only it was that simple."

Yll joined the hug, then Regg. Lar put his hand on Regg's shoulder, as he rubbed at his eyes. Ryn felt their warmth engulf her. For a moment, everything was going to be alright. Then the embrace ended, and Ryn felt cold and alone.

Lar's hand slid to Regg's elbow. "I came to find you. Paxon is requesting an audience for us with the council. I'm leaving as soon as I get the approval. I'd like you to come with me. It might be the last chance to see him." Lar's voice choked.

"I want to go. Please let me go," Ryn said.

"Me too," Yll added.

"A Viator Traveler can only take three," Clayr said.

Just then a Travel magic messenger appeared.

"That was fast," Yll said.

"Lar de Ingis?" the messenger asked.

"That's me." Lar held out his hand for the message.

He scanned the paper then folded it and put it into his jacket pocket. "We have permission to go."

Ryn sagged into Clayr.

Yll threw herself into Regg's arms.

Regg crushed her to him. "I won't be long. I have something to give you when I get back."

A tear choked laugh escaped Yll as Regg pulled away far enough so he could kiss her with such passion Ryn shifted, feeling like she was invading a private moment.

"Ahem," Clayr said.

Regg and Yll pulled away, both of them red-faced and breathless.

Clayr embraced Regg and Lar. "Be safe. Fight for Zo, he's worth fighting for."

At that Ryn teared up.

Lar engaged the messenger to take them to the House Sano. Ryn stepped up to join them.

The Travel messenger put out his hand. "Only family are permitted. You're not family."

Ryn took a step back. Her breath stolen from her like she'd been punched in the gut. Didn't her mother's engagement make her family? Of course it didn't. It was a nice thing to say—you're my family—but when dire circumstances arose, only blood was family.

Lar turned to her. "The approval only permits Regg and I to go."

Through tears she barely saw them leave. Dust and dirt pelted her face and hands from the spinning wind of the Travel magic. Then they were gone.

* * *

Once the air cleared from the Travel magic, Ryn took off running across the Library grounds. She could barely see where she was going. When her feet stopped, she found herself in front of Zo's door. She wiped her eyes and knocked like a fool. All was silent. She drew in a deep breath and lifted the latch. It was dark inside, cold and empty. Beardsley rubbed against her leg. She bent down and scooped him up, hugging him tight to her chest. There was no way to light Zo's lanterns, because, of course, he didn't need something to light them. She sat on his bed in the dark with Beardsley on her lap while she petted Jinx. Her mind was blank. Her body numb. She couldn't put any thoughts together. Eventually she laid down, pulling the blankets over her, and drifted off to sleep.

* * *

She was on that warm beach. The one her mother had shown her. The one where she had seen Zo in her dream, and he had told her about Jak and Dan's Library break in. The sound of the waves crashing onto the shore drained her strength, and her legs buckled beneath her. The sand was warm, almost hot in the sunshine. It seeped into her bones. She took in a deep breath of the cool, salty air. She closed her eyes and dug her hands deep into the sand to find where it became cool to the touch. She thought about Zo. How he loved the beach. She sent her mind out to him, trying to summon him to her. It was nighttime. He must be asleep somewhere. If she filled her mind with him, surely he would appear. She brought an image of his toothy grin, standing in the sunshine, breeze ruffling his hair. She smiled. He would be there. The sand crunched beside her like footsteps approaching. Her eyes fluttered open—to an empty beach. Her eyes scanned the shore in both directions, but there was nothing, not even a seagull. The sun began to set as her head dropped to her knees.

* * *

A furry tail under her nose twitched her out of her dream, but she came fully awake to the sound of the door opening. She squinted at a dark shadow silhouetted against the sunshine filled door.

"There you are." Fergus' voice was filled with relief. "I've been looking everywhere for you."

Ryn covered her head with the blankets. She didn't want to face the day.

The floor creaked at Fergus' footsteps announcing his crossing the room and coming to sit in the chair by the bed. The one she had used to sit next to Zo. She took a deep breath to fight the tightness threatening to crush her chest.

"Hey, are you alright?" Fergus asked.

Ryn said nothing. What could she say to that?

"Of course you're not alright. That was a dumb thing to ask. I'm really sorry Ryn."

She peaked out from under the blankets that smelled of Wilmar's with a hint of fire. She fought to keep the tears from rising.

Fergus held out a crock of fish, and he suddenly became Jinx and Beardsley's best friend.

"I brought some food for the cats, I wasn't sure if anyone was taking care of them."

"Thank you," Ryn whispered, fighting to keep her voice in control.

He got up to find a spoon in Zo's chest of drawers, then scooped the fish into the cat's bowls.

"Madame Curator sent me to find you to tell you to take a day or two off if you want. She understands it might be difficult for you to focus right now," Fergus said.

Ryn sat up. "Great! Then I have time to go to Eileansano. If I get a Viator Traveler I could spend the next couple days there. Maybe if I tell them I know something about what happened they'll let me stay. Maybe I could see him. I could be there." Ryn threw the covers off and got out of bed.

"She also wished for me to remind you that House Viator is not one you can trust, and that you shouldn't let them take you anywhere." Fergus gave her that stern look he always had when she was up to something she shouldn't be.

"You could come with me! If you're with me, they wouldn't dare try anything."

Fergus put his hands on her shoulders. "What's happening at House Sano is not going to be pretty."

"I don't care." Ryn lifted her chin glaring into his eyes.

Fergus sighed. "I didn't want to have to pull this, but Madame Curator knew you were going to insist so she gave an order and specifically forbade you from going. Not only is she the head of the Library, and your superior, but she wanted me to remind you that your mother has given her charge of taking care of you in her absence."

Ryn stomped her foot like a toddler. "I don't care. I am of age, I don't need a minder."

Fergus dropped his hands from her shoulders.

Her face immediately flushed with embarrassment at her behavior.

"She can't do this to me. I have to go."

She plowed forward, but Fergus shuffled backward, staying in front of her.

"Stop Fergus, please move."

He kept in front of her till his back hit the door.

"Let me go."

"I won't let you throw away your career at the Library."

She started beating on his chest. "My career means nothing right now. Let me go!" She dissolved into tears. "I have to go."

Fergus put his arms around her and held her close. His right hand cupped her head and held her gently to him.

"Please," she sobbed into his uniform, she couldn't hold it back anymore.

He just held her. He didn't let go while she cried and raged.

Eventually her sobs dissolved into hiccups. The hand on her head stroked her hair. His head bent to her, and he whispered how strong she was, and how she was going to get through it, and how much he admired her. She pulled her arms tight around him and breathed in the scent of his uniform. The smell of wool and outdoors in the spring. She inhaled a cottonwood seed stuck on the trim and sneezed. Fergus gave her a handkerchief that matched the one he'd given her last fall after the whole Master Wes disaster.

She blew her nose and wiped her eyes.

"I'm sorry," she murmured.

"I understand, Ryn." He bent down so he was eye level with her. "It's not fair. You do something amazingly heroic and you're punished for it. If I could spare his life, if I could trade places, I would do it. If for no other reason than to see you smile."

Ryn blew her nose again and looked at Fergus through tear-gummed eyes. The sunshine creeping in from around the curtain made his hair almost glow. His eyes had tears in them. She didn't know what to say that wouldn't be dismissive of what he just offered to her, so she threw her arms around him and buried her face back into the wet spot she'd made on his uniform.

He wrapped his arms around her again and they stayed that way for a long time.

Eventually Jinx started playing with the hem of her skirt, getting his claw stuck in the fabric. She had to let go of Fergus to disentangle Jinx.

"I need to get back to my duties, but if you need me, just ask Errol where to find me. Anytime, day or night. I'm here." Fergus gave her a kiss on her forehead.

Ryn nodded. "Thank you."

Fergus slipped out the door so the cats wouldn't escape, and Ryn was left alone. As soon as the door closed the room felt suffocating. She scooped up Jinx and set him next to Beardsley on the bed then scurried out the door.

* * *

She wandered the Library grounds trying to get lost in the web of walkways through the budding flower beds. She thought maybe if she walked enough, she could out distance what was happening in her mind, and the stress in her heart. Eventually she found herself in front of the Boiler Room. She remembered the night her and Zo snuck into the Library through the underground tunnels, and the Protector of the Library chased them till Zo was hit with a fire lesson that threatened to burn down the Library, and how ridiculous he looked being carried out over Fergus' shoulder. Ryn smiled, then her heart squeezed and she hurried away to the west gate and out into Waatch. She wandered past the Library supply shops with papers, pens, and notebooks. Normally she loved to stop and look, but today, none of it appealed to her. She found herself passing Thax's tailor shop. She paused briefly at the windows outside. She considered going in, but she couldn't bear to talk to Tory or Thax right now. Any kind of small talk felt like a huge chore, and she absolutely couldn't discuss what happened. She would have to tell them later, if they didn't already know. Jak, Tory's friend and Brynd's ex-boyfriend, had made it clear that the citizens of Waatch knew everything that happened in the Library.

She went up the street and turned a corner and somehow ended up in front of Zo and Iden's favorite breakfast place. Her gaze took in the sign over the door, but her brain refused to read it. She fled down the street, deliberately turning down a street she knew she'd never been down before. She wanted to escape into something unfamiliar, yet every street she passed, and every turn she made, she expected to see Zo coming down the street toward her. He should be there, walking the streets, going from one job to another. She finally turned a corner and realized she was at the westernmost end of the street Wilmar's place was on. She was approaching it from a different direction than normal. Her feet carried her quickly down the street. Maybe she could sit with Wilmar. He was always a great comfort, and maybe, just maybe this was all a bad dream and she would find Zo sitting at Wilmar's worktable grinding herbs into potions.

Once she was halfway down the block she could see the long line outside Wilmar's office. When she passed by, one glance through the window told her Wilmar was alone seeing patients. He was too busy for her. She hurried past and decided walking wasn't helping her take her mind off everything. She decided to go home and change into a fresh dress and go to her job. The thought of endlessly reading to Lyssa surrounded by books in her loft sounded enormously appealing.

* * *

Ryn rushed up the steps and pushed the bookcase door open to find Lyssa running her fingers over the spines of the books on a shelf behind the couch. Lyssa startled at the sound of someone entering the room, and a book fell onto her head.

"Ouch! Who's there?" Lyssa said, rubbing the spot where she got hit by the book.

"It's me, Ryn."

"I thought you weren't coming," Lyssa said, holding the back of the couch to bend down and feel for the book she dropped.

"Wandering around isn't helping me, so I thought working might be a good distraction. At least I can get lost in House Viator's past troubles."

Lyssa must have found the book, because she straightened and started for her desk.

"I'm glad you came. I've been puzzling over your white-haired man, and I couldn't help but start doing some research." Lyssa sat at her desk and pushed a few books toward Ryn's chair. "I made Kay come in and read these to me."

"*Wild Magic Creatures and Where to Find Them, Who Has Wild Magic, How to Catch a Watersprite*—you think the white-haired man came from the wild magic?"

Lyssa gave a small shrug. "The story I remembered translating was about a wolf seen with the sprites, but look at this." Lyssa ran her fingers over the cover of the where to find magical creatures book, then opened it to a marked page.

On one side of the page was a drawing of a wolf, on the opposite was a passage on wolf lore.

Wolves at one point roamed the land in abundance. Said to be the offspring of the dragon and Ancestor women, they were fiercely loyal to their father and would do his bidding. In ancient times if a wolf was near, the dragon was not far behind. The wolf has faded into the mists of time as a myth, and no wolves have been seen for centuries. House Vivus has been accused in the past of attempting to use their animate magic to bring these wolves back to life, but they have fiercely denied that rumor.

Ryn sucked in her breath, her hand flying to her mouth. "Prym is House Vivus. What if she was involved in resurrecting those wolves that attacked us? She was scared of something out on Viatoro. What if she knew what was happening in her own House?"

"Interesting to ponder, isn't it?" Lyssa seemed to be like everyone else in the Library and Waatch—she seemed to know everything that happened, even though she was secluded up here in the fourth-floor attic.

"What if the wolf attack on Zo wasn't an accident? What if they were deliberately trying to take out the one person who has a mental link with the Library Protector? It would mean that…"

"They set him up to be killed," Lyssa finished.

Ryn tried to swear like Zo, but her brain froze and nothing came out.

"I've heard the stories of what happened that night, but I don't understand how you're related to this Zo person. He sounds dangerously fun." Lyssa giggled.

"He's my broth…" Ryn started, then remembered how she'd been told she was only a friend and not family. She wasn't family to anyone. No one was her blood relative. She was nothing, no one. Even Jett, her brother by adoption, had rejected her. Tears welled up in her eyes, she was grateful Lyssa couldn't see them.

Then in her mind she saw Zo, bending down to look into her in the face outside the orphanage.

Courage, little sister, I will always be your brother.

She heard his voice clear as the day he said them. As if he was standing there saying them to her now. A tear trickled down her cheek.

The door down to Kay's office burst open. Brynd came flying in, white-blond hair sticking out in all directions, her blue grey eyes wide and scanning the room, finally settling on Ryn.

"They've done the unthinkable! Come quick!"

Chapter Ten

Then we learned how a year past, the beast had come,
Shattered and weary in human guise;
He demanded at once that bread be supplied,
And protection from men lest his need become.

I have often wondered and feared about this. If the dragon of old could appear as a human, could a new dragon do the same? And if they did...could there be a dragon living among us?

- From the journals of Moult de Dico

Something that smelled like the worst cat pee he'd ever smelled brought Zo back from a deep dreamless nothing.

"He's coming around," a woman's voice said.

His eyelids were red from the light on the other side, but he struggled to lift them. He tried to shift his body, but found he couldn't move anything. He peeked through the small slit he was able to open.

There was a woman in Eileansano Healing robes hovering over him. "Zo, we need you to wake up."

That didn't sound like a great idea to Zo. There were weighted blankets holding him down, dragging him back into sleep. His eyes slid closed again.

Another shot of the pee smell roused Zo to wakefulness.

"That's better. Drink this, the Council investigators want to see you." The Healer put a cup to his lips.

Zo's parched mouth and dry lips eagerly took in the liquid. He coughed, choking on it going down too fast. The Healer did something to the bed he was lying on and Zo found himself propped up, but still unable to move. She put the cup to his lips again and he drained the cup.

"That's good. You lie there and wake up, and I'll go let them know you'll be ready soon."

He heard a door open and close, and a feeling of isolation rushed in. He blinked, wishing he could rub the sleep out of his eyes, but he still couldn't move. He found if he worked a bit he could wiggle his fingers and toes slightly, but that was all. The room he was in was brightly lit by the kind of lanterns Healers use to see their patients' wounds better. They were hurting his eyes and giving him a headache. There was a small table that had a cloth covering what must have been some instruments, but otherwise the room was empty. The walls were white, the ceiling was white, it was all very barren of life. It didn't have the homey feel the recovery rooms had in the Waatch Healing House. The light shining in through the window high up on the wall was barred.

There are bars on the window. The thought floated in and out of Zo's mind. *Maybe if I sleep some more this will all make sense.*

The sound of keys jangling in the door lock brought Zo fully awake.

The woman Healer and two men in House Sano uniform entered the room. They all wore thick looking gloves that had so much padding they could probably withstand holding hot coals in their hands. Zo didn't understand. Wrapped up as he was, with his hands pinned to his chest, there was no way he could use his Fire magic.

The Healer brought in some chairs, then closed and locked the door. The two men sat. One of them removed a glove so he could write in a notebook. The Healer took something sharp looking and came to stand next to Zo's head.

Zo swallowed.

"State your name for the record please," the man whose uniform had many bars and tassels on it asked.

"Zo de Ignis," Zo's voice croaked like it was waking from long disuse.

"We are going to ask you a series of questions. You have been given something that will assist in telling us the truth. We recommend you do, because lies will only make things harder for you," Bars and Tassels said.

The second man began scribbling in his notebook.

Something flashed in the Healer's hand near Zo's cheek. He tried to flinch away but still couldn't move. His heart picked up the pace.

"Advocate," Zo's voice failed. He cleared his throat. "Don't I get an advocate?"

"You will have one at the trial. For now, we are just taking your statement. We would like to hear your side of the story," Tassels said.

Zo's thoughts were swirling. He was pretty sure he needed someone to defend him in the state he was in, but couldn't formulate the words to argue.

"Where am I?" He asked.

"The House Sano Healing House on Eileansano."

"How did I get here?"

"By boat. Enough now, we will be asking the questions."

Zo's head swam with thoughts. If he could distract them long enough for him to think straight, maybe he could talk himself out of trouble.

"Where's my mother?" He asked.

Tassels shifted in his chair. He frowned at Zo. "You will get to see your family if you answer my questions truthfully."

Something flashed near Zo's cheek. He managed to tilt his head away slightly.

"Now tell us, where were you on the afternoon that the Library worker Tammy de Illiso was killed?"

Zo cleared his throat again. "Asleep. I've been working double shifts at the Library and helping the Waatch physician."

Scribe guy's pen started scratching in his notebook.

"Do you have anyone who can prove that?"

"My cats Beardsley and Jinx."

Tassels made a strangled noise in his throat. "Anyone else?"

"The Library guard, Fergus, woke me up to come and examine the body."

Scratch, scratch, scratch went the pen.

"That's easy to verify. How about the evening Regent Jordan was found dead? Where were you then?"

"Again, I was asleep." Zo didn't dare tell them he'd just finished his last magic lesson. He didn't want to open that conversation. Nor did he want to tell them about his dreams of killing. "After my nap I went with my sister to a party at the physician's place." He avoided mentioning his birthday.

"Why haven't you been taking your Healing lessons at the Waatch Healing House?"

"I told the headmaster I didn't want my mother informed of my enrollment. She showed up anyway. We fought, so I haven't been back."

Tassel's gloved hand reached across to push Zo's hair back. He turned Zo's head to the right and the left, examining him.

"Why do you look sickly? Your magic should heal you, even while you're asleep."

Zo tried to pull his head from the man's grasp, but failed. He said nothing.

Tassels released him and nodded to the Healer. She brought another glass of liquid to Zo and forced him to drink it. Tassels sat with his arms folded while Zo's head swam like it was submerged underwater. The heavy weighted blankets were overheating him. Sweat beaded on his forehead. His vision blurred, and saliva trickled out of the corner of his mouth. The Healer wiped it away with a cloth.

"Now." Tassels leaned closer to Zo's face. "You will tell me everything you're hiding."

Zo took a deep breath, and everything he never wanted to say to anyone, much less these two jokers, came spilling out of him like a flood.

* * *

When Zo had finished spilling his guts, the Healer let Tassels and his scribe out of the room, then locked it again. A tear trickled from Zo's eye. He couldn't believe they had forced all that information from him. Not just the details of killing the wolf, but all of his deep, dark, private fears. His stomach flip flopped at the thought of what they would do with that information.

The Healer wiped the tear from his cheek, then fed him some mush. His stomach protested the food at first, but after a few bites he stopped feeling shaky, and nauseous.

When he was done eating there was a knock at the door. The Healer unlocked and opened the door. There was a heated whispered discussion, then the Healer opened the door wide.

Fyri de Sano, Zo's mother, entered the room.

Zo groaned.

"Oh, my poor baby boy!" Zo's mother rushed over and sat next to him on the bed, her hands feeling his forehead and the sides of his neck. "He looks terrible. Why hasn't anyone Healed him?"

The Healer sucked in her breath. "Touching someone with Killing magic is death." She pulled over a chair. "You should move away, and put on gloves."

Fyri sniffed at the gloves. "My son doesn't have Killing magic. You all are being absurd. He's overheated and far too warm in all of these wrappings. I demand you remove them."

"No." The Healer put her hands on her hips, nostrils flaring.

Fyri turned red. "I am a member of the Healing Council, I demand you release my son."

"My orders are from the Head of Council herself. If you want his treatment changed, you'll have to take it up with her."

"I shall! At least get me some ice to cool him down."

The Healer huffed and left the room.

Zo's mother turned to him. "Quickly tell me what happened. I need to know what defense to mount."

Zo's jaw tightened. "Can't you read what they just forced me to tell them?" The violation was grating on him.

"No—they will use that only to condemn you. I have powerful friends. Tell me everything so I can save you." He'd never seen his mother sound so desperate. He wondered if she really cared about him, or just her reputation.

After her behavior in Waatch he didn't feel like he could trust her motivations, but at this point he supposed her motivations didn't matter.

"I killed that wolf at the ball with Healing magic." He watched her face to see behind the mask.

The smile she gave him looked plastered on her face. "See, I was right. It was just an animal, you're fine."

"My Healing bead disappeared. Madame Sano abandoned me and I didn't finish my lessons."

His mother sucked in her breath. "No."

He almost hesitated to tell her the next bit, but he had already told Tassels and the Scribe so she would find out anyway. Besides, he was almost gleefully ready to twist the knife.

"I dreamt that I killed Tammy and Regent Jordan at the same time the murders took place."

Fyri turned as white as the walls behind her. She rose from the chair and shifted to the corner of the room, her back to Zo. She stood still as Praedo's statue for so long Zo was sure she would walk out as soon as the Healer returned. Finally, she turned on him.

"I'm going to fix this," she said.

"What's there to fix? What's done is done. In order to save my family, friends, and half of Waatch I violated some ancient law that, by the way, nobody told me about because it's *forbidden* to talk about. I hate this magic so much. I wish I hadn't been born into it," Zo spat.

Fyri reeled back like he had slapped her. She took a deep breath then reached up to smooth her hair.

She sniffed. "I know you don't mean that. I will get you released and then you will do as I say to get this fixed. You will keep your mouth shut during the trial, and I will take care of the rest. Do you understand?"

"Get this fixed? There's no fixing the fact that I'm over eighteen and didn't finish my lessons. My Healing is gone, and you can't do a thing about it. Get out Mother, I've accepted my fate," he said it, even though he wasn't sure he had at all.

The Healer unlocked and opened the door just as Fyri turned and stormed out.

Zo sunk down deeper into the bed. He wasn't certain making an enemy of the one person who could probably save him was a great idea, but he wasn't going to let her control him. Not now, not ever.

"The rest of your family petitioned the Council to see you, but they were denied," the Healer said as she shoved an ice pack under the heavy blanket.

Zo shivered at the sudden cold. "Good, I don't want them to see me like this."

"You've seen everyone for the last time." the Healer said before she left the room, keys sliding the deadbolt in place behind her.

Chapter Eleven

I found the door! I'm certain it leads to the chamber where Praedo's beads of bone rest, but there's no lock and no latch. The only markings on the door is a carving, and I have no idea what it means. I have not encountered such a carving anywhere. The only thing close to it is the strange carvings on that odd door with no latch in the Library, but those carvings shift and change. Who knows what goes on behind that door. I'm thinking of sending a description of this carving to Ryette and Clayr. Those two have access to more extensive knowledge than I have.

- From the journals of Moult de Dico

Ryn hurried after Brynd down the main hall of the Library Board of Regents to the doors that led to the Regent's Chamber. Yll was standing outside the doors pacing, her arms hugging herself.

It wasn't something Ryn was accustomed to doing, but she went straight to Yll and put her arms around her. Yll was shaking as she clung to Ryn.

"What's happening?" Ryn asked.

Yll hugged Ryn tighter, then pulled back. "It's Mother. They're…" Yll let out a sob.

The latch lifted on the chamber doors, and Norm, who was standing guard, opened the door just enough for Fergus to slip out.

"It's a vote of no confidence," Fergus said.

"What?" soft-spoken Brynd yelled, her eyes bulging.

"It was unanimous. Between the fiasco with Master Wes, the fire battle in the Heart of the Library, and now two murders on Library grounds, the Board has returned a unanimous vote of no confidence in Clayr. She has been stripped of her title and will be escorted off the grounds. Any personal belongings will be collected and returned to her at her cottage in Sooke." Fergus said.

"But…what about Yll?" Ryn asked.

"As Clayr's daughter she has been dismissed with her. They are deliberating now on the fate of all the Ordinary workers. I have to be honest Ryn, it doesn't look good."

Ryn's gaze went from Fergus' downturned eyes, to Norm's shaking head, then stopped at Brynd's hand covering her mouth. Losing Zo had shifted the ground of her world beneath her feet, but this crumbled it. Her knees gave out and they hit the tiled floor hard, sending a sharp spike of pain through her hips. She ignored it.

"But…where will we go? What will we do? My family depends upon my job." Brynd's voice broke.

Ryn was lost without the Library. It was her whole world. The Library was her family.

Fergus helped Ryn to her feet. His strong arm went around her waist and helped her limp to a bench outside the door. With his thumb he wiped a tear Ryn hadn't realized she'd shed from her cheek.

"Maybe everything will be alright. I'll talk to Errol and see what can be done." With that, Fergus slipped back into the Regent's chambers.

Ryn couldn't stay sitting. She limped back and forth in front of the doors, while Brynd dropped into the spot Ryn had vacated on the bench, and Yll resumed hugging herself.

"What will we do?" Yll asked. "The Library has been my whole life. My mother has been curator since before she adopted me."

The doors remained closed for what felt like days. Ryn was sure she had worn a path in the tile pacing. Finally, when the light was long gone from the windows high above the hall, and it felt like midnight, the doors opened and Fergus emerged shaking his head.

Errol, Captain of the Library guard, emerged escorting Clayr. She held her head high, with Errol's arm around her shoulders. His gesture felt protective rather than punitive.

"Please escort Ryn and Brynd to their room to collect their things," Errol commanded Fergus, his voice breaking.

"Yes sir." Fergus' response was quiet and slow.

"That's it?" Ryn's anger flared. "Just like that we're being thrown out? After everything we've done to save the Library?"

"All Ordinaries are to be expelled," Errol said. "They are returning to an Ancestor descendant staff only. Please make sure you collect Zo's things as well. He won't be returning."

Ryn's heart squeezed at the way Errol said that so matter of fact.

Regent Jeris, Prym's father, exited the doors in conversation with another regent.

"Get this garbage out of here." Jeris waved at Ryn and her friends, then continued his conversation as they strode down the hall.

Yll followed Errol and her mother.

"But where will we go?" Ryn turned to Fergus and Norm. "It's too late to travel back to Sooke, and Mother hasn't been there in moons—who knows what critters have moved into our cottage?"

Brynd put an arm around Ryn. "I have an idea."

* * *

It was the middle of the night by the time Ryn, Brynd, and Fergus stood in front of the tailor's shop with several bags, trunks, and three cats in their arms. Fergus was battling Jinx who kept trying to climb up on top of his head.

"Where did your brother get this cat?" Fergus asked. "He's like a petite fire monster."

"Oh, he's being good. He prefers men to women," Ryn said.

"Perfect cat for your brother," Fergus grunted. "Ow, ow ow." Jinx tried to climb the side of Fergus' head with his claws out.

Brynd pulled the rope to ring the bell inside the shop again. They'd rung a couple times already.

Finally Tory, Thax the tailor's assistant, opened the door. Her dark hair stuck up in places and her eyes squinted at them as she held a lantern up to see who was at the door in the middle of the night.

"What are you doing..." Tory started, then she seemed to take in the cats and the luggage. Her eyes went wide. "What's happened?"

Ryn looked around at the sleeping shops on the street with their quiet residences above them. "Can we come inside? We'll explain everything."

Tory nodded and held the door open for them.

Once inside, Fergus gave up his fight to hold Jinx and let him go. Jinx zipped around the shop then into the back behind the curtain. Abby, Ryn's cat, and Beardsley quietly eyed Jinx's antics from Ryn and Brynd's arms.

"I hope he doesn't spill my piss bucket of dye," Tory grumbled.

"I'm so sorry Tory, we didn't know where else to go," Brynd said.

"What are you doing here with so many bags and the cats?" Tory asked.

The stairs creaked and Thax came down into the shop. He took in the scene rubbing his eyes.

"They've thrown you out," Thax said.

Ryn nodded, not trusting her voice to say anything.

"No," Tory gasped.

Fergus was putting his fingers to his face and pulling them away, looking for blood. "They've dismissed Clayr, and had all the Ordinary workers terminated and escorted out."

"In the middle of the night," Ryn added, heat flushing through her body.

Tory swore.

"We were hoping..." Brynd started.

"Of course you can stay with me!" Thax opened his arms and threw them around Ryn and Brynd. "I have an extra room. Tory, will you go remove the dress form and the bolts of fabric from the spare room, and put clean sheets on the bed?"

Tory opened her mouth like she was going to protest, but took in Ryn and Brynd, and closed it. She put her arms around the girls.

"It'll be so nice to have someone around besides this grumpy old fart." She squeezed them tight, then she headed off up the stairs.

"Hey—who you calling old?" Thax said.

Fergus put a hand on Ryn's shoulder. "I'm sorry, but I have to get back to my post at the Library."

Ryn nodded, reluctant to let go of Fergus' familiar presence.

Fergus hugged her tight. "Don't worry, I know it looks bad right now, but things are going to work out."

Ryn sniffled as she held onto Fergus. "Wait—you're ordinary, why aren't they kicking you out?"

"Since the Library was founded the Library guard has always been made up of Ordinaries from Waatch. It's only recently that Clayr has allowed Ordinary Library workers," Fergus said over the top of her head.

Ryn nodded slowly. Fergus kissed the top of her head then left, the shop bell tinkling as the door opened and closed.

Thax moved to lock the door behind him. "Let's get you two settled, shall we?"

Something crashed behind the curtain to the back workroom.

"What was that?" Thax asked.

"Jinx," Ryn and Brynd said at the same time.

Thax blinked slowly. "Does somebody owe somebody something?"

Ryn and Brynd giggled.

"No, it's Zo's cat, Jinx," Ryn gave him a pleading smile.

Something else crashed.

Thax rubbed his forehead, eyeing Abby and Beardsley in Ryn and Brynd's arms. "Right, looks like cat hair is going to be the new Waatch fashion statement this season."

* * *

The next morning Ryn woke stiff and sore. The bed was small for one person, but for two people with three cats it was tiny. Ryn tried to stretch out, but her feet hit Abby. Jinx hissed at her and batted her hair with his paw.

"Alright, alright, I'll get up and out of your way you little monster." Ryn slid out of bed and Jinx took over her pillow.

Ryn followed the smell of bacon into the kitchen where Tory was making breakfast.

"Morning love, still on Library time I see." Tory smiled.

"More like the cats forced me out." Ryn yawned. "Do you always cook breakfast?"

"It's the easiest way to wake up Thax. The smell of food gets him every time."

Tory put a plate of food and a mug of chamomile tea in front of Ryn, then sat in the chair opposite her at the table.

"Before Thax stumbles out here, tell me what's going on," Tory said.

Ryn picked up a piece of bacon and nibbled on it. "Zo has been accused of killing people."

"So we heard. I've known many killing types in my life, and Zo isn't one of those. It can't be him." Tory poured herself a cup of roasted barley tea.

"He's not. He dreamed he killed them, but how can you kill someone in a dream?"

"You can't," Thax said from the doorway.

Tory stood to fix a plate, putting it on the table as Thax sat.

"Plus the fact that Zo barely knew Tammy and didn't know Regent Jordan at all. What reason would he have to kill them?" Ryn picked up her fork and started on the eggs.

"Hmmm—do they have any other suspects?" Tory asked, resuming her seat.

"They said there were others at the Waatch Healing House who were under suspicion. I know one of them was that Keir guy. Zo spent some time with him. He gave me the creeps when I met him, but Zo liked him. I didn't understand the fascination." Ryn sipped her tea.

Thax tried to hide his smile behind his mug.

Tory cleared her throat and shot Thax a look.

"What?" Ryn asked.

"You dated Dan, sweetheart. People might question your fascination there." Thax patted Ryn's hand.

Ryn's shoulders slumped. "I suppose."

The conversation died as Thax attacked his breakfast. Ryn swirled the runny egg yolk around her plate with her fork.

"I wish I could prove Zo didn't kill those people. I want him to come home." Ryn's voice broke.

Tory sat up straight, then gave a sly smile. "I know just where to go to get that proof."

Ryn knew exactly who Tory had in mind and her heart leapt at the thought of seeing them again. Then it sank. "Oh. Oh no. I haven't talked to them in moons, and I'm pretty sure they're mad at me."

"But who else knows everything that happens in Waatch—especially if it's nefarious?"

"Jak and Dan," Brynd said from the kitchen entry.

"Eat up. We're going to go roll those two out of bed. I owe them a visit anyway," Tory said as she fixed Brynd a plate.

Ryn swallowed hard. Jak and Dan were fun when she was dating Dan, but since then they seemed like a lot more trouble than she could handle.

* * *

They hurried to get dressed, and were on their way out the door when a carriage pulled up outside the Thax's shop. The carriage door opened and Clayr stepped out.

"Ryn, I'm so glad I found you! We are on our way to Sooke, we can give you a ride home," Clayr said.

Ryn could see Yll inside the carriage. She was slumped to the side and looked asleep, bumpy carriage ride and all. The desire to see her home in Sooke suddenly gripped Ryn. Then an image of an empty cottage without her mother, or Jett, and without Lar and the boys in their cabin came to her mind. The image was dark and lonely.

"I thought you left last night, so I arranged to stay with Thax for a while," Ryn said.

"Sorry, I was able to convince Errol to let us stay in the Curator's cottage for one last night. He and Norm stayed with us and made sure no one found out we didn't leave straightaway. It gave us time to pack." Clayr glanced back into the carriage at the sleeping Yll. "We didn't get much sleep."

Ryn's eyes dropped to the cobblestoned street. It was damp. It must have rained a bit last night.

"I really appreciate you tracking me down and offering the ride, but I need to stay in Waatch for a while. I have a few things I need to look into," Ryn said.

Clayr looked both ways up and down the street, then pulled Ryn into Thax's shop.

"I hope you're not thinking about getting involved in anything to do with Zo's case. I may no longer be curator, but I am still your temporary guardian. Stay out of that mess, there are dangerous forces involved. It was their final effort to have me deposed and it worked."

Ryn fought hard to keep her face from flushing red. She didn't think she succeeded.

Clayr leaned closer and whispered even though Thax was still upstairs and Brynd and Tory were outside the shop waiting. "I must tell you, just before they pulled me into the Regent's Chambers for the vote, I received a letter from your father. It was marked urgent. I am suspicious of the timing of their call for a vote of no confidence. I fortunately locked it in the secret compartment in my desk drawer so I could read it later when I was less likely to be disturbed, but they came and dragged me away. It's still there, and it might contain important news. I will find a way to retrieve it. As soon as I do, I will let you know what it says, so you don't need to stay here, we can take you to Sooke where you'll be safe."

Ryn shook her head. "I need to be here, at least for now. Information will come to Waatch first. I can't stand to be out there in the dark not knowing what's going on."

Clayr sighed and gave Ryn a tight hug. "I should force you to come, but I understand and I can't bring myself to do it. Stay close to Thax, he'll keep you safe." Clayr gave Ryn's shoulder one last squeeze, then she bustled out the door and back into the carriage.

"Love ya!" Clayr called from the carriage window as the carriage drove off.

Ryn's mind was spinning trying to process this information. As far as she knew there had been no formal communication with her father for a long time. Of course, her mother didn't tell her everything, so there could have been. Clayr seemed to think this letter was important though.

The bell tinkled as Brynd opened the door and stuck her head inside. "Are you coming?"

Ryn shook herself, not realizing she had drifted off, and gotten lost in thought. "Yes."

* * *

They hurried down the street on Tory's heels. Tory's stride was full of purpose as they entered a part of town where the buildings were worn, and the people looked more worn. The area wasn't familiar, but Ryn realized she must have been this way before with Jak and Dan. It had been dark at the time, and she had been more concerned with sticking close to Dan than paying attention to where they were. When they turned off the main wheel spoke of a street that led from the Library, toward the otter wall, they found themselves on a close narrow street with rundown buildings on each side. Tory stopped, put her fingers to her mouth and gave a series of low whistles.

A girl melted out of the shadows next to them. Ryn jumped, heart pounding.

"Sammy!" Tory said.

"It's good to see you." The girl gave Tory a brief hug.

Brynd's hand was pressed to her chest. "You scared me to death!"

Ryn nodded in agreement.

"What brings you here?" Sammy asked.

Tory glanced up and down the street. "The boys. We need to see them."

Sammy's lip cured a bit as she looked Brynd and Ryn over.

Ryn thought she recognized Sammy. She was pretty sure she'd seen her before.

"He's not going to like this." Sammy folded her arms.

"Does it look like I care what he likes? I'm here before first bell. Tell him to get his butt up." Tory's voice was a low growl.

"Fine, your funeral," Sammy said, and led them down the street.

The street was empty except for one lone figure in a dark suit. His head was down and his arms were crossed like he was hugging himself. When he passed, he stepped out into the street. After Sammy passed him, he stepped back—right in front of Ryn.

She looked up into his face as she went to step around him, then stopped.

"Jett?" Ryn asked. It was hard to tell if it was him, because he had a thick beard and long hair under a hat.

He startled, and their eyes met. Those same dark brown eyes she'd known most of her life. He tried to push past her, but she stayed in front of him.

"What are you doing here? I thought you were on Viatoro playing grandmama's favorite."

He frowned at her. "I'm here running errands."

"Are you going to go home to Sooke?" She asked, the words slipping from her mouth.

"Why would I do that?"

"I've been let go at the Library. I don't have anywhere to go but home to Sooke, and I don't want to be alone," Ryn said.

"I told you not to work for the Library. They don't want Ordinaries there," he snapped.

Ryn stepped back from him, her mouth open.

Jett's gaze met hers. "Go to Viatoro. They'll take you in."

"Grandmother made it clear she didn't want an Ordinary for a grandchild."

Jett shrugged. "At least you won't be alone."

"I'm done feeling like throwaway leftovers." Ryn frowned. She moved out of his way, and he continued down the street.

A few paces away he turned and called over his shoulder. "Think about it. There's a better side to be on."

Ryn huffed, and hurried to catch up with everyone else.

* * *

The hallway outside of Jak's office looked different in the light, and a lot more empty without Maus sitting behind the desk in front of the office. Maus was Jak and Dan's faithful messenger and friend. They treated him like a little brother and were protective of him. Zmej had taken him as leverage to get Jak and Dan to break into the Library to discover how to access the Heart Tree. Ryn felt guilty she didn't have better news to bring Jak and Dan about where Zmej had taken Maus, whose whereabouts was still unknown. She put her hand on the top of Maus's desk while Tory knocked on the door.

No one answered, so Tory opened it and walked inside.

Jak was in his chair behind his enormous desk kissing a red headed girl. Dan was at a smaller desk writing something.

"Ahem," Tory said.

Jak only slowed his lips, and cracked open one eye at them.

Ryn glanced over at Brynd to see her blushing red. Only a couple moons ago it was Brynd in Jak's lap in that chair. Ryn winced.

Dan glanced up from his work, then shot to his feet. "By the idiot Ancestors, Tory, what are you doing?"

Jak slowly finished his kiss, then sat back, the girl still clinging to him. "What do you want?" He asked, licking his red, swollen lips.

"We have a murder to solve," Tory said, hands on her hips.

"Well." Ryn's voice shook. She couldn't believe she felt nervous with them, when just a short time ago she had felt comfortable. "Two murders. We need to find the murderer."

"You mean you need to prove Zo's innocence," Jak said.

"Yes." Ryn's head dropped.

"He didn't do it," Jak said.

Startled, Ryn's eyes met his. "How do you know so surely?"

"Because Regent Jordan was Clayr's biggest supporter on the Board, and Zo had no reason to kill him." Brynd said.

Ryn's gaze shot to Brynd, whose eyes were fixed on Jak.

Jak's lips worked their way into a slow lopsided smile. "You got it. Get rid of Clayr's support, and you can get rid of Clayr."

Ryn's eyes narrowed. "Of course, I should have known that."

Jak nodded.

Brynd folded her arms. "And they did that, before Jordan's body was even cold, they called a vote of no confidence."

Tory put her hands on her hips. "But who would kill him? And how?"

Jak and Dan exchanged a look. The one they used when they were mentally discussing what information they should and shouldn't share. Ryn didn't like it.

"Tammy and Regent Jordan weren't killed with Healing magic," Jak said.

"How do you know?" Brynd asked, her gaze flashed quickly to Ryn's.

Jak examined his fingers that were intertwined with the girls. "There is another magic that can kill without leaving a trace. The Healers are too arrogant and quick to assume it's the Killing magic. They haven't seen anyone killed with Healing magic in several decades."

As Jak spoke an image flashed through her mind. It was an image of that Spirit teller saying words and yanking on her spirit, separating her body from her spirit. Could she have died because of that? It made sense, Zo needed to heal her at the time. She wished she could talk to him and ask exactly how he healed her.

"So we're looking for someone with Spirit magic?" Tory asked.

Dan stepped up to Jak's desk. "Yes, I know a Healer within the Waatch Healing House. I had them take a look at the bodies. They confirmed—it wasn't Healing magic."

Ryn turned to look at Dan, but her throat closed and she couldn't bring herself to ask her question. She hadn't contacted Dan since the day after the attack on the Library, and she could tell by the sharpness in his eyes that he was not happy with her.

Luckily Brynd asked the question for her. "How do you know the signs?"

"Waatch lore says the victim's heart is exploded," Jak said.

"And I talked to one of Keir's followers before they were all arrested," Dan added.

"How could the Healers have missed it? I'm sure they know this Waatch lore," Brynd asked.

"Killing with Healing magic is such a forbidden act that they keep no records of past incidents," Dan said, staring right at Ryn.

Ryn lowered her eyes from Dan's. He had asked if they could still be friends, and she didn't really give him an answer. Now she needed his help, and she felt bad she hadn't done more to reach out to him before now.

Ryn rubbed her forehead trying to cover her emotion. "I'm so sorry I haven't been a good friend, but I really need your help. Is there a way you could present this evidence to the Healing Council?" Her voice choked, she looked up, but couldn't see through tears.

Jak barked a laugh. "Presenting ourselves in court is a good way for us to find ourselves in prison."

"You have pissed a few people off," Tory cracked.

Ryn nodded. The movement caused a tear to run down her cheek.

Dan sighed. "I'll see what I can do to get the evidence submitted to the court."

Ryn's heart lifted. "You will?"

Dan sat heavily back into his chair. "Yeah. Not that you all deserve it after the way you treated us like yesterday's trash."

Ryn bit her lip, and nodded. She wanted to hug him, but was too intimidated to approach him. "Thank you so much, I can't tell you how much this means to me."

"Eh—I suppose we owe Zo for saving us from the wolves," Jak said, then resumed kissing the girl on his lap.

They took that as their signal to leave, but Ryn remembered the information she had for them.

"Lar returned from their hunt for Zmej. He didn't see Maus, but there was a little girl with Zmej," Ryn said.

Jak and Dan exchanged a look.

Dan nodded. "Thanks for the information."

With that, Ryn turned and fled the office.

Chapter Twelve

In shadows deep, where ancient echos sing,
Shores were cursed by the serpents wing.
Where the beastly dragon ruled the land,
The most majestic mountains stand.

Again, I know this is a secondhand account of Luc's writing, but I'm desperate for a clue to open the door. Echos sing? Maybe there's a song involved in opening the door? The carving looks like a sword and a tree. If the sword is Praedo's all hope is lost. There's no way that sword can be removed from the Origin.

- From the journals of Moult de Dico

Zo stood in front of the Healing Council twisting and bending as he tried to work out his cramped and stiff muscles. Lying in one spot for days, unable to move, had left every part of his body protesting. His knees popped as he yawned to shake off the last of the sleepiness from the drugs they had given him. A new drug was coursing through him. One that was making him fully awake and ready to stare down the council, knowing full well they held his life in their hands.

A prissy ancestor type with a dark suit strode through a side door and rushed up to Zo. His shirt was cut low so it was unmistakable what magic he had, two of the most powerful houses, Sano and Viator. The room tilted. A vibrating tension coursing through Zo's veins made him take one look at the man's dark spiked hair, strong jawline, and the hint of muscle filling out the suite, and a desire to kiss him washed over him. He knew there would be a punishment for such an act, but as hyper altered as Zo was, he did not care.

"I'm sorry I'm late, I'm to be your advocate for these proceedings," the Dark Suit said. He was wearing gloves and noticeably avoided the normal handshake that would accompany an introduction. Instead, he switched to grabbing Zo under his arm and holding him up.

Zo was watching the man's lips while he spoke, and fantasizing about getting him alone in a closet.

The man waved his hand in front of Zo's face. "What did they give you?"

Zo shrugged.

"Great. My client is drugged out of his mind. How am I supposed to defend this?"

Zo shrugged again. "Don't?"

Dark Suit made a strangled noise in the back of his throat. Zo found it cute.

"We can beat this. They have no real evidence against you. You can't kill someone in your dreams," Dark Suit said.

"Whatever you say."

Dark Suit pulled out a satchel of papers and started sifting through them. The slight stubble on his jawline was making Zo crazy, swaying where he stood.

A door opened and Keir was ushered in by a couple men in white shirts. His eyes darted all around the council chamber like he wanted to flee, but he stayed where they placed him next to Zo. Keir's hands were bound in a sack. Zo looked down and noticed his hands were in the same sort of sack. He wondered why he hadn't noticed that before.

Keir's face turned to Zo. "This is all your fault. You did this. You weren't supposed to tell!" Keir spit.

Someone rapped a wood hammer against the council desk. The council sat in a large semicircle, and each member wore their Healer's robes. Zo noticed his mother and Keir's parents were missing. Maybe they weren't allowed to decide on his fate.

"Members of the council," the head council seated directly in front of Zo and Keir began. "We are here to test the accused, Keir de Sano, and Zo de Ingis, for evidence of the killing madness, and to try them for the deaths of one Tammy de Illusio and the honorable Library Regent Jordan. How do the defendants plead?"

"Not guilty," another man, not nearly as attractive as the advocate for Zo, said.

"Council." Dark Suit bowed a bit. "Not guilty."

Zo started. "Who said I'm not guilty? Looks like I'm guilty." Zo held up his wrapped hands.

Several members of the council flinched back.

Dark Suit rubbed his forehead, then turned to the council. "Clearly my client has been given too much of something. We should adjourn until some of the drugs can wear out of his system."

"Denied." The head council said. "We will take into account how much medication they have been given. They will be tested for the Killing magic. The state they are in is for the protection of those present."

Zo's advocate threw up his hands. Zo just wanted to sit and watch him move, but there were no chairs to sit in.

"Proceed." The head council waved toward a side door.

Two carts were wheeled out.

"If you have the Killing touch, you won't be able to resist killing again."

An attendant removed the black cloths which covered two cages. Both held birds that looked to be injured, with broken wings.

"Heal the birds and you will be deemed innocent," the head council said.

Zo began to sweat. He knew from previous attempts that he could no longer heal. The magic was gone and Madame Sano, as promised, never returned to finish his lessons.

The bag was removed from his hands and one of the birds was pushed closer to him. It was grey with black beady eyes that stared at him in terror, its wing bent at a strange angle to its body. Zo found his eyes swimming in tears. He related to the bird. He felt himself broken inside, wanting to be healed and return to who he was just a few short moons ago. If he could only return to that night and let the wolf kill him...

Dark suit cleared his throat and pressed in closer to Zo, but still arm's length away. "Just reach your hand inside the bars."

Zo lifted his fingers, pushing them inside the cage between the bars. He stroked the soft feathers, gently talking to the bird, telling it not to be afraid. Again, just as when Ryn was struck by the wagon, he reached for his healing magic. Once again all he felt was an empty hole. A tear slid down his cheek.

"I'm sorry," he whispered to the bird.

Keir's bird started flapping noisily inside its cage—its wing completely healed. Zo wasn't surprised. For some reason, probably because he was double Healing magic from both parents—a forbidden practice—Keir had still been able to heal despite his use of the Healing to kill. It had to be something like that. Why else would Keir be able to kill and still be able to heal?

Unless there is something wrong with me, Zo thought.

"Interesting." One of the council members said, leaning back in their chair.

The other council members started talking amongst themselves.

"Order! Let's come to order!" The head council banged the hammer down. "Will the advocates please approach?"

Dark Suit joined Keir's advocate in front of the head council member. Zo was appreciating Dark Suit's backside when one of the orderlies forced Zo's hands back into the bag.

"Hey—that's too tight," Zo complained.

The white shirt orderly glared at him, then withdrew.

The head council made a sharp cutting gesture and the advocates returned to their clients.

"The test is inconclusive..." the head council started.

"But my client has no beads and no bead scars for Healing magic," Keir's advocate said.

Keir's head jerked toward his advocate. "Hey—I thought you were on my side."

The head council pursed his lips. "But he healed the bird. Let us begin the trial of the murders." Again the head council waved, and a House Sano official, and a Waatch official entered the room.

"In the case of the murders of Tammy de Illisio and Regent Jordan, what has the investigation found?"

The official from Waatch began to speak. Zo shifted his legs, which had seen little use in he didn't know how long. They were restless and tired of standing. He really wanted to sit—or run for his life.

"A recent development in the investigation has led to the conclusion that the deceased persons were killed using Spirit magic, not Healing magic," the Waatch official said.

More stirring occurred among the council members.

"How do you know that?" the head council asked.

"The records of crime in Waatch indicate that when something is killed with Healing magic their heart explodes..."

"This is true," Keir interrupted, nodding.

"That's not helping you," his advocate whispered.

"Neither are you," Keir shot back.

The Waatch official glanced back at them then continued, "We have had it verified through two different sources, including the Waatch physician, that Tammy de Illisio, and Regent Jordan's hearts are, in fact, intact."

Zo started at that. In order for Wilmar to confirm that he would have had to cut their chests open. Most Ancestor descendants found that profane and would never let that happen. They must be desperate to prove they murdered these people.

The head council's mouth hit a flat line, and his brow creased. The council member next to him leaned over and whispered in his ear.

"The council will adjourn to deliberate," the head council said.

Dark Suit stepped in front of Zo. "I would remind the council that my client was asleep at the time of the murders and has no magic capable of killing in a dream."

"And my client was with his parents at the time. They are here ready to testify to that fact," Keir's advocate added.

The head council only nodded, and the council members stood, filing out into a room behind the semicircle desk.

Dark Suit put his hand in his artfully spiky hair. "Oh this is not good. They're going to want someone to blame for the deaths. If they give Keir a pass they are going to come down hard on you. The Library Board is demanding a conviction. They need someone to blame."

Zo sagged, his legs giving out. The orderlies rushed forward to grab him. A chair appeared and Zo sat.

Dark Suit put his hand on Zo's shoulder. He must have been convinced by the bird demonstration that it was safe to touch him. His touch sent a shiver up Zo's spine. Dark Suit crouched before Zo, so they were eye to eye.

"Whatever they ask you, do not answer. I will answer for you," Dark Suit said.

Zo was enchanted by his lips, then he shook his head to clear it. Whatever they had given made him alert, but hyper focused. Iden's face swam before Zo's eyes. Those perfect full lips with that sweet lopsided grin he liked to give Zo. Another tear leaked from Zo's eye. Dark Suit wiped it away, a gesture that caused more tears to flow. Iden deserved someone whole. Someone better. Zo's bagged hands pressed against the promise necklace hidden under his shirt.

"You didn't kill the bird, so I'm sure the council will be lenient," Dark Suit said with a sad smile that was probably supposed to be encouraging. It wasn't.

"What are the options?" Zo asked.

"Not much about Killing magic is documented by House Sano, but the one thing we do know is that eventually the desire to kill will become overwhelming. It's unusual that you don't have it. Those who've used Healing magic to kill are dangerous. There's only two options—death or be dociled."

Zo's stomach clinched, and his head spun. This was it. He wished for the wolf to have killed him. All he did by killing the wolf was prolong his death by a couple moons. And what had he accomplished in that time? All he had done was grow sicker, and weaker, and now break Iden's heart.

"Wait—dociled? What does that mean?" Zo asked.

"A Mind Healer will sever all the connections and wipe your memory and most of your thought processes. You will be as the word says—docile with no independent thought, doing whatever you're told," Dark suit said.

Zo swore.

"I've heard it's a peaceful existence."

"I'm sure the people they've done this to don't think so," Zo said.

Dark Suit stood and shrugged. "That's the only option for those who are a danger to the public in House Sano."

The side door opened and Zo's mother came rushing into the room. She hugged Zo's head to her chest, her hands pressing his head tight to her.

"My baby, they're not going to take you from me, I won't let them," she said, bending down to kiss his head, then resting her cheek on top of it.

Zo said nothing, realizing this was the last family member he would ever see. Where was his father and his brother? He wished he could tell Regg to make better choices with his life then he had. He would never have the chance.

The council chamber doors opened and a man stepped out. "All rise. The council has reached a verdict."

Zo's mother and Dark Suit helped him stand.

The council members filed in and sat.

The head council shuffled some papers and held one up to read. "In the case of Keir de Sano, son of Myrta de Sano, we find the defendant guilty of the Killing magic. The destruction of his Healing beads and absence of bead scars proves he is guilty of using Healing magic to kill and that the Ancestors have rejected him. The compulsion to kill will eventually take over, therefore the council sentences you to..."

"Wait!" Keir's mom shouted, rushing the head council.

A whispered discussion ensued between the head council and Myrta. The head council's face turned red. He leaned over and consulted with the councilor next to him.

Zo's attention shifted to Keir. Something about his posture seemed to say he knew his mother was going to get him released. Keir glanced over at Zo and gave him a smirk and a wink.

The head council shook his head then pointed at Keir. "Please resume your place next to your son, or I will have you removed from the chambers."

She backed away slowly, her shoulders shaking. Zo couldn't tell if it was anger, tears, or both.

"Keir de Sano in light of your parent's service to the council..."

Here it comes, Zo thought.

"We sentence you to be dociled."

"What?!" Keir's mother shouted.

Zo watched Keir's face turn a sickly pale white.

"The procedure will take place as soon as the head mind Healer can prepare himself," the head council finished.

Keir swayed and his mother grabbed his arm. Clearly it was not the outcome they thought was coming.

The head council signed the paper he had been reading and handed it to the assistant that had announced the council's return to the chamber.

The head council picked up another paper. Zo felt an icy cold wash through his gut.

"We find the defendant Zo de Ingis, son of Fyri de Sano, guilty of using the Killing magic. His lack of his Healing bead, and the incompleteness of his Healing studies is evident, and therefore he has been rejected of the Ancestors. You have been deemed unsafe to the public. We sentence you to..."

"Death," Zo said. He thought it was a whisper, but the startled looks on the Healing Councilor's faces said they heard him.

"No!" His mother yelled.

"So be it." The head council nodded, wrote on the paper and signed it.

"No!" Zo's mother flew to the head council, yelling something about her son, and her position being higher than Myrta's on the council. The head council stood and exited the chambers.

Time seemed to slow for Zo. He watched Keir being led away—reaching after his mother, shouting something to her. Zo's mother was in front of him, tears streaming down her face. She was also shouting something at him, but he heard nothing through the blood rushing in his ears.

Dark Suit stood motionless watching the orderlies pry Zo's mom off him and lead him away.

The hall they led him down became a tunnel slowly darkening until everything became black.

* * *

They came for Zo in the middle of the night. He was groggy from whatever they had given him after the trial. They removed all the blankets and wrappings and helped him to his feet.

This is it. This is how it ends, Zo thought.

His stomach turned to liquid ice and his legs became wobbly. Two people supported him on either side to help him down the hallway. Zo's stomach was bad and he suddenly needed a toilet. The Healing House pants he wore were light and loose. They wouldn't hold in what was threatening to come out all over the floor. His sweat made him start to shiver.

They turned a corner and there was a figure dressed in black holding a sword low and across his body. Zo had briefly wondered how the Healing House could kill someone. They certainly weren't using Healing magic to do it.

The sword flashed in the low light and Zo's legs gave out. He landed face first on the floor in darkness.

Chapter Thirteen

She came to me. I did not send to her in her dreams. I was looking at the book. The one someone left at the orphanage and asked that it get passed on to Ryn. I've long suspected it was her story, but seeing her here in my cave looking like a spirit projection, I have little doubts. If it's true the magic she could possess is unprecedented. I told her to come and I would give her the book, but now I'm not so sure. What will that much power do to my sweet pumpkin?

- From the journals of Moult de Dico

Ryn left Tory at Thax's, while Brynd went to send a letter to her parents telling them she would no longer be able to help support the family and their apple farm.

The thought of just sitting upstairs in their room at Thax's doing nothing made Ryn's head swim. To ease the tightness in her chest, she let her feet take her wherever they wanted to go. Without even thinking about it, she found herself walking on the beach, looking out across the water wondering what was happening on Eileansano. The islands weren't that far, really. If the water wasn't so frigidly cold and her swimming skills so terrible, she would jump into the water and swim for it. A wave broke and rushed up the sand almost to Ryn's boots. She crouched down and put her fingers in the water. It felt like melted ice. Her fingers came away reddened. She definitely wasn't swimming for it. She resumed her walk, dragging a stick along in the wet sand, till she came to the edge of the woods. She stood there thinking about the pebbled beach where she and Zo had screamed away all their frustrations into the water. That sounded really good right now, but for the first time she was afraid to enter the woods alone. There were too many unknown things out there.

A flash of white between the trees confirmed her fears and she turned to flee. A hand caught her arm and stopped her. Ryn sucked in her breath and pulled her arm.

"Shhhh, lady Ryn. Shhhh...no need to fear."

Ryn turned to find the man Schiz holding her arm.

"What are you..." Ryn started, then annoyance bubbled up inside. "Look, I appreciate your concern for me, but I really don't have time to listen to you ramble about us and *Them* today."

Schiz let go of her and backed away, lowering his head. "I haven't seen you since...and you managed to escape *Them*...but he sent his sons to attack you...I thought for sure...you faced him...you're braver than I."

Ryn shook her head trying to understand what he was saying. "What sons attacked me?"

"No matter, you are safe now. But...it's time. I can take you to your father. He wants to see you." Schiz glanced back at the woods, shifting from foot to foot.

Ryn hesitated. She had no idea how this strange man who lived in the wild could know where to find her father.

"I would love to see him," she said. An image of her father as she dreamed of him sitting in the chair in the library of the Viator guest house came sharply to her mind.

"Good, let us go," Schiz held out his hand.

Ryn stared at it. It was surprisingly clean for a man who slept on the ground, but the back of his hand was scratched and scarred. The idea of leaving everything behind and running away sounded more appealing than Ryn dared to admit to herself.

She sighed. "I'm not ready. I'll let you know when I am." She didn't think she would ever let Schiz take her somewhere, but she didn't have anyone to travel with to visit her father, and she had an increasing desire to see him. Perhaps when she wasn't needed in Waatch anymore, but by then she could probably get someone she trusted more to take her.

Schiz withdrew his hand with a frown, and a slight bow. "As you wish."

Ryn nodded, but something about the sadness in his eyes kept her from turning and leaving.

"How do you know my father?" she found herself asking.

Schiz looked back toward the woods behind him. "We grew up together."

Ryn's brow furrowed. Her father had never mentioned having such a strange friend growing up.

"He is like a brother to me. I would do anything for him." Schiz's eyes welled up with tears.

Ryn felt the words pierce her heart—*Like a brother*. Tears came to her eyes.

She nodded. "I understand."

Schiz's body shifted, like he wished he could hold her.

Without thinking, Ryn threw her arms around Schiz, reveling in his smell of fresh cut wood.

A twig snapped somewhere in the woods, and Ryn thought she heard a low growl. The hair on her arms stood up.

Schiz's body went ridged and he lifted his head, sniffing the air. "Get back to Waatch. I'll find you soon."

Like a spring that snapped, he took off, disappearing into the trees.

Ryn turned and fled back to the safety of Waatch.

* * *

Ryn's feet carried her to the Library gates. They had almost taken her onto the grounds and toward her old dorm room, but she quickly realized where she was and stopped. She rested her hands on the bars of the west gate, trying to catch her breath. Ed was on guard there. He glanced at her, then looked away, his head bowing.

"I'm really sorry Ryn," Ed said.

"I know." And she did know. The Library guard had always been supportive of her, even when she had caused them some trouble. Everything she'd done was a step toward protecting the Library. Recently, the guard had used her connection to the Protector of the Library to help repair the damage done by Zmej and the wolves. They valued her, and it felt good.

"Can I help you with something? Do you want me to fetch Fergus for you?" Ed asked.

The thought of a Fergus hug sounded great, but she said, "No, I don't want to bother him."

Ed's gaze held hers for a long time. He frowned, then looked in toward the Library grounds, and back at Ryn. "Stay here and guard the place, I'll be right back."

"But..." Ryn looked out into the streets of Waatch.

"I'll only be a moment," Ed said, then he strode off toward the guard house.

Ryn's eyes watched up and down the street wondering what she would do if someone like Jak and Dan, who were banned from the Library, tried to enter while she was the only one on guard.

Ed returned a few minutes later with Fergus in tow. Once Fergus saw Ryn, he jogged up to her.

"Are you alright?" he asked.

Ryn nodded, barely holding back the tears.

Fergus gathered her up into his arms and held her. Her tears disappeared and she found her heart beating fast. She was acutely aware of every place on her body his arms touched her. Fergus had always been kind to her. Sometimes he was stern when she broke Library rules, but he had protected her and stood by her. She buried her face deeper into his wool uniform which smelled of outdoors and fire.

"You've been guarding the boiler room," Ryn said into his soft wool.

Fergus just hugged her tighter, then let her go. "I have to get back, but stop by anytime and have Ed come and get me."

Ryn nodded. Out of Fergus' arms, the tears returned.

"Oh, my sweet Ryn," Fergus hugged her again, then jogged off.

Ed was standing by the gates, his eyes shifting from Ryn the minute she looked at him.

Ryn walked over and put her hand on his arm. "Thank you Ed."

He nodded, but a huge grin slowly spread on his face.

* * *

Ryn arrived back at Thax's to find Yll pacing in the tailor's shop.

Ryn's stomach clenched. "What's the matter?"

Yll crossed the shop to her. "Oh, thank goodness you're here. Mother got word that a package from your father was delivered today to the curator's office. Her assistant was able to take it and conceal it, but now Mother's worried not only about the letter your father sent, but also the package."

"How is she going to get them?" Ryn asked.

Yll threw up her hands. "There are lots of people loyal to her, but many who are afraid they'll get caught. Nobody else wants to lose their job." She started to pace between fashion displays. "There's gotta be someone who can retrieve them." She stopped. "What about that guy you were dating? The one who broke into the underground?"

"Dan? They both gave a vow never to set foot on the Library grounds again. If they do, they'll go to prison. I doubt they would risk that."

"Not even for you?"

"Especially not for me. We aren't exactly on the best of terms. I have been too focused on my work lately, and I'm afraid he hates me for ignoring him." Ryn's eyes dropped to her hands. She rubbed the back of her hand with her thumb.

Swearing came from behind the curtain that led to the back room of the shop. Thax emerged holding Jinx by the nape of his neck.

"Can you do something with this cat? He almost dumped a huge container of sulfur!" Thax's red face and flared nostrils made Ryn cringe inside.

Ryn ran over and scooped up Jinx from Thax's outstretched hand. "Sorry!"

Yll gave a loud sigh, which brought Ryn's focus back to her. "There has to be a way. It's information from your father—aren't you curious?"

She was curious. She was more than curious. The letter from her father could answer a lot of questions, or open more. She needed to know what he had found. If he sent a letter directly to Clayr it had to be important, but getting into the Library without permission was almost impossible. Getting around Fergus alone...

Fergus's frown drifted into Ryn's mind. He cared for her, but had proved many times his loyalties were with the Library.

She petted Jinx, who tolerated being held and petted for once.

Then she had another thought.

Ryn reached out and grabbed Yll's arm. "I have an idea, but we can't do it today. I was just at the Library gates and I don't want to raise suspicion. Do you have a place to stay in town?"

Yll nodded. "We're staying with a friend of Mother's. Once she got the message that the package arrived, we left Sooke and came straight back."

"Good. Meet me here tomorrow morning after first bell."

* * *

To Ryn's great delight, the next morning dawned with a misty spring rain. Ryn wrapped herself in her cloak with the hood up—perfect to hide inside. She met Yll at the pen shop Dan had taken her to which was across the street from the west Library gate.

"I still don't understand how you're going to get us into the Library," Yll said.

Ryn gave her a wide grin, but the truth was her stomach was doing flip flops. If they got caught, there was no one to protect them. Jeris would delight in having a reason to throw Ryn into prison. Ryn shook out her shaking hands, pulled her hood over her head and led the way across the street to the west gate. As Ryn hoped, Ed was standing guard. Ryn brought tears to her eyes. It wasn't hard, all she had to do was think about all the bad stuff happening to her at the moment. One thought of Zo was all it took.

"Ryn," Ed said. "Back so soon?"

Ryn nodded, wiping her eyes. "Would you mind getting Fergus for me?"

"What's wrong?" Ed asked.

"Too much," Ryn answered, her voice choked a bit. It was all true.

"Stay here, I'll see if I can find him." Ed strode off toward the Boiler Room.

"He's just leaving us here with the west gate unprotected?" Yll whispered.

"Makes you wonder how Jak and Dan got on the grounds last winter." Ryn gave Yll a sharp look. "Now's our chance."

Ryn took Yll's arm and strolled onto the grounds like they were clients on their way to an appointment with a researcher. Ryn tried to walk slowly, but she was afraid Ed would return with Fergus before they could make it to their destination. Fortunately, mounting the back steps always required a bit of a rush to get up them, so hurrying didn't look too suspicious—she hoped.

Once at the top, Ryn found the panel behind the statue. The wall slid open and she ushered Yll inside.

"What is this place?" Yll asked once the door shut behind them.

"Secret passage," Ryn answered.

"Well obviously, but..."

Ryn ignored Yll and opened the door to the stairway. Once at the top of the stairs, huffing and puffing from climbing them too fast, Ryn pressed her ear against the bookcase door. She didn't hear anything on the other side, but she wasn't sure she could through the books and the door. Pressing the door open just a crack she peeked inside the room. Lyssa was at her desk, her fingers drifting over the bumps in a book. Ryn opened the door.

Lyssa looked up. "Ryn! I thought they banned you from the Library—How are you here?"

"We snuck in. How did you know it was me?" Ryn asked.

"You always smell of pine trees and chamomile. You shouldn't be here. If they catch you, it will be trouble for all of us," Lyssa said.

"I know. I'm sorry to drag you into this, but there's something that is Clayr's that we need to retrieve. Will you help us?" Ryn asked.

"Who's we?" Lyssa's gaze drifted over toward Yll.

"A friend," Ryn said. She wanted to keep as much information from Lyssa as she could in case they found out about Ryn and Yll's visit. The less she knew the better.

"Right, friend who smells a lot like Clayr, you're in luck. I believe the third-floor supervisor is out today. You should be able to pass through her office. The rest will be up to you. I suggest you use as many secret passageways as you can."

"The only one I know of is in the middle of the third-floor collections and we'd have to pass the reference desk to get to them," Ryn said.

"There's a stairway across from Kay's office. I know because they use it to take me to Clayr's office so no one knows I'm here. Pull on the lantern in the hallway."

Ryn bent down and wrapped her arms around Lyssa. "Thank you! I'm sorry I couldn't finish helping you transcribe."

Lyssa sighed. "Story of my life. At least you didn't leave because you hated it."

Ryn laughed. "I would gladly come back. The Library is my home." Her voice broke off at the last word.

Ryn started toward the door down to Kay's office.

"Wait!" Lyssa said.

Ryn turned back. "What?"

Lyssa moved to her desk, picked up a book and handed it to Ryn.

"*How to Kill Dragons*?" Ryn asked, raising an eyebrow that Lyssa couldn't see.

"Yes, there's a paper in there that I had Kay copy from the book for you. I think you'll find it interesting." Lyssa's smile had a hit of mischievousness to it.

"Alright, but I don't know why we need to know how to kill a dragon, there's no dragons here." Ryn tucked the page into her pocket inside her skirts.

Lyssa patted Ryn's arm. "Best get going before someone finds you here."

"Right." Ryn led Yll to the door at the opposite side of the room, then she stopped and turned back. "What will happen to you? Will they throw you out as well?"

Lyssa's head turned in their direction. "No, my parents pay the Library too much to keep me here. I'm sure Regent Jeris would like to continue that income."

Ryn nodded, started toward the door, then turned to give Lyssa a hug. "Thank you."

She was halfway down the staircase before she felt an odd weight in her skirt pocket.

* * *

Ryn peeked into Kay's office from the painting door. The room was dark and quiet. Ryn's heart raced as they crept across the floor. The hallway outside the office was clear, so they stepped into it, Yll pressed close behind Ryn. Kay's office was at the end of the hallway, so Ryn hoped with her gone no one would come this way. There were two lanterns on the wall, only one was lit. It was too far up for Ryn, so Yll reached up and pulled on it. The wall paneling slid to the side revealing another staircase down.

Ryn checked to make sure no one had heard the panel open then started down the stairs.

"How do I close it?" Yll whispered. She was pushing on the panel trying to slide it back in place.

Ryn stepped back up to Yll and ran her hands along the walls. "I don't feel anything."

Voices and footsteps drifted down the hall to them.

"Ryn!" Yll's voice rose.

"Just reach up and push the lantern back up, then duck back inside." Ryn's whisper was louder and harsher than the intended.

Yll reached out the door. The panel started to slide shut on her. Ryn grabbed Yll's arm and pulled her into the stairwell, almost sending them toppling down the stairs.

The voices and footsteps came muffled through the paneling.

"That was close," Yll mouthed.

Ryn nodded, lifted a lantern from a hook on the wall and raised the wick.

They descended the stairs.

At the bottom was a door that opened into an office. Ryn swallowed.

"How do we know whose office this is?" Ryn asked.

Yll peered through a crack in the door, her head shifting this way and that, as she took in the whole office.

"It's Mom's assistant," Yll said.

"Are you sure? If we walk into the wrong office..."

The normal office door opened and shut. Clayr's assistant, Dyana, and Prym entered the office having a heated discussion.

"You better not be hiding anything from Daddy," Prym said. "Your loyalties are to the Library, not that Ordinary ex-curator. I will see you dismissed if I find you've taken that package. Daddy wants it, and mail delivery says they left it in the curator's office. The only people with access to the curator's office is Daddy and you."

Clayr's former assistant rolled her eyes. "If you leave the curator's office unlocked, as your father often does, everyone has access. Now, if you're quite finished, I have a large amount of work formally changing all of the curator's correspondence from Clayr to Jeris."

"That's Regent Curator Jeris to you." Prym lifted her head and flounced out the door, slamming it as she left.

Dyana let out a long breath, shaking her head, then she turned to the door where Ryn and Yll were listening.

"You can come out now," she said.

Ryn started, as Yll pushed the door open.

"How did you know..." Ryn started.

The assistant held up her hand. "I know my office and I know when that door is open." She looked Yll up and down, her lips pursed and her brow furrowed. "You shouldn't be here. If you get caught it will be bad for all of us."

Yll approached Dyana's desk. "My mother sent me to retrieve the items sent by Moult." Yll waved her hand at Ryn. "Moult is her father."

Dyana went very still as her eyes stared at Yll and Ryn. She took a deep breath, went to her door, and locked it. She pulled her keyring from a pocket and unlocked a drawer, but instead of pulling out the package from Ryn's father, she took out a tiny carved wood box. The assistant pushed on different spots of the box and the lid sprang open. She pulled out a very small key, which she took to her bookshelves. At the very bottom right hand corner Dyana pulled a large tomb off the shelf. It was titled, *Curator's Finances*.

She placed it on her desk with a chuckle. "Nobody cares about the bookkeeping for the curator's office. Well, except the Board of Regents, but they would never come looking for it themselves."

Dyana pushed her key into top of the book's cover. It fit into a small hole, then turning three times the cover sprang open revealing the book to be a box. Dyana reached inside and pulled out a package wrapped in skins. She placed it into Ryn's hands.

"Here's what your father sent. I haven't been able to retrieve the letter that arrived before the package. Jeris has the curator's office carefully watched."

Ryn clutched the package to her chest. She hadn't held anything of her father's for years. She suddenly felt more connected to him than in her dreams of him.

"Thank you," Ryn whispered.

"Now, back into the hidden stairway before someone finds you," Dyana said.

"How do we get out of the Library?" Yll asked.

Someone knocked at the office door. The voice on the other side sounded like Jeris'. "You found a way in, you can find a way out," Dyana whispered, then closed the secret door on them.

"Great," Yll whispered.

Chapter Fourteen

As spies we sent disguised as birds,
Who brought us news from the eastern plain:
The armies advanced with fire and chain,
Yet the dragon was not seen or heard.

Is this a hint in the GP at the so called 'Wild magic' that Praedo's companions had? It could be Praedo's magic projected onto his friends, but it could also be their own magic.

- From the journals of Moult de Dico

Ryn started back up the stairs, when a slight stirring in the air caught her attention. She glanced around, but couldn't see anything that might have moved the air. The air brushed against her hands again. Ryn took the lantern and held it up to the wall behind Yll. It seemed like a solid wall of wood, but there was a gap at the bottom between the paneling and the floor. Air was flowing through the crack.

"What..." Yll started, but Ryn put her finger to her lips and pointed to the door to the office.

Ryn ran her hand along the wood paneling searching for a crack or something off. About halfway down the wall from where she started, she found a small hole. She leaned down to peer into the darkness inside the hole. They would need a key. She frowned, holding in an exasperated breath she wanted to let out. Shoulders slumped, she turned to go back up the stairs.

Yll's hand reached out and caught her arm. To Ryn's astonishment she held up Clayr's curator's keyring. The one Ryn had stolen from Clayr last fall. It felt like a lifetime ago. The ones Clayr should have given to Errol or Jeris when she was kicked out.

One by one Yll sifted through the likely keys until she found one that fit. She crossed her fingers and turned the key—the lock clicked and the door opened.

Ryn's heartbeat sped up. The assistant's office was right next to the curator's. Ryn pressed her eye to the crack the open door created—and she saw the familiar giant desk, the wall of windows that looked out across the courtyard to the guard house, and the walls lined with bookshelves.

"This is it!" Ryn whispered.

"Shhhh," Yll hissed.

"Looks empty." Ryn didn't see anyone in the office. The voice outside Dyana's office had sounded like Jeris. "I think we're in luck."

Ryn opened the door fully and they slipped inside the office.

Yll pointed to a drawer in Clayr's old desk. Ryn nodded. She had searched Clayr's desk before, and she knew its hidden secrets. Ryn crawled under the desk and pressed a latch that released a hidden panel in the bottom drawer. Yll pulled out the drawer all the way to reveal the hidden compartment and a small wooden box. She took the curator's keys and unlocked it. A letter was folded up inside. Yll, handed it to Ryn, closed and locked the box, then shut the hidden panel and the drawer.

"Let's get out..." Yll was saying when the door burst open.

Ryn froze, heart hammering in her chest.

"Jeris, so help me, I'm going to murder you for what you've done," Iden said as he strode through the door.

When he caught sight of Ryn and Yll standing there like deer in a hunter's sights, he quickly turned and shut the office door, then rounded on them.

"What are you two doing here? Are you trying to make things worse for everyone?" Iden rushed up to them.

Jeris' voice boomed in the hallway somewhat muffled, but they could make out Iden's name and some derogatory words about him.

"No time!" Came Ryn's harsh whisper.

Ryn grabbed Iden's arm and dragged him into the secret passage just as the door began to open. The last thing Ryn wanted was for Iden to stay and confront Jeris. Who knew what trouble Iden's temper would stir up. Ryn said a prayer to Praedo Jeris didn't hear the click the door made as they shut it tight.

With her heart hammering Ryn pushed Iden up the stairs to the third floor. By the time they got there, huffing and puffing, they could tell something was wrong. Shouts could be heard in the hallway outside the secret door.

"He's on to us," Yll whispered.

"You should have just left me in his office," Iden said. "The guards saw me go in."

"Fantastic." Yll's voice dripped with sarcasm.

"Sorry, I panicked." Ryn frowned.

Iden's posture shifted as he smirked at them. "Fortunately, I know another way."

* * *

Iden led them halfway back down the hidden stairwell, then opened a door into the second-floor documents collection. There was the sound of voices and feet stomping about, but Iden managed to get them through the rows of document shelves to, of all places, one of the small cubby hole doors where Zo took the Library's temperature.

"Inside," Iden whispered, tripping the lock that held the small door shut.

Yll crawled across the table in front of the cubby door, put her feet first into the hole and started down the ladder.

"Are you going to fit?" Ryn asked Iden.

"Just get in!" Iden helped her up onto the table.

Ryn slid in easily, but was worried they would have a similar mishap to what happened when she and Zo snuck into the Library. Fortunately Iden, despite having a bigger build than Zo, slid right through the door behind Ryn and pulled it shut.

"Down!" he called with a barely hushed voice.

Ryn climbed down the ladder as fast as she could without stepping on Yll's hands.

"I still don't know how we're going to get out. There's no way they're letting us through the Boiler Room," Ryn said, as she focused on hurrying without falling.

Once at the bottom of the ladder, Ryn let go and fell the last few feet. Yll was rubbing her hands from the hasty climb. When Iden dropped to the bottom, he took off down the tunnel. Ryn was hopelessly lost, not having spent as much time in the tunnels as Zo did. They turned a corner—and ran right into the Protector of the Library.

The protector was in its smoky claw form. Iden jumped back, but Ryn stepped around him with her hand up. The protector immediately changed to its human form. It started gesturing wildly.

Ryn shook her head. "Too fast, I can't understand."

The Protector slowed down, but Ryn still didn't catch it. She shook her head. The Protector pointed to Yll.

"Madame Curator? She's been thrown out by a vote of no confidence," Ryn said.

The Protector dropped its hands and hung its head. After a moment it pointed to Ryn and Iden, then held its hand at Zo's height.

"Zo's...gone," Ryn's voice broke, her hand going to her mouth.

The Protector took a step back, its dark form seemed to tremble. Its hands flashed wildly about again. Ryn couldn't understand it.

"I'm sorry, I don't know what you're saying, but if you're concerned about the Library under Jeris, we all are," Ryn said.

The Protector held out its hand. Its smokey essence formed the shape of the sword. The Protector pointed upstairs. Then the blackness swirled into a branch. The Protector pointed at Ryn.

She held her hands up and shrugged. "Clayr has the stone. I don't know what you mean about the sword and the branch."

The Proctor made a motion with its hand like it wanted them to follow. Its head shifted back and forth between them. Then it did something that made Ryn's heart stop—it threw its arms around Ryn, enveloping her in its shadow, then it shot up into the ceiling of the tunnel.

The three of them stood frozen in place. Ryn waited, wanting the Protector to return and protect her.

"That was wild!" Yll said.

"Come on, we're losing time." Iden pushed past Ryn.

They followed him to a pool of water and a barred gate.

"Of course—I forgot about the water entrance." Ryn felt really stupid.

"Yes, and the rain has been light lately so we shouldn't have to get too wet," Iden said.

Iden was right—although Brynd's dress had been soaked to her knees when she had entered the tunnels with Jak and Dan, the water only came to Ryn's ankles. They waded through the waters, and Iden unlatched the door, and waved them through. Ryn was first outside and climbed the steps—to find Fergus standing at the top, arms folded, his cold hard eyes fixed on Ryn.

* * *

"Fergus..." Ryn started. "I can explain."

He reached out his hand and took her arm.

Ryn began to tremble. Fergus had caught her again, and this time she knew no one was around to save her.

Fergus unhooked his cloak at his neck and swung it around to Iden.

"Hurry and cover up. I need to get you off Library grounds as quickly as possible," Fergus said.

Ryn's jaw hung open. Fergus's hand switched from her arm to briefly wrapping itself around her waist. Once Iden secured Fergus's cloak they all lifted their hoods, keeping their heads down as they headed toward the nearest Library gate, which happened to be the north gate.

In their favor was the fact that most workers at this hour were in the Library, so they didn't pass anyone who might report that Fergus was seen ushering clients out. Ryn desperately hoped that Fergus wouldn't get into trouble for helping them. She couldn't bear the thought of him losing his generations-held position in the Library because of her. She was sure his family wouldn't be pleased.

Once they were through the north gate and off the Library grounds, Fergus stayed with them all the way to Thax's shop. As they approached the shop, Ryn caught a glimpse of someone inside whom she recognized as part of Jeris' household in Sooke. Yll gasped in recognition. The girls pulled the guys down the street and around the corner. Ryn's hands were shaking and she was breathing hard.

"Do you think Jeris sent them looking for us?" Yll asked.

"I don't know, and I don't want to find out," Ryn said, peeking down the street at Thax's door.

"Great." Fergus rubbed his forehead.

Ryn turned to him. Wishing she had something comforting to say, but she was sure they were all in big trouble this time.

"They left," Yll said, from the building corner where she'd taken up watching Thax's shop.

Fergus joined her, saying nothing until Jeris' servant was gone.

Iden stood shielding Ryn as he watched the street behind them.

"Let's go." Fergus waved them forward.

When they entered Thax's shop, Thax immediately closed all the blinds and locked the door, putting out his closed sign.

"What have you all done?" he demanded.

Ryn shrank, and Fergus put an arm around her shoulders.

"We retrieved what my mother needed from the Library," Yll said, lifting her head.

"You stole from the Library?" Tory entered the room. "Now that's bold. Bolder than Jak and Dan would do."

Fergus dropped his arm and frowned at Ryn.

Ryn gazed up into his face. "It's not what it sounds. It's a letter and a package my father sent to Clayr. They don't belong to the Library, and because of what my father is researching, we're afraid it might be something important that we don't want Jeris to get his hands on," Ryn said.

"Let's see." Fergus held out his hand.

Ryn pressed her hand to her pocket, feeling the weight of the package, plus something else.

Besides the package and the letter, there was the paper Lyssa had given her, plus a small book. Ryn pulled out the package and the papers. She left the book in her pocket. That was definitely a violation of Library rules. Lyssa must have slipped it into Ryn's pocket when Ryn gave her a hug. How Lyssa had managed that she couldn't fathom. Ryn had been too worried about sneaking around to pay attention to the weight in her pocket. She moved to the counter to set everything down.

Everyone gathered around her.

Ryn picked up the paper Lyssa had given her first. It was a passage about old theories about how to slay a dragon without magic. One theory had someone hide in a trunk. Once the dragon was tricked into swallowing it, the person emerged and slew the dragon with a sword from the inside out.

Yll shivered. "That's disgusting."

"And how would you get out? What if the dragon took off in flight, you'd plummet to the ground?" Fergus asked.

Iden nodded. "Sounds like death for the slayer as well as the dragon."

The next entry was about convincing a dragon to swallow sulfur, and igniting it. The theory proposed that the dragon would then explode.

Thax looked toward his back room. "I've got sulfur. I mean, it burns, but seems like you'd need to get it extremely hot to get it to explode like that."

Bam, bam, bam!

Everyone jumped at the pounding on the door.

Yll peeked out the blinds, gave a squeak, then turned the lock and let in a wet and soggy Regg. It had begun to pour rain outside. She pulled him in and relocked the door.

Despite him being soaked, Yll threw her arms around him. He stiffly put one arm around her. His eyes were red, and his face was a mask of deadness.

Ryn's pulse sped up and her stomach dropped.

"You have news." Ryn's hands shook.

Regg started crying and buried his face in Yll's shoulder. His arms coming around to hold her tightly to him.

"No," Ryn whispered.

Tears began streaming down Iden's face. He reached out and gathered Ryn to him, holding her tight.

"The sentence was death. Zo's gone," Regg sobbed.

Ryn stood there frozen, blood rushing in her ears. She tried to shake her head even though it was pressed against Iden.

"It can't be. They didn't even listen! Jak and Dan said they would send witnesses that you can't kill in dreams!" Ryn cried.

Regg was gasping with sobs.

Ryn pulled away from Iden and backed up into a dress form with a, of all things, cow hide on it.

"It's my fault. As soon as I saw that Keir guy, I knew he was trouble. I should have stopped him. I should have said something. I was so wrapped up in my own stuff. What kind of sister am I? Of course I'm not his sister. I'm nobody's sister." Tears flooded Ryn's eyes, but she managed to find the door, fumbling with the lock.

"Ryn, wait! They might be out looking for you!" Fergus called after her, but it was too late, she was already running down the street.

* * *

She ran blindly, heart hammering so hard it felt like it would burst from her chest. When she turned a corner and saw where she had run, she dropped to her knees before Wilmar's door. An ugly cry welled up from the depths of her soul and escaped her throat as a horrific screech. Wind swirled around her, stirring up old dead leaves from the corners of the doorway. Her scalp tingled as she fell forward onto Wilmar's doorstep, the wind dying down to a calm.

The door opened and Wilmar stooped to lift her.

"Ryn?" His brow furrowed as his eyes searched her face.

She stumbled to her feet, letting him guide her into his exam room.

Nix was there. His broad slumped back was to her. He didn't even stir to look at her when she entered.

Ryn was shaking uncontrollably. Wilmar sat her in a chair and took her pulse, while he checked her eyes and felt her forehead and neck.

"She's going into shock. Hand me that blanket, will you?" Wilmar said to Nix.

Nix's hand enfolded a blanket on the shelf, then he handed it back to Wilmar without shifting.

Wilmar wrapped the blanket about Ryn, then vigorously rubbed her arms to warm her.

"We heard. That girl Ayn came over and told us the news." Wilmar kissed Ryn's temple.

"Let me make you some chamomile tea." Wilmar stood, passing through the curtain into his living quarters.

Ryn remembered the last time she was here, and watched Zo push through those curtains to answer the door. If she could go back to that day. She would take him and run away. Back to Sooke maybe, or maybe Brynd's family apple farm. Someplace safe, away from all the awfulness. If she had done that, he would still be here. Tears streamed down Ryn's cheeks.

Wilmar returned with the tea. He set it on the table next to Ryn, just as a knock came at the door. Wilmar wiped his hands down his face then went to answer it.

Brynd came rushing in.

"I thought I might find you here." She knelt next to Ryn, her hand running through Ryn's hair. "Are you alright?"

Ryn picked up the chamomile tea. Her favorite. The scent of the flowers steeped in hot water relaxed her muscles, but her stomach was still tight. She took a sip hoping the tea would calm her stomach.

"No," Ryn said.

Brynd nodded, tears forming in her eyes. "I got to Thax's right after you left. The guys sent me after you. They've gone back to Eileansano to help Fyri with memorial service arrangements. I doubt she'll take their input, but Iden is insisting they honor every aspect of Zo's life."

Ryn set her mug down. "I want to go."

Brynd put a hand on her arm. "They said they would come back for us when everything is set. In the meantime, we need to get you out of Waatch before Jeris confirms it was you in the Library, and I need to go home. I was wondering if you'd go with me?"

Ryn stirred at that thought. "I had just been thinking that if I had taken Zo to your apple farm none of this would have happened." Ryn's voice broke.

Brynd smoothed Ryn's hair. "Let's not think about that." Brynd pulled the package, letter, and Lyssa's notes from her pocket and handed them to Ryn. "Tory's collecting the rest of your stuff from Thax's. We don't feel it's safe for you to go back there."

Ryn nodded. "Where's Yll?"

Brynd lifted her hands in a shrug. "She went to find her mother."

Wilmar came over and took Ryn's pulse again. "At least stay the night here. I don't think you're ready for a road trip yet."

Ryn snuggled down deeper into the blanket. "I think you're right."

Chapter Fifteen

Got a letter today from Ryette about Jett. I know he's not my son, but I raised him. I love him deeply. I've told Ryette for years that she needs to tell the kids where she's from. I'm glad we were honest with Ryn about her being adopted. I know Ryn feels a connection with her mother because they're both 'Ordinary'. I knew it was going to be bad when the kids found out, but I'm surprised Jett chose to side with House Viator. I guess I didn't realize how much he desires power.

- From the journals of Moult de Dico

The light was so bright it penetrated Zo's eyelids. His hand came up to cover the light before he carefully opened one eye a crack. A man who looked like the male version of Madame Sano stood over him, dressed in white robes that almost glowed in the light.

"I've gone to the ancestors?" Zo croaked, his voice gravely from disuse.

The man chuckled. "Not quite."

"Oh good. I knew there was no such place."

The man shushed him. "I'll be back."

The light faded and everything became quiet and dark. Zo rested his eyes. His head was starting to throb.

"Great, I can't even rest in peace," he mumbled.

The light returned with the Sano look alike and his mother.

"Oh Mother, they got you too?" Zo said, a strange sadness welling up inside to think that they had killed his mother too. His heart started pounding, and he tried to sit up. "Did they get Dad and Regg?"

Fyri sat next to him. "Shhhhh." She traced her fingers through his hair, starting at his hairline and smoothing back around his ear. "It's alright. Everything is fine."

"Of course everything is fine—we're dead. Who cares anymore." Zo laid back and let his mother stroke the same lock of hair over and over.

His mother turned to Sano guy. "How long will it take?"

"Well, we have to get all the drugs out of his system, but after that it shouldn't take more than a few days—so long as what you say is true—he only killed an animal."

"It was a wolf." His mother's voice was making Zo's head pound harder.

Sano guy's eyes got all buggy. "They don't exist."

"They do, I saw it," Fyri said.

Sano guy ran a hand through his hair. "I can't say for sure. I've never treated a case that wasn't an animal or a human. I guess we'll find out."

"Wait." Zo lifted his head again. "I'm not dead? How am I not dead?"

His mother gently pushed him back down. "Shhhhh. Rest now. Master Rocco is going to fix you."

Master Rocco choked, then coughed. "I'll see what I can do, but your mother is right, you need to sleep off what House Sano did to you."

Zo cracked one eye open at him. A guy who looked like the embodiment of House Sano, but sounded like he was against the council? Strange.

His mother ran her fingers through his hair like she did when he was a kid and hummed a familiar lullaby tune. He drifted back to sleep.

* * *

The nightmares began. The giant mouse was chasing him again. The cry that escaped his throat when the mouse caught him woke him from his sleep. He closed his eyes and the wolf killed him, then he watched as the wolf tore out Ryn, Regg, and their parents' throats. He rolled over and the dream shifted. He was in the underbelly of the Library. The Protector of the Library appeared, and its claw-like hands sliced open Zo's stomach. Zo doubled over from the pain, and his knees hit warm soft sand. It was the beach he had dreamed of briefly before. The one where he had met Ryn and told her about Jak and Dan breaking into the Library.

He looked up and down the beach. The sand was golden yellow and the waves broke, rushing up the beach. The sand reached up the mountain behind him, as if a giant wave had once deposited it there, but there was no Ryn. His stomach still stung, and he clutched it, watching blood drip onto the sand. Maybe he really was dead. Maybe the scene with Fyri and Master Rocco had been the dream. The warm sand felt good though. Maybe he could just lay down here and soak the heat in. He contemplated laying down and letting go. His life was over, no matter what his mother thought. He put his bloody hands into the sand, his head yearning to make the warmth his pillow...

Someone sniffled. Strange that he could hear such a soft noise over the crashing of the waves. He looked up to see Ryn sitting on the beach staring into the water. Her rough voice called his name. The anguish in her scared him. He opened his mouth to call out to her...

"Wake up darling, you've slept for two days. It's time to get you up and get you moving." His mother's voice brought him back.

His stomach still hurt, but there was no blood. His mother gave him some water to drink. The iciness of it turned his stomach and he broke into a cold sweat. After a few minutes though, he began to feel better.

"What happened?" he asked.

"I called in every favor I was owed and got you out. I brought you here to the island of Receptum. It's a small island off the coast of Eileansano. There are Healers here willing to work outside the boundaries House Sano has set. I used to hate what they stood for, but I couldn't ignore the rumors they could possibly heal you," his mother said.

Zo sat up. His head spun, and his muscles shook. He'd spent too long lying down. His back was raw from bedsores.

"I feel like death," he said.

"Thank goodness I could save you from that. Let's get you up. Master Rocco is waiting for you," she said.

Standing was worse than sitting, and Zo wobbled back against the bed. His mother, who was much shorter than him, managed to get her arm around his waist and support him. He took a couple shaky steps before an attendant came and helped. They walked him down a hall to a larger room. Master Rocco sat cross legged on the floor, his eyes closed, seemingly in deep meditation.

"Should we disturb him?" Zo asked, his voice too loud in the quiet space.

Master Rocco opened his eyes. "You're not disturbing me. Come. Sit."

Zo's mother and the attendant helped him sit before the master. Zo's knees protested the bending.

"Ow, ow, ow," Zo said as he tried to fold himself.

The Master gave him a serene smile. "Please leave," he said to Fyri.

Zo's mother opened her mouth to protest, but the attendant took her arm and pulled her away, shutting the door behind them.

Zo sighed, trying to relieve the heavy weight in his chest that his life had become.

The master patted his knee. "Come, it's time to heal."

"But I can't heal, the ability is gone." Zo's gaze dropped to his hands in his lap.

"That is because of guilt and shame. Those who have no guilt can still use their Healing magic despite the act of killing with it."

Zo looked up sharply at the master. "That's why Keir…he could still heal even though he had killed. I thought it was because he was an inbred Healer."

"Take my hands."

Zo reached out to the master, pausing just before they touched.

"You're not afraid I'm going to kill you?" Zo asked.

Master Rocco smiled. "You killed a wolf attempting to save a room full of people it was ready to kill. I think I'm safe."

"Why couldn't the Healing Council see that?"

Their hands connected…and the guilt washed over Zo like a sneaker wave, pulling him under and drowning him.

Awash with emotion, Zo struggled to connect with Rocco. Zo had joined minds with Madame Sano and Keir to heal in the past, but both of those experiences brought pain. Reflexively Zo flinched away from Master Rocco's Healing magic. It hurt to feel it and not be able to meet it with his own.

"Relax. Let go of your thoughts," the master said.

Zo shifted, his legs growing uncomfortable.

"Deep breaths. Clear your mind."

Zo breathed in deep, but his head was full of scenes—Keir showing him how intoxicating the power of killing was, Zo's attraction to Keir's power, Keir suggesting he kill Jinx...That split second decision to kill the wolf instead of letting it kill him...

"That's it—that's the one. Let that memory flow out of your mind," Rocco said.

But Zo held it, caressed it—couldn't let it go.

"Breathe in with me," Master Rocco said. "One, two, three, four, hold it."

Zo held his breath. In his mind the wolf's teeth were digging into his throat.

"Now let it out—four, three, two, one, push the memory out with it."

Zo breathed out, focusing on counting, and the sound of Rocco's voice, but the wolf still had a hold of his throat.

Master Rocco went silent and still.

"I'm sorry," Zo said.

Master Rocco shook his head. "This thing you encountered. It's not an animal, and it's not human, yet it's both."

"What does that mean?" Zo's stomach tightened.

"It means we'll have to dig deeper, but you can't do that with all the pains distracting you. I will need to ease those, but not completely. As part of your recovery, you must heal yourself from all your wounds."

The Master's Healing magic flowed into Zo. His nausea and pains eased. Sores and knotted muscles relaxed into relief. His stomach growled with hunger.

Master Rocco chuckled. "Let's go find you something to eat."

Zo unfolded himself with a grace he'd never felt before, or hadn't felt for a long time. He marveled at how he was better than he had been in moons, but the heaviness wasn't gone. The heaviness in his heart was still there.

* * *

The next few days Zo worked with Master Rocco during the day, and his mother hovered over him all night. He didn't catch a glimpse of her anywhere during the day. He wondered where she went during that time—not that he wanted her around all day. There was a strange tenseness to their time together in the evening. As if she was trying to win him over and make up for all the years of terrible parenting. The things she had done last winter were inexcusable, but Zo found himself comfortable in her presence. He didn't completely trust her, but he let himself pretend he was five years old again and allowed her to attempt to ease things between them.

Zo also continued to have nightmares. Sometimes he was achingly close to Iden, but couldn't touch him. Other times he was on the beach again. Ryn sitting with her knees pulled up to her chest. She stared out across the water at the setting sun. She no longer called for him. He thought that was for the best. She needed to get on with her life. Progress was slow, and Zo feared he would never heal. It was best if he just let her be. It was better than facing rejection from her and everyone else. He needed to take care of himself. No one else was going to do that.

He turned and walked away down the beach.

* * *

Zo sat cross legged on the mat in the meditation room. Master Rocco was next to him, his breathing regular and mindful. Zo was attempting to copy the master's rhythm, but his mind was filled with images of Ryn and the bird that he couldn't summon his Healing to repair.

Zo took a deep breath, intending to clear his mind, but words tumbled out of his mouth instead. "What if I can't fix my Healing?"

"Then you spend your life doing your job of keeping the temperature correct at the Library. It's a prestigious job, and I've heard you are invaluable." Master Rocco's voice was low, and barely above a whisper.

Zo shifted his legs back and forth. He was important to the Library. He was one of the few people who had seen and communicated with the Protector of the Library. For some reason it was no longer enough. He hated his old self who wished to be rid of his Healing magic. If he could only go back in time and strangle that kid he had been.

"I can't live with that," Zo whispered.

"Hmmmm—what are the alternatives?" Master Rocco asked still in that light airy voice of meditation.

Zo thought for a while. "If only there was a way to get another Healing bead and take the magic back. Start all over and take the lessons."

"That would be nice. If only it worked that way. Sometimes we have to work through our consequences, and find a new path. I've heard you were studying to be a physician. If you still want to heal you should return to pursuing that."

Zo's heart sank. He loved Wilmar, but he also loved sneaking in some Healing magic with the herbs. He sighed and laid on his back. His gaze taking in the huge, exposed wood beams overhead. If only there was a time travel magic. Something he could use to go back in time and erase all of his mistakes.

Master Rocco nudged his leg. "It's almost lunch. Finish up your meditation so we can go eat."

Zo put his hand over his eyes, counted to ten, then took a deep breath and sat up. His only hope at the moment was to hope he could fix what was broken.

* * *

Several days into his recovery, he went into his session with Master Rocco and found his mother in a heated argument with the master.

"He should be healed by now. You promised he would be healed by now." His mother's face was red, her eyebrows pointed the way they did when she was furious.

"I told you it would be complicated. We have made progress. He is able to heal himself, but he's still unable to access his magic fully," Rocco said.

"That's not good enough. If he's not completely healed, I cannot bring him back to House Sano. That is the only way they will pardon him. If they find out he's alive they will send agents to kill him." Fyri was pacing the practice room.

"It's going to take time…" the master began.

"We don't have time!" Fyri shouted. "His brother and that idiot who calls himself Zo's boyfriend have been digging into my affairs, suspicious that there's no body. They managed to get someone to talk…" his mother stopped and glared at Master Rocco. "I can't have them find him here. They will lead Sano authorities to him. I need him healed now!"

Zo shifted, and the door he stood next to creaked.

Fyri's head whipped around to find him there listening.

"Iden and Regg are looking for me?" Zo asked. "I thought no one cared."

"Everyone thinks you're dead," Master Rocco said.

"What?" Zo was having trouble processing everything they were saying. His mother brought him here without telling anyone he was alive?

"It's for the best…" his mother started, but Zo just shut down. This was her. This was always her trying to run his life the way that she thought he should live it.

"I'm not listening." Zo turned to leave.

Fyri moved with more speed than he thought she was capable of, and came around in front of him.

"I'm sick of your disrespect. I'm your mother. I saved your life. You will do what I tell you to do."

Zo's fists clenched. "So nothing's changed."

Master Rocco was suddenly between them, his back to Zo, he put out pleading hands to Fyri. "This isn't helping the healing process. He can't get rid of his guilt and shame if you are adding to it."

"You stay out of this." Fyri wagged a finger at Rocco. Her eyes met Zo's. They flashed with anger. "Let me tell you this, son. This island that we are on, it's close to Eileansano's shore. This is a hidden colony of unconventional Healers, but every member of the Healing Council is aware of its existence. If someone leads the Council here looking for you, you're dead. I suggest you find a way to restore your Healing magic, or you will need to hide for the rest of your life, because they *will* come for you to carry out their sentence."

With that, Fyri spun on her heel and disappeared down the hall.

Master Rocco sighed. "Well, that ruins any chance for calm meditation and healing for today."

Zo's pounding heart agreed.

Chapter Sixteen

Then magic primeval was spoken aloud,
The vast plain trembled, the soil was riven,
The level was raised by the might of heaven,
And mountains eternal arose from the cloud.

I have often wondered, beyond the desolation that is the Origin, how much of the land was changed by Praedo and the dragon? This verse in the Canticum Tarrae in the GP indicates that Praedo's arrival changed the land.

- From the journals of Moult de Dico

Yll burst through Wilmar's door just as Ryn and Brynd were saying their goodbyes, getting ready to leave for Brynd's parents' farm.

"Oh good—I'm so glad I found you here! Mother has a message for you." Yll handed Ryn what felt like a book wrapped in paper, with a note attached.

Ryn opened the note:

Ryn
I just got the news. I know you must be hurting right now, and possibly prepared to do something unwise (like breaking into the Library yesterday), but I'm going to plead with you to get out of town for a while. Somehow Jeris knows it was you in the Library. He suspects you have 'stolen' your father's package and letter. He's demanding their return and is searching Waatch for you. I also suggest you don't return to your home in Sooke, Jeris will look for you there. Staying with Thax right now will be dangerous for both you and him. Please be smart about this.

Also, Lyssa begged I send this book to you. She says you wished to see it, and after re-reviewing its contents she thinks you need this information. For what, I don't want to know at this point. I suspect it's a Library book that shouldn't be out of the Library, but I'm not the curator anymore, so the fact that it's out of the Library is on Jeris' leadership. Please be safe out there.

Love ya!
Clayr

Ryn unwrapped the book to find it was the history of the Library that she'd found on Lyssa's shelf. The one she hadn't had a chance to look at. She clutched it to her chest.

"Tell your mom we are way ahead of her. We're on our way to Brynd's family. Please keep us updated—especially about the funeral. I want to be there." Ryn fought to keep the emotion from her voice, but didn't succeed.

Yll nodded and gave Ryn a hug. "I'll let you know." She turned to Brynd. "How do I find your farm?"

While Brynd gave Yll directions, Ryn tucked the history book in her bag next to her father's things. If they could find a ride, she would read everything on the road.

Wilmar gave Ryn one last hug. He didn't have to say anything, the tears in his eyes said it all.

Wilmar sniffled. "I'll send you a note through Yll if I have any news Clayr doesn't."

Ryn nodded, and Wilmar pulled away to blow his nose.

"Give Nix a hug for me," Ryn said as her and Brynd filed out the door.

"Of course," Wilmar said, then turned to his work bench.

Outside on the street Yll also gave Ryn a hug. "See you soon."

Then so quickly it startled Ryn, Yll turned into a robin and flew away.

Brynd put her arm around Ryn's shoulders. "Let's get out of this town and get on the road. Walking out of Waatch into the smell of cedar trees and forest has a way of clearing the mind."

Fortunately, they were only partway down the road west toward the peninsula when Brynd saw a neighbor farmer to her parent's orchard. They were able to jump in the back of his wagon and hitch a ride. While they bumped their way down the road, Ryn tried to forget how she had rode in the back of a farmer's wagon with Zo headed in the same direction, not so long ago.

To distract herself Ryn took out her father's letter.

> *Clayr,*
> *My connection with Ryette is gone, and I must urgently get in touch with her. Or perhaps you can help me. I've found the cave at last! It's taken ten years of work, but I'm certain I've found the cave where Luc left the original beads of Praedo. However, the door is sealed. I've tried everything, but cannot open it. There's a symbol on the door. I'm wondering if you've seen it before, or if you could do some research on it. The symbol is a circle bisected by what looks like a sword (or maybe a fence post?) surrounded by leaves of a tree I don't recognize. If you could get this information to Ryette, or if you have knowledge of this symbol, please send the information you have via the usual route.*
> *I'm worried about Ryette and her absence. Please send to me what you know of her whereabouts as soon as possible.*
> *Moult*

Ryn sat forward.

"Brynd! My father found the cave! The one with..." She looked over her shoulder at the farmer driving and lowered her voice. "Praedo's beads."

Brynd's jaw dropped. "Are you kidding?"

Ryn shook her head, and took out her father's package. There was a note attached to the package.

> *Clayr,*
> *Zmej is here. He's got Ryette, and a man I don't know with him. He's threatening to harm them if I*

don't bring the key and open the door for him. I've told him I don't have the key. (I still don't understand the symbol, but I think maybe the sword is Praedo's?) I fear he will find the key if he gets a hold of my journal of notes, so I'm sending it to you for safe keeping. Perhaps you can solve the mystery of the key to opening the door with the resources of the Library? But be careful whom you trust with this information. He has followers everywhere, some you would least expect. Zmej and the others are deeper in the cave and closer to the door. I'm not sure how he's keeping Ryette and that man from leaving, because I can't get close enough. There are wolves roaming the caves, and it's difficult to leave my cave home. I'll try to hold him off as long as I can, but I'm going to need help. I've put instructions about how to find the cave in my journal. There's a tree growing out of a giant log at the entrance. You can't miss it. Please send help!

Moult

Ryn sucked in her breath. "Zmej has my mother, and my uncle."

"Oh no! Should we turn back to Waatch and get help?" Brynd asked.

"How far are we from your farm?"

"Actually, we are closer to the farm than to Waatch at this point," Brynd said.

Ryn considered what was best to do. If they went back to Waatch they risked getting caught by Jeris and that would be no help to her parents.

"Do your parents have a way of sending messages to Waatch?" Ryn asked.

"Sure, they send me messages all the time via courier, but there are shapeshifting messengers for hire."

"Alright, let's get to your parents and we'll send a message to Clayr that my parents are in danger."

* * *

Several days at the apple farm and Ryn still hadn't gotten any word from Waatch. She walked between rows of apple trees in full bloom. Their sweet yet tangy scent swirled around her with the light breeze. A petal floated down and landed on her nose. She felt like she was present, but not there at the same time. She focused her attention on the white and pink blossoms making the trees look like fluffy clouds. The thought of all the apples that would come later in the summer made her stomach growl. Here was life. It burst into bloom, then bore fruit, then withered and died. They should all be so lucky to live long enough to wither.

The apple trees were life, but Ryn felt numb. In the days since she left Waatch she couldn't stop thinking of Zo. At least when they first took him, she had hope the council would find him innocent, and she would see him again. The finality of his death ripped her heart out of her. Brynd kept reminding her there were lots of people who loved her, and she knew that, but time and life seemed to have stopped for her. There was no moving on from this point. She was stuck here forever.

It didn't help that she'd sent multiple messages to everyone she could think of in Waatch, and no one was responding. Yll hadn't even brought the promised message from Clayr. Where were they? Her parents were in danger, and everyone was ignoring her. She was just an Ordinary, with no power to overcome Zmej. She needed help to rescue her parents, but no one had come. If someone didn't respond soon, Ordinary or not, she was going to have to do something to save her parents. Too much time had passed since her father had sent that package to Clayr. By now her parents could be dead, then who did she have left in this world? She was staying in Brynd's family's house with Brynd's parents and eight siblings, but Ryn felt all alone.

Ryn found the stump she had grown fond of sitting on under the canopy of blossoms. She took out the book Lyssa sent with her on the Library's history and read, hoping to distract herself.

> *In the year 529 Dom was chosen as curator by the newly formed Board of Regents...*

Ryn yawned and closed the history book. She took out the package her father had sent. It was his journal. It was filled with notes and thoughts on the different sources he had read about Luc as well as Praedo's beads. It described how the beads were distributed to Praedo's companions. She wondered what Praedo's companions had been like. They must have been brave to fight the dragon with ordinary weapons and no magic. She had skimmed the information Yll had written from her memory of Luc's many journals, but hadn't paid much attention to the stories. She wished now that she had. Were they jealous of their powers as their descendants are? Or were they more giving and generous with their magic?

She turned the page to where her father recounted how Luc had refused to take upon himself the magic. Her father had the same thoughts she did—perhaps Luc had feared the corruption of power. And yet, because he didn't take a bead of magic, the companions trusted him as keeper of Praedo's beads. He oversaw the building of the Library as a sanctuary and protection for the beads. It seemed a similar bead ceremony to the one Ryn had been a part of at House Viator used to take place in the Library. Everyone thought Praedo's beads had run out, because the cask of them in the Library was empty, but her father had spent years proving there were some that still existed. Hidden deep inside the mountains of the peninsula, they were there, the original beads made from Praedo's bones. The ones that held all the magics within them, and Zmej wanted them. She needed to do something. Sitting waiting for someone to come and help her was going to get her parents hurt, or worse. Ryn had almost been roasted by Zmej's fire. She had been powerless to do anything to save herself and the tree. It was a good thing Zo had found her...

A deep sadness swelled inside her chest. His toothy grin and his eyes that twinkled with mischief floated in front of her.

She put her father's journal to the side, and pulled out the book Lyssa claimed was Luc's original journal. The one with the bumpy writing on it. Ryn carefully compared Luc's Gesta Praediana journal with the copy her father had made of it in his journal. Everything was word for word the same. The only difference was the raised bumps. Ryn ran her fingers over them again. She didn't really remember the bumps and what letters they represented, but she remembered what they said.

The Branch is the Key. TLTRP

She still didn't know what it meant, and her father's journal made no mention of the finger writing. Maybe it was a clue he didn't know about. Ryn's heart sped up. She needed to get this information to him. He could figure out what it meant. It could be the clue they needed.

Ryn started collecting her books, but her hand paused on the Library history book. There had to be a reason Lyssa sent it. Lyssa knew well the consequences of sending Library materials outside the Library. Luc's book was important. The history book had to be too.

She started flipping through the pages, not knowing what she was looking for. Partway through the book something caught her eye on the corner of the page. It was the finger writing, just a letter or two. Ryn didn't know what letters it was, but she instantly knew it was Lyssa's way of marking the page for her. On the page it read:

Praedo's sword which resides in the Library...

Ryn scrunched up her nose. *But Praedo's sword is buried to its hilt at the Origin. How could it be in the Library?* It didn't make any sense, certainly this was some weird Library folklore.

She flipped through more pages and found another page marked. This page said:

It's rumored that the magic of the wild has the ability to turn the dragon's children into humans. Beware gray haired men who look far too young to have gray hair.

That was the only passage on the page that was out of the ordinary. The rest followed in the same dry manner of recounting Library history as the rest of the book. It was out of place, and Ryn didn't understand why Lyssa found it so important she sent it to her through Clayr. Ryn shrugged.

Gray haired young men brought the image of Zo fighting the wolf. Its jaw was around Zo's neck, as it bit down it went still...and because of that Zo was now cold and still somewhere. Did they bury him yet? Had she missed it being away? Desire to see his face one last time overwhelmed her. They had left her out and she would never have that chance to say goodbye.

Ryn clutched the books to her heart and doubled over. Her sobs echoed through the orchard. Somehow, she had to escape the pain.

She leapt up and ran back toward Brynd's family home. If she ran fast enough maybe she could outrun it all.

Chapter Seventeen

A fog dense and bitter enclosed the shore,
A darkness of salt, of shadow, of grief;
No light could pierce through its ghostly relief,
Nor sight could avail us a step or more.

Oh, how I have felt this darkness...

- From the journals of Moult de Dico

Zo had perched himself on the wall in the gardens facing the sea. His legs were folded, and his hands rested gently on his knees. Even with his eyes closed, he could see the water, feel the ocean, and hear the waves that beat to the rhythm of his breathing against the rocks below. He was trying to find peace. A calm that would overcome his doubts. Since Zo found out people were looking for him, he wanted off this island in the worst way. When his mother had left, she had taken the only mode of transportation off this rock and stranded him there.

He took a deep breath and attempted to let it out slowly. Once again, his mother had thought only of herself and what she wanted. Healing Zo had nothing to do with Zo's wellbeing, and everything to do with her position of power on the council. It was taking every bit of Zo's control to keep from snapping and yelling at everyone he encountered. He knew they didn't deserve it, but oh, it would feel so good right now.

A commotion began off to Zo's left in the direction of the Healing facility. People were yelling and doors were slamming. It wasn't completely unusual, sometimes patients became difficult—the way Zo wanted to be difficult.

Someone yelled, "You can't go out there."

The sound of booted feet pounding on the garden flagstones finally drew Zo's attention. He opened his eyes to see two people running at him. Before he could process it, he was being lifted bodily off the wall and wrapped in a hug that squeezed him so tight he was unable to breathe.

The pressure on Zo's chest eased a bit and he sucked in a breath. The scent of Iden, salt air with a hint of old books, filled his nostrils. Zo relaxed into his embrace.

"Hey! What about me?" Regg couldn't get Iden to let go, so he joined the embrace.

Zo pulled his arm out from between them and wrapped it around his brother. He felt Regg's tears trickle down his ear. His left shoulder was already wet from Iden's.

They stayed like that for a long while. For the first time in a long time Zo could reach out and feel Regg's Healing magic, but the best part was that Iden's thoughts were once again flowing into his mind.

Wildfire! Wildfire! I thought I lost you, Iden said.

Zo inwardly rolled his eyes. *Everyone says that in the story books.*

It's true though. I can't believe you're here.

Zo hugged him tighter.

At last, Iden released him and held Zo's face in his hands. "You look well."

"Better, but not complete, the Healers here have restored my ability to heal myself, but I still can't heal other people," Zo said.

"The fact that you're alive and looking better than you have in moons is such a relief," Regg said, rubbing his eyes.

"How did you survive? We heard the Council sentenced you to death," Iden asked, dragging Zo over to a table and chairs next to a full yellow blooming forsythia bush.

Zo's gaze shifted to Regg as he sat. "Mother. She arranged to get me out of there and bring me here. These Healers claimed they could heal me."

"Can they?" Regg looked toward the Healing compound.

"They got me this far, but I'm stuck. I just can't seem to heal my magic enough. They said maybe in a few years I could work through it all and be well, but they can't guarantee it." Zo sat back, turning his neck one way, then the other to crack it.

"Well that won't do. We only just managed to get here ahead of the agents of House Sano. They've found out where you are and they're coming to finish the job." Iden looked back over his shoulder as if he was expected the agents to burst out into the garden at any moment.

Zo fixed his gaze on Regg. "How did you get here?"

"By boat. It's a fast one." Regg started to rise.

Zo looked down at his patient loose shirt and pants. "I need to change."

Iden nodded. "Let's hurry. There's not much time."

Zo changed back into his winter solstice suit—it was what he had been wearing the night of his birthday. His mother had brought it along because it was a Thax original. Zo dropped by Master Rocco's meditation room on their way out.

"I'm leaving," Zo said, startling Master Rocco who was deep in meditation.

The master cracked an eye open. "It's too soon."

"I don't have a choice, agents of Sano are on their way here for me."

Master Rocco stood. He put a hand on Zo's shoulder, his head bowed deep in thought.

"Good luck," the master said at last. "I don't know if it's possible to heal your magic. Even if you had the power of the Ancestors, it would still be hard, but I do hope you find a way."

Zo nodded, then gave Master Rocco a brief hug. "Thank you for restoring what you could. I'm grateful to be able to heal myself again."

Master Rocco led Zo to the door. "Go now, be safe."

Zo gave the master one last look, then followed Regg and Iden through the Healing facility and down the stairs to the docks. He inhaled the sea air and took in the sparkling sunshine on the water.

At the end of the docks there was a man with a small boat waiting. There was no sign of any other boat on the horizon, but Zo didn't want to take any chances. The faster they could get away, the more likely he could stay alive.

"Welcome," the boatman said. "The Ancestors have blessed us with a fine sailing day."

"I thought you were using your air and wind magic?" Regg said.

The boatman laughed. "By the grace of the Ancestors and what they have bestowed upon me." He stopped and winked at Zo. "Good weather also helps."

What the Ancestors have bestowed. Hmmmm, Zo thought.

Iden startled and looked over at him. He must have caught Zo's thought.

"Where to?" The boatman asked Zo.

"Home."

* * *

Two days later, Zo stood in Jak's office, arms folded with his eyes looking down his nose at the man. Zo poured as much menace into his stance as he could. He'd come here to get answers, and he wasn't leaving till he got them.

"Come on, I know you know who killed Tammy and Regent Jordan." Zo had asked nicely, but Jak was being evasive.

Jak held up his palms. "Suspicions only, I can't turn someone over without hard evidence."

Zo turned to Fergus. Zo'd left Iden at Thax's with Jinx, Beardsley, and Abby. Someone needed to stay back who knew where they'd gone. Zo chose to bring the most intimidating person he knew besides Nix, whom Zo hadn't seen. Zo was trying to keep his whereabouts secret. Rumors had it that agents of House Sano had been seen in Waatch looking for someone of Zo's description. Fergus was the next best choice for the job. He looked just fine in his uniform with the Library sword at his side.

"We don't care about evidence, we need to know who's going to stick a knife in our backs." Fergus's hand rested on the pommel of his sword.

Jak shook his head. "I can't be sure, but Jett was here about a moon back. He was pressing me for information about Moult's location. I told him Moult was his dad and he should know better than I do. I also told him to tell Viator to shove it. He said he wasn't working for House Viator and left."

"So who's he working for?" Zo started to sweat. Jett was Ryn's brother and had Spirit magic—the kind of magic that could kill without leaving a trace. He'd seen it. He'd seen the Spirit-teller rip a spirit from someone's body.

Jak shook his head. Dan stepped forward and sat on the edge of Jak's desk.

"We can't be sure." Dan and Jak got faraway looks on their faces. Zo had seen it before, on Iden when he was speaking to Zo's mind.

Zo's eyes examined both Jak and Dan's necklines, but their collarbones were covered in the fashion of Ordinaries.

"Come on, I know you have your suspicions." Fergus shifted legs.

Jak and Dan consulted mentally again. Dan lowered his head, but Jak spoke out loud.

"Evalesco. We suspect he's working for Evalesco," Jak said.

"Evalesco, isn't Zmej at the head of that?" Zo asked.

"He could be. It's hard to tell," Dan said, but the way he sifted made Zo think he was lying in some way.

"I don't believe Jett would work for Zmej. He's Ryn's brother," Fergus said.

"We have answered your questions. Now, we have an organization to run, so if you don't mind." Jak stood and held his hand out toward the door. Dan moved to open it.

"One more question," Fergus said.

"We are not a repository of information like the Library." Jak folded his arms.

Zo was done with this guy, but they needed more information. According to Yll, Ryn said they would need the stone, the sword, and the branch to retrieve Praedo's beads—and Zo had become very interested in retrieving those beads.

"You remember what you found at the heart of the Library? How it talked about the sword, the stone, and the branch? I'm guessing you have looked for those objects—what did you find?" Zo leaned forward on Jak's desk.

Jak and Dan exchanged a startled glance. "Well, you took the stone from us. We have no idea what the branch is—possibly part of the Heart Tree? The sword...well, we have our suspicions."

"I thought it was the dagger that Zmej carried. It seemed to vanish him from the Library," Zo said.

Dan shook his head. "We don't think so."

"The stories say there were two swords." Jak's grin had his mischievous bent to it.

"How do you get it?" Fergus asked.

Jak laughed. "You're asking me, Library boy?"

"Right." Zo turned to go.

"One thing." Dan stopped them.

He exchanged one of those looks with Jak. "I don't know if you remember, but Zmej took someone important to us. We've tried everything, but Zmej still has them. If the information we gave you leads you to Zmej, we want our person back."

Fergus nodded. "Who is it?"

"Their name is Maus. They're just a child and don't deserve to be caught up in all of this." Dan's eyes were misty.

Jak let out a half laugh, half choke. "They were probably picking Zmej's pocket when they got caught."

Zo could get behind this kid. "We'll do our best."

Chapter Eighteen

Through journeys uncounted, through lands without end,
We found ourselves lacking for council or meeting;
Our voices grew faint, our plans retreating—
We needed a bond our thoughts could send.

Lands without end...how far did they travel? Did they see those distant lands where legend says other trees of the Wild magic exist? If they did, what did they find? And yet, it couldn't have been too far if Praedo's Mind magic still reached them. Of course, I've already discussed how much greater his power was.

- From the journals of Moult de Dico

Ryn wiped her eyes, then opened the door to Brynd's home. It was slightly bigger than the cottage Ryn had grown up in, but certainly wasn't big enough for as many brothers and sisters Brynd had. Brynd's father, Olvan, was in the kitchen making dinner, dancing around a toddler who was wandering the kitchen trying to catch hold of his leg. Brynd's mother, Xylia, sat with one of Brynd's younger sisters on her lap, while she poured over the financial books for the family's apple farm. Something about being in their home made Ryn feel at peace, even if Brynd's younger brothers were swinging sticks around pretending to be sword fighting, and another sister was attempting to read a book while churning butter.

Olvan glanced over at Ryn when she came through the door. "Ah Ryn, can you come entertain this little one so I can finish cooking?"

Ryn shrank back. Being the youngest, she didn't have any experience with small children. She didn't really know what to do with them.

"Sure," she agreed, because she appreciated that they had taken her in, fed her and let her stay.

Ryn peeled the toddler's arms off his father's leg, and the toddler instantly started wailing. Ryn picked him up and tried to soothe him, but he only cried harder. Eventually Brynd's mother held out her arms for him. Ryn gratefully released the child to his mother.

Brynd's parents were unlike any other Ordinaries Ryn had met. They certainly weren't like Jak and Dan, or even Wilmar. There was something that felt timeless about them. As if everything they did was a continuation of something magnificent, but Ryn couldn't determine what exactly. Brynd said it was because they were keepers of the old Wild magic. The magic that the people held before the dragon and the slayer came. The magic that was the foundation of the Library Heart Tree.

Brynd came in the door with some of her siblings, looking hot and sweaty.

"We were able to remove that dead tree in the second grove, but there's no indication what killed it. You should take a look at it, papa," Brynd said, washing her face and hands in the washbasin.

Her father nodded. "I'll look at it tomorrow."

Brynd and her father wore the same furrowed brow. Brynd had told Ryn that if a disease killed the tree it could spread to the other trees in the orchard. That could be disastrous for the farm.

Brynd stepped into the kitchen and helped her father take the pots of food off the fire. Ryn helped Brynd's mother entertain the toddler. He was happy to let her shake a rattle at him as long as he was in his mother's arms.

Once dinner was on the table and every chair, bench, or box was brought to the table so the family could sit, Olvan began the song of praise and gratitude to the Heart Tree. Each member of the family took up the song in turn. The tree at the Heart of the Library came to Ryn's mind. Its leaves rustled to the sound of the song. She closed her eyes and joined the song. She had learned it quickly, and it seemed to flow about her like the living water at the tree's roots. She sang the last note, savoring the moment of peace the tree brought her.

She opened her eyes to find everyone staring at her. She blushed, and Xylia cleared her throat and began passing dishes of food.

"We sing the song of our heart," Olvan had told Ryn her first night at Brynd's. "Most of those called Ordinaries by the Ancestors have lost their connection to the tree. Xylia and I have spent our lives trying to restore the magic that once connected us to the Heart Tree. The song helps us remember and give thanks."

That first night it had seemed strange, but now she loved the tradition.

Tonight for once, the usually boisterous table was quiet, which made it easier, yet more awkward for Ryn to speak up. She didn't want to seem rude, but she needed to do this. Her stomach tensed.

"I've sent messages for help back to Waatch, but no one has answered. I'm scared something terrible will happen to my parents if something isn't done quickly. There's no more time to wait for help, and certainly no time to go to Waatch and come back. It's been far too long since my father's letters were sent." Ryn took a deep breath. "I've decided I need to go to the peninsula and find my father. I would like to leave as soon as I can."

Olvan tore off a chunk of bread and dipped it into the gravy on his plate. "We can help you with supplies, but that's a long road to walk through a rough wilderness on your own. You really shouldn't go by yourself."

"I know, but—what else can I do? Someone has to help them," Ryn said.

"And how do you expect to help your parents?" Olvan eyed her over a bowl of squash.

Xylia reached over and put her hand on Ryn's. "We will send for Brad, to accompany you. At least wait till we hear from him."

Brad was Brynd's brother who used to sell apples to Ryn in Sooke.

Brynd stirred her carrots on her plate. "Mama, Brad has hired out to make extra money for his betrothal. Let me go with Ryn."

Olvan took a deep breath. "And what do you two think you're going to do against the dragon?"

"The dragon that destroyed everything." Brynd's curly haired little sister whispered as she raised a spoon to her mouth. The piece of meat fell off before it got to her mouth.

Ryn shook her head. "Dragon?"

A knock came at the door and Brynd's younger sister, who was closest to the door, slid off her box to answer it.

When the door opened, Yll came tumbling in, feathers drifting in after her.

"Yll!" Ryn and Brynd hurried over to give her hugs.

Ryn picked a feather out of Yll's hair. "The shapeshifting still needs work," she giggled.

Yll grabbed Ryn's arm and dragged her outside. "We got your messages, and we've come to help."

"We?"

In the fading light of the spring sunset the air in front of the house began to swirl into a dust funnel. The leaves of the nearby trees rustling in the breeze. The swirling dust resolved into three people clinging to each other. A Viatoro Traveler stepped back from the other two, his back to Ryn. She wondered how this porter knew how to find Brynd's house. That sounded bad for the prospect of hiding from Jeris's ire.

The porter stepped to the side and Iden kissed someone on the forehead. Iden turned to Ryn with a grin that lit up the yard. Then Ryn noticed who Iden had his arm around...

Ryn's knees gave out and she almost tumbled back onto the porch, but Yll grabbed her by the waist and held her up.

"What? Is this real?" Ryn whispered. "I fell asleep in the orchard and I'm dreaming."

Zo crossed the yard to her and scooped her up into his arms. His hug was so tight her eyes bulged, and she was struggling to breathe.

"Very real, parva soror," Zo whispered into her hair.

Ryn's heart hammered in her chest. She would have thought him a spirit, but his squeeze rooted her in his presence.

"I...What? How?" Ryn continued to flounder.

Iden stepped up next to them. "Rumors of his death have been greatly exaggerated."

Zo chuckled.

Ryn squeezed him back as tight as she could, inhaling the smell of cedar and sea air on him. She couldn't believe she was awake and it was real. Maybe they had all died somehow and they were now back together? She clutched at the back of his coat, putting her ear to his chest. She listened to his heart beat strong and steady.

"You're real," was all she could think to say.

She listened to his laugh, loud and a bit distorted through his chest. "I am indeed."

Ryn was filled with emotion, but the surprise coursing through her body kept it from showing.

A spinning dust funnel appeared next to the spot where Zo and Iden had arrived, resolving into Regg and Fergus with their own Travel magic porter.

"Ah man, we missed it!" Regg said. "You should have been faster."

Their porter shrugged.

"How did you all find us?" Ryn asked.

Zo grinned. "Apparently, I'm not the only one who had a crush on Brynd's brother. Iden here had his eye on him for a while, and has been here to try to woo him. He was turned down flat."

"Yeah, yeah, yeah," Iden muttered.

"Plus, I have the directions," Yll added.

Ryn tightened her grip on Zo and buried her face in his chest. "I'm just glad you're here."

She couldn't stop smiling even with the daunting task of saving her parents hanging over her.

"We heard you needed some help," Regg grinned.

Fergus stepped up to the porch and Ryn noticed he was holding a large sword in its scabbard.

Ryn gasped. "That looks like Praedo's sword? How did you get to the Origin?"

"Nope," Iden said. "It's the so-called replica from the Library. Jak gave us a clue. Clayr did some research, we're not really sure how, given she's banned from the Library. The lady has skills. Anyway, it seems that this 'replica' may be more than a 'replica'. There is evidence it could be the sword spoken of by the Protector of the Library."

"Right! Of course it's the one for the Library." Ryn felt silly that she had thought they could get to the Origin and take that sword.

Then she remembered that Lyssa had mentioned one of the books she had translated mentioned the sword. In fact, it was the history book Clayr had sent her. Clayr must have looked through the book before sending it. Ryn needed to do some fast skimming of that book.

...And the Protector had formed the shape of the sword in its palm and then pointed upstairs. Ryn felt dumb that she hadn't put it all together before.

Ryn leaned in to examine the sword more closely. It was the one she'd seen many times lying in the case in the Objects Room.

"How did you..." Ryn started.

Iden grinned. "Fergus and I liberated it from the Library. We just got out. We all came here as soon as we had it."

"What about the stone?" Ryn asked.

Yll pulled the roughly pitted black rock from her pocket.

"And the branch?" Brynd asked, picking up the toddler and swinging him onto her hip.

Ryn glanced behind her to see all of Brynd's family on the porch or in the doorway, silently taking in the visitors. Brynd's mother was wiping her eyes. Ryn and Brynd had told them their stories.

Ryn wasn't sure how to answer that. Something inside of her stirred, but she couldn't form the words. The branch was close, she knew it.

Regg sniffed at the air. "Is that dinner I smell?" His stomach growled.

Brynd's father laughed. "Come on inside, there's plenty for everyone."

* * *

Ryn sat on the porch swing after dinner with her head on Zo's shoulder.

"I don't understand, I thought they sentenced you to death," she said.

"They did. My mother saved me. She took me to a group of unconventional Healers to try and fix my magic."

Ryn raised her head and looked him over. He looked so much better than he did on his birthday when they took him.

"Did the Healers fix it?" She asked.

"I was able to get back my ability to heal myself, but I'm still unable to heal anyone else."

"So your mother's on your side now?" Ryn asked.

Zo sighed. "I thought there for a brief few days that maybe things were different—that maybe the scare of losing me changed her."

"But it didn't," Ryn said.

"Before Regg and Iden showed up on the sanctuary island, my mother informed me that House Sano is hunting me, and if I don't fix my magic and prove I'm not a threat to society, they will kill me. I can't return to my life until I fix it."

Ryn relaxed her head back onto his shoulder. "How are you proposing to fix it?"

"Well, you see there's these beads of Praedo's bone..." Zo started.

Ryn jumped up. "By the Ancestors!" She paced. "Whoa, whoa, whoa. Wait...How...That's..." she turned to Zo and stared into his soft brown eyes. "That's more than just healing power. That's...everything! That's all of the magics together."

Zo cracked his knuckles against his leg. "What else can I do?"

"What makes you think that taking on one of Praedo's beads will give you your Healing back? If it could do that, why not just take another bead from House Sano?"

"Well, first of all House Sano wants to kill me right now. I doubt they would give me a bead, but I don't know. I have this feeling that Praedo's beads and magic are different than the Ancestors."

The door opened, and Regg stuck his head out. "The kids are in bed and everyone's ready."

Zo stood. "Let's get this thing planned."

Ryn watched him disappear into the house. She took a deep breath as a wave of emotion flowed over her. She looked out into the night. This past moon had felt as black as the darkest night, but the frogs were croaking to each other, beginning their spring mating dance, and life turned. She was so grateful to have Zo back. Life without him had lost all of its color. She almost had to live the rest of her life without him. She wasn't prepared for that. Now, now that her heart wasn't racing with excitement, the tears welled up inside and flowed down her cheeks.

She took a deep breath. She didn't know how they were going to save her parents and restore Zo's magic, but she was going to do everything she could to make it happen.

Yll stuck her head out the door. "You coming?"

Ryn wiped her eyes and went inside to join the others.

Chapter Nineteen

With wings bestowed by the magic of Praedo,
We roamed through the islands, through caverns and caves,
Through mountains, through valleys, by air and by land—
Yet no trace nor shadow the beast ever gave.

I have to wonder if this is how Luc found this cave.

- From the journals of Moult de Dico

Despite the seriousness of the meeting, Zo couldn't help but smile at those gathered around the table. Somehow in this place he'd never been before, it felt like home. He put his hand on Iden's knee and squeezed it. He didn't want to let Iden out of his sight again, but he also wanted Iden safe. The decisions they were going to make this evening were not going to make him happy, no matter what was decided, but he enjoyed the moment of being together.

Ryn was reading her father's letters, and selections from the journal he had sent. Zo wished he could have been there to help her steal them from the Library. He was grateful Iden had stepped in to help.

Ryn followed up with reading passages in the Library history book about the sword.

"So your father claims to know where to find Praedo's mythical beads, and the dragon has your mother, and by now possibly your father." Olvan thoughtfully pulled at his beard.

"Dragon? You've said that before. What do you mean dragon?" Ryn asked.

Olvan sat forward. "Those of the wild magic claim Zmej is the next dragon sent to conquer." He waved his hand at her father's journals. "Your father copied Luc's poem into his journal. Read it more carefully."

Ryn turned to the pages with the poem. Then she read out loud.

"In the Canticum Mutiationis it reads:

> *Then we learned how a year past, the beast had come,*
> *Shattered and weary in human guise;*
> *He demanded at once that bread be supplied,*
> *And protection from men lest his need become."*

Ryn's eyes got wide. "The dragon can change into human form?"

"Let me see that." Yll pulled the journal to her, reading through the poem, she choked. "I mean, I memorized the journal, but I didn't notice this before. It can't be real. Certainly, we would have known he was a dragon."

Olvan's smile was sad. "He's fooled the Ancestors. Done it for who really knows how long he's been here. He's playing with them, causing the division between Ancestors and 'Ordinaries,' making us weak."

Regg shifted in his seat. "It's not the same dragon, is it? The one Praedo killed?"

"No, that dragon is dead. This one came…who knows when." Olvan folded his arms. "Some sailors have visited distant lands and claim Zmej has destroyed Heart Trees elsewhere. It is only a rumor, but as we have traveled to sell our apples, we have collected what stories we can. The fact that he produces blue fire is the best evidence. All the stories of old mention the blue dragon fire. I believe you've witnessed it." Brynd's father's eyes locked with Zo's.

"Yes. I did find it strange, but I've had other issues to deal with lately, and haven't given it much thought," Zo said.

"I've heard Ryn and Brynd's stories over the past several nights. You and Ryn are apparently the only two people in generations to have seen the Heart Tree at the center of the Library." Olvan leaned back.

Ryn stared out the darkened window, seemingly lost in thought.

"If Zmej is a dragon, we're all in over our heads," Regg said, his face drained of color.

"Indeed," Olvan said.

"If the dragon has so much power, why would he need Praedo's beads?" Iden asked.

A valid question, Zo thought at Iden. Zo searched the faces of Olvan and Xylia for the answer.

Regg leaned in. "Obviously to increase his power."

Olvan shook his head. "I don't believe it works that way."

"To keep the power out of our hands," Iden answered his own question.

Regg leaned back, rolling his eyes.

Iden pointed his finger down on the table. "No, think about it. If what you say is true, and Zmej has been stirring up trouble between the Houses and the Ordinaries for decades? Centuries? Who knows? And his end game was to divide and conquer, it would make sense that all he needs the beads for is to destroy them."

Olvan, fingers stroking his chin, nodded. "You have a point. If the children of the Ordinary are the only ones who could use the dragon slayer's beads, it would be advantageous for him to dispose of them."

Zo pounded his knuckles against his leg. *Children of the Ordinary?* Maybe his plan to restore his magic wouldn't work.

Iden took his hand and squeezed it. He had heard Zo.

"We need to get to the beads before he does. We're powerless against him if we don't have those beads." Ryn said, her eyes on the table with that far away thinking look on her face.

Ryn's an Ordinary, Zo thought. *She deserves those beads. She deserves the magic more than I do.*

Hey, there's more than one bead. She can gain the magic and you can fix yours, Iden's thought caressed his mind lovingly.

Zo met Iden's eyes, then gave Iden a halfhearted smile he didn't really feel. Something told him it wouldn't be that simple.

"We have the stone and the sword. We have what we need to find the beads," Yll said.

"But not the branch," Brynd added.

"Fine—most of what we need," Yll added.

"The history book claims the sword is Praedo's. That he had two swords. Fine, but what does it do? Why do we need it to find the beads?" Fergus put his hand on the sword which leaned against his chair next to him.

Ryn took the journal back from Yll and flipped through the pages. "According to my father, he believes Luc created the lock in such a way as to require proof of Praedo's blessing. Maybe that's why?"

Yll picked up the stone. "And what about this? It clearly does weird things to the Library's protective magic, but what is it?"

Olvan took it from Yll's hand. "This is Wild magic. Magic from the center of the world."

Zo exchanged a look with Iden. He could feel Iden's mental eyeroll. They both didn't know what to make of Olvan and Xylia. They were on the odd side.

"When I saw the tree." Ryn's eyes seemed to be focused somewhere else, as if she was seeing the tree again. "There was a branch cut off. It was dripping sap. As if the tree was crying."

"You must seek out the sprites," Brynd's mother piped in from the corner where she was rocking a small child.

Ryn sat up straight like she'd been jolted by Lightening magic.

This was too much for Zo. "What in the name of the Ancestors I don't believe in are sprites?"

Olvan grunted. "They are the wild of the Wild magic. They only care about cultivating the earth and its magic. They do not associate themselves with Ancestor descendants who stole their land, destroyed their magic, and imprisoned the Heart Tree. You'll be fortunate if they don't kill you upon approach."

Ryn shuttered. "I've heard of sprites in children's stories. I never believed they were true, but..." She looked from Olvan to Xylia. "I think maybe they're true." Her brow furrowed as she ran her fingers across it.

"Of course they're true. I have seen them. A few of us have tried through the years to restore the Wild magic to us

Ordinaries who've lost it. The sprites will help. They'll know what the branch means, and where to find it," Xylia said.

Brynd's father looked between Ryn and Brynd. "It's too dangerous."

"But to open the door, to unlock the power that could save my parents—and possibly all of us if Zmej really is a dragon—we need the branch," Ryn said.

There was an awkward silence around the table as everyone either rubbed foreheads, examined folded hands, or stared up at the ceiling.

"And what about the Library and Waatch?" Yll asked. "My mother is still in exile, and there's no one to protect the Library. We never did find that killer who killed Tammy, because—as Brynd discovered—she was researching how to kill dragons, and Regent Jordan, who was my mother's firm support on the counsel. Without him, they were able to oust her quickly. Someone killed those people to take down my mother and the Library."

Zo exchanged a look with Fergus.

"We went to see Jak about the killer. He thinks he knows who it was," Fergus said.

Zo shook his head at him.

"Seems like it would be dangerous to track down this killer," Brynd said.

"You should leave that to the authorities." Xylia nodded.

"And yet, despite what we went through at the winter solstice, someone is still actively trying to take down the Library," Yll said. "They've managed to have my mother, the Library's strongest defense, removed."

"My parents have been in Library leadership for many years. I'm certain the Ancestor descendants think they are helping the Library, and themselves," Iden added.

"They are not," Brynd said.

"Of course," Ryn said. "Zmej needs to destroy the protection the Library offers the tree so that once he has the power, he can destroy it."

"So we need to save Ryn's parents, find Praedo's beads, and potentially protect the Library from an attack by the dragon," Regg said.

"Who said the dragon would attack the Library?" Brynd asked.

"He tried once to destroy the tree, I'm sure he'll try again. Especially after he's secured the beads and knows we can't defend against him," Fergus answered.

"We drove him off before," Zo said.

"We surprised him, and attacked him with his own dagger. I'm sure he won't be surprised again," Ryn countered.

Zo pushed against the table, cracking his knuckles.

Iden sat forward. "Regg, Fergus, and I will return to Waatch, track down the killer, find out if he's working for Zmej, and see if there's a way to stop the dragon, and set up defenses for the Library."

Zo's heart quickened. They would be going up against someone who could kill with a touch. He took in Iden's profile, the curve of his cheekbone, his full lips, and his sparkling blue eyes. Zo's promise necklace warmed. Iden's thought entered his mind.

Don't worry.

But Zo was worried.

Fergus shook his head. "No. I need to carry the sword to this cave, and see it safely returned to the Library."

Although he hadn't said it directly, Zo suspected Fergus wanted to protect Ryn. She had expressed her displeasure for those who thought she couldn't take care of herself. Fergus wisely chose a different argument for him to go.

Iden slowly nodded at Fergus.

Ryn stirred as if she'd hadn't been listening. "Zo and I will seek out the sprites, and then rescue my parents."

"With me," Fergus said.

Ryn looked at him with wide eyes. She really hadn't been listening.

"Right." She nodded.

"I'm going too," Yll said.

Ryn shook her head. "Go with Regg and Iden and help protect your mom and the Library."

Yll's eyes sparkled. "I can do both—I will be your messenger bird. I will go back and forth between you and Waatch. I'm certain you are going to need to stay in touch, and we don't want to trust this information to paid courier sources."

"Perfect," Iden said.

Brynd looked between her mother and her father, bowed her head, and frowned.

"I'm going back to Waatch," Brynd announced. "Even though I was dismissed from the Library, I'm not wanted by the authorities, and I can cultivate my connection with Jak and Dan to get their help." Her eyes locked with her father's. "I'm sorry to leave you again."

Olvan pressed his fingers together and held them to his frowning lips.

"Now that we don't have your Library income, we really need you here," he said.

Brynd's mother stood with the child in her arms and put an arm around Olvan. "I've been over our accounts and I'm tightening our budget. If we lose the Heart Tree to the dragon, all will be lost. The tree is the last defense against the dragon. If it's gone, the power of this world will be gone. Go. Help your friends."

Brynd stood and went to her parents. They exchanged tearful hugs. Zo shifted in his seat. His heart and his mind were warring with each other. His heart wished for a family that cared for him like that. He thought for a moment he had it with his mother. His head knew it wasn't reality and he needed to focus on taking care of himself.

Ryn sat up tall. "Good. Zo, Fergus, and I will travel out onto the peninsula, visit the sprites, hopefully locate the branch, then we'll go rescue my mother and father from Zmej. Yll will start with us, and then fly to Waatch in a day or so." She pointed to Iden. "You, Regg, and Brynd will go back to Waatch as see what you can find. Send us messages through Yll as often as you can so we can stay up to date on what information we find. Agreed?"

Everyone nodded.

Xylia turned to Ryn. "I will take you as far as the entrance to the sprite pools. After that I need to return home."

Olvan looked down at his tight folded hands. Zo thought for a moment he was going to object, but they really needed someone to show them the way to find these so-called Wild magic sprites—if they even existed.

Olvan sighed and kissed his wife's hand.

Ryn rocked back and forth, then placed her hands flat on the table. "We are set then. We will leave in the morning." She stood.

Iden squeezed Zo's hand. *Let's take a walk.*

Zo nodded and the two of them slipped out while Brynd's parents directed sleeping arrangements and bedding for the added number of guests.

Iden and Zo walked hand in hand into the darkness, the sound of frogs croaking to each other spoke to water being nearby. It was cloudy with no moon, so they didn't walk farther than the lights from the house reached.

Iden stopped at the fence that led into the orchard, then pulled Zo into an embrace that led to kissing, which ignited a deep longing inside of Zo. Despite the chilly spring evening Zo was hot, ready to ditch his waistcoat and shirt.

Iden slowed their kissing, then buried his forehead into Zo's shoulder.

"I can't believe you're here. That you're alive, and I can hold you in my arms. I didn't think that would ever happen again," Iden whispered.

Zo tightened his arms around Iden. "I can't believe I'm alive either. There was a moment, when they came for me, I saw someone with a sword. I thought I was dead. I guess it was just whoever my mother hired to rescue me, but wow...in that moment...I was sure my life was over."

Iden pulled Zo closer and kissed him passionately, tasting, exploring everything, taking him in and possessing him with need. Zo had never felt so alive. He met Iden's fervor and added his own.

Iden broke free, panting. "Wow, you've been holding back on me." He gave a short laugh, then pressed his forehead to Zo's with a moan. "I don't want to let you go."

"I'm dead if I don't go. I would always be running. That's no life, and I wouldn't ask you to share it."

Iden pulled back and the light from the house windows reflected on tears streaming down Iden's cheeks.

"Promise me you'll come back," Iden said.

Zo chuckled. "If I come back it will be because I hold more power than anyone since the original Ancestors."

Iden let out a tearful laugh. "You'll be impossible to live with, I'm sure."

Zo grinned.

Iden pulled Zo in again.

"And you," Zo said into Iden's shoulder. "You protect yourself from that killer. Whoever they are, they are dangerous. I've seen through their eyes while they were killing, and they are cold and ruthless."

Iden nodded. They kissed again, and Zo wished the house was empty. He was just wondering if Brynd's family had some kind of shed or barn when Ryn opened the door.

"Zo...you need to come choose a pack and a walking stick," she yelled out into the dark.

Iden kissed Zo on the forehead.

"There will be plenty of time when you get back. We're going to grow old together like Nix and Wilmar." Iden fingered Zo's promise necklace around his neck.

Zo laughed and took Iden's promise necklace into his hand. "I do need an assistant."

Iden grinned. "It's a date then."

They turned and walked back to the house, arms around each other's waists.

Once inside, Zo did ask about other buildings on the farm, but everyone who could show him where they were had already gone to bed.

"Rats," he mumbled, while Ryn pulled him away to help her pack.

Chapter Twenty

I've met the man at last. I'd heard many stories about him from Ryette when she was growing up on Viator, but from those tales he could have been any power-hungry Ancestor descendant. Now that I've seen him in person, I believe he is more. Dragon is a cursed thing to call someone, but who else would be surrounded by wolves—the legendary dragon offspring. The story of the wolf and the water sprite is looking all too real. I don't want to fear him, but I do. I'll hold out as long as I can.

- From the journals of Moult de Dico

Ryn didn't sleep well that night. Brynd had insisted she take her bed since Ryn would be sleeping on the ground for a while, but Ryn couldn't relax enough to get a good sleep. She was up all night worrying about her mother, somewhere out there with a dragon. Then there was Iden, Brynd, and Regg heading to Waatch where a killer lurked, and Yll planning to fly back and forth between them. She'd never done that much flying before—what if something went wrong? And Fergus and Zo—the sprites didn't sound friendly, and she and Zo barely survived their last encounter with Zmej. If he was a dragon, what other magics did he possess besides fire? It took Praedo, with all of his magic, and twelve companions to take the first dragon down—how was she going to do it with no magic? She would need to distract Zmej and lead him away from Zo and Fergus. Ryn refused to lose Zo again, and Fergus deserved to live his life as his forefathers—protecting the Library. For Ryn, she knew she wasn't anything, or anybody. Some called her a brilliant researcher, but there were lots of brilliant researchers.

When the windows began to lighten, Ryn gave up and crawled out of bed, tiptoeing around those sleeping on the floor. She decided to start getting ready, but when she tipped a bit of water from a pitcher into the basin to wash up, the noise made a sleeping Regg stir. She decided to wait to get ready till more of them were awake. She walked as lightly as she could across the room, trying not to make the floorboards creak, then opened the door and stepped out into the chilly, dew filled morning.

She inhaled sharply when she found Fergus sitting on the porch swing, sharpening Praedo's sword. She still couldn't believe it was real and not a replica. She let her breath out and shut the door carefully before coming to sit next to him. She didn't expect to find anyone up, but she was grateful for the company. She had spent too much of the night inside the fears in her head.

Fergus didn't say anything, just kept running the stone down the length of the blade. The birds were twittering to each other in the trees in anticipation of the sunrise.

"I feel bad you left your position at the Library, and got involved in this mess," Ryn said. "Your family won't be happy with you." She bowed her head, looking at her feet dangling close to the porch decking.

"If there's no Library left to defend, my family won't be happy," Fergus grimaced.

Ryn nodded. "I just don't want to get you in trouble with your family, and I don't want you to lose your job because of me."

Fergus stopped, and she looked into his eyes. "I'm here because I need to be. I want to be, and it's important. The last dragon almost destroyed the world. If Zmej really is the next dragon, we've let him get too close already." He held up the sword. "Everything is balanced on the edge of a knife. Two Ordinaries, plus a guy who can shoot fire from his hands, against the most powerful being we've seen in a millennia. We need every power we can call upon for help."

Ryn looked away from his warm eyes. "So there's no way I could persuade you to go home?"

"Ryn."

She looked back at him. His fingers traced a line from her forehead down her cheek, gently brushing a stray hair back behind her ear. Then he bent forward and their lips met.

Ryn's heart raced. Her breath was completely gone as his lips moved gently against hers. Something shot through her body and pulled at her gut. Fergus sat back and looked Ryn in the eyes.

"I'm staying with you," he said.

Though only their lips had touched Ryn was breathless. Her heart pounding, she smiled and he returned it.

"Ahem."

Ryn turned to find Brynd poking her head out the door. "Everybody's getting ready. I suggest if you want some hot bath water you get it now before it's gone." She gave Ryn a knowing smile, and Ryn felt herself blush.

Fergus stood and helped her up. "I like that color of red on you. Maybe I should induce it more often."

Ryn's blush deepened.

* * *

The sun was up, shining between the distant mountains and the clouds above, turning them pink and purple. They were all ready to go, standing in the road in front of Brynd's family farm. Olvan and Xylia were hugging their daughter. None of her siblings were up yet, despite all the commotion getting ready. Regg was holding Yll tight and kissing her, the sunlight glistening on a tear on her cheek.

"I'll see you soon. I still have that thing I want to give you." Regg kissed Yll's forehead.

Yll giggled. "I don't think you're ever going to get the chance."

"Oh, I will."

Zo shifted from one foot to another, adjusting the pack on his back. Ryn tried to remain calm despite his apparent uneasiness.

Iden didn't seem to care, he strode right up to Zo and kissed him full on the mouth with a kiss so passionate, Ryn felt she was intruding on something intimate. She shifted her gaze to the fading color on the clouds as the sun climbed higher and the clouds covered the light. Her eyes found Fergus looking at her. She blushed again.

Iden held Zo's head. "Be safe."

Zo's hand was wrapped in Iden's shirt. He pulled Iden close and kissed him again.

Ryn shuffled her feet, kicking a rock.

Iden broke away, laughing. "Alright, alright." He gave Zo another quick kiss then he moved to join Regg and Brynd. "We'll hitch a ride into Waatch as soon as we can find one."

Regg gave Zo a hug, and then Ryn. He kissed Yll's hand, then Regg, Brynd, and Iden headed off down the road toward Waatch.

Ryn sighed. She threaded one arm through Zo's arm and one around Fergus's.

Xylia gave Olvan a quick kiss and a hug. "I'll be home night after next. Wait up for me."

Olvan smiled and nodded, wiping a tear from his eye, he squeezed Xylia's hand. "Come home whole."

And they were off down the road to the peninsula. Each footstep filled Ryn with dread and excitement. She felt too small to do much good, but she was going to try.

* * *

As they walked, Ryn's worry for her parents grew. They didn't seem to be traveling fast enough. She wished Jett was with them and could Travel magic them to where they needed to go.

"What is this Wild magic?" Yll asked once they had walked for a while, and the silence between them all had become oppressive. "My mother's Ordinary, but I've not heard about any other kind of magic than Ancestor magic."

Xylia stirred from her quiet contemplation of the road ahead. "It has always been here. It wells up from the earth. That's why the hot springs are full of it—the water is heated next to the molten part of the earth below. That stone you have." Xylia pointed her chin at Yll. "It's lava rock. Powerful with the magic, though that specimen does not come from this part of the world. It must be from somewhere the earth and the magic are actively spewing forth from the ground."

Yll pulled the stone from her pocket, examining it.

"How do you use the magic?" Ryn asked.

Xylia raised her eyebrows at Ryn. She cleared her throat. "Well, I can't say for the sprites, they seem to access it naturally, almost like breathing, but for the rest of us Ordinaries, it helps to call upon nature, the tree, the sprites—it comes when needed."

"So how powerful are these sprites?" Fergus asked, his fingers fidgeting with the hilt of his Library issued side sword.

Xylia breathed out slowly. "Hard to tell. If you listen to them, Praedo lost his life because he relied only on his magic to defeat the dragon."

"But his companions were 'Ordinary,' and they allegedly helped in the battle," Fergus said.

"Yes, but they were not sprites. Praedo kept the sprites from the battle," Xylia sighed.

"Why?" Yll asked.

"Praedo married one of them. A particularly beautiful watersprite named Eladorys," Xylia said.

Ryn rubbed her forehead. "I've heard that name before. Where have I heard that name?"

"History books maybe?" Yll offered. "Didn't you say Lyssa had a book on sprites?"

"She did, but I never got a chance to look at it." Ryn shook out her hand and took a drink from her water bottle.

Xylia must have sensed her anxiety and began to sing a walking song. One Ryn had never heard before. Yll joined her, then after a few refrains, Zo joined in. He gave it his usual silly spin, making Ryn laugh. Eventually she and Fergus joined them. It passed the time and the day away. The clouds were dark in the direction they were headed. The sky ahead reminded her of what she was getting herself into. Storms were coming.

* * *

As the light faded, Xylia led them to a clearing under a group of large oak trees off the side of the road with a fire ring in the middle. She explained it was where most travelers stopped for the night when on the road to the peninsula. The ground was hard and cleared of any debris. Fergus and Yll went looking for kindling to start a fire. Someone had left some split logs next to the firepit.

"Maybe we should keep going," Ryn said to Xylia. "We need to get there as fast as we can."

Xylia gave her a lopsided smile, that seemed sad. "We can't walk all night. There are creatures out there in the dark. Don't worry, we'll pick up the pace tomorrow."

A cool breeze made Ryn shiver. She gazed off in the direction of the peninsula mountains where they would find her father's cave. They seemed too far off, and she felt too late.

She watched Zo light the fire and was grateful to have him around again. She had missed the instant fire when she needed it.

Xylia pulled out a pan and some food out of her pack, preparing to cook a meal. Ryn hadn't noticed the large pack Xylia was carrying before. It was larger than hers, and Xylia was only going to be on the road a couple days. Now Ryn realized why. Xylia was doing what moms do—taking care of everyone. They all had food in their packs, but Xylia was planning for meals of more than dried fruit, smoked salmon, and hard-boiled eggs. The thought made her smile and worry about her own mom.

Fergus returned and dumped a load of twigs and branches next to the firepit. He removed Praedo's sword from where it was strapped to his back, but kept his Library issued sword on his hip. His Library sword was his father's, and his father's before him. Zo paused setting up the tarp over their sleeping area long enough to feed the fire and increase the heat. Ryn moved over to the flames and warmed her hands.

Fergus came and stood next to her. The energy between them crackled like static, but neither one of them moved closer, or away. Ryn snuck glances at his face, staring into the fire, his hands on the pommel of Praedo's large heavy sword.

Yll brought her pile of kindling and set it by the fire. Her brown eyes danced in the firelight. As she passed Ryn she put her hand on her shoulder. "I approve," she whispered in Ryn's ear.

Xylia brought her pan and a wire rack to the fire. "Alright you two, out of my way. Go help Zo over there." She shooed them away from the fire.

The cold air hit Ryn's hot face as she turned away toward Zo who was tying off a rope around a tree. A shiver ran up her spine. Despite the trees, the place felt too open and vulnerable.

* * *

After the best meal Ryn thought she had ever eaten—Xylia said everything tasted better when cooked outdoors over a campfire—they sat around the fire, Zo and Fergus were trading Nix stories, while Xylia, Yll, and Ryn laughed. The laughter eased the tension from her worry. When a lull in the talking came, Ryn stared into the fire, watching the flames lick at the wood the way they licked at Zo's hands.

"What are they like, the sprites?" Ryn wanted to know more.

"Being children of the Wild magic, they seem to move with it. Some say they are born from the earth itself, though I don't know how that would work. The water sprites seem to almost flow like water, but they are as real as you and I. Their magic is elemental, as far as I can tell. They could be hiding more. The hot spring I'm taking you to—they say odd things can happen to a person if they enter that spring. Grandmother Eladorys leads them. She had ten children with Praedo." Xlyia paused to catch everyone's eye before stirring the fire.

Ryn frowned at that. *How could Praedo's wife still be alive?* It seemed like a folk tale.

"I never heard of Praedo having a wife and children," Ryn said.

"Myths and legends," Yll said.

Xlyia's eyes locked on Yll. She shrank on her log seat.

"I doubt it is knowledge that was written down. Pradeo kept it secret to protect his family, and few people attempt contact with the sprites these days. In the old times, before the Ancestors, the people of Waatch used the wild magic, and consulted the sprites for their knowledge and wisdom. Now only a few of us here on the peninsula know where to find them. They have become guarded and protective of their own. It takes knowledge to approach them and not get drowned in their pools."

An owl hooted somewhere in the trees, making Ryn jump.

Ryn's brain was spinning. Here was knowledge she'd never heard, nor had she run across it in the Library, and they had done some exhaustive searches on the history of Waatch and the Library last winter.

The sound of an animal moving in the bushes drew Ryn's attention. Something cold ran up her spine. She shuddered. The darkness beyond the fire, the unknown, made her heart beat faster.

"Enough of story time. It's time to get some sleep. When we reach the entrance to the pools tomorrow, I will tell you all you need to know to approach them safely." Xlyia stood and stretched.

Footsteps crunched on the road outside the campsite.

Fergus came alert immediately, standing and drawing his sword.

"Stand down," Xylia warned. "It could be a weary traveler."

Fergus held the sword low and moved to the edge of the darkness. Zo came to join him, flames licking at his fingertips.

A disheveled man with leaves and twigs in his hair entered the light, holding his hands up.

"Schiz!" Ryn exclaimed.

Zo shook out the flames and put a hand on Fergus' sword arm.

"Mistress," Schiz bowed low to the ground in front of the group.

Ryn moved to crouch in front of Schiz. "What are you doing way out here?"

Schiz lifted himself from the ground and shook his head. "I...saw you leave. We were worried." Schiz tapped at his temple.

Ryn tensed, heat rushing through her. She didn't like the sound of the word 'we' and although they were few in number and power, she couldn't think of how Schiz could help them. He claimed his Travel magic was broken. She stood.

"I have plenty of protection here." Her jaw muscle twitched under her clenched teeth.

"Yes, mistress." Schiz bowed low again.

"We? What does he mean by we?" Yll asked the question.

From the darkness behind Schiz a white shape approached, eyes shining in the dark. Ryn's pulse quickened as it came into the light. It was a snow-white wolf, head hung low.

"Kill it!" Fergus yelled and brought his sword up, ready to swing.

Fire filled Zo's hands as he began to spin a fireball.

"Wait!" Schiz jumped up in front of the wolf, holding his hands up. "We are here...in peace. Don't...don't..." Schiz shielded his face against Zo's flames.

Yll turned into an eagle and the wolf growled. Fergus took a step forward, sword swinging. Schiz danced out of the way. Yll flew into his face and knocked him to the ground.

"It's open. Get it!" Fergus said.

Zo's fireball was fully formed. He pulled his hand back to throw.

Ryn stared into the piercing blue eyes of the wolf. They were bluer than Iden's and there was something infinitely sad there. The wolf lowered his head and laid on the ground. Something about the wolf felt familiar.

"Stop!" Ryn yelled, jumping in front of the wolf.

"Ryn, you'll be killed!" Zo shouted.

Fergus reached out and grabbed Ryn to pull her out of the way, as Yll dived at the wolf and took a chunk out of its fur, causing it to yelp.

Zo lowered his arm.

"Maybe we should hear them out," Zo said.

Ryn struggled against Fergus' iron grip. "Let go Fergus, I think it's alright."

Fergus relaxed his grip and Ryn ran to help Schiz up. There were tears flowing down his cheeks.

"Not the way..." He wiped his eyes. "Not the way I wanted..."

"It's alright, Schiz. Please introduce us to your friend." Ryn said.

Schiz wiped face on his sleeve. "Lady Ryn, this is Remus, my most trusted friend and companion."

Remus sat and lifted his paw to Ryn. She looked to Schiz, who nodded encouragingly, so she took Remus' paw and shook it.

"Nice to meet you," Ryn said. It had to be one of the strangest experiences she'd had. Here was this monster, of the kind they had fought and been almost killed by just a few moons back, but she was shaking its paw and it looked like it was grinning at her.

Zo gripped her shoulder from behind. She could feel the tension in his grip. He wasn't as sure of this encounter as she was. She turned to tell him it was going to be alright. Somehow she felt at peace with the wolf...

"We're not alone," Xylia warned.

Shining eyes appeared in the dark. They were surrounded.

Chapter Twenty-One

The wolves pound at my door day and night. Zmej knows I'm in here, and he's sure I know where the bead cave is located. I do know, but I won't tell him. I'll take the secret to my grave if I have to. I must find a way to hide my research.

- From the journals of Moult de Dico

Zo spun in a circle, holding his fireball aloft. In the darkness, just beyond the light were eyes, and movement, and a deep growling. He recognized that growl. He'd heard it before—just before he was attacked by the wolf. Zo broke into a cold sweat. He only had a portion of his Healing powers. He wasn't prepared to lose even that little bit again, but the number of eyes out there staring at him—there was no way they could defeat all of them with Fergus' sword and his fire. The need to kill rose inside him, and his body yearned for it. He gasped as the need overwhelmed him.

Remus circled them, baring his teeth and letting out a deep growl into the dark.

One wolf darted out into the light. Remus attacked it, baring his teeth. There was biting, and fur flying. One gray wolf against Remus' stark whiteness. The two wolves were a blur of action, but eventually the gray wolf yipped and withdrew. Remus resumed his pace around Zo and the others.

"Handy," Fergus said.

"Against one, there's at least a dozen sets of eyes out there," Zo said.

"If they attack all at once..." Ryn started.

Zo had a flash of memory of Schiz's beadscars. He turned to Schiz. "You're House Viator—take the women and get out."

"*No.*" Ryn glared at him.

Schiz shook his head. "Magic's...broken."

Zo swore.

He turned and faced the dark, bringing flames to both hands.

Another wolf attacked, and Remus launched at it. The noise between the two wolves was deep and guttural.

Another wolf came at them. Zo launched a fireball. Fergus put Ryn and Xylia between him and Zo's backs. Yll took flight from the branch she was perched on. Zo saw Fergus' sword flash in his firelight, and heard a wolf yelp. Schiz was doing something with his hands and water was rising from what must be a nearby stream. Zo launched another fireball, as Schiz made a sharp gesture with his arm that sent water flooding under several wolves, knocking their legs out from under them. Zo's fireball found its target and sent the wolf running away.

But more took their place.

"They're too hard to kill," Fergus yelled at Zo, thrusting his sword at a wolf. "You're the only one who's killed one."

Zo's insides screamed at him. Half of him wanted to kill—the other half panicked at the thought.

Yll's eagle form harassed the wolf attacking Fergus from behind. Fur and feathers went flying.

Another wolf raced out of the dark, coming straight at Ryn. She gasped and pressed close into Zo's back. He shot a fireball at it, sending it rolling. Sweat poured down his face. If he could just keep the wolves far enough away, he could handle them with fire, but he was growing thirsty. He tried not to think about it.

Remus broke from the wolf he was fighting and limped close to Ryn's side. The wolves began to circle them, closing in tighter and tighter.

"This is bad," Fergus said.

Xylia stepped out in front of Zo.

Zo reached for her. "Get back."

Xylia began to call out into the darkness:

"Sisters! My sprite sisters! Come to me! Save us from the dragon's abomination!" Xylia called out into the darkness.

The night went still and quiet. The wolves stopped pacing.

Zo glanced over his shoulder as he felt Ryn's back leave his. She was crouched on the ground, her eyes on Remus' bloody leg, but her hands were pressed against the hard packed earth.

Xylia began to sing a song about the sisters of the Heart Tree. Zo had never heard a song like it before. It was rhythmic, but soft and high, and sweet. Her eyes were closed and her arms lifted toward the tree branches above her. The branches and new spring leaves began to shake, and swing violently, but there was no wind.

Zo, Fergus, and Schiz ducked down beside Ryn. Yll landed next to them. Xylia remained standing with her hands up, still singing her song, faster and higher. Ryn was gasping, looking like she was about to be sick, one hand gripped Remus's bloody leg. Zo put his hand on her neck, but of course his magic didn't come to him.

The swinging tree branches connected with one wolf, then another, sending them flying out into the darkness. Every wolf close to Zo and the others was hit and sent flying. The rest yelped and fled. One lone wolf stared at them from the edge of the darkness until a branch swung at him, and he fled into the night. Ryn collapsed backward into Fergus' arms.

Zo hovered over her. "What happened? The sight of blood never made you ill before."

Ryn gave him a weak smile.

Zo turned his attention to Remus's wound. He needed to get it covered quickly, because apparently Ryn was having a problem with the sight of blood. He found his pack by the tent and pulled out some bandages Olvan had given him.

"Anyone else hurt?" he asked, while he bandaged Remus's leg.

Everyone shook their heads. Xylia had collapsed to the ground, but without his magic Zo could only discern that she was winded.

"What was that?" He asked, helping her sit up.

"I have visited the sprites often enough that I can occasionally call upon their help in dire situations," Xylia said.

A shiver creeped up Zo's spine. That was the oddest sort of magic he'd ever seen. He shook it off.

Zo turned to Remus. Once his wound had been cleaned and wrapped, Zo went to find Ryn, sitting on a log by the fire, Fergus's arm wrapped around her waist.

Zo held her arm and felt her pulse while he looked into her eyes. Color was returning to her bone-white cheeks. "What happened?" He asked her again.

"I don't know. I looked at Remus' wound and I felt dizzy. Then I felt something pulling at me. I thought I was going to be sick there for a minute," Ryn said.

"You look sick. Have you felt this way before while at Wilmar's helping out?" Fergus asked.

Ryn paused. "Maybe a little, but not like this."

Zo shrugged. Her pulse was slowing and her eyes were clear. "Maybe you're becoming more sensitive."

Remus padded up in front of Ryn and laid his head on her lap. His eyes looked up at her with an adoring look, and maybe tears? They were glassy like they were tearing up.

Ryn smiled and let him sniff her hand like she would a cat, then petted his head.

"You were so brave," she said to Remus.

"The wolves will be back," Zo said. "We should pack up and move on."

"I agree," Ryn added.

Xylia and Schiz shook their heads.

"Best not move in the dark, where they can see us, but we can't see them. We'll stay here by the fire. I doubt they will return again to these trees tonight." Xylia said.

Yll came flying in from the darkness, transforming into her human form as she landed. She was getting really good at it. "I followed them, but lost track of them at the foothills. They were still running."

"See? We gave them a good scare—they won't return." Xylia said.

Zo wasn't as sure, but he knew the foothills were a good way off.

"Alright, but we should have two people keep watch." Zo didn't think he could sleep tonight. Adrenaline was still coursing through his veins.

Fergus nodded, then stood, pulling a reluctant Ryn along to make up beds with the blankets they brought. She clearly still wanted to pack up and go. Yll went with them. Remus took up a post by the tent, sitting there staring out into the darkness. Schiz and Xylia stayed with Zo. Xylia's shoulders slumped, and there were dark circles under her eyes. Whatever she'd done with the trees had clearly drained her.

"I'll take the first watch. Why don't you get some sleep?" Zo said.

Xylia's eyes shone. She shook her head. "Can't sleep now."

Zo understood that.

Schiz came and sat next to Zo by the fire. Zo still didn't know what to think of the man. He was strange in so many ways, but he didn't feel threatening. The fact that he showed up with a wolf though, that was concerning.

"How is it that your best friend there is a wolf? Is he some kind of shapeshifter?" Zo asked.

A leaf fell out of Schiz's hair as he shook his head. "We've known each other...since we were pups."

Zo raised an eyebrow at that, but Schiz just stared at Remus.

"How do you become friends with a wolf?" Zo tried a different angle.

Schiz shrugged. "Our mothers were best friends."

Zo turned away from Schiz and rolled his eyes. Xylia caught it.

"The wolves are the offspring of the dragon and a woman of Ancestor descent," she said, using a stick to stir the fire.

"Children's tales meant to keep young women out of the woods at night," Zo said.

"But clearly real," Xylia said.

Zo didn't know what to think. Only a few paces away from him sat a mythical creature he'd only heard about in stories meant to scare young children into learning their magic properly. Yet the thought of a dragon getting together with a woman. Unless Zmej really was a dragon, but how could that be? Didn't the dragon of old fly in and roast half the countryside? And the power of his destruction had created a crater so deep and steep it could only be accessed by Travel magic. He snapped his fingers and let small flames curl around his fingers. He supposed what he did with magic would seem pretty incredible to Ordinaries who never saw Ancestor magic. He glanced over at Xylia. The so-called 'Ordinary' had put on quite the display of power tonight. It was all very confusing. He really didn't know what to believe anymore.

"Even if Zmej is a dragon, why would his offspring be wolves? And how many women was he with if there are that many wolves out there?" Zo asked.

When Xylia didn't reply, he looked over to find her with her chin on her chest and snoring softly where she sat.

Schiz patted Zo's knee like Zo was his grandson or something.

"Everything...is going to be fine. They are...together at last." Schiz smiled at Ryn.

Zo stared at the stick in Schiz's hair. "Um...sure," he said.

Oh boy this is going to be a weird trip, he thought, adding another log to the fire.

* * *

The next morning, they came to the village where Ryn's orphanage stood. The one they had visited a few moons back.

"Do you want to stop in?" Zo asked Ryn as they approached the village. "Maybe they've found that book that might have clues about your family."

"No, I have reason to believe my father might have that book," Ryn said, her gaze fixed and her voice sounding far away.

"I think it's worth checking, but whatever you say," he said.

They drew stares as the road took them through the village. It was later in the day than the first time he and Ryn visited, and there were more people going about their business. Admittedly they were strangers, and maybe looked like an odd group, even if Schiz and Remus had taken a trail through the forest to avoid the road through the village. No telling what the villagers would do if they saw a wolf strolling by.

They passed the spot where, after their visit to the orphanage, Ryn had swerved into the road and was hit by a wagon. It was the first time since he killed the wolf that he had failed to Heal. He glanced at Ryn's arm. It was still cold enough that she hadn't worn short sleeves yet, but he knew that cut must have scarred. He frowned. If he could have Healed, her scarring would have been minimal to none. If he could go back in time and do something different. In an instant he was back in that ball room, reaching out with his magic to kill the wolf...

Fergus nudged him. "Hey, I think we're being followed."

Zo looked over his shoulder. There were villagers chatting with each other, working in gardens, or loading wagons. There were lots of eyes on their group, but Zo didn't see anyone actively following them. Then he saw it—the flash of a couple dark green uniforms changing course to go between the orphanage and the house next to it. Zo's pulse quickened.

"Agents of House Sano," Zo said.

Ryn startled, grabbing Zo's arm she looked around, up and down the street.

He gently shook her off, flames coming to his fingers.

Fergus grabbed his elbow. "Not here. Let's duck into the woods. Hopefully the sight of Remus will scare them off."

Zo nodded and their group hurried past the orphanage, and slipped off the road into the woods.

"How did they find me all the way out here?" Zo asked.

He hadn't seen any agents in Waatch while they were there, nor had anyone followed him since he left the Sanctuary island. *Why now?* His heartbeat pounded in his ears.

"Someone must have tipped them off," Fergus said.

"But who?" Ryn asked.

Once they were well off the road and into the woods, Schiz and Remus joined them.

"There are guys in green after Master Zo here," Fergus said.

Schiz nodded. "Understood."

Remus took off toward the road growling.

"I don't like this. Even if Remus scares them off, they've seen Zo and can report back to whomever sent them," Ryn said.

"Maybe I can figure out who that is," Yll said. "Nobody from House Sano knew where you were going. There must be someone in Waatch. The others should be getting back to Waatch soon. I'll fly back and let them know what's happened, and try to stop House Sano from sending more agents."

Ryn nodded. "How will you find us when you return?"

"Xylia said the entrance to the springs isn't far from here. My eagle eyes will help me catch up." Yll gave Ryn a hug.

"Be safe," Ryn whispered, almost too low for Zo to hear.

"You too." And with that, she released Ryn and changed into a hawk the same color brown as her hair.

Yll flew off through the trees, and Remus came back with his tongue hanging out the side of his mouth looking really pleased with himself.

Schiz knelt to pat Remus' head. "We are...safe for now, but we should stay off the road for a while."

Schiz led them down a trail going deeper into the woods, then changed course and walked on a trail closer to the road. It took longer, and wasn't as straightforward, but it was better than fighting House Sano agents. Remus brought up the rear. The sound of Remus's near silent footsteps behind Zo made the hairs on the back of his neck stand up. Every time he glanced behind him all he saw was Remus's teeth. Zo's spine tingled. He tried to shake it out of his body. He put a hand to where the puncture wounds on his neck had finally healed. He didn't like having a wolf at his back, but he couldn't deny Remus had kept them safe.

* * *

When the sun through the leaves indicated it was late afternoon, Xylia stopped them, her head cocked to one side, and her nose sniffing.

Zo inhaled a deep breath. There was something in the air. Something that vaguely smelled of rotten eggs.

"The springs are near. Here is where we must rejoin the road," Xylia said.

They left the woods behind and crossed the road to an unusual sight—there were vines hanging long down the sheer mountainside. Xylia led them to the vines and pulled them back to reveal a narrow crevasse between two steep granite walls.

"Here is the entrance. It is too late in the day for the journey between. You will need to wait until morning to enter. Do not bring the wolf, the sisters don't take kindly to the dragon's children. Be cautious, magic bubbles up from the earth here. Follow the crack in the mountain to the waterfall, then take the trail beside the falls to the pool. Tell them I sent you to ask for their help. Hopefully they won't drown you," Xylia said.

"Shouldn't you go with us to introduce us?" Ryn asked, her voice rising in pitch.

Xylia shook her head. "I have approached the sprites already recently. The sprites can be sensitive to visitors. My name holds worth with them."

Zo didn't like the sound of that.

Xylia took off her pack. "I will cook us something to eat, then I will be off. I need to get back to the farm and my family."

She stopped and took a deep breath, then she gathered Ryn up in her arms.

"You've only been with us for a short time, but I feel you are family." Xylia kissed Ryn on the forehead. "I wish there was more I could do for you, but calling upon the sprites last night took every ounce of magic I have collected over the past years. I wish I had more to give. I'm certain the sprites will give you what you need. I fear the fate of the Heart Tree rests in your hands."

Zo didn't quite know what to make of Xylia. She had helped them get this far, but all the talk of Wild magic and sprites was straight out of all the stories he'd heard as a kid. Unless these sprites could defeat a dragon, which it looked like they couldn't since Praedo had to defeat the first dragon, he didn't see the point of all this. Except for the part where he needed the sword, the stone, and the branch to find Praedo's beads. If they really existed. He glanced out of the vines toward the road. He hoped they were thick enough to hide him from House Sano. They really were determined to kill him. If Praedo's beads weren't real, he didn't know what he was going to do.

"If you could be so kind as to start a fire for me," Xylia asked him.

Zo looked nervously toward the road again.

"Don't worry, no one can see through the vines."

Zo wasn't so sure, but there was a firepit near the entrance, and Zo started a fire in it. While Xylia began to cook, Ryn and Fergus sat on rocks by the fire, deep in conversation. Remus took up guard between them and the vines, while Schiz sat tapping his head and muttering something.

Zo was drawn to the crevasse. The walls looked like they had been thrust up from the earth, and the late afternoon sun glistened on the walls like they were wet. Zo put out his fingers to touch the walls, but pulled them back when he got a shock stronger than when you shuffled across carpet then touched a metal latch. He shook out his hand, his gaze searching the deep shadow that was the crack. The darkness pulled at him. Like a gaping mouth of blackness, he felt sucked into it. He grabbed a tree next to the entrance and hung on as his feet left the ground, pulled toward the entrance. Just as Zo was about to lose his grip and get sucked down the dark tunnel, the pull stopped, and he was once again standing at the entrance as if nothing happened.

Heart pounding, he stumbled back toward the fire.

"And that is why you don't enter the gate in the darkness," Xylia, chuckled as she stirred the vegetables in the pan.

Chapter Twenty-Two

The dragon took flight to the high, empty sky,
Calling to kin with a roar full of dread;
Two more dragons arose, terror widespread,
Later, Praedo discerned the illusion nearby.

The fact that dragon magic can create illusions is disturbing. Here in the dark, chased by wolves, I wonder what is real?

- From the journals of Moult de Dico

Ryn gazed up at the sheer granite walls, the morning sun glinting off its surface. Something about the place sent a thrill through her body. Zo said it had shocked him when he touched it, but all Ryn felt was energy coursing through her.

"We will...wait for you here," Schiz said. "If you don't see us, just whistle...We will come."

"If I knew how to whistle," Ryn mumbled under her breath, still in awe of the sheer height of the walls before her.

Fergus rubbed the back of his neck. "I don't know. We don't know what's in there. Having the wolf around has been handy."

"Xylia said we couldn't bring him. If we're asking for help, I don't want to cause trouble," Ryn said.

Zo cracked his knuckles against his leg. "Daylight is slipping away, let's get to it."

Ryn looked over at him. Despite the morning chill, there was sweat on his brow. "The sun is barely up, we'll make this as fast as we can."

Zo's cheek twitched, but he nodded.

Fergus went first, and Zo brought up the rear.

"Don't you think I should lead us?" Ryn asked.

Fergus shook his head and drew his Library sword. "Don't know what's ahead."

The boys had her sandwiched between them, which meant she couldn't see much. Ryn reached out her hands and ran her fingertips along the walls. They weren't smooth, but they were flat. The small path of the crack between the walls was even, like a path was deliberately cut through the mountain. If she couldn't see, at least she could feel. The walls crackled beneath her fingertips and her hair stood on end. She couldn't help smiling at the uplifting sensation that flowed through her body. She felt like she could do anything, even fly.

"Why do I only see darkness ahead, and I feel like the path is tilting, rolling to the right," Fergus said.

"I don't know. All I see is your backside," Ryn said.

"I felt that too, last night. Like the blackness was sucking me in," Zo said.

"I don't feel sucked in, I feel like I'm walking through a rolling barrel." Fergus stumbled over a rock.

"Just keep going. It can't be too far," Ryn said.

Ryn tried to peek around Fergus, but the way was too narrow. She stared at Praedo's sword on his back. In the past she had only briefly noticed the intricate scroll work on the hilt, but now she was transfixed by it. The swirls and flourishes seemed to dance to a music she couldn't hear. Her head swam in the dance, her eyes following one swirl, then another, around and around. Time stopped, or faded, or accelerated—she didn't know where she was, or when.

"Ryn!"

She looked up into Fergus' concerned face. There was a roaring in the background she'd never heard before.

Fergus frowned. "Are you alright?"

Ryn shook her head. "Yes?"

"We're here," he said.

He moved aside and Ryn saw the source of the roar. It was water cascading down from high above. Cold water spray prickled at her cheeks and hands, bringing her fully back to the present.

Ryn laughed. "This is incredible!"

A second fall of water cascaded down the cliff like a sheer veil dancing in the breeze.

"That's quite the climb," Zo said.

Ryn followed his gaze to a set of steps that led up the side of the waterfall. It wasn't quite straight up, but it wasn't a gentle angle either.

Ryn wiped misty spray from her face. "Let's get started."

Zo groaned.

"Think of the thick legs you'll get." Fergus winked.

"I'm gonna look like a tree trunk," Zo complained.

Ryn shifted her pack and took a deep breath. "We're here to find the branch so we can save my parents and get you your magic back. We're just going to have to dig in deep and do it."

Fergus laughed. "We're just being whiny. Lead the way so we don't leave you behind."

Ryn eyed him. "You mean, so you can catch me if I fall."

"That too," Zo said.

Ryn started up the steps. There were ropes strung on each side of the stairs. Ryn started up full of energy, and ignoring the ropes. The first dozen or so steps weren't too bad. Then she started to get winded. She thought all those moons of going up and down the Library stairs would have prepared her better for this. It apparently did not. She glanced back at the boys following behind her.

"Keep going," Fergus said from below her. "If you stop it will be hard to get going again."

Ryn reached for the ropes at the side of the staircase and pulled herself onward. Eventually she found reaching forward and pulling on the rope before each step up made it a little easier. When she finally came to the end of the stairs, her legs felt like jelly, or maybe jam. Tea and tea cakes at the tea house sounded so good right then.

At the top of the falls the ground was flat rock. A river tumbled over the side, becoming the waterfall. Ryn looked back down the falls and stumbled to the side. The sight made her dizzy, and the spray coated everything, but it was no longer cold. Everything up at the top was warm.

Zo took the last couple stairs quickly and moved off to a large pool to the right of the river. Mist hovered over the pool.

"It's a hot spring." Zo held his hand over the water, but didn't put it in.

"That's not mist, it's steam." The thought popped out of Ryn's mouth.

There was something about this pool and the misty steam. Something niggled at the back of her brain. She felt like she'd been here before.

Fergus crouched down next to Zo. "A bath sounds nice. I wonder how hot it is..." He started to put a finger in it.

Zo grabbed his hand. "That's a thermal hot spring. It could be hot enough to melt your skin off."

The smell of rotten eggs became strong as Ryn moved away from the waterfall mist, closer to the pool.

"I don't think you'd want to take a bath and then smell like that." She wrinkled her nose.

"Shhhh," Zo held up a hand to them, staring into the foggy steam.

"What...?" Ryn began, but cut off as soon as she saw the dark figure moving in the fog.

Fergus started to draw his side sword, but Ryn put her hand on his arm to stop him.

The figure wasn't in the water, but it wasn't on the water either. As it got closer it resolved into a man, the pool gently swirled around his feet till he stood before them.

Zo inhaled sharply.

"I...I thought the sprites were sisters," Ryn said.

The man before them, who seemed to be made of water, or maybe steam, laughed. "I am Tertius." His gaze shifted to Ryn. "We have been expecting you, daughter of the Tree. The waters rejoice that you have chosen to come to us."

Ryn frowned. How could he be expecting her?

Tertius turned to Fergus. "What brings you here, son of the Tree?"

Ryn bowed to the man. "Xylia sent us. She said you could help us. We've come to ask for your guidance and wisdom."

Tertius turned to Zo. "Do you find my form appealing, Follower of the Slayer?"

Ryn watched Zo turn red all the way to the tips of his ears.

Ryn cleared her throat. "Um—we were hoping the sprites might know where we can find the branch that is missing from the Heart Tree."

Tertius stumbled back a step without disturbing the water. "There's a branch missing from the Tree?"

"Yes. I was there with the tree at the Heart of the Library. I saw the cut. It drips sap like tears." Ryn was surprised at the sudden heaviness in her chest that rose to choke off her words.

The fog swirled around the man, but Ryn thought she saw tears in his eyes. "You are a fortunate daughter that the Tree let you approach."

"I was there, too." Zo's voice was higher and rougher than usual.

Tertius shifted back to Zo, his gaze moved up and down Zo. "Highly unusual, child of the Slayer's magic."

Ryn took a step forward. "My mother is being held captive. We need the branch to free her."

"She is not your mother," Tertius said.

Ryn took a long step back from the water's edge. "I was adopted. How do you know?" Seeing Zo's beadscar told everyone he was of Ancestor descent, but how did this man know she was adopted?

Tertius stared off over the river, into the mists of the waterfall. He was silent for a long time.

Ryn shifted. She had a weird feeling, like she was being weighed and measured.

Tertius' eyes sifted to find Ryn's. They were a deep grey blue that matched the spring water.

"It is forbidden. I cannot speak in the place of my sister. All will be revealed at the Tree. Follow the path back to the Tree." Tertius turned to go back into the pool.

"But what about the branch?" Ryn asked.

Tertius met her gaze again. Ryn shivered, despite the heat.

"Put forth your hands," he said.

Ryn reached out and took Tertius's warm, yet dry hand. He dipped down and poured water into her cupped hands.

The water was there, but not there, like the life water around the Heart Tree.

"The branch is yours. The gate will open," Tertius whispered.

"And how do we stop the dragon?" Fergus added in a rush.

Tertius glared at him.

"Do you not know there's a dragon out there?" Fergus pointed out into the mist.

Tertius opened his mouth, but nothing came out.

Zo swore. "They don't know."

Fergus paced the water's edge, then stopped. "Might I, a son of the Tree, recommend that you sprites take a look outside of these mountains and discover what's going on out there."

"You have no proof." Tertius held his head high.

"In human form he shot blue fire at the Heart Tree," Zo said.

Tertius paled and sank to his knees into the water. "He will come for the egg. I must consult with the sisters."

And then the fog engulfed him, and he was gone.

The water in her hands began to glow, and she remembered her dream. She was at the Heart Tree and the sap teardrop glowed in her hands. She pulled her hands to her chest and the warmth flowed into her.

Daughter of the Tree, a voice whispered.

She turned to Zo and Fergus. "Um, that went...well?"

Zo swore. "Are you joking? He told us we have the branch and then we find out he has no idea there's a dragon out there."

Fergus had a far off look in his eyes. "He called me a son of the Tree." He turned to Ryn. "And you, the daughter. Maybe we do have what we need."

"What do you mean, we have what we need?" Zo's eyebrow was raised. Clearly not happy with all the strangeness of their encounter.

"If Fergus and I are part of the tree, maybe we're the branch?" Ryn offered.

Zo snorted.

The fog thickened like a wall, pushing them back toward the stairs.

Zo put his hand against the fog wall.

"Ow!" He shook his fingers. "It's hot. How could fog be hot?"

Fergus shrugged. "It's a hot spring?"

The fog shifted and Ryn took one last look at the spring. Something about it pulled at her heart. A drop formed on her cheek like a tear, but it wasn't hers. She wiped at it, marveling at its silver brilliance on her finger.

"I'll be back," she whispered, not really knowing why she felt that so strongly.

"What do we do now?" Fergus asked.

Ryn watched the river flow. It seemed slow till it plunged over the side. "We get back on the road. We can't delay finding my mother any longer. We need to go."

Fergus nodded.

The trip down the falls proved trickier than the climb up. The stairs were wet and slippery. Ryn lost her footing halfway down and landed hard on her backside.

Fergus reached a hand down to help her up.

"Ow," she said.

Fortunately, instead of the long tight squeeze that it was when they entered, the crack in the walls seemed to push them out when they got to the bottom of the waterfall. They were through it to the entrance faster than when they went in.

The sky was barely lit, the tree line deep in shadow.

"Is it night already?" Fergus asked.

The dark forms of Schiz and Remus melted out of the forest.

"Morning," Schiz said as the first rays of sunlight burst over the trees.

"How did we lose a whole day?" Zo asked.

"These mountains are strange." Schiz nodded, fingers tapping his temple.

"But it didn't get dark while we were there. How was there no night?" Ryn asked.

"Time moves differently in there," Schiz said.

"Fantastic." Ryn forced as much sarcasm into her voice as she could. "Let's hope the sprites will use their strangeness to think about what they can do against the dragon."

"Did anyone else notice that sprite mentioned an egg?" Fergus asked.

Ryn's brow furrowed. "Maybe?"

Zo shrugged his shoulders.

Ryn was completely drained, and moody. She desperately wanted to have Zo's fire magic and light something on fire—and then sleep by that fire for the rest of the day, but they had lost a whole day, and they still had a long way to go to find her father's cave.

She hefted her pack, repositioning it on her shoulders. "Let's go."

"Where do we go?" Fergus asked.

Ryn pulled out her father's journal, then showed everyone the map her father had drawn. "That way down the road till we find a tree growing on top of a giant hollowed log."

Zo traced the road on the map with his finger, taping his finger on the drawing of the tree. "Seems straightforward enough. It definitely looks like a cave entrance."

As they walked, the morning sun rose above the trees and Ryn turned her face to it. She needed the light and the warmth to calm her desire to make them go faster, or to speed up time so they could be there already.

Schiz was watching the ground in front of him, rubbing his forehead, muttering something under his breath. Ryn shifted her focus and searched for something she could say to him. The awkwardness stretched between them for most of the morning.

Once they passed one tree growing out of a log, and determined there wasn't a cave behind it, she finally thought of something she could ask Schiz. "Is it true, what they say about how wolves are born?"

Schiz looked over at her, then back at Remus. "The dragon...is his father. His mother—my mother's sister."

Ryn worked at keeping her face neutral. She didn't want to offend him. She still didn't believe Zmej was a dragon. There was something about Zmej that made her skin crawl, but she'd met more than one man who did that to her—Master Wes came to mind.

"As with all who mate with the dragon...the birth...eventually takes the mother's life," Schiz said.

Remus' head hung low.

"I'm sorry," was all Ryn could think to say.

"Born at almost the same time...Remus and I grew up together. He is a brother...of sorts."

Remus stopped, his head pointed toward the forest beside the road, his fur raised. A low growl started deep in his chest.

Ryn searched the trees off to the right side of the road. The left side was still sheer rock of the mountain.

"I don't see anything..." Ryn said.

"Wolves," Fergus whispered right up close behind her, making her jump.

Zo swore.

"Should we run?" Ryn's voice shook.

"You can't outrun a wolf." Schiz shook his head.

Fergus was eyeing Ryn's short legs. She swallowed hard.

"Just keep moving." Zo called back to them. "If they attack, then we deal with it."

Ryn picked up the pace, not running, but walking as fast as she could. Fergus was right behind her, hand on his Library guard sword, and feet almost tripping over her. His presence behind her forced her forward faster. Remus prowled the edge of the woods, still growling. Zo's long strides took him further ahead of them. Ryn started to get winded. Her weariness dragged her down. The distance between them and Zo grew. Fergus took her elbow and hurried her along.

Ryn tried to speed up, while keeping an eye on the forest. The sun broke through here and there, but it only made the dark places more shadowed. At one point the trees grew tighter together and the forest darkened. The sunlight on the road made it hard to see into the forest. Remus barked and darted into the trees. Schiz followed him.

"Great," Fergus said, and picked up the pace.

The surge of fear gave Ryn energy to move faster. They almost caught up with Zo. There were small flames dancing around his fingertips.

When it got to be late afternoon, Ryn's legs felt like they wanted to fall off, and her stomach was grumbling.

"Let's take a break," she said.

"The road turns to the left up ahead and diverts away from the forest. We can stop there," Zo said.

They hurried around the corner and the forest ended as the side of the road dropped away into the ocean below.

"Look, there's a way down to the beach up ahead." Fergus pointed to where the road dipped down to almost the beach level.

The beach was mostly pebbly, but there was sand where the waves rolled up onto the shore. There were also many driftwood logs. It would make a great resting spot to defend against the wolves.

After Ryn dumped an armload of wood by the firepit Fergus dug in the sand, she walked across the rocks to a driftwood log and plopped herself down on it. She stared out across the water. There was land out there in the distance. It must be one of the ancestral islands. Despite how many times she'd studied the mosaic map of the islands on the floor of the grand foyer of the Library, she didn't know which island it was. She hoped it wasn't Viartoro or Eileansano.

Zo sat down next to her. "What're you feeling, lil sis?"

"Worried, scared, tired, hungry—mostly hungry."

He chuckled his deep chuckle. "We're going to get through this."

"Even if we do, what will become of our families? Of the Library? Of Waatch? What is life going to look like from here?"

Zo gazed out across the water. "And what happens if we both get Praedo's magic? We would be like the Ancestors of old. What do the history books say about what they did with that power?"

Ryn blinked. "I...don't know. I don't think I read anything about them, I've only read about Luc and he didn't have magic."

"Part of me would really love to make House Sano lick my boots," Zo smirked.

"Right after I make House Viator lick mine," Ryn frowned.

It sounded good, but she knew she'd never do it.

"What would you do with all that power? Become Curator of the Library?" Zo turned to face her.

Ryn thought of the tree, and the tear. Something burned in her heart and pulled at her stomach like a string. She wanted to see the hot springs again. Something about it felt like it was where she belonged, even more than the Library. The Library was familiar, but she was done with the Ancestor attitudes about her. Kicking her out felt like her breaking point. She loved the Library, but the hot spring and the sprites—there was something there she wanted to know more about.

"Have you ever been someplace you've never been before, but felt like it was home somehow?" Ryn asked.

Zo's eyebrow raised. "Not that I can think of."

Ryn nodded. "I tried to take an Ancestor bead before, and it rejected me."

"But this is Praedo, this is different."

She looked into his warm brown eyes. "Something tells me it's not."

Zo glanced at Fergus feeding the fire, and digging through the food sack Xylia had left them.

"Things are always changing. I promise you, you're going to be alright." Zo squeezed her shoulder.

"What about you? I'm scared Zo. I got a taste of life without you and I don't like it."

He bent down so his eyes were level with hers. "I don't have a death wish. I will do my best to avoid being killed by wolves or House Sano, and restore my magic so I can go back to Waatch and...I don't know...maybe take over from Wilmar? I think he wants to retire."

"That sounds nice, but can you do that? With all that power?"

"I don't know."

He straightened and she hugged him around the middle. "Don't leave me ever again," she mumbled into his chest.

"I won't on purpose." He hugged her back.

* * *

Just as they were sitting down to the meal Fergus cooked over the fire—dried fish and roasted vegetables—eyes appeared out in the darkness coming from the road. Ryn stiffened, and Fergus drew his sword.

Remus trotted into the firelight with his tongue hanging out to the side. That seemed to be his triumphant look after a fight. Schiz came into the light with his hands up. Fergus put his sword away.

Then Ryn noticed the blood on Remus' shoulder. Ryn gasped, jumping up to rush over to him.

"What happened?" She gasped.

Remus sat and let her push back his fur to try and get a better look at his injury. Zo joined her. He put his hand on Remus' neck. Her insides quivered as she stared at his closed eyes. He opened them and shook his head. He still couldn't Heal.

Remus' blue eyes searched hers as Zo's more expert hands took over the first aid of cleaning and bandaging the wound.

"We were able to chase them off," was all that Schiz would say.

Fergus offered him a cup of hot mint tea, and Schiz shuffled over by the fire.

Ryn went to him. "Are you hurt?"

Schiz sipped at his tea. "Nothing a good night's rest won't cure."

Still, Ryn noticed what might be bite marks through his pants.

Something dark swooped down from the sky to land on the log next to Fergus. He jumped to the side, and Ryn shot up, ready to run.

The hawk on the log cocked its head, one way, then the other, then transformed into a familiar form.

"Yll!" Ryn rushed over to give her a hug.

"Whew, it was hard to find you in the dark, but there aren't many campfires way out here." Yll gave them a slight smile.

"What's happening?" Ryn asked.

Yll frowned. "Best you read these letters."

She held out a thick sealed envelope.

"Why do I feel like I'm not going to like this?" Fergus asked.

Chapter Twenty-Three

The beast in its anger commanded the wave,
From the newborn waters drew lances of ice;
He hurled them at Praedo with lethal device,
Yet Praedo made snow of the weapons he gave.

Sometimes I sit back and marvel at how epic this battle was. If I had half this skill and bravery...

- From the journals of Moult de Dico

Zo went to Ryn's side as she unsealed the envelope, which had Clayr's Library curator seal on it. One of the letters inside was addressed to Zo in Iden's handwriting. Ryn handed it to him while she opened the one from Clayr.

Iden's writing looked steady. Zo hoped that was a good sign. He read:

My Wildfire,
I hope Yll finds you safe. I don't like the sound of wolves and assassins. I would rush out there if I could get there quickly enough. I'll have to trust Fergus, and content myself with finding our killer.
Jak is such an arrogant prick, but Tory was able to help me work with him without me killing him. (Seriously!) I'm sure glad Brynd and Ryn aren't dating those two anymore. ANYWAY I went with Jak and Dan to this amazingly seedy bar (we should seriously go there sometime, just for the entertainment of it). They had heard of a new agent for Evalesco in Waatch, and had tracked him down to the bar. Unfortunately, after we tried to lean on him for information, he was found dead in the alleyway. So another dead end, killed in the same manner as the rest—no blood, just magic. Jak has temporarily inducted me into his little band of criminals, and I've

gone on patrol with them multiple times. (no, I'm not sleeping much, but we're in a hurry and we've got no leads, except for someone who said the Evalesco agent met with a young, tall man with black hair shortly before we arrived) I'll keep searching. I'm troubled that the description of the potential killer does sound like you. Possibly why you were accused of the crime.

I hate that I can't feel your presence in my mind at this distance, but my promise necklace brings me comfort. I'm going to find the killer and get your name cleared for good. Be safe my love. What I wouldn't do to have you here with me right now. Oh, the things I want to do…

Yours forever and always,
Iden

Zo felt his promise necklace grow warm. He knew they were both thinking about each other. The last part made him ache with need. He kissed the letter then folded it into his pocket. He looked up to see Schiz giving him a strange look. As if Forest Man could judge Zo for being strange.

He peeked over Ryn's shoulder to see she was now reading. Turned out it was not from Clayr, but from Regg. Zo recognized his brother's surprisingly neat handwriting:

Ryn and Zo,
After Yll brought us the information that agents of Sano were chasing you, I was in to see the Headmaster of the Waatch Healing House. He still feels bad about what happened to Zo. He unfortunately hasn't seen any House Sano agents in Waatch, though he admits, because he allowed so many students to be seduced by Killing magic, that he's out of favor with the Healing Counsel. They are sending a supervisory committee to oversee him and the Waatch Healing House for an indefinite length of time. I feel bad because he always seemed fair to me,

or at least listened. I remember the headmaster of the Sano Healing House. He was awful.

Dead end there, so I went to the docks to ask if anyone had seen a group of House Sano agents land. Also no luck, but I did see something interesting. On my way back to town I thought I saw what looked like Jett? And he was in the forest with a bow and arrow and what I would swear was a wolf, even though I didn't get a good look. I ran over because I thought he might need help, but when I got there, I couldn't find anyone. So strange.

I'm sorry I haven't been able to find the agents and call them off. I'll keep trying. Hopefully the task Clayr gave me will flush out those agents if they exist.

Luck of the Ancestors be with you!
Your brother, Regg

"Your brother knows archery?" Fergus asked.

"A long time ago. It was something he picked up as a kid, but I haven't seen him with a bow in years." Ryn frowned. "Maybe it wasn't him."

Zo grunted as Ryn folded up the letter. "Was there a letter from Clayr? What did she say?" he asked.

A half giggle escaped from Ryn. "Yes. Um—it seems that work at the Library is grinding to a halt. Most of the collection managers, as well as upper management, were Ordinaries. Jeris promoted all the lower-level Ancestor descendants, but none of them know what they are doing. They are spending more time bossing each other around. He promoted Prym to head of the research department, but..."

"She's never actually done any real research," Fergus said.

Ryn nodded. "As we saw with Master Wes and how she stole all *my* research to get ahead. I guess she thought as head of the department all she had to do was boss everyone around. Unfortunately, all the junior researchers don't know what to do either, so there's an angry mob of clients who've scheduled, sent out invites, and hired caterers for their bead ceremonies, but are unable to attend them because they can't get their bloodlines documented."

Zo chuckled at the thought of all the spoiled Ancestor types throwing tantrums in the grand foyer of the Library.

Fergus's frown was deep though. "This will only support the cause of moving the Library to Viatoro, even though it's their fault everything is a mess."

Yll picked a feather out of her hair. "My mother is talking to the town's people, in case Zmej really is a dragon. She's hoping to get support to defend the Library if it comes to that. Most people want to see her back as Curator, so they are ready to storm the Library right now. She's enlisted Regg, Brynd, Jak, and Dan to help."

"We need the support of all the Ancestral Houses. Waatch is made up of mostly Ordinaries. They're not slaying a dragon with pitch forks," Ryn said.

"I don't know, we've seen some pretty unusual stuff the past few days, all of it way outside of what I understand as magic," Zo said.

"That was the Wild magic in the wild," Ryn said. "And if Wild magic could have defeated a dragon, wouldn't it have done so with the first dragon?"

Fergus rubbed his brow. "He called us children of the Tree. Praedo's companions were from here. They had to have been 'children of the tree' right? Perhaps we need his magic, plus Wild magic."

"Yes!" Schiz stepped close to the fire, half of his face in the firelight's shadow, it made him look like a scary campfire story come to life. "There is much power together!"

"Which is why the dragon has worked to tear us apart," Yll said.

Ryn's brow furrowed.

Zo cracked his knuckles against his leg. Could Ryn and Fergus have some sort of magic in them? Ordinaries have never exhibited any kind of ability. In fact, Luc says nothing of his companions having magic until after Praedo bestowed it upon them.

Yll yawned. "Let's get some sleep. I've been flying half the day."

Zo pulled the tarp out of his sack. There weren't any standing trees on the beach, but some of the logs by the fire were bigger around than he was tall. If he could secure the tarp to the logs...

Thwap!

Zo was knocked backward against a log. Something had hit him. He looked down to find an arrow sticking out of his shoulder.

"Zo!" Fergus shouted, then turned as a man in a green cloak rushed into the firelight of the campsite.

Fire leapt into Zo's hand and he swirled it, forming a fireball. He shot the fireball at the man, as Yll turned into a hawk and flew into the man's face. Remus turned into a white blur as he bore down on two wolves who emerged from the forest behind the man. Another fireball formed in Zo's hand, and he hit one of the wolves. Fergus went after the green cloaked man, his sword smashing the man's bow, as Schiz pulled water from the ocean and sent a wave over everyone's head. The wolves were washed up the beach into the dark.

Remus turned on the man Fergus was fighting. Green Cloak turned and fled, his hood flying off.

"And don't come back!" Schiz yelled.

Yll followed the man till he was lost to the darkness, then she circled back, shifting into a human as she landed.

"Ryn, I think that man was Jett," Yll said.

"What? It can't be. Regg just saw him in Waatch. How could he be all the way out here?" Ryn's eyes were wide.

"Ryn! Your brother is House Viator." Yll eyed Ryn up and down like she was looking for something wrong with her.

Ryn's eyes got big and her mouth clamped shut.

"Right," she said.

A sharp pain shot through Zo's shoulder, and he slid down the log to sit on the sand.

Ryn's wide-eyed face appeared in front of him. Her hands went toward the arrow, then stopped, her fingers opening and closing.

"What do we do?" She asked.

"Pull it out." Zo gritted his teeth, the pain was really starting to hit him now. "I can heal it if you take it out."

"But what if you pass out? You can't heal it if you're unconscious. That's what happened to Regg with the knife on the steps of the Library," Ryn said.

"It's just my shoulder, I'll be fine," Zo panted.

Fergus swore as he knelt beside Zo. "I got it. This is going to hurt...a lot."

Zo nodded, then grit his teeth. Ryn squeezed his hand.

"There're bandages in my bag. Pack the wound with them and put pressure on it to stop the bleeding. It didn't hit anything vital, so I should be fine going into deep meditation to heal myself. I'm going to look like I've passed out, but I'm not."

Fergus pushed the arrow. Zo screamed. Ryn went white as a sheet.

Yll ran for Zo's bag and came back with the bandages. Zo lay back struggling to change his short, shallow breaths into deeper ones. When he got ahold of his breathing, he let his mind drift inside of himself. It followed the nerve pathways, easing his pain, till he found the hole in his shoulder. He fought back the shock of seeing a hole in his body, then eased his mind into the work of repairing it.

* * *

Zo came back to himself to the sharp sound of raindrops hitting the tarp overhead. He cracked an eye open. It was beginning to get light; no one was up yet that he could see. He tried to roll over and wished he hadn't. They had piled blankets on him to keep him warm, but the weight of them reminded him of his time in the House Sano Healing House. His heart raced and he threw off all the blankets. He sat up panting and shaking. He looked over and saw that he had dumped all the blankets onto Ryn. She uncurled and let out a sigh in her sleep. She must have given him her blanket and been cold.

He felt his shoulder. It was sore. It would need more work when he had more time, but for now it was good enough. He shifted to sit up, leaning back on the log, his muscles stiff from his unmoving, deep healing sleep. He watched the rain come down outside the tarp. He shivered and took one of the blankets back from the pile on Ryn. She rolled over.

As the raindrops fell, he contemplated how fortunate he was that Master Rocco was able to restore his self-healing. He could only imagine the trouble they would be in if he had to continue on wounded. He looked over at Ryn. He knew Ryn needed his help, and he needed to heal his magic, but having Green Cloak after them, whoever he was, didn't help. The thought that it was the giant, quiet Jett was disturbing. That he would attack his own sister.

Zo ran the fight from the night before back through his mind. Green Cloak hadn't actually gone after Ryn, just Zo. What had Zo ever done to him? Maybe Jett objected to his cooking that night when they'd met. First impressions were important. Zo chuckled at his own joke.

If he could get one of Praedo's beads he would have all the magic. He burned to have more than just fire. If he had all the magics last night, there would have been no contest. He doubted Green Cloak would have dared attack him. Zo would be able to protect everyone, and himself. The Ancestors, Praedo's companions in the fight against the dragon, weren't children when they took on his beads. Zo was counting on that meaning he could take them on, even though he was eighteen. That was, if the beads were real and did exist. He really hoped they did, because he was in a world of trouble if they didn't. If Ryn and Fergus were the branches, Green Cloak must want them to get the beads. The race for power was real. Ryn was right, they needed to hurry and get to this cave where her father was staying. Zo wondered how much further they had to go. Between the wolves and the Sano agents they had plenty of motivation to move fast.

The sound of footsteps crunching on the pebbles made Zo tense. He relaxed when he realized it was Schiz's shoes showing below the tarp. Remus appeared from behind him, shaking water off. Schiz bent low to see into their makeshift tent.

"Master Zo...you look better."

Zo put his hand to his shoulder and gently rolled it. It protested, but not too badly.

"I've...collected some wood...would you?" Schiz pointed to a new fire ring that was just outside, partially out of the rain.

Zo wasn't ready to move close to it, so he made a fireball and shot it at the wood.

Despite the dampness, the wood caught fire and began to crackle. Zo felt the warmth flood into the tent.

Fergus began to snore.

"Is the sun up yet?" Zo asked.

"Hard to tell in the rain...but it's still early." Schiz said, feeding more wood to the fire.

"We should get moving as soon as we can." But Zo relaxed into the warmth the fire was giving off. The thought of going out into the rain and being wet and cold all day did not appeal.

Ryn inhaled deeply and reached out and grabbed his arm. Her eyes opened a crack. "Are you healed?"

"Well enough."

"Good." Her eyes drifted closed again, as she snuggled deeper into the blankets.

"I should get up and make breakfast," Zo said, but he leaned his head back against the log and drifted back to sleep.

* * *

Someone touched Zo's shoulder, and he startled awake. Ryn held out hot eggs wrapped in bread to him.

"Eat. We need to get moving," she said.

The rain had stopped and everyone else was already packed up. Startled, Zo moved to jump up, but his stiff body protested. He settled for slowly climbing to his feet. Fergus folded up the tarp and put it in a bag.

"How late is it?" Zo asked.

"Don't worry about it," Fergus said.

They started back toward the road, Zo picking his way over the rocks so he didn't twist an ankle on top of everything. When they hit the road, they were going at Ryn's pace. It was on his lips to protest, but his body was grateful.

Everything dried out and the sun peeked out. Zo kept his eyes out for wolves and Green Cloak, but they didn't see anything all day.

"What does the entrance to the cave look like again?" Yll asked.

Ryn pulled out her father's journal. She turned to a picture and compared it to the rocky hillside on the left of the road.

"There's a fallen, hollowed out cedar tree somewhere just off the road. It looks like this."

"There's lots of cedar trees growing out of logs out here. We've checked each one," Fergus said.

"But this one you're supposed to be able to walk through." Ryn pointed to the dark hole in the picture of the cedar log.

"And you haven't traveled down the road far enough, if this map is accurate." Yll's finger traced the winding line that represented the road.

Ryn frowned and stuck her nose in the map. "I think we're close."

"We could have passed it already." Yll looked back down the road.

"I don't think so," Ryn said.

Zo cracked his knuckles on his thigh. His impatience flared inside him. His feet hurt, and his shoulder was aching carrying his pack on his back. He gazed back down the road. Nothing moved back there.

"Let's find this tree," he said, walking faster down the road.

The rest of the day was damp and windy. There was still no sign of the wolves or of Green Cloak. Schiz shrugged it off, saying Remus had scared them away. Zo's gut told him differently. He didn't like it. Remus had chased them before, but the wolves had come back. Just when they rounded another corner that jutted out close to the water, Yll returned in her eagle form from scouting ahead.

"It's there." She pointed to a dark spot along the coastline up ahead.

"Thank the Ancestors, let's get there before it gets dark." Fergus hiked up his pack and started off down the road.

Zo didn't like it. He began to wonder how many people knew about this cave. If the wolves really were Zmej's children, did they know about it as well?

He whistled to Fergus, who turned to glare at him. "We need to approach cautiously. Remus—take the lead. Let us know if you sense anything."

The wolf nodded, then put his nose to the ground, sniffing ahead.

They got to the hollowed-out cedar tree, and it indeed had a small tree growing out the top. The roots hung down inside the tunnel the hollowed-out cedar created. Remus sniffed at the giant log, sneezed, then sat with his head cocked to one side.

"Remus...hasn't smelled anything," Schiz said.

It started to rain. Zo looked up at the cloudy sky. His feet were already cold. He sighed.

"Inside we go, nothing else we can do, just be on the lookout," he said.

Ryn nodded but climbed into the hollowed-out tree a little too eagerly. If there was a trap set for them, they were walking right into it.

Chapter Twenty-Four

Ryette came. She's been chasing Zmej. She says he is a dragon for sure. Zmej used blue fire against my sweet daughter. I'm so glad Ryn's safe! The tunnels have been quiet for a while. I've been able to leave the cave a few times. I thought it was safe to show Ryette the way to the bead cave. I was wrong.

- From the journals of Moult de Dico

The cedar log tunnel was dark. Rain dripped from the roots hanging in the tunnel. The ground was a soft carpet of mulched cedar that stuck to Ryn's boots. This was it. The place where Ryn would find her father, and hopefully her mother. A shiver ran up her spine at the thought of facing Zmej again.

Ryn glanced back at Zo. "Um—a little light please?"

"Well, since you asked nicely," Zo said, squeezing past Fergus.

Ryn moved to the side, her hand pressing against the log wall, so Zo could get by her.

"Are you sure this goes somewhere?" Yll asked.

"That's what Dad's journal says." Ryn waved it over her shoulder at them.

Zo lit a flame that he cupped in his hand. Their shadows danced on the walls of the tunnel, but the way ahead was still dark. Remus brushed Ryn's legs, almost knocking her over to get in front of her and Zo. They walked a surprisingly long way until the tree tunnel opened into a cave. Ryn pulled out the journal and held it to Zo's light.

"There should be a tunnel off of this cave," she said.

Zo increased the intensity of his flames and held the light up. The cave was a dark grey like the mountainside, but felt more like a larger tunnel.

"There!" Yll pointed to the far side of the cave.

There was indeed a black hole in the cave wall.

"There's also one over here." Fergus pointed to the right of the tunnel entrance where there was another uninviting hole to nothingness.

Ryn consulted her father's journal. All her father said was to follow the tunnel after entering the cave.

Remus whined, and Ryn knelt before him. "I need to find my dad. Do you smell any humans in here?"

Remus' eyes were glassy in the firelight. His usually happy face had a frown. He turned from her and smelled both tunnels. Eventually he sat next to the tunnel on the far side of the cave.

"I hope he's right about this. I don't relish the idea of us getting stuck in a small confining tunnel," Fergus said, sweat beading on his forehead.

Ryn couldn't understand why he was sweating when it was icy cold in the cave.

"If we run into a dead end, we'll just backtrack," Ryn said, as Zo and Remus led the way.

They traveled long enough that Ryn started to feel the weight of the mountain on top of her. In the tunnel ahead, Zo and Remus stopped.

"What is it?" Ryn asked, she was directly behind Zo and couldn't see anything ahead.

"It's a door," Zo said.

Fergus poked his head past Ryn and around the corner. "And another tunnel to the right."

There was an iron knocker on the solid looking wood door. Zo lifted it and knocked. The sound echoed down the tunnel. Remus gave a low growl.

"Shhhh!" Ryn said, as if shushing the door knock would do anything.

"I hope nobody heard that." Fergus gazed down the darkened side tunnel.

There was the sound of a lock turning, and the door cracked open.

"Who are you?"

Ryn recognized her father's voice and pushed past Zo. "Dad!"

Moult looked older, and paler than he did in her dreams. His dark hair had grey shot though it, and was sticking up at odd angles like he hadn't combed it in a while. His pants were worn at the knees, and his shirt was frayed at the edges. His face was thin. Ryn swallowed hard.

Her father's face changed from one of bewilderment to a smiling surprise. "Ryn!"

He opened his arms wide and scooped her up.

"Oh, how I've missed you," Ryn whispered into his bony shoulder.

Her father gave her a hug that crushed her to his chest.

She felt her father's head shift back and forth.

"Come in everyone. Quickly, before we have unwanted visitors," her father said, opening the door wide.

Once they were all in, Ryn's father shut and bolted the door. He startled at the sight of Remus, but didn't say anything. There was a fire in the fireplace that vented up somewhere into the mountain. Ryn moved close to warm herself. She hadn't been warm since they left the sprite's hot spring.

Her father crossed the room to stand beside Ryn. He had tears in his eyes.

"I didn't think I'd ever see you again except in my dreams," he said.

Ryn reached out and put an arm around his thin waist. "Me too."

Her father turned to everyone there. "I'm Moult, Ryn's father. I recognize Yll there, but no one else."

Ryn turned to face her friends. "Oh sorry, this is Fergus, he's a guard for the Library."

Her father shook Fergus' hand.

"And this is Zo—he's um..." Ryn searched her brain for a way to tell her father her mother was dating another man.

Zo stuck out his hand. "Stepbrother to be."

Her father just nodded.

"And that's Schiz and Remus." Ryn pointed to the wolf and his companion lingering in the back by the door.

Moult rubbed his forehead. "Are there more of you outside somewhere?"

"No, it's just us," Ryn said.

Her father frowned, took Ryn's hand and squeezed it. There were tears in his dark eyes again.

Ryn squeezed his hand back. "We came as soon as we could. Where's Mother?"

Moult was silent, and Ryn didn't like his silence. "Why don't you all make yourselves comfortable. I'm sure you all are hungry, I will make something to eat." Moult went to the other side of the cave where there was a cooking fireplace, and a couple of tables.

Ryn followed him, while everyone else moved closer to the fire to warm up.

"Dad, what's happened? Where's Mom?" Ryn demanded.

Moult was trying to get a spark from his firestarter, but his hands were shaking.

"Zo, could you come and help?" Ryn asked.

Zo came and lit the kitchen fire with a snap of his fingers.

Ryn took her father's hands. When Zo had returned to the others Ryn whispered, "What's wrong?"

Her father removed his hands from Ryn's and leaned hard on the table. She took a moment to absorb his appearance. She couldn't believe how much he had aged since he'd been gone. In her dreams he seemed the same as she always knew him, but here in person his black hair was shot with grey, his face had begun to wrinkle.

He gave Ryn a sad smile then patted her hand. "I'll explain after everyone's stomach is full."

"Do you need help?" Ryn asked.

"No, you go take a rest. You've traveled a long way."

Fergus vacated a large stuffed chair so Ryn could sit. She was there for only a few minutes before the warmth and the comfort had her drifting off to sleep.

* * *

In her dream she was with a tree that looked just like the one at the heart of the Library, but the place felt different. The air was different. It was warm, wet, and heavy. Zmej was there. A girl who looked about the same age as Ryn stood between Zmej and the tree. Fire shot from Zmej's hands. The same blue fire Ryn had seen him use before. The girl battled back with an astonishing array of magic. Fire, water, air, earth—one right after another. Ryn couldn't believe it, but the fire was winning. The girl dropped to her knees, crying out in a strange language, an obvious plea for help...

* * *

"Ryn."

She opened her eyes to see Fergus standing over her shaking her awake.

"Are you alright?" he asked.

Ryn rubbed her eyes. "Yes?"

"You were crying in your sleep," Zo said. He was standing just behind Fergus.

Yll pushed past the boys and came to sit next to her on the couch, wrapping her arms around her in a hug.

Ryn didn't realize how tense she was till she relaxed into the warmth of Yll's embrace.

"Dinner's ready," Ryn's father said.

Ryn unfolded her legs from under her and stretched as she stood.

Her father had made a soup of smoked salmon, with carrots and potatoes. It was filled with herbs that tickled Ryn's nose and made her stomach growl.

Yll touched her fingers to her forehead. "Thanks be to the Ancestors."

"Thanks be," Ryn's father said.

The soup was simple, but delicious. The warmth of it unknotted Ryn's insides and the muscles in her chest and neck. She felt sleepy again.

"Where did you get the food? I thought you were trapped here?" Ryn filled her bowl with another scoop of the soup.

"These are from my storage. I don't get out much, even when I'm not trapped here, as you said. I stock up on food so I don't have to leave," Moult said.

"When we arrived, you said that we should come inside before we had unwanted visitors. Who would that be?" Fergus asked Moult.

Moult set down his spoon, and folded his hands over his bowl. He glanced at Remus who was lying by the fire. "There are wolves in the tunnels. They have tried to get at me. Fortunately, my door is strong."

Ryn put her hand on her father's arm. "What's going on?"

"I found the cave where Luc hid the beads. I'm sure of it. It's taken me years of research and searching, but I finally found it." He looked at Ryn. "I sent a message to your mother, because it has carvings on the door which I believe are the keys to opening it, but I didn't understand them. She's the best researcher I know, and I knew she could puzzle it out. The next thing I know, she's standing at my door." His gaze shifted to Zo. "I'm guessing it's your father she's with."

"That's Uncle Mik," Ryn added. "Her brother."

Her father shook his head. "I wouldn't know, I've never met any of Ryette's family."

"Uncle Mik has red hair, and was with her chasing after Zmej. Where is he?"

Moult shrugged his bony shoulders. "The man she's with has black hair like your friend there." He pointed at Zo.

Zo cracked his knuckles on his leg. "How could my dad be here? He was just with me...or at least that's what I was told while I was in the Sano Healing House."

Yll stared at him. "You were gone for almost a moon."

Zo rubbed his eyebrows. "Hmmmm, I guess I was out of it for most of that time."

"Where's Mom?" Ryn asked.

Her father shifted in his seat. "I made the mistake of showing them the path to the door with the carvings. We were followed. Zmej was tracking her. He caught up to us before we got to the door. He took your mother in order to force me to tell him where the door to the beads is located.

He wants to destroy the beads so no one can rise to oppose him."

"Where's my dad?" Zo demanded.

Her father turned tear-filled eyes toward Ryn. "We fought to get your mother back. Zmej took her down an unexplored tunnel. Your father sent me for help. He went after Zmej. I haven't seen them since."

Zo swallowed, his knuckles still on his leg. "My father has fire, but I've fought Zmej before—it's something completely different."

Moult nodded slowly.

"We've been told he's a dragon," Yll piped up.

Moult sat back, fingers rubbing his forehead. "I suppose that makes sense. I should have seen it. I've never run into him before, but your mother told me many stories about him from her childhood. Some of those stories seemed unnatural."

"So what do we do?" Ryn's voice rose in pitch.

"I was hoping you brought more people to fight. We aren't going to be enough." Moult gestured to everyone at the table.

"There's trouble at home," Yll said. "Jeris has taken over the Library and thrown all the Ordinaries out, including my mother."

"We had to send half of our help back to Waatch," Ryn said.

Her father folded his arms, rubbing his chin thoughtfully. "The wolves are hard to kill, and Zmej…even harder."

"We brought the stone." Ryn dug in her pocket and produced the black pock-marked stone that had negated the Library's protection and allowed magic to be done within its walls.

"And the sword," Fergus pointed to the corner where he'd propped Praedo's sword against the wall.

"We think they are the objects in your drawing from the door to the bead cave," Ryn said.

"Let me see." Moult held out his hand to Ryn.

She gave him the stone. He eyed it, holding it close to his eyes. "I've seen this kind of stone before. It's not from around here. You did magic inside the Library with it?"

Ryn nodded. "Mother used Travel magic with Yll and I inside the Library."

"Fascinating. Can I see the sword?"

Fergus stood and brought the sword to Ryn's father. Moult pulled it from its sheath. Lying it on the table, Moult went to his desk and came back with a magnifying glass. He studied the sword from tip to pommel, occasionally making exclamations, but never explaining. When he was done, he shuffled over to his desk, digging through a drawer till he came back with a small book that looked like one of Luc's journals.

"You see." Moult pointed to a picture in the journal. "Here is the only reference in existence that says Praedo had *two* swords. One that was buried into the dragon, then driven into the stone at the Origin when the dragon's magical energy exploded, and one..."

"That's hidden in plain sight," Fergus said, running his fingers reverently over the sword lying across the table.

"Look!" Yll pointed to the picture of the sword in the book. "The markings are the same."

The boys and Yll moved in closer to get a good look. They did indeed look like the same sword.

"Well of course it's the same. I mean, they claim it's a replica," Zo said. "It could still be a fake."

Mould nodded. "Possible, but let us hope it's not." He turned to look into Ryn's eyes. "For your mother's sake."

"So what...are they supposed to do?" Schiz spoke up for the first time since they'd entered Moult's cave.

Moult frowned at him. "Who are you anyway?"

"I...think you know," Schiz said. Ryn was finding his vague answers annoying.

"I can't give it to her. I'm not ready," Moult said.

There was a long pause while Schiz and Moult seemed to size each other up.

"What about the branch?" Yll broke the silence.

"And how do the three work together?" Zo asked.

Moult shook his head. "I'm not certain. That's the part I was hoping Ryette would find the answer to. Maybe she did."

"I don't think so. Clayr received your letter after Mother was gone."

Remus stood from his spot by the fire. He padded over to stand next to Moult. He whined.

"It's time," Schiz said.

Moult turned away from them, resting his palms lightly on the sideboard. "I thought I was ready. Seeing her now, I'm *not ready*."

"You have it...I know you have it...she needs to see it," Schiz said.

Ryn was reminded of one of the dreams she'd had of her father. He was sitting right there, at his desk. He'd told her he had a book to show her.

"I dreamed you told me to come see you. That you had a book I needed to see," Ryn said.

"Yes!" Schiz tapped his temple.

Moult bowed his head. "In the morning. You all are tired from your journey. I'll get you all some skins and blankets to sleep on."

"What about Mom? We let you feed us, but we need to go, Dad. We don't know what Zmej is doing with Mom." Ryn tapped Fergus's arm and motioned toward the door.

"She's fine. We can leave once you've rested." With that, Moult went into his bedroom and shut the door.

"What was that all about?" Ryn glared at Schiz. Sometimes he really made her upset.

Remus pressed up against Ryn's leg. She reached down and dug her fingers into his soft fur. Petting him reminded her of Abby. She hoped her cat was getting along well with Thax and Tory. In that moment she wished to be home, back in her cottage by the stream, skipping stones across the river.

Moult returned with an armful of blankets and skins. Yll took them from him and set them out on the floor in front of the fire.

"I really think we should leave now." All Ryn could think about was Zmej throwing fire at her mother, or worse...she wasn't sure which magics a dragon had. She'd only seen his fire. Could he do the same things the Slayer's magic could do? She looked at Zo suffering from the effects of using Killing magic. Was there a cost to the dragon for doing such magic? Somehow, she doubted it.

Moult's gaze took in the group. Ryn did too—and realized they all looked exhausted.

"Get some rest first. We'll need all our strength." Moult gave Ryn a tight hug. "It's so good to see you, pumpkin." Then he released her and went to his room, shutting the door once again.

Remus whined.

Ryn dropped back into the oversized chair fuming. Her father had called for them to hurry up and get there, and now that they were here, he was acting like they had all the time in the world. She was tempted to wait till she knew her father was asleep then take everyone and go. She opened her mouth to tell everyone to get ready when Remus growled. Nothing too loud, just a low guttural noise from deep inside his chest. Ryn might have missed it, but she felt its rumble because Remus lay against her chair with his back pressed against her feet.

"What is it?" She whispered.

Remus stood, making his way to the door, the growling intensified.

The hair on Ryn's arms stood up. Something was out there, just on the other side of the door.

Schiz stood and went to the door, pressing his ear to the wood. Ryn thought that was ridiculous because the wood was almost as thick as her forearm. She didn't know how he could possibly hear through it.

Schiz and Remus locked eyes on each other.

"Wolves," Schiz said.

Fergus was instantly on his feet, reaching for his Library side sword.

Zo and Yll jumped to their feet

The door to Moult's room banged open, and he flew to a cabinet by the cave wall.

"A dozen or so wolves out there. They haven't been able to break down my door yet, but they've never come with so great a number before." Moult pulled some spears and a small sword out of the cabinet.

Adrenaline rushed through Ryn. Her heart beat fast, and her eyes swam.

"Is there another way out?" Ryn asked.

Her father shook his head. "No. If they break through the door, we have to make our stand."

"We're trapped in here," Zo said, small flames licking at his fingers.

Ryn swallowed her panic and took a spear from her father. She had no idea how to use it, but something was better than nothing.

Chapter Twenty-Five

> *Ha! In an old volume of the history of the peninsula and its surrounding areas I found reference to the sprites. The author seems to feel they are real, and that their magic is powerful. If that's true—where have they been? And why did Praedo fight the dragon with his magic alone?*
>
> - From the journals of Moult de Dico

Bang! Bang! Bang! The door to Moult's cave shook. Something was working hard to get in. They were trapped. The walls seemed to close in on Zo. He broke into a cold sweat. His breathing became shallow. He forced himself to take deep breaths.

The hinges on the door groaned.

"They're going to get in," Fergus said, taking up a position next to the door.

Moult took the kitchen table and dumped it on its side. "Behind the table!"

Ryn and Schiz ducked down between the table legs, Ryn holding a spear pointing toward the door. Yll changed into a small hawk and perched on top of the sideboard.

Zo took up a position next to the overturned table, his hands spinning fire into a ball. The act of pulling heavily on his fire magic calmed his sudden claustrophobia.

The pounding on the door intensified. The hinge bent with an audible groan and a wolf snout appeared in the opening between the cave wall and the door. Fergus brought his sword down on the wolf's head. It yelped and withdrew.

More pounding on the door shook the whole cave and the door came crashing down, almost on top of Fergus as he danced out of the way. Remus leapt at the first wolves through the door. Fergus slashed. Zo swore a long stream of expletives, then launched his fireball over their heads at the wolves in the tunnel. Feathers were flying as Yll's talons tried to claw the eyes out of a wolf trying to get behind Fergus. A wolf launched over the table, but Schiz stuck it with a spear, while Moult hacked at it with a sword. Zo had another fireball in hand, but didn't want to hit Ryn and the others. Zo's heart hammered in his chest as the wolf turned on Ryn. Fortunately, Ryn got her spear under the wolf and was able to push it back over the table.

The wounded wolves limped out of the way, as fresh wolves took their place. They seemed endless, and exactly like the wolves in the Library, the wounded ones recovered quickly and were back at it.

Fergus' arms were covered in wolf blood and the cave smelled of singed fur. Two wolves snuck past Fergus, in the middle of sticking his sword into the chest of a third wolf who knocked him backward with their momentum. Before Zo could stop them, the two wolves were around the table, taking on Schiz and Moult. Remus came shooting back into the cave in hot pursuit of the biggest wolf Zo had ever seen. Zo shot a fireball at it, but it didn't slow the giant wolf down. It launched itself over the table and Ryn stuck it with her spear, dead in its chest. It should have stopped the wolf. It didn't. The wolf came crashing down on Ryn, pinning her to the ground, its jaw open with its teeth right at Ryn's neck.

Zo saw himself at the Solstice Ball in the same position. In that moment he could care less about never healing again, his vision red. He reached out his hand and grabbed the wolf by the neck...

"*Stop!*" A voice boomed through the cave.

The wolves stopped in the tracks and sat where they were. The wolf on Ryn remained with its teeth just hovering about her throat.

Jett appeared in the doorway. Wolves laid down obediently at his feet. Yll flew at him. Jett smacked her out of the air. She hit the wall of the cave hard and slid to the floor, returning to her human form as she fell.

"I said *stop*." Jett's voice was low and deadly.

Fergus lowered his sword.

Zo kept his hand on the wolf's throat. He wasn't taking any chances.

"Surrender now, or the dragon's first born will rip her throat out," Jett said.

"Surrender now, or I'll kill his first born," Zo said.

Jett's hand shot out. Zo felt a pull on his spirit, trying to separate it from his body. Zo sent a fireball at Jett, who dodged it, letting it shoot down the tunnel behind him, but the pull on Zo's spirit stopped.

Jett whistled and the wolf let go of Ryn.

She sat up dazed. "Jett—what is going on? What are you doing?"

"Serving the one who will give me power, and let me use it," Jett said.

Zo rubbed at his chest where he'd felt the pull on his spirit. "You're the one. You killed Tammy and Regent Jordan."

"Yes," Jett said so matter of factly that both Ryn and Moult gasped.

"But…Wait…Why? Why would you do that? You didn't even know Jordan," Ryn said.

"The master needed them out of the way. No more foolishness. Everyone up. I'm taking you to what we all want, and we shall open the treasure. Shall we?" Jett moved to the side of the doorway and gestured down the tunnel.

Fergus helped Yll up, who was holding her head. The wolf backed off Ryn, and Moult and Schiz helped her to her feet. They both stood protectively on either side of her. Remus shook his head and growled.

"Don't start with me, you're in enough trouble already. You'll be lucky if your father doesn't dispatch you." Jett glared at Remus.

Remus barred his teeth, and the wolf next to him bit him on the hind leg. Remus yipped, limping to follow Fergus and Yll out the door.

Zo got back on his feet. He bristled when he saw Jett grab Ryn's arm.

"Master Zmej was angry when you delayed his triumphant defeat of the tree." His frown turned into a wicked smile.

Zo got right up in Jett's face. "I'm more of a brother to her than you are."

Jett knocked Zo out of his way, and forced Ryn forward down the tunnel, causing her to stumble. Fergus' neck and arm muscles bulged out.

"Calm down, Ordinary, or I'll kill you on the spot," Jett said to Fergus as he pushed Ryn past him down the tunnel.

Ryn looked back at Zo, her eyes wide. Zo's fire curled around his fingers. He couldn't believe the gentle giant who used his Spirit magic to commune with animals was dragging his sister toward Zmej. Zo wanted to punch his face in, but all he could do was follow and hope for an opportunity to take Jett down. The giant wolf brought up the rear behind Zo, his eyes shining in the dark. The wolf growled every time Zo looked back at him.

Jett and another wolf took the lead. If they at one point had been lost in the tunnels, they knew where to go now. It was darker than night, a total absence of light. Jett held a lantern to light the way. Zo tried to use his fire, but as soon as flames came to Zo's fingers, Giant Wolf behind him snarled at him.

They came to a tunnel that split off from the first and continued downward. It was narrower, and Zo felt the tunnel walls press in on him. He breathed deep, trying to calm the panic starting to rise in him.

"What did Zmej promise you?" Ryn asked Jett. "He will never give you one of Praedo's beads. He only wants to destroy them. He wants all the power."

"And what are you doing here, *sister*? Do you think you're getting Praedo's beads? The power you've always wanted? Don't make me laugh! You can't handle power."

"I can handle it better than you! I can't believe you've become so power hungry you would kill someone!" Ryn spat the words at him.

"Shut up!" Jett yanked on Ryn, pulling her faster down the tunnel.

They traveled so deep Zo thought they must be at the very root of the mountain. Jett stopped at a barred door.

Ryn's wide eyes looked back at Zo. "Jett, let us go before..."

Zmej melted out of the darkness.

In the light of the lantern flames Zmej's shadow appeared to have wings. Maybe the stories were true. Maybe he was a dragon.

"Ah good, everyone is here," Zmej said.

Remus started barking. He flew past Zo, almost cutting his legs out from under him. Up ahead, Remus got between Ryn and Zmej, barking and baring his teeth.

Zmej backhanded Remus, who yelped as he flew down the tunnel.

"I'll deal with you later," Zmej snarled at Remus.

"Foul creature, I'm not helping you," came a voice from behind the bars.

"Momma?" Ryn asked.

Ryette rushed forward, holding her hand up to shield her eyes from the light. How long had Zmej kept her in the dark? Zo wondered.

"Ryn!" Ryette reached through the bars and hugged her daughter. Both of them burst into tears.

"Zo?" Lar came to the bars, staring slack-jawed at his son. "I didn't think I'd ever see you again."

Zo took one step forward, but Giant Wolf growled.

Zmej pulled Ryn away from her mother's embrace. "So touching. Tell us the combination so that we can open the vault door."

"Take me with you, I'll show you," Ryette said.

Zmej put his hand around Ryn's throat. Fergus took a step forward, and Remus growled.

"No. Tell me now."

Ryn's hands scratched at Zmej's hands, her eyes bulging.

"I'm losing my patience." Zmej shook Ryn like a rag doll.

Lar pounded on the bars. "We each memorized a piece of the sequence. You need both of us."

Zmej's grin was cold. "I doubt that, but since you are all eager to suffer the same fate, why not?"

Jett took a key ring off the wall and unlocked the door.

Ryette engulfed Ryn in a hug. Lar wove his way between Fergus and Schiz to get to Zo. The look on his father's face was one Zo had never seen before, not even when Regg lay bleeding to death on his lap. Tears flowed freely down his cheeks, and Lar alternately wiped them with his hands like a small child. Lar embraced Zo, holding him tight like he was scared Zo was some image conjured by Zmej's magic.

"I thought I'd lost you," Lar said into Zo's neck.

Zo's skin tingled and his heart raced. His father had always been quiet and stoic. He'd never shown Zo any emotion except anger and disappointment. Zo squeezed his father tight. Memories of him in that darkened hallway of the Sano Healing House flooded his mind. He had been certain he'd never see his family again. He wanted to feel relieved, but he knew this might be the last time he hugged his father. Zo patted his father on the back then released him.

Jett and Ryn's words to each other echoed in Zo's mind. They all wanted Praedo's power. All of it. All of the magics. Travel, Healing, Fire, Water, Air, Earth, Lightening, Spirit, Shape shifting, Illusions, and Mind magic. If he could get a bead, and it would still teach him even though he was eighteen, he would be more powerful than any Patriarch or Library Curator, or Head of Council. And he was so close to it. Any moment now it could be all his. Zo's head spun.

The only thing that stood in his way was Zmej. Shadows and stories could lie. At the hot springs they'd seen that there are other types of magic out there in the world. Their only hope was if they could overpower Zmej. Maybe his behaviors just led people to believe he was a dragon.

"Moult!" Zmej yelled.

Zo started as Moult pushed past him down the tunnel. Zo hadn't realized Moult had followed them.

Zmej pointed his hand down the tunnel. "After you."

Moult looked at Ryette, whose deep frown conveyed much of her feeling toward Moult. Ryette pulled Ryn closer to her, protective arms wrapping around Ryn.

Moult nodded, then started into the darkness.

The group proceeded down the tunnel that wove its way to the left and the right, passing many branches that led off in different directions. Zo was so lost, there was no way he could find his way out without help. They finally came to branch off to the left. Moult held up his lantern. At the end of the tunnel was a small door made of stone, barely taller than Ryn. The tunnel narrowed down to the door.

Zo broke into a cold sweat. The full weight of the mountain pressed on him, but the door was there. His freedom was there, right in front of him. He could feel the power that laid beyond. It pulled to him. It sang to him. His healing would be complete. What Zmej and his wolves took from him, would finally be his again—and more. So much more! The feel of it made Zo salivate.

Zmej pushed Ryette forward. "Do your job."

Ryette stood in front of the door studying it. One hand brushed dust off the symbol on the door. The one with the Stone, the Sword, and the Branch. Her brow furrowed in an echo of the way Ryn's did.

"Do your part of the sequence. I need that door opened." Zmej took hold of Ryn again.

Zo and Fergus bristled.

Moult moved in next to Ryette. He was staring at her, while she stared at the door. She shook her head slightly. Zo remembered Moult had Mind magic. They were communicating.

"Open the door!" Zmej's finger became a claw that pressed into Ryn's throat.

Lar stepped forward. "These are metal hinges on the door. Maybe we can lift the door off the hinges?"

Moult shook his head. "I've tried. The door is too tightly fit into the doorway."

Blue fire erupted from Zmej's fingers. It shot toward the door and hit Lar square in the back. His coat burst into flames.

"Dad!" Zo shouted as he leapt forward. He put out his hand to absorb the fire. He wondered how much dragon fire would cook his insides, and if Master Ingis would chuckle when he told his future students about the idiot kid who thought he could extinguish dragon fire.

As Zo started pulling the fire from his dad's back into himself, a flood of inky black ice water washed down the tunnel, knocking everyone's feet out from under them and smashing Zo into the door. The water receded. Zo stood, shaking water off his hands as he held up a fireball. Schiz stood at the end of the tunnel next to Remus, who was shaking water out of his fur.

Zmej was steaming.

Actual steam was rising off him.

He put his fingers to his mouth and whistled. The sound was piercing. Ryn clutched her ears. Eyes shown in the dark. Remus's furious bark echoed down the tunnel as he turned and attacked the wolves behind him.

"I'll take care of this door. Melting it off its hinges won't hurt the most important object in that chamber." Zmej raised his hands. Blue fire danced around his fingers.

"Wait!" Ryn ran out in front of the door, just as Zmej released a stream of fire at it.

"No!" Zo and Fergus screamed.

Chapter Twenty-Six

Even if I could get around Zmej and the wolves to the door, I don't know how to open it!

- From the journals of Moult de Dico

Ryn threw her arms up as Zmej's blue fire raced toward her. This time she didn't have the Heart Tree's life water to protect her, and no amount of water Schiz could find in the cave was going to disperse that fire stream. It was strange. Ryn saw her mother, reaching for her like she could protect her. Lar firing a fireball at Zmej. Zo and Fergus were yelling something. Where had her father and Yll gone? Ryn watched the flame come down the tunnel toward her. She saw the hair standing up on her arm in the blue flame's light. She squinted her eyes. In a moment it would be over. *This is how it ends...*

The flames hit an invisible wall in front of Ryn and went out.

Ryn opened her eyes fully. Zmej and the others were on the other side of a wall that shimmered and flowed like water. Schiz's hand was pointed at her. She grinned her thanks. She didn't know how he did it, but she was grateful.

"Wait!" She shouted again as Zmej pointed his flames at her. "I think I have the answer to opening the door." Ryn pulled out Luc's journal, the one Lyssa had given her.

"You've got until my patience wears out." Zmej put his hands down.

Ryn turned to face the door.

Ryette and Lar stepped up beside her.

"What do you think you're doing?" Ryette whispered.

"I thought you knew how to open it," Ryn said.

"We were stalling. This is your father's work. I was counting on him opening this door," Ryette said.

"Where is he?" Ryn couldn't see beyond the light of fire in Lar's hands.

Lar shrugged. "I lost track of him when the tunnel flooded."

Ryn's fingers traced the carvings on the door. "There's a tree, the sword, and a stone—or maybe the tree is the branch. You said there's a sequence. What's the sequence?"

Lar shrugged. "We just said that to get Zmej to let us out."

"*Great.*" Ryn's frustration came as sarcasm.

A tiny bat fluttered in and hung upside down from the tunnel ceiling. Ryn raised her eyebrow at it, and the bat transformed into Yll.

"The bat's new," Ryn said.

Yll shrugged, pressing her hand to the carving. "I like to try new things."

Ryn started flipping through Luc's journal.

"Don't bother." Yll recited from memory:

> *"Follow these verses to where they shall end,*
> *Where both our stories shall join and resign,*
> *And may his old bones your strength now refine,*
> *When the dragon rises to battle again."*

"That's the one," Ryn said, as she ran her fingers over the carving then continued down the door.

Her fingers froze. Beads of sweat appeared on her forehead. It could be just the roughness of the stone, but it seemed too regular for that. She couldn't read the finger language, but she thought she recognized the pattern. She ran her fingers over the bumps on the title page of Luc's journal. It was a match: TLTRP.

"The Stone, the Sword, the Branch," Yll whispered as she examined the carving. "What's this?"

Ryn examined the spot Yll was pointing to. It looked like a divot in the stone.

Ryn pulled the stone out of her pocket. It fit perfectly into the divot, then melted into the stone door, morphing into a vertical crack, like someone had shoved a sword into the stone. Ryn ran her finger down the slot.

"Fergus!" she called.

Fergus started from his tense stance in the background. He had his hand on the grip of his side sword and was staring at Zmej like he was ready to pounce. It said a lot about Zmej's power that no one had taken Fergus's swords from him. Clearly Zmej wasn't threatened by them.

Ryn gently touched Fergus' arm, then traced her finger down the slot.

Fergus nodded. He unstrapped Praedo's sword from his back, pulled it from its sheath, and plunged it into the wall.

Nothing happened.

"What next?" Fergus asked.

Ryn ran her finger over the bumps on the door. "TLTRP."

"Turn it?" Yll suggested.

Fergus got a good grip on the sword and twisted his wrist. Nothing happened.

"Maybe he's not strong enough?" Lar suggested.

Fergus pursed his lips, but didn't say anything.

Zmej was right behind Ryn. She could feel his hot breath on her head.

"Give it to me." Zmej held out his hand.

Fergus hesitated.

Zmej back handed Fergus across the face, sending him stumbling backward away from the door.

Zmej grabbed the sword's grip, and immediately released it, shaking out his hand.

"How is there a dragon slayer's sword here? The only one on this planet is buried in the place my mate was murdered," Zmej yelled.

Ryn tilted her head to one side, and raised an eyebrow at Yll, who shrugged. Ryn looked back at Ryette and Lar. Ryette raised her hands. Ryn knew Praedo's sword that Fergus had was real, but the origin was where Zmej's...mate? Lover?...was killed? A memory of Lyssa talking about the destruction of a dragon egg as a way to kill dragons. Was that real?

"I'm done with this." Zmej brought fire to his hands.

Ryn grabbed the sword. "TLTRP," she whispered. The sword began to glow.

What does it mean? What does it mean?
Blue light sharpened her shadow on the wall.
Turn.
The word came to her mind. "Turn left." She twisted the sword to the left. "Turn Right." A twist to the right. "P." She stopped.

"Push!" Yll yelled.

Ryn shoved hard on the sword, but it slid easily into the door.

The carvings in the door glowed white just before the door began to glow.

"That's it!" Zmej pushed Ryn out of the way.

He reached out to push open the door just as the light from the door reached full intensity.

Ryn squinted her eyes and held up her hand to the light.

Right when Zmej touched the door, light and power shot out from it.

Zmej took the full impact of the power. It was like Zmej's blue fireballs, but in the form of a giant wave. It burst forth from the door and, faster than lightning, its impact sent everyone flying back down the tunnel. Remus yipped in surprise. They all crumpled to the ground—except Ryn. She stood there, heart pounding. What happened? They all looked pale in the light of the door.

Zmej stirred.

Ryn swallowed.

Push, came the word to her mind again.

She pushed her palm into the symbol on the door and it melted away around her. She stumbled forward into a cave brightly lit by the glow of a being who seemed to be completely spirit...and Ryn recognized him from the painting door in Kay's office.

"Luc?"

He turned a smiling face toward her. His hand was upon a large cask on a stone altar in front of him.

"Are those...the beads?" Ryn drifted forward, reaching out her hand to lift the lid off the cask.

The image of Luc shook his head and pointed toward the hole in the doorway that Ryn had come through.

Zmej appeared there, fire steaming off of him.

"At last!" Zmej knocked Ryn into the wall as he scooped up the cask. "Where is it?" he yelled, looking behind the altar and running his hands along the walls. "I know you have it, you bastard, give it to me!"

Zmej's hand found a spot in the wall that melted away around it. There, in a small alcove, sat what looked like a stained-glass window blown into a ball the shape of an egg. Bits of orange swirled in what looked like glass. Inside, something moved.

"Evren!" Tears flowed down Zmej's face.

He set the cask of beads down and cupped the glassy egg to him.

Ryn took a step back when a sob escaped Zmej's lips. He curled around the egg and rocked it back and forth.

"Evren, my love, I will keep this one safe. This one will survive. This one will eat the blood of that tree. I will make sure of it. I will burn that cursed Library down and the ashes of the tree will nurture our son. This time I won't fail." Zmej rocked back and forth, his hands producing flames that made the egg glow.

Ryn crept forward, slowly reaching her hand toward the cask of beads. Zmej continued to cry and rock the egg. She was almost there. Her fingers touched it...

Zmej turned on her. "Child of this abominable world that took my life-mate," he snarled, snatching up the beads. "I will at last exact my revenge, and with this, no one can stop me." He held up the cask and stormed out the door.

Ryn followed him out into the tunnel. The others were starting to move, shaking their heads, or favoring an arm or a leg.

"Stop him! He's got the beads!" Ryn yelled.

Zo got to his feet and started toward Zmej, who shot a trio of fireballs at him in rapid succession, knocking Zo off his feet again.

"Oh no you don't." Zmej held up the cask. "I shall enjoy picking my teeth with the last Heart Tree's charred branches."

Ryn cocked her head at that statement. The tree's branches weren't toothpick size.

Jett appeared in front of Zmej. "Give me my reward. I have earned it."

Zmej looked down his nose at Jett. "No one can have this power. It's the last thing standing between me and that tree. I made sure House Viator couldn't add magic to themselves, and now I will make sure the last of that idiot dragon slayer is gone. I will finally bring this world to its knees as I promised the dragon horde I would. I have waited long for this moment, out of my way." With that Zmej knocked Jett into the wall.

There was a sickening crunch with Jett's impact.

Ryette screamed and ran to Jett. Ryn's heart raced as she took a step toward them.

Zmej whistled and wolves formed a screen to block the tunnel. He walked through them and into the darkness.

Lar and Zo both swore.

The wolves paced back and forth, keeping their eyes on all of them. Remus growled. The wolf that was the largest, the one Jett had called Zmej's first born, came from the back of the pack to stand in front of the rest. He locked eyes with Ryette. She gasped.

Then he turned and started barking at the wolves, growling and foaming. The wolves backed away. The giant wolf chased them down the tunnel. There was yipping and yelping, then silence.

Out of the darkness the giant wolf returned with a huge grin on its face.

The wolf sat and morphed into Moult, Ryn's father.

Ryn gasped and ran forward, throwing her arms around him. "How did you do that?"

Moult shrugged. "I coaxed the big one to chase me back to the cage Zmej had set up for Ryette. I locked the wolf in and came back in disguise. I used my mind magic to communicate with them and convinced them to leave."

Ryn clapped her hands like a little girl. "Brilliant!"

"Hurry, we've got to catch Zmej before he leaves with those beads." Zo ran past everyone down the tunnel.

"Wait—you don't know where you're going!" Moult shouted and ran after him.

Ryn started to follow, but something caught her eye. Luc's spirit was standing in the melted bead chamber doorway beckoning to her. She went to him. He put his hands on her shoulders. She felt nothing, because he was just a spirit, but when he pressed his lips to her forehead, she could feel a warmth flood her from the place where his lips touched, flowing down her face, her neck, into her body, arms and legs. Energy surged through her like she hadn't felt since she was a small child. Then he hugged her to him, briefly before letting her go. He gave her the stone, then squeezed something else into her hand, pressing a finger to his lips as if to tell her to be quiet, and winked at her.

Then he was gone.

Ryn turned to find everyone had followed Zo and Moult. She ran to catch up.

Remus was waiting for her at the first tunnel junction. He turned and she followed him. She was running as fast as she could to keep up with him. They turned a corner, and the tunnel opened up into the largest cave Ryn had ever seen. The walls sparkled in the light of Zo and Lar's fire. They had Zmej surrounded.

"You're trapped. Give us the beads," Zo said.

Zmej laughed.

Something in the air shifted and changed. It was like the air in the cave was being sucked toward Zmej. Ryn's hair whipped at her face, her skirt slapping at her legs. Remus leapt at Zmej just when a burst of power, like what came out of the door—only a cloud instead of a wave—swirled around Zmej. Remus hit it and bounced off.

The cloud of energy grew and expanded, till it almost filled the entire cavern. The others ducked or rolled out of the way.

Then the cloud collapsed and what it left behind...Ryn had only seen in paintings, especially on the ceiling of the Library foyer.

It was a dragon.

Huge and horned, it was a black nightmare lizard with wings. It sucked in air till Ryn was gasping for breath, then it screeched so loud her hands shot to her ears. With the screech, came fire blasted at the cave wall. The rock melted into a giant hole.

The dragon popped the cask of beads held in its talons into his mouth. He chewed, turned to give Ryn a wicked pointy-toothed grin, then took off through the newly formed hole in the mountainside, clutching the glass blown egg to his chest.

Ryn collapsed to her knees, her mouth working without sound. Out of the corner of her eye she glimpsed Zo lying on his side, shielding his eyes from the outside brightness streaming into the no longer dark cave.

The beads were gone. They were Zo's last hope. She knew she should be worried about Waatch, and the Library, and the Heart Tree, but watching Zo's hope of healing fly away was like a knife to her gut. Tears welled up in her eyes, and she looked away back toward the open door. She took deep breaths to try and hide the fact that she was crying.

Fergus swore.

Zmej's wolves, who had entered the chamber in time to watch him take flight, took off down the tunnel that led from the chamber, yipping and barking like they were off for a fine day of play.

Ryn squeezed the object in her palm tight, then opened her hand. There it sat. Zo's hope was gone, but Ryn's was in the palm of her hand. The spirit of Luc had given her a bead. It was the last bead now. Praedo's bead looked different from any others she had seen. The bone was discolored with age, which made her wonder how long ago the Ancestor's beads were made. This bead was smooth, but irregular. It was her redemption. From now on no one could exclude her. She held in her hand greater power than anyone else had seen in two millennia. She squeezed her hand tight, wondering if she could start her lessons fast enough to protect the Library and the Heart Tree from Zmej.

"Where do you think he's gone?" Lar asked, looking up through the hole in the ceiling.

"To burn down the Library and the Heart Tree so he can hatch his dragon egg," Ryn said.

"What?" Ryette said.

"Dragon egg?" Yll asked.

Ryn stared up at the blue sky through the hole above her. "It's what Zmej was really after. There was an egg in the wall of the room."

Moult mopped at his forehead with a handkerchief. "How did we miss that? I've searched every record there is, every journal of Luc's. He never mentioned an egg."

"Except one small mention in an obscure book about killing dragons which apparently nobody took seriously, because it resides with an outcast girl on the fourth floor of the Library." Ryn's eyes dropped to her father's.

Zo swore.

"Zmej was crying over the egg," Ryn said.

Moult paced the cave floor. "The tree, the Library...the ancient dragon."

"Evren was what Zmej called her," Ryn said.

"A female dragon?" Ryette grabbed Moult's arm, stopping him.

His jaw was working.

"Considering how many wolves there are, Zmej must not be missing her that much." Zo's gaze fell on Remus, who whined and sat next to Schiz.

"Or he does too much," Fergus said next to Ryn, his hand lightly brushing her arm.

"Wait, wait, wait." Yll rubbed her forehead. "So the old dragon that Praedo killed was a female dragon, who had laid an egg...here?" Her gesture included the cave and the mountain.

Ryn shook her head. "Zmej said something about burning down the Library and needing the ashes of the tree to hatch the egg. I can only assume he means the Heart Tree."

Moult's eyes got wide. "The Library to protect the tree—this Evren was going to lay her egg in the Heart Tree, but Praedo killed her."

"So how did the egg end up here?" Yll asked.

Ryn's brow furrowed. "Luc must have brought it here for safe keeping. Maybe destroying an egg isn't as easy as the Killing Dragons book suggests."

"It doesn't matter now." Lar put a protective arm around Ryette. "The dragon Zmej wants to burn down the Library and hatch an egg in the tree. We need to return to Waatch as quickly as possible."

"We're going...to need help," Schiz spoke up.

"I've already set that in motion. I sent my brother Mik to my mother when I realized what we were up against. Help should already be in motion, we just need to point it in the right direction," Ryette said.

Ryn's gaze took in everyone gathered in their little circle. She swallowed hard, as her chest tingled and her heart pounded. She could lose someone in this circle fighting the dragon. She gulped for air and reached out a hand to Fergus. He took the hand and kissed it.

"I'm here," he whispered.

"Let's get back to Waatch," Lar said.

Yll's weight shifted legs. "I'll leave now. I'll see you all there." She turned into a hawk and flew out the hole Zmej had created.

"I'll join her." Moult said as he turned into an eagle and soared up through the ceiling.

"How are the rest of us going to get back, mama? You can't take all of us," Ryn asked.

"Remus and I will find our way." Schiz stepped forward, knelt before Ryn, pressed his forehead to her hand, then disappeared down a tunnel with Remus. The wolf whined as he looked back at Ryn, before the darkness took him.

"That's still too many," Lar said.

Something moved in a dark corner of the cave. "I can take you." Jett stepped into the light.

Zo shifted. He opened his mouth, but Ryette cut him off.

"Great, you take Lar and Fergus. I'll take Ryn and Zo. We'll meet at Thax's shop," Ryette said.

Jett's head hung low as he nodded. He reached out his arms and engulfed Lar and Fergus. The air swirled and they disappeared.

Ryn's mother held out her arms to Ryn.

A thought struck Ryn. "Wait! What happened to Maus?"

Ryette shook her head. "Who?"

"Zmej... he had a boy...girl..child with him. What happened to them?" Ryn asked.

Ryette shook her head. "I saw a girl early on in our chase, but I haven't seen her since."

Ryn fought back tears. One more casualty of the dragon. She clenched her fist around her bead, and ran to her mother, who swept them up into the swirl of Traveling as Ryn fell into her arms.

Chapter Twenty-Seven

I'm sending my journal to Clayr at the Library, and praying to the ancestors someone can come to help.

- From the journals of Moult de Dico

Zo's heart squeezed in his chest as Ryette's Travel magic battered him on the outside. He had seen a real live dragon, but his mind was on the cask of beads the dragon swallowed. His one hope to restore his Healing magic and clear his name. The loss of those beads meant more than the victory of the dragon, it meant his life would never be what he had come to want. He had trained with Wilmar and could become a physician, healing with no magic—but would House Sano let him live once all was said and done? And would anyone in Waatch trust someone to heal them when he had been accused of murder? Of course there was always his Fire magic. It was unlikely the Library would allow him back into the Boiler Room, but he could do as his father had done—burn fields, clear brush, and fight fires. It was funny because a year ago that was all he wanted to do. Fire had made him feel powerful. Now it seemed like a step back, a let down. The thought of leaving Waatch, Iden, Ryn, Regg, Wilmar, and Nix was like a knife wound to his chest. He never thought he would want so badly to have the ability to Heal.

The swirling stopped outside of Thax's shop in Waatch. Ryette let go of them, pressing her hand to her chest, looking breathless. Instinctively Zo reached out his hand to check on her, then remembered he couldn't use his magic on someone else, and pulled it back.

Ryette saw it and held up her hand. "It's alright, traveling this distance is just a bit tiring. Give me a moment."

The bell tinkled as the Thax's door burst open and Clayr emerged from the shop.

"Oh my goodness! I was so afraid I would never see you all again." Clayr tried to wrap her arms around everyone, but her arms didn't reach.

Clayr put her hand on Zo's cheek. There were tears in her eyes.

"Where's Yll?" Clayr asked.

"On her way," Ryette said.

"What's happening?" Lar asked.

Clayr gaze shifted to Zo, then looked up and down the street. "Come inside."

* * *

Thax's shop was in a state of organized chaos. Display mannequins were shoved toward the front of the store. Bolts of fabric were stacked off to one side. In the middle of the shop was Thax's worktable from the back of the shop. On the table was what looked like a map of Waatch. Standing around at one end of the table having a heated discussion was Iden, Regg, Thax, Jak, Dan, and Tory. When Tory saw them enter, she crossed the shop to Ryn and engulfed her in a hug.

Iden let out a whoop and rushed Zo, causing Zo to stumble back into the mannequin with the white and black patched cow skin dress.

Zo opened his mouth to say something. He couldn't remember what, because Iden was kissing him so hard their teeth clanked together. When they finally broke apart, Zo was breathless.

"I missed you too," Zo gasped.

Iden threw his head back and laughed, then wrapped his arms tight around Zo. "I was so worried."

I'm here, Zo said into Iden's mind. It was so nice to feel that mental closeness again.

Thax came over and wrapped his arms around the both of them. "Ah, young love." He squeezed them both.

Zo laughed.

The bell tinkled again and Lar and Fergus entered. Jett stood outside on the street.

"Excuse me," Ryette said as she went out the door to her son.

Tory and Ryn were chatting excitedly. Fergus had his arm around Ryn's shoulders as he glared at Jak and Dan, who were deep in conversation, ignoring Fergus.

"Why are we here?" Zo asked Clayr.

"When in exile, dress fashionably," Thax answered as he moved to join the rest of the crowd at the table. "Tory dear, will you get some chamomile going for everyone?"

Tory glared at him. "I will not. I'm not your tea fetcher."

Ryn took Tory's hand. "I'll help."

The two of them climbed the stairs to Thax's living quarters.

A gray streak shot across the floor from the back room and leapt up on the table, batting his paws at the map's rolled up corner.

"Jinx!" Zo shouted, scooping the kitten up in his arms. "You little ball of havoc, I've missed you so much."

Zo smothered the kitten with kisses, then placed Jinx on his back in the crook of Zo's arm. Jinx tolerated the belly rubs for a moment, then wriggled out of Zo's arms and ran back behind the curtain into the back room. Zo smelt his hands.

"Why does Jinx smell like the hot springs?" he asked.

Thax swore. "He's gotten into my sulfur again!" He followed Jinx into the back.

"Sulfur?" Zo asked.

Ryette entered the shop with Jett on her arm.

Ryn and Tory came down the stairs with a tea pot and some mugs.

"Gather around please," Clayr said, waving everyone to join her at the table.

Iden kept his arm around Zo's waist as they stepped up to the table.

Clayr turned to Ryette. "Report. What happened out there?"

"Zmej is a dragon," Ryette said.

Thax and Tory gasped. Jak threw his head back and laughed.

"Of course he is," Jak said.

Ryn narrowed her eyes at Jak over a mug of tea.

Clayr frowned. "So it's true. There is a dragon and he might attack."

Lar cleared his throat. "Will attack. I'm surprised he's not here already."

Clayr's gaze took in the group newly returned from the cave out on the peninsula.

"He told us he would burn down the Library and the Heart Tree to incubate his dragon egg," Ryn said.

Dan leaned in over the map. "Dragon egg, interesting." His eye locked on Jak's. They were clearly Mind talking to each other.

Ryette placed her hands on the table. "A quick summary is: the dragon of old was Zmej's mate. An egg was produced and was supposed to be incubated in the burning of the Heart Tree, but Praedo killed her. Looks like Luc hid the egg from Zmej and he's been searching for it ever since."

Regg ran his hands over where the Library was on the map. "So every Heart Tree on this world was killed to incubate a dragon egg."

Everybody turned to stare at Regg.

"What?" Regg shrugged. "I was listening at the apple farm."

Zo swore.

"By the Ancestors," Fergus said.

Lar held up his hands. "Doesn't matter. What matters is we need to protect Waatch, the Library, and the tree from an incoming dragon."

"How do we do that?"

Everyone turned to see Jett, leaning up against a stack of bolts of fabric holding a mug of tea. His eyes looked distant, like his mind wasn't present.

Fergus folded his arms. "You tell us."

Jett's laugh sounded hollow. "I wouldn't know."

Jak stepped around the table, stopping right in front of Jett.

"Where's Maus?" Jak demanded.

"I don't know what you're talking about," Jett sipped his mug of tea.

Jak knocked it out of his hands. "Liar. You killed those people and you kidnapped Maus for Zmej. I have proof it was you." He grabbed Jett by the jacket and got right up in Jett's face. "I'll only ask one more time. Where's Maus?"

"Who? The little girl?" Jett asked.

Jak and Dan exchanged looks. "Who told you she was a girl? No one knows that but us."

"The dragon knew. He knows everything. He made her put on a dress."

Jak shoved Jett away from him. "I'll kill him."

Dan punched Jett in the face. "Where is Maus!"

"Hey!" Lar yelled.

Ryette ran over. Dan held her back.

Jett rubbed his jaw. "Exile. He left her on the island of Exile."

Thax whistled. "Ancestors help the dragon."

"I don't think they would," Iden said.

"Let's go." Jak grabbed Dan's arm.

"We'll deal with you later," Dan spat at Jett.

"I'm coming too!" Tory ran up to them.

Jett smiled. "Good riddance. You'll never come back from that place. No one is allowed to leave."

Jak glanced at Clayr. She shook her head.

"Come on, I helped you out. A pardon from the Curator of the Library could free Maus," Jak plead.

"I'm not the curator anymore."

Jak gave her a lopsided grin. "They don't know that."

Ryn put her hand on Clayr's shoulder. "Please. Maus is a friend."

Clayr turned to Ryn, then her shoulders slumped. "Alright, give me my bag. I'll write a pardon."

Once Clayr was finished, Jak, Dan, and Tory were out the door. Right after they left, the bells tinkled again.

"Did you forget something?" Ryn called.

But it wasn't Jak and Dan, it was the Waatch guard. "We're here to collect a murderer."

Zo ducked behind Iden.

Jett ran for the back room. Before anyone could move, he was out the back door and gone. Ryette ran after, and Lar followed her.

The guards were right behind them.

* * *

Sometime after the Waatch guard finished questioning everyone, Yll and Moult flew in.

Yll's gaze took in everyone in the room. "What did we miss?"

Clayr ran over and crushed Yll to her. "I'll tell you later."

Regg was next. He enfolded Yll in a hug and rocked her back and forth, kissing her on the head. He was whispering something in her ear that Zo couldn't hear.

Yll slapped him on the shoulder. "So I still don't get my whatever it is you have for me?"

Regg blushed.

Clayr cleared her throat. "Now that everyone is here— Where's the beads?"

"The dragon ate them," Lar said.

Iden moaned and put his arm around Zo's shoulders pressing his temple to Zo's.

I'm so sorry, Wildfire.

Zo didn't respond. His hands and feet had gone cold and his stomach dropped. Standing in the cave it had seemed surreal. Here in Thax's store it was all too real. It was over. House Sano would come for him. Maybe it was best if he died fighting the dragon.

I don't like that thinking, Iden thought at him.

Clayr took a deep breath and closed her eyes. When she opened them, they sparkled. Zo couldn't tell if it was determination or tears.

"No matter. The dragon is coming to burn the Library down and we must prepare to fight him." Clayr's voice rang out loud and clear. "Are you with me?"

"Yes!" Thax's place rang with their voices.

Zo shoved his disappointment aside and joined in with a resounding, "Yes!"

Chapter Twenty-Eight

For many long months we searched without rest,
Yet our labor was noble, our purpose true;
Through villages freed from the shadow's cruel hue,
We struck at the curse that oppressed the oppressed.

Gesta Praediana—Luc's Epic Poem

"First things first, we need to take back the Library," Ryette said, her voice flat.

Ryn watched her mother carefully. Ryette had returned without Jett. Her posture was uncharacteristically stooped, and worry lines ran across her forehead. She was standing at the table with her hand over the Library on the map, but Ryn could tell her mind was elsewhere.

Ryn didn't understand. Her brother Jett had been incredibly stupid, and had sided with the dragon in the name of power. Somehow his longing for his second magic had consumed him enough that he wanted more—or maybe it was their grandmother's attempt at imprinting more magic upon him. He had seemed off since then. His lust for Praedo's beads was his undoing. Ryn had a hard time feeling bad for him. She couldn't understand why her mother would still care after all the awful things Jett had done.

"Impossible. Jeris has control of the Library," Clayr said.

Fergus shifted. "If I may, Madame Curator—the guard is on your side. Say the word and we'll come to your aid."

Clayr shook her head. "But Jeris has sway over the Ancestor workers. They won't follow me."

"I think there's more support there than you think, and once the workers hear a dragon is coming, I bet they abandon Jeris quickly." Iden jammed his finger on the center of the map which was the Library.

Moult rubbed his chin. "I've been away for a long time, but the Library leadership in Sooke always supported you. I bet you could rally them."

"Yes! My parents would return in a heartbeat. Let's message them," Iden said.

Ryette took Clayr's hands. "It's our only hope. We must go to the Library and call an all-hands meeting. We need to persuade the workers to follow you to fight the dragon, or leave."

Clayr's hands gripped the table. She put her head down and took a deep breath. "Alright. Iden, you contact your parents and have them gather as many supporters as they can from Sooke. Have them meet us at first bell. Fergus, take the word to the Library guard. All hands meeting in the meeting hall when the bell rings for the start of the day."

Lar opened his mouth, then frowned.

"What?" Clayr asked.

Ryette answered, "We don't know when the dragon is going to attack. Shouldn't we call the meeting for closing bell tonight?"

"No. Closing bell tonight is not enough time to gather the numbers of supporters we need here. We'll just have to risk a possible dragon attack in the night."

Ryn took a deep breath and resisted the urge to pace the room.

"I'm on it." Fergus strapped Praedo's sword to his back and headed for the door, stopping when he got to Ryn.

He scooped Ryn up and held her tight. "I'll come find you when I can."

She held him tighter. She wanted to keep him there with her. She wanted to protect him. That seemed like an absurd idea, but it was what she felt.

"Be safe," Ryn said.

He let her go and was out the door. Ryn was glad he didn't look back. She wasn't sure she'd have let him leave if he did.

"While you work on your speech, I have the perfect outfit for you." Thax moved the cow dress mannequin aside and dug through a rack of dresses.

Ryn pulled out the paper of notes from the Killing Dragons book. "Thax? Do you have more of that cow hide?"

Thax waved his hand toward the back room. "Sure, loads of it. It's for my coming fall collection."

Ryn scooped the rotten egg-smelling Jinx off the floor. "I think I'm going to need it."

* * *

Visitors came and went all night to Thax's shop. Brynd got back from running errands early enough to help Ryn cut and stitch together cow hide. Thax wasn't thrilled. He complained about how much time he'd spent selecting the perfect pieces for his new fall designs. Ryn kept reminding him it was for a good cause.

Zo and Iden were deep in conversation over a map of the Library that Errol, Captain of the Library guard, had brought. They paused, looking into each other's eyes. Iden went in for a kiss when the doorbell jangled.

Nix entered eyes wide. He crossed the floor in two strides, grabbed Iden by the scruff of his neck and threw him out of the way. Nix engulfed Zo in a hug. Zo's arms and red face said Nix was crushing him. Tears glistened on Nix's face when he let Zo go, holding him at arm's length.

Nix opened his mouth to say something, but instead, crushed Zo to him again.

"Alright, alright, you're going to suffocate the boy," Wilmar said, putting his hand on Nix and moving him out of the way. "My turn."

Wilmar embraced Zo, whispering something into his ear that Ryn could not hear.

Nix blew his nose. "You came back and you didn't tell us."

Zo turned red while Wilmar still hugged him.

"House Sano still wants him dead. We were trying to keep his location quiet," Iden said.

Zo grabbed the edge of the table as he lost his balance when Wilmar finally let go. "It's good to know you're missed."

Ryn giggled, then went to give Nix and Wilmar her own hugs.

Nix took Zo by the chin and examined his face closely. "You look well."

Zo frowned. "Well enough until House Sano catches up with me."

Nix folded his impressively thick arms. "They'll have to get through me. I'm not losing my grunt again."

Zo rolled his eyes, while Ryn pulled Wilmar aside. "We went after Praedo's beads. Zo thought the beads would restore his Healing magic, and get House Sano off his back. The dragon ate the beads."

Wilmar gazed at Zo, wiping his eyes again. "I'm just glad he's alive. We'll give him Nix and my cabin in the woods. He can stay there. It's well hidden. No one will find him."

Ryn nodded, her hand feeling for Praedo's bead in her pocket. The magic she had always wanted, and she didn't feel sick handling it like she did the Ancestor beads they had tried to give her on Viatoro. The magic would work for her, she was sure of it. Everything she had always wanted. No one would make fun of her again. Prym and her father would *have* to respect her.

She watched Nix enfold Zo in another hug, mussing up Zo's hair like he was a little boy. Zo's smile was lopsided. The weight of everything was in the creases around his eyes, and the tightness of his jaw. He was going to fight the dragon with a death sentence from House Sano hanging over his head. Ryn feared Zo would see he had no reason to make it out of the battle alive.

The doorbell chimed and everyone froze as Schiz and Remus walked through the door. Errol drew his sword, but Moult put a hand on his arm.

Ryn ran to embrace Schiz and Remus. "You made it! How did you make it so fast? That walk takes days."

Schiz tapped the side of his head. "We found our way out of the cave...Remus reminded me I used to Travel magic. Said no...can't...broken...but I did it."

Schiz's wide smile lit up the room.

Ryn clapped her hands and gave him a hug.

"A wolf? I don't recall anyone mentioning a wolf." Clayr frowned.

"Sorry! Yes, this is Schiz and Remus. They're with us," Ryn said.

"One wolf against however many Zmej has isn't much, but I guess we'll take it," Clayr said. "What about magic? We need magic."

"My brother has gone to gather as many from the Ancestral Islands as he can," Ryette said.

Clayr nodded but the frown on her face conveyed her skepticism. "Hopefully they get here soon."

Errol stepped forward and pointed to the Library map on the table. Everyone gathered around. "Our biggest problem is that the dragon attacks from the sky. We don't have any defenses for aerial attacks."

Clayr shared a look with Ryette. "The Library holds many secrets only the Curator knows. Hidden in the attic of the Library are harpoons, bigger than the ones for giant fish, plus other equipment to launch giant fireballs." She pointed to the Library roof. "Here, here, and here the roof slides away to allow for the defense of the Library against a flying attack. I didn't see any use for it till now. I'm grateful the Ancestors prepared for a distant future."

"The Boiler Room is loyal to me. I will bring my grunts to man the fireball launchers," Nix said.

Errol nodded, stroking his chin. "The Library guard will man the harpoons."

Clayr held up her hands. "First, we have to take back control of the Library. If we don't have the majority of the worker's support, we will lose the battle."

Errol grunted. "You will need to present the workers with their marching orders when they agree. We need to plan out every detail."

Errol and Clayr went on to debate logistics.

Ryn yawned. She made sure Brynd had all the pieces she needed for her sewing project then headed up the stairs for some quiet. She was running out of time to learn the magic from the bead. She had to start now and hope she could learn enough to help fight the dragon. She got to the top of the stairs and closed the door to the room her and Brynd had briefly shared. Abby and Beardsley were both laying on the bed. Their eyes glanced at her sleepily. Ryn ran over and petted both of them, praising them, and telling them how much she missed them. Abby stretched lazily and meowed at her. She probably wanted to eat. Ryn stood to go find some food in the kitchen, but Beardsley's yellow eyes held hers. He was Zo's older cat. He'd known Zo longer than Ryn did. His eyes were wide, but his face said nothing, and yet in his eyes Ryn saw Zo as a little boy wanting to play with fire, and hating his healing. Zo fighting to heal the lady they found stabbed on the street. Zo with dark circles under his eyes, unable to heal Ryn from the cart accident. She put her hand over the scar her sleeve hid. She dreaded the warmer weather and the short sleeves that would reveal it to him.

She nodded to Beardsley and went back downstairs.

* * *

A small, cold hand took Zo's. He looked over to find Ryn there. She was pale and her frown was deep. When she looked up into his eyes, they were glassy with unshed tears. He thought he should comfort her in some way, but it just wasn't in him at the moment. She tugged on his hand and dragged him up the stairs to a small bedroom. She pulled him inside and shut the door.

"Beardsley!" He scooped up the cat and kissed him all over his head. "I've missed you so much."

He buried his face in Beardsley's fur. Tears prickled his eyes as he wished for his old life back.

"You too, Abby." Zo petted Ryn's cat.

"What's up, parva sor?" Zo asked, sitting on the bed, loving on both cats.

Ryn paced, her hands clenched in fists. She brought one hand to her forehead. "Ancestors help me," she whispered.

Zo stopped, his insides squirming. "Tell me."

With tears streaming down her face, she opened her palm to reveal one bead of bone sitting in the center. She had clutched it so hard it left an imprint on her palm.

"Is that...no, it can't be," he said.

She nodded. "In the bead chamber I saw Luc as a spirit. Right before we left, he appeared to me again—and put this in my hand."

"You've been holding onto it since the cave. Ancestor beads make you sick. How are you not sick?" Zo asked.

She shrugged. "It's not an Ancestor bead. It's from Praedo."

Zo stared at it in wonder. The legendary beads. His one hope. The hope that was lost.

"This is great! You can use it to gain all the magic and maybe we can defeat the dragon." Zo grinned.

"Take it." Ryn held out her palm to him. "Heal your magic."

Zo froze. His chest tightened.

"No." His shaky voice sounded distant in his own ears.

"I want you to have it." Ryn reached for Zo's hand.

He whipped it out of her reach.

"*No*. This is your dream, Ryn. Your chance. Everything you've ever wanted. *All the magic.*" He stared into her tear-filled eyes. "I won't take this chance from you."

He watched Ryn swallow. "I know. It seems ridiculous to give up such power, but...I can see it in your eyes. I know what you're planning. You think dying a hero will be better than at the hands of House Sano, but I got a taste of life without you in it and I don't want to do that again. I can't. *I won't.*"

She grabbed his hand and pressed the bead into it. "Praedo come! Teach my brother your magic!"

Zo stared at the small bead. So tiny, yet so much power within.

Ryn searched through the drawers in the room. "There has to be some cording here somewhere..."

He had wanted the power so badly, but now—the potential was terrifying.

He opened his mouth to say, "I can't" and hand it back to Ryn, but everything went black.

* * *

Zo was floating, but not in water. His feet didn't touch any floor, yet he was still upright. Blackness surrounded him, with an incalculable number of pinpoints of light. Somehow, he got the impression they were stars, but the light didn't dance the way it does on a dark starry night. He shook his head and tried to clear it, to make the light of the room return, but the velvety blackness remained.

"It's beautiful really—all that water," a deep male voice said behind him.

Zo floated around to see a glowing, curved sphere that spanned the horizon. It was blue, and green, with white streaking across it like a marble.

Standing in the darkness was a man, one arm folded, the other propped against his chin, contemplating. Zo took in his sandy-blond-e hair and his chiseled features, and recognized him instantly from so many statues and paintings.

"By the Ancestors," Zo gasped.

Praedo turned to face him, chuckling. "They would have loved that their descendants swear by them."

Zo felt himself blush. He couldn't believe he was feeling intimidated by this person so many worshiped as the savior from the dragon, so he turned his gaze upon the sphere.

"What is this place?" He wondered.

"Oh—that's your world. It looks quite different from space." Praedo resumed his contemplation of the sphere.

Zo wasn't sure if he believed Praedo, but it certainly was a strange experience.

"Why am I here?" Zo asked.

Praedo shifted his contemplation to Zo. "Perspective."

Zo rubbed at his eyebrow.

"Holding one of my beads is a lot of power, and you should see what's at stake to protect. I came to this world to help defend it against the dragon. Zmej arrived on your world with the first dragon. They were slowly killing every Heart Tree filled with the native magic of your world. The trees were good nourishment for their offspring. They had to be stopped. Your world and its magic was dying with each tree's death. I drew a proverbial line in the sand here with the Library's tree. I was able to kill the dragon and take her egg, but Zmej was furious. He was positioning to take another tree out there across the ocean to the west when she died. My only regret is that Evern took me with her. I hoped bestowing my power upon my companions would combine with the natural Wild magic to defeat Zmej. Unfortunately, Zmej sowed the seeds of discord between the local population and my companion's descendants. That rift needs to be healed if you are to save the tree."

"What can we do? I've fought him, he's too strong. We can't even stop his children." Zo cracked his knuckles against his leg.

Praedo's eyes followed Zo's hand hitting his leg. Zo stopped.

"You managed to kill one of his children." Praedo's eyes shifted Zo's.

"And destroyed my Healing magic in the process."

Praedo nodded slowly. "Sometimes the consequences are heavy."

"Am I going to get it back now?" Zo couldn't keep the hopeful rise out of his voice.

"You have my magic. A power that hasn't been seen in generations. You will learn a great many things."

"But Zmej is about to attack the Library now. How can I use a magic I haven't learned?"

Praedo inhaled, as if waking from a dream. "We're going to do a bit of on-the-job training."

Praedo's grin was definitely a bit unhinged.

Fantastic. I'm about to learn the most powerful magic from this spirit, Zo thought.

"But first..." Praedo's hand swept across the glowing sphere. "Remember what's at stake."

"Oh," Praedo paused. "And tell my granddaughter I'm so proud."

* * *

When Zo's eyes fluttered closed, Ryn grabbed his arm, guiding his body down onto the bed. She put her hand on his chest as his breathing became quiet and regular.

Ryn stood, her hand covering her mouth. She couldn't believe she'd done it. She couldn't believe she'd given up her one chance at magic. She squeezed her eyes shut as tears poured down her cheeks. There was nothing left for her. She was still the orphan drifting through life with no anchor. She loved her parents, and she knew they loved her, had chosen her, but there was still that disconnect. Her grandmother's rejection of her had proved that. It would have been nice to not need ancestors to have magic. To have it straight from Praedo. No one could dispute her power.

She looked down at Zo and remembered how lost she felt when they took him away. Wandering the streets hoping he'd just appear around the next corner. No matter what choice she made she lost in the end. She chose Zo. Her life didn't really matter, but his did. She would do whatever it took to keep him in her life, and now he would be the most powerful Ancestor descendant since the original group of twelve. No one could touch him. Not anymore. That thought brought her peace.

She closed the door to the room and went downstairs. She didn't know how long his lesson would take. She hoped it wouldn't be long, as the night was quickly passing. Soon it would be morning and they would go to the Meeting Hall, and hope everyone would follow Clayr.

* * *

"I thought you said you were going to train me while I fought," Zo said to Praedo. The ghostly figure was dressed in the same old style as Master Ingis—short pants cut off at the knee and a shirt with long flowing sleeves, but with an otherworldly flair. The scarf at his neck shimmered in a way Zo had never seen any fabric do before.

Zo was glad Thax couldn't see the scarf. Thax would drive himself mad attempting to replicate it.

Praedo cleared his throat. "Yes, well—it's been so long since I trained anyone in magic, I almost forgot this step is critical. I'm a two-thousand-year-old spirit of the best dragon slayer there ever was, things are a bit hazy. Patience, dragons like to play with their food before they eat it."

"I think a couple thousand years is enough playing." Zo pounded his knuckles on his knee—or he would have if he could have moved his arms. "I don't think Zmej is in the mood to play anymore. I think he's just angry now."

"Mmmmm hmmmmm." Praedo was distracted, formulating the next package of information to imprint on Zo. It started as waves of his hands, and became glowing symbols representing each type of magic, surprisingly similar to the symbols on the Ancestor beads. It seemed as though the ancestors had tried to copy it from memory, but the symbols only appeared briefly before Praedo sent them shooting at Zo straight into different parts of his body. Fire had been first. The symbol for fire bored into his belly. He barely felt it as a warming sensation that spread. This time, the Mind magic hit him right between the eyes with such intensity that his head wanted to explode. It was a cacophony of thought and sound, and his head felt like it was splitting open. His hands grabbed his head to hold it together. The headache was so bad he leaned over and vomited. Then as quickly as it came, the pain ended, and his head felt strange. Like there were multiple thoughts and people inside.

Praedo was using his hands to form the next symbol. "Don't worry, I'll show you how to shut out the background noise, but first…"

Zo took a deep breath right before the Spirit magic hit him in the chest.

Time passed as Praedo hit him with one magic after another. Zo didn't know how much time it was taking. He lay on the ground, his hands traveling from one spot of pain to another. Every magic known to the Ancestors had been inserted into Zo—except one. He heard himself moaning but couldn't feel himself making the sound. His half-seeing eyes saw Iden kneeling next to him, holding his hand tight. Zo didn't feel that either.

Praedo's wickedly grinning face appeared over him. "What? You thought that after generations of the dilution of my magic you could take it on so easily?"

Zo shook his head, but the movement made him want to vomit again.

Praedo's smile faded. "It is a painful process, and it probably was mean of me to withhold this magic till the last, but I enjoy being dramatic."

He began to form a symbol in the air over Zo, who groaned, and tried to put his arm between himself and the symbol. It would do no good. Zo flinched as the symbol became whole and bright before his eyes.

"It's time to Heal," Praedo said, and pressed the symbol into Zo's neck.

Something inside of Zo, a wall, or a flood gate, crumbled to dust and Zo felt the healing flood through his body and mind. Every hurt, every pain from taking on Praedo's magic, fled the wave of light that penetrated the darkness inside of Zo. A darkness that had come with the temptation to use the light of Healing to kill another creature. Zo began to gasp and shake. Iden gathered him up in his arms, holding him tight. Tears were flowing freely down Zo's face. All that was once broken, was now healed—even the parts of him that once hated his Healing magic because of his mother. He felt light radiate from him. He was surprised Iden didn't see it.

Zo stopped shaking, took a few deep gasps of breath, then sat up, examining his glowing arms in wonder.

Praedo laughed. "Sorry for the drama, but I do love that part."

Zo gazed into Praedo's face. Part of him wanted to hate him for putting him through all that pain before relieving him, but the joy that filled him with the return of his Healing couldn't be overshadowed by the annoyance he felt.

"Now we're ready," Praedo said, releasing Zo from the magic lesson.

* * *

Zo's eyes opened to Regg's pale face hovering over him with his hand on Zo's throat.

"I'm fine," Zo tried to say, but nothing came out of his mouth.

Regg's frown deepened. He closed his eyes. Zo felt his brother's presence spread from his neck throughout his body. When it found the bead in Zo's hand, Regg leapt back from Zo, shaking his hand out.

"What was that?" Regg examined his hand.

Zo closed his eyes. He reached inside for his Healing magic.

Not that way, that's such a primitive form of my magic. Use it this way, Praedo's voice came into Zo's mind along with an image of the exact way to heal himself. It wasn't the creeping tendrils of Healing magic slowly making its way through his body, but a holistic approach. At once he saw everything about his body—the old injuries as well as the block set up that stopped the flow of his Healing magic. Praedo gave him an image of Zo whole and healed. Zo applied it to himself.

Zo inhaled deeply and sat up. His eyes opened to find Regg, Ryn, and Iden hovering over him on the floor. Worried frowns and furrowed brows turned to surprise as he leapt to his feet.

"What are you all standing around for? We've got a dragon to slay." Zo's grin felt like Praedo's.

"Sorry, you were out so long I began to worry," Ryn said.

Zo looked toward the small window in the room. "What time is it?"

"Sun's coming up," Iden said, pulling his arm out from under Zo's shoulders.

Ryn hovered next to him, her brow still furrowed.

"I'm fine little sis. In fact—better than ever."

Ryn folded her arms. "It takes years to study and learn magic."

Zo's fingers closed around where Praedo's bead had been in his hand, but was now gone.

Zo felt for his collarbone. "Don't worry, I've got help."

His scar for fire at his collar was also gone, replaced by a new one. Slightly bigger than the Ancestor's scars, his fingers probed it gently. He couldn't see it that close to his neck.

"I think I just became the most powerful user of magic," Zo said, his finger tracing the symbol.

Praedo laughed in his head. *Not yet.*

Chapter Twenty-Nine

At last had come the hour of dread,
The long-feared battle would soon begin;
Never again would such strife be seen—
The hero and dragon in fury wed.

Gesta Praediana—Luc's Epic Poem

The morning dawned clear and the Dragon Mount was pink from the coming rays of the sun. Ryn joined the throng of workers filing into the Meeting Room. She tried to look like she belonged, but she kept watch on those around her, waiting for someone to object to the Ordinary being there.

Fergus put an arm around her. "Relax, half the people here are the Ordinaries Jeris kicked out. If he wants to start a fight, he'll get one."

Ryn nodded. She didn't trust her voice. Her stomach was in knots. She hadn't slept all night and soon they would face the dragon. The old story of the dragon slayer killing the dragon, but then dying himself, did not inspire confidence.

"We can't lose this," Ryn whispered.

"I know." Fergus pulled her closer to his side.

Once inside the meeting hall, the chill of the early spring morning melted into the heat of many gathered bodies. Everyone was talking. Ryn and Fergus found Yll and Regg by the platform at the front of the room. Iden strode through a side door.

Ryn put a hand on Iden's arm. "How's Zo?"

Iden shook his head. "We got halfway here and that Praedo guy remembered something else he needed to teach Zo. No wonder the dragon defeated him. I hope he doesn't do this in the middle of the battle. Zo's grabbing something to eat at the mess hall. He'll be here soon."

Ryn stood on her tip toes to try to get a look out the door. She was overly hot and her stomach was churning. She hoped Zo would hurry up.

Iden put a hand on Ryn's shoulder. "Thanks for what you did. I know what you gave up for him. I'm pretty sure no one else in this room would have done the same."

Ryn bowed her head. "I decided living without magic was easier than living without Zo."

Iden squeezed her shoulder and released it.

"Where's Mom?" Yll asked.

"I thought she was ahead of us. She should be here by now," Regg said.

Zo poked his head in the side door by the podium. Ryn breathed a sigh of relief.

"I think you all need to see this," Zo said.

They went out the side door and around the building. In front of the main entrance was a sight Ryn was sure hadn't been seen before, except maybe at the founding of the Library.

On one side was what could only be described as those who were "Ordinary" or the sprites of the wild magic. Ryn saw Tertius there, along with Brynd's parents. On the other side, led by Ryn's grandmother, was a delegation from what had to be every Ancestor island. Ryn couldn't be positive about that, because she wasn't sure she had met someone from every island, but it certainly looked that way. In the middle was Ryn's parents, and Clayr.

"We don't need their kind." Uncle Mik pointed at Tertius and a woman Ryn thought she'd seen in a dream.

"Good. We will take down the dragon the way it should have been done the first time," Tertius said, arms folded with his head held high.

Jeris came striding across the grounds from the Library to stop next to Ryn's grandmother. "You are trespassing on Library grounds. Get out."

Ryn wasn't sure if he meant Clayr or the sprites.

"This land belonged to our people before the dragon and the slayer," Tertius spat, pointing to the Library. "That is our Heart Tree."

"And our Library protects it. Without us your tree would be dead," Jeris yelled.

Library workers started pouring out of the meeting hall to see what was happening.

Clayr held up her hands. "This compromise was made over two thousand years ago. It is what it is. Right now, we have a dire situation. The dragon has retrieved his egg and wishes to hatch it in the ashes of the Library and its tree."

The elderly woman sprite next to Tertius stepped forward. "We must save the tree."

"The Library is more important," Jeris countered.

Moult stepped forward. "I have studied Luc's writings all my life, and I only recently discovered that the dragon has been playing us all for fools for a millenia or more. This is what he wants. He wants us to fight amongst ourselves so that we can't fight him. He's powerful. Praedo in all his power barely took him down, but he left us a clue with Luc."

Moult gestured for Fergus and Ryn to approach. Moult tapped the sword on Fergus's back. "The sword, the stone, and the branch. The sword of the Slayer, the rock from the earth, and the branch from the tree. They are the keys to unlocking our power. We must combine our power to win. It's the only way."

"Preposterous. I'm not working with these primitives." Jeris started to walk away.

Ryn's grandmother, Jayne, put her arm in front of Jeris. "You will listen and cooperate."

Jeris' face turned red. "You're not the Library Board of Regents."

"I *am* the Board of Regents, they all follow my direction." Jayne's voice was deep and full of warning.

"Well, that confirms that," Yll whispered.

"Enough." Clayr stepped forward with a crossing sweep of her arms.

A silence fell over the crowd.

"I am taking control of this battle. I have spent decades fighting for the Library. The recent battles against pests and saboteurs were the worst, and I pulled the Library through. Who will follow me in defending Waatch and the Library from the dragon?" Clayr held her head high.

"I am the curator, and you're banned from the Library." Jeris turned to the closest Library guard, which happened to be Bart. "Escort this woman and her friends off Library grounds."

Bart turned wide eyes to Errol, who had just stepped up next to Clayr.

Nobody moved.

Ryn's grandmother smiled. "I believe you have your vote of confidence, Clayr. Give her the curator your keys, Jeris."

"What? No!" Jeris shouted.

Jayne put her hand out. "The keys, before this wonderful crowd of people start thinking your protestation is a sign you're with the dragon."

Jeris dug in his coat pocket and pulled out his curator's keyring. He threw it on the ground at Clayr's feet, then stormed off.

Errol picked them up and handed them to Clayr.

She turned to the sprite delegation. "I have searched the records and there's no mention of the sprites visiting the Heart Tree for centuries. Would you care to see it?"

The older female sprite stepped forward. "I am Eladorys, wife of Praedo and mother to his children. I accept your invitation, Madame Curator, and pledge the support of the wild magic to the cause of slaying the dragon."

Clayr curtsied deeply to Eladorys.

"Those of us here of Ancestor descent also pledge our support to protect the Library and its contents," Jayne said.

Clayr turned to the crowd of Library workers gathered outside the doors of the Meeting Hall. "And you, my dear colleagues. Will you help me defend the Library?"

The crowed shuffled, looking at each other. Ryn imagined a bunch of record keepers were wondering how they could fight a dragon.

Ryn and Yll looked at each other, grinning, they shouted, "Yes!"

The rest of the workers joined in their shout of affirmation, which quickly became screaming.

Ryn turned back toward the Ancestor delegation. Schiz and Remus were running through the crowd.

"Dragon!" Schiz yelled, pointing at the sky.

A black dot on the horizon was moving in fast toward them.

* * *

Zo swore.

"Not now, my love." Iden gave Zo his lopsided grin.

"Everyone into the Library!" Errol shouted.

Clayr started shouting orders as Norm and Ed hustled her toward the Library front entrance.

"We need to get everyone inside and man the defenses before the dragon gets here," Clayr said to Errol, who barked orders at his guards to get both front doors open wide.

"We need to calm these people down, so they don't stampede," Zo said as he strode beside Iden and the others.

"There's my dad, I'll see what we can do." Iden jogged off into the Library worker group which was still mostly clumped together.

Out of the Ancestor group Fyri, Zo's mother, emerged making a beeline for Zo and Regg.

"I don't have time for you right now, Mother," Zo said to her.

"You'll make time for me or House Sano will take you down right here," she screamed at him.

Zo pulled down the collar of his shirt, revealing Praedo's bead. "I would advise against that. I have Praedo's power now."

Zo left his mother frozen with her mouth hanging open.

* * *

Once inside the Library, people were running this way and that way. Clayr, Errol, Ryette, and Lar were attempting to gain some kind of control over the situation.

Zo drifted off into the corner behind the statue of Dico.

Praedo, how do I help Iden and his dad calm the crowd? Zo thought.

Tricky. You have the power, but no training. I'll give you my best short cut. Praedo answered, to Zo's relief.

Zo spent a rushed moment learning how to project thought waves from his brain that skimmed the surface of those around them. Everyone's movements slowed and became more deliberate.

This is handy, Zo said.

When Zo blinked back out of his mind and into the real world, Iden was standing in front of him.

"That was impressive." Iden grinned.

"Where's everybody gone?" Zo asked, walking over the foyer mosaic on the Ancestral islands.

"The map room is where they've set up. Something about it being the center of the Library." Iden kept pace with Zo.

* * *

The Library's map room was filled with people, and overly warm. Ryn wiped sweat from her forehead.

Fergus stepped up and drew Praedo's sword from its sheath. "This is the twin sword to the one at the Origin. It slayed one dragon, I'm certain it could slay another."

"Or lay the area to waste like its twin did," Clayr said.

"Right." Lar stepped away from his vigil at the door. "I'd say the sword should be a last resort."

"Who knows if it will actually have the same effect," Moult said.

Clayr gathered herself and straightened her back. She wasn't much taller than Ryn, but the presence she projected commanded the room.

"I want Nix, Lar, and Zo, in charge of launching the best fireballs we can muster at that dragon. Errol, I want troops on the ground as well as in the attic. Defend the doors, we can't let that dragon inside. Errol, send a contingent to the Waatch tower. Tell them to prepare to defend the walls of Waatch as well as the walls of the Library—and tell them to work with Jayne. The people from the islands need to team up to defend the streets."

Jayne pointed to the giant map of the region. "We should also put House Mare on the defense of the bay. They can keep the bay clear for the use of water to put out any fires."

Ryn's insides twisted. Dragon fire would result in burning buildings. In her mind's eye she imagined all of Waatch on fire.

Clayr nodded. "Good thinking."

"Regg and Yll, round up Wilmar and bring House Sano to the Dining Room to set up for incoming wounded," Clayr said. "The Dining Room is closer to the Library, but far enough away to hopefully be out of the direct line of fire."

Yll opened her mouth and started to protest, when Clayr turned to Regg and pointed at his chest. "You are to make sure my daughter stays safe."

Regg nodded slowly.

"Mother, let me be your messenger. I can be of better service helping you coordinate the battle," Yll pleaded.

Clayr shook her head. "Stay with the Healers."

Fergus cleared his throat. "She's been a fierce fighter in our battles with the wolves."

Clayr shook her head. "No."

"The young ones need to prove themselves," Moult's voice came from the corner.

"They absolutely do not," Ryette shot back at him.

"Everyone has their assignments. Let's get moving. The dragon should be almost on top of us," Clayr said.

"Let's hope we have enough time," Ryette added.

Clayr lifted her head to talk over the chatter. "If I didn't give you a specific assignment, you're with me and Ryette at the command center."

Everyone started to file out of the map room.

Ryn stepped up to Clayr. "What about Lyssa? Nobody knows she's there. What if they left her on the fourth floor?"

"I'm sure her supervisor got her out," Clayr said, turning to talk with Tertius.

But Ryn wasn't so sure. Ryn had to find out if Lyssa was safe.

As Ed was headed out the door, Ryn grabbed his arm. "Will you check and make sure Lyssa got out? Her study is on the fourth floor."

Ed startled at that. "I had no idea, but I'll send someone to check."

"Thank you." Ryn smiled.

Fergus took Ryn's arm and pulled her outside the map room and into a reading alcove. She looked up into his blue eyes as he ran a hand through his hair. He squeezed his eyes shut, and when he opened them again, they had fear behind them.

"In case I don't have a chance to tell you, I just wanted to say that you're the most extraordinary person I have met. There's something about you. Something that connects with the Library. Something that fits. I hope that I get a chance to explore that connection with you, but if I don't—keep working. Keep fighting. You're amazing." Fergus' face was full of worry, but also caring.

Ryn swallowed hard. She couldn't say they would all be fine, because she'd faced Zmej before, and had nearly been roasted alive by him. So she swallowed her platitudes and just nodded.

Fergus hugged her to him and kissed her on the top of the head. She looked up into his face and he bent down, his lips gently touching hers. It was soft and sweet, then his lips moved, testing, tasting. A thrill ran down the center of Ryn, straight to her toes. She pulled him closer, her breathing coming quickly. Fergus' tongue parted her lips. Ryn stopped breathing.

"Ahem."

Fergus pressed his forehead to Ryn's, but still clung to her.

"You're needed up top," Norm said.

Ryn pulled Fergus tight to her chest. Norm waited.

"I have to go." Fergus kissed the top of her head again.

Ryn hugged him harder. Despite his words, he clung to her.

Finally, Ryn knew the time had come. She took a deep breath, inhaling the smell of cedar and sea, and musty cave on Fergus. It imprinted on her mind as she let him slip from her arms and slowly walk away. She didn't want to think about what was to come. All the people she loved most dearly were here, and they were up against something only the Dragon Slayer of old had defeated.

* * *

The Library floor vibrated beneath Ryn's feet as she entered the map room.

Iden looked up at the ceiling. "The dragon has come."

Nix came bursting through the door behind her. "The fireballs are keeping the dragon at bay, but none of the harpoons have hit their mark. The Library's protective barrier is holding, but the intense heat from the dragon fire has overwhelmed some of the Library guards. My grunts don't let a little heat bother them. I'm concerned about the heat and the windows—that it will eventually shatter the glass."

"Moult, you've studied the Library's history in depth—is there a defense for the windows?" Clayr asked.

Ryn's father nodded. "I believe there are hidden shutters."

"Go with Nix and find them," Clayr snapped, and Moult followed in Nix's shadow.

Ed returned to the map room.

"Did you find Lyssa?" Ryn asked.

Ed shook his head at her on his way to Clayr's side.

Everyone was busy in some sort of deep conversation, either within their minds or with each other, so Ryn slipped out the door and headed for the grand staircase. Dust and soot covered the workers and guards running up and down the staircase. Two Library guards carried a stretcher between them that contained someone in a Library uniform. Ryn veered toward them, till she saw it was someone with black hair. Her heart still hammered in her chest. It wasn't Fergus—yet.

By the time she got to the third floor the smell of hot wood and fire permeated everything. Nix said the fire wasn't getting through, but that's not the way it smelled. Ryn found the research manager's office and went straight to the hidden door behind Luc's painting. She didn't have the key, but the door opened for her. She raced up the stairs calling Lyssa's name.

"Here!" Came a weak reply.

Ryn threw open the door to a room that was blazing hot. Lyssa was lying on the couch with sweat glistening on her face and arms. Ryn ran to her. She was burning hot to the touch.

"I'm here. I can lead you out," Ryn said.

"I feel sick." Lyssa rolled to her right and vomited over the side of the couch.

Ryn panicked. She didn't think she could carry Lyssa, even though she was only slightly taller than Ryn.

"I'll help you, but you're going to have to walk," Ryn said.

Something hit the roof above them hard. Ryn was certain it was about to collapse.

"Leave me. There's no use in an Ancestor descendant who can't do magic," Lyssa said.

Ryn was taken aback. Lyssa had always displayed so much confidence in herself. Did she really think about herself that way? Had she let them get to her, being locked up in this tower the way she was?

"Lyssa, you're the hardest working researcher I've seen. We need you. I need you." Ryn pulled Lyssa to a sitting position and put her shoulder under Lyssa's arm. "We're the misfits of the Library, and we're going to prove them all wrong about us."

Ryn got Lyssa to her feet and stumbled toward the door. The Library shook and Ryn and Lyssa slid down the stairs to the third floor, ending up in a tangle of arms and legs.

"Ow," Lyssa said.

"See, I told you we would make it," Ryn said.

Lyssa started to giggle.

Ryn joined in, till tears streamed down her face.

"What's going on out there?" Lyssa asked.

"Dragon attack," Ryn said, as she pulled Lyssa to her feet. "Did you read those pages I gave you?"

"Yes." Ryn put Lyssa's hand on her arm.

"I think the one with the cows might work…"

"On it! Let's go!"

* * *

"How sure are we that this thousand-year-old Library can withstand a dragon attack?" Iden asked.

Clayr frowned at him.

Zo's eyes scanned the room, taking in the people coming and going with Clayr and Ryette at the center directing everything.

"Where's Ryn?" Zo asked.

Ryette's head turned toward him, and Moult turned in a slow circle.

"She was right here. Um—I guess that was some time ago," Moult said.

"You were supposed to be watching her," Ryette shot at him.

"Clayr sent me to find the shutters for the windows," Moult shot back.

At that moment Ryn strolled through the door leading a girl on her arm. They were both sweaty, with their hair matted down to their heads, and Ryn was limping.

Ryette rushed over to Ryn, her hands feeling Ryn's forehead.

"I'm alright, I just twisted my ankle falling down the stairs," Ryn said.

"*You fell down the stairs?*" Ryette shouted.

The girl on Ryn's arm giggled. "It was quite the ride."

Clayr came around the table to examine the girl with Ryn. "Are you hurt, Lyssa?"

Lyssa shook her head, and Ryn managed to lead Lyssa to a chair at a table. Lyssa put out her hand to feel the back of the chair before she sat.

Ryn's eyes found Zo's and she limped over to him to hug him tight. "I'm so glad you're back."

Zo chuckled. "I never went anywhere."

As Zo hugged Ryn to him, he felt the Healing magic flow into her. Ryn rotated her foot and her grin lit up her eyes so they sparkled like sunshine on the ocean. She hugged him again, then took a paper out of her pocket and sat at the table next to Lyssa. They bent their heads together in deep conversation.

Yll and Brynd strode through the door, Yll taking a position across the table from her mother.

"Dragon fire has taken out two groups of Waatch citizens. The Healers and Wilmar are overwhelmed at the Dining Room." Yll pointed to two spots on the map.

"I'll go." Zo started for the door.

"No." Clayr's voice was stern. "The best way to help the Healers is to prevent more casualties. We need you up top defending against the dragon."

Zo chafed at the command. The Healing magic coursing through his veins made him so relieved and happy, he wanted to Heal every person who had been hurt.

"I won't be gone long. I'll be quick." Zo started for the door again, but a strange light was coming from beyond the doors.

A figure walked by the door. Everything about her flowed—her hair, her dress, the way she walked...there was also a faint glow about her. Another figure walked past, and this one was one Zo recognized. Tertius, the man they had met at the hot spring. The sprite contingent was in the Library.

Ryn ran for the door as two more flowing and glowing people walked past.

The woman in front of the procession looked back at Ryn and smiled. "Follow, the dragon comes."

"I think the dragon already came," Iden whispered to Zo.

Ryette put a hand on Ryn's shoulder. "How do you know these people?"

Ryn's eyes seemed unfocused when she turned to her mother and said, "It's like a dream."

Everyone followed the procession till it stopped in front of the door to the Heart Tree. The woman in the lead waved her hand over the carvings and they changed into a crisp picture of the tree as Zo remembered it from Solstice night when he fought Zmej.

Standing next to the door was Schiz and Remus.

Tertius put his hand up and swept Schiz aside. "This ceremony does not require the father."

Remus growled.

The woman turned to Ryn and smiled. "Come."

The door didn't open so much as melted, as the sprites and Ryn walked through. Ryette tried to follow, but the door became solid wood again. Zo put his hand to it like he had that winter's night, but it didn't give way to him this time.

Ryette pounded on the door. "Let me in!"

The door didn't budge, and the carving reverted back to its vague outlines and characters.

Clayr ran a hand over the carvings. "Nothing more we can do here. Let's hope they can help defend the Library somehow. Back to the map room."

Zo turned reluctantly away from the door. He would just have to hope Ryn was safe inside. As he started back, he saw Yll frowning and Brynd hugging herself. A low growl filled the bookshelf aisle.

Herb came running down the aisle. "Wolves are in the Library!"

Errol and Ed drew their swords, grabbed Clayr by the elbows, and rushed her back down the aisle of books.

Zo swore.

"Didn't we just do this like a couple moons ago?" Iden asked.

"We can't do magic in the Library," Yll said, swallowing hard.

"Where's Fergus and that cursed sword when we need it?" Zo said.

Brynd groaned. "I don't want to run all over the Library again."

"Wait..." Zo had a sudden realization. Before when he had a fire magic lesson it had waited until he was *outside* the protective magic of the Library—and hadn't he just healed Ryn *inside* the Library?

"...I think..." Before Zo could finish a wolf came sliding around the endcap of the bookshelves, nails clacking as it scrambled for purchase on the slick Library floors.

"Help me, Praedo," Zo whispered under his breath as he reached for a magic he'd never used before.

His hair stood up on end as he thrust his hand out to shoot lightning from his palm straight at the wolf. The bolt hit it dead in the chest and the wolf went down.

Yll's eyes were wide and staring at Zo. "How did you...I can't shapeshift."

Another wolf came from the opposite direction. Zo shot another bolt of lightning and took out that wolf.

* * *

To Zo's utter astonishment, Iden, Yll, Brynd, Ryette, and Moult moved as one to protect the Heart Tree door. Zo stepped in front of them.

Remus bolted after another wolf, and Schiz followed him.

Zo reached for a magic he'd only seen his father use to fight fire. From somewhere beneath the floor of the Library the earth heaved, and clay dirt formed in Zo's hands. He launched the clay hardened like daggers at another wolf.

"I think I'm going to enjoy this too much," Zo whispered under his breath.

Two more wolves shot down the aisle at them. Zo turned into a huge black bear and stood in front of everyone. He took the brunt of their leap full in the chest, knocking him off his feet.

"Zo!" Iden yelled and stepped in front of the wolf racing down the aisle at Zo's back.

The wolf leapt over Iden and went straight for Zo's head. Another wolf came around the corner and tackled Zo to the ground. Zo bit and scratched four wolves with his sharp teeth and bear claws, but the wolves were on him, bearing him to the ground, biting and tearing at his hide. Zo didn't dare change out of bear form, or the wolves would have him for sure.

All this magical power at his fingertips and he was going to be eaten by wolves.

Chapter Thirty

The sun ascended the flaming tide,
Staining with fire the shore and the sea;
Yet brighter still, unceasingly,
The dragon's wrath against us cried.

Gesta Praediana—Luc's Epic Poem

Ryn walked barefoot on the squishy moss that surrounded the Heart Tree. An abiding peace seeped into her soul. She took a deep breath and put her arms around the tree, pressing her cheek to its bark like an old friend or long-lost family.

"I see you've met before," The sprite who had led them there said.

Ryn nodded.

"This tree is one of the last anchors of the Wild magic. We must defend it at all costs, but first, we must heal what has been broken." She reached out a hand to Ryn.

Ryn reluctantly let go of the tree and walked to the gathered circle of sprites.

"I am Eladorys, first among the magic. I was born before the dragons came. This is my son Tertius, you have met him before, and these are some of my other children." The lead sprite indicated the others with them in the circle. "Do you know why you are here?"

Ryn rubbed her forehead. "I'm not sure. I feel like I belong in a strange way, yet I don't know you."

Eladorys nodded. "The Wild magic is your family." Eladorys looked up into the branches of the tree. "You should be a part of the tree." Her gaze returned to Ryn. "I'm sorry you were cut off. It was my fault. My decision. I didn't think you would survive. I've watched you for a long time now. I was mistaken."

Ryn turned back to the tree, her heart racing. How could she be a part of the tree? Cut off she definitely felt. She glanced at Eladorys. *She* was the reason Ryn didn't feel like she belonged anywhere? The reason when anyone talked of family, Ryn felt excluded from the conversation. Ryn didn't look like her mother. She didn't talk like her father. Her friends whom she loved and counted as family sometimes reminded her that she wasn't real family. It hurt. Perhaps Zo wished he was adopted and had a different mother, but then he wouldn't have that Healing magic he had come to love so much.

Ryn turned back to Eladorys. She needed to ask, but the words were stuck in her throat.

"So...you're my family?" Ryn finally forced the words out.

Eladorys smiled.

Ryn looked at the sprites in the circle. They all had a kind of shimmer that spoke of magic.

"I have magic?" Ryn asked.

Tertius laughed. "You have been manifesting it all your life, did you not notice?"

Ryn's brow furrowed. "How?"

"When the wolves attacked you on the road and Xylia called upon us, did you not feel the power from the earth making the trees move?" Tertius asked.

"Um...I thought that was Xylia," Ryn said, her heart pounding in her ears.

Eladorys's slight smile spoke of amusement at Ryn's ignorance.

"The circle must be complete," Tertius said, holding out a hand for Ryn to take.

Eladorys pointed to the missing branch of the tree. The one where sap dripped like tears.

"It was not so long ago that the branch was cut from the Heart Tree. It was a mistake to let it be cut. At the time, it seemed the best option, but we soon came to regret it. We must heal it now if the tree is to survive and the dragon is to be defeated," Eladorys said, in an ethereal, dreamlike voice

"But a dragon came before and he was defeated by the slayer, not the tree," Ryn said, struggling to understand what was happening.

Tertius scoffed. "That is because the slayer sent us away to protect us. We are his family, his children, he was worried. We can see now that we must combine with the slayer's magic to defeat the dragon. Zmej is not such a fool. It will take the union of the slayer's magic, and our magic, the magic of this world, to defeat him. We see now—all divisions must be healed."

Eladorys' cool, soft hand took Ryn's and the circle became complete. Tertius began to sing a low note deep from his abdomen. The female sprite next to him took up a note one step up, still quite low for a female voice. The next sprite began and the next, around the circle till Eladorys sang a crystal-clear high note that floated above the rest, but fit like a piece to a puzzle. Once they were all singing, Eladorys and Tertius squeezed Ryn's hands. Somehow, she knew they wanted her to join in the song, but where did she fit? Was it high? Or low? Or somewhere in the middle? Ryn took a deep breath, opened her mouth, and just let her voice join in the song. She found herself singing something that sounded like the Heart Tree's song. It dipped and flowed and soared to new heights. She had enjoyed singing as a child, but hadn't sung much as she got older. But now—now she flowed with the song of the tree, supported by the notes of the circle of sprites. The tree joined in.

The song of the tree vibrated in Ryn's chest. It was like the sound of waves as the wind blew the treetops, but also the crack of ice falling from its branches after an ice storm. Then it became a song and sound she'd never heard, but now understood—the sound of sap coursing up through the branches of the tree, and the roots growing deep into the soil. It was life. It was joy. It was family.

"Heal the tree, return the branch!" Eladorys' singing was a shout. The life water from the tree's roots surrounded them swirling in a blurry sparkling circle. All at once it shrank and engulfed Ryn. She struggled to continue the song. The life water wasn't wet, but was thick and shimmery like water. The life water spouted off Ryn and found the cut branch on the tree. At once Ryn was a part of the tree, but also herself.

Something of who she was flowed with the life water between her and the tree. She saw faces, some welcoming, some stern, some full of wild abandoned joy. They were all unfamiliar, yet she felt the pull of recognizing something of herself in them. Her rounded face, her brown-green eyes and her short stature. She had never seen a group that looked like her before. It made her smile, and comforted her that she wasn't alone anymore.

The life water retreated and flowed back to the tree's roots. Ryn gasped for air like she had been underwater for too long. When she got control of her breathing, she saw Eladorys smiling at her, and everyone else admiring the new branch on the tree that had once been missing.

Ryn walked to the branch and ran her fingers along it. There was a name carved onto the branch.

"Cya?" Ryn turned to see if she had pronounced it correctly.

"Welcome home." Eladorys opened her arms to Ryn.

Ryn went to her and hugged her. It was warm, but not familiar. She hoped it would someday become familiar.

"Dearest Cya, I am your grandmother." Eladorys's smile was warm.

Ryn looked at the faces around the circle. "Where's my mother?"

Eladorys exchanged a look with Tertius. "She couldn't make it. She wanted me to ask you..."

Something banged against the door to the Library interior.

"The Dragon's abominations are here," Tertius said.

Eladorys squeezed Ryn's hands, a question in her eyes.

In Ryn's mind she could see wolves attacking Zo just outside the door. Ryette, Yll, and the others prepared to defend the door with chairs, and step ladders. The Protector of the Library standing in its dark smoke form before the group of defenders. Part of her brain said she should be questioning how this was possible, but she did not. It was like some part of her had been asleep, and now it was awake. Was the Protector a sprite? It was hard to tell.

"You may stay and help nourish the tree's roots, or you can leave to defend it. It is your choice," Tertius said.

Ryn gazed up at the tree, soaring into the upper lofts of the Library. She felt at home here. She needed time to explore it. To understand who she was and her family. She never wanted to leave.

"But how? How can I defend the tree? How do I use the magic?" Ryn asked.

Eladorys bent closer to Ryn. "It's there inside you. Do you feel it now?"

Ryn's mind traveled through her body from top to bottom. There was something familiar there. Something that had always been there, but now she saw it in a new way.

Her face scrunched up. "I think so."

"Dig down deep and enter the flow of it, just like you added your voice to the song. You will have what you need," Tertius said.

"I'll go," Ryn said, holding Eladorys gaze, who nodded as Tertius took Ryn's hand and led her to the door.

Ryn took a deep breath, and they stepped through...

* * *

On the other side of the door, they walked right into a wolf launching itself at the door. Ryn threw up her arm and a shield of earth appeared on it. Tertius circled his hands and a sphere of swirling air surrounded the wolf, sending it spiraling away.

Ryn stared in wonderment at the shield on her arm. She had barely even thought of something to protect herself and it had appeared. She reached a hand out and shocked the wolves attacking a bear next to her. They both yelped and took off running.

The bear transformed into Zo, and he came to stand next to her scratched and bloody. Ryn lifted an eyebrow at him. He put his hand to his bleeding forehead, then pulled it away to examine the blood. His brow furrowed, then his skin took on a white-blue glow before everything healed.

More wolves appeared to join the other two.

"Get behind me," Zo said.

"What are you talking about?" Ryn said.

Zo looked over at her and did a double take. Ryn's clothes and hair were floating, like she was underwater.

Zo swore. "What happened?"

Ryn shrugged. "The branch came home."

The pack of wolves launched themselves at the group just as Nix, Lar, and Fergus ran up from behind Ryn and Zo.

"Watch out!" Fergus said as he lifted Praedo's sword and placed himself between the wolves, and the others.

Nix stepped up next to Fergus and swirled his hands like he was about to whip up a firestorm.

"Nix! You're in the Library, not on the roof!" Ryn shouted.

Nix turned a wide-eyed face toward them. He clearly had forgotten he couldn't call his magic here. He turned as the giant wolf, the one that was Zmej's first born, tackled Nix to the ground.

"Nix!" Zo yelled, diving for the wolf to pull him off.

But, the massive wolf had already torn out Nix's shoulder and part of his neck. Zo rushed over, putting his hand to the gushing wound, but just as he did, the giant wolf tackled Zo to the ground.

Ryn zapped the wolf with lightning, but it wouldn't let go of Zo. Fergus rushed forward, running his sword through the wolf.

Zo shook his head and scrambled back over to Nix.

"We need to take this outside. We can't fight properly here without getting everyone killed and damaging the Library," Ryn said.

"Tell that to Zmej. I'm sure he sent his wolves in here to open the way to the Heart Tree," Fergus said as he swung at another wolf trying to get past him.

Ryn heard wolf nails on the floor behind her. Her heart sank as she turned to face a wolf attack to their rear, but the new wolf that came bounding over all of their heads to take on the wolf pack was all white.

"Remus!" Ryn exclaimed. She had never been so grateful to see a wolf.

Schiz was right behind Remus. He put a hand on Ryn's shoulder, and tapped a finger to his head.

"I got this. Give me the stone," Schiz said, then charged past Remus fighting his wolf brothers.

Ryn reached in her pocket and pulled out the stone. Schiz took it and ran. Ryn regretted giving it to him, and her stomach dropped. Instinctively she knew this was going to be bad. Tears came to her eyes as she shouted at Schiz. He turned and smiled at her as he tackled the giant wolf and half the pack.

"No! No!" Ryn was running toward them, tears streaming down her face.

Fergus was right behind her, swinging at wolves that snapped at her.

The giant wolf howled and the rest of the wolves turned and ran toward it. There were too many of them. Schiz would be torn to shreds.

The wolves engulfed Schiz. All Ryn could see was Schiz's hand clutching the stone. Schiz's travel magic enveloped the wolves and they were all gone.

"No!" Ryn screamed.

"I'm sure he's fine, we just need to find where they went," Fergus said to her when she turned in a circle.

"No, this is bad. Something is wrong. I know it," Ryn said.

Yll was there with Lar. "We're ready to fight. I'm sure they're outside somewhere. Let's go."

Ryn saw Zo focused on Nix. He had healed Ryn so quickly, if Zo was still healing Nix, it must be bad. She decided to leave him to it.

Ryn nodded at Yll. "Let's go."

* * *

Outside, Zmej was flying toward the Library, the wolf pack jumping and yipping below him. Enraged, the dragon threw something at the ground. After it hit, Ryn knew what it was.

Her heart stopped. Schiz had been this strange man, always in the shadows for several moons. He had frightened her at first, but once she had gotten used to his ways, he had grown on her. In her mind she could see his quiet focused face as he tried to explain himself.

Remus ran out the Library doors and shot past Ryn. He circled Schiz's body, howling, then he laid down next to Schiz's twisted and broken form, and placed his head on Schiz's chest.

Ryn's heart broke.

The dragon screeched, taking in air to breathe out fire. Ryn shot a wall of water between Remus and the dragon fire.

Fergus went still next to her. Ryn looked over to see him wide-eyed, staring at the water flowing from Ryn's hands.

Ryn would have laughed if the situation wasn't so dire.

Yll turned into an eagle and flew up toward the dragon.

"Yll, don't be stupid!" Ryn called to her.

Just being a distraction.

Ryn could hear Yll's thoughts in her bird form.

If you get yourself killed, I will kill you! Ryn sent back.

Ryn raced down the Library main entrance stairs hoping to draw the dragon away from the Library. The dragon tracked Ryn and started to dive toward her.

Yll in eagle form got in the dragon's face, pecking at his eyes. The dragon swung its wings at her.

Fergus shadowed Ryn. They both slid to a stop next to Remus. Ryn got one glimpse of Schiz's open, unmoving eyes and wished she hadn't.

"Remus, we need you!" Ryn squatted down to put a hand on Remus' fur.

Lar and Moult joined them with Tertius appearing seemingly out of nowhere. Ryn jumped back from him, her heart pounding.

Moult shape-shifted into a hawk and joined Yll at harassing the dragon. The two birds flew off and the dragon chased them.

"Great, I hope they don't get themselves killed," Ryn said.

Lar waved a hand for attention. "Alright, we have my fire, and earth. What else?"

"Praedo's second sword." Fergus held up the replica that was real.

"Ryn and I can handle this," Tertius said.

Lar frowned and gave Tertius a side-long look. "This is a joint effort, remember?"

"He's not going to pursue Yll and Moult long, we need a plan," Fergus said.

"It's simple, now that the tree is healed, we launch all our firepower at once and overwhelm the dragon," Tertius said.

Lar shook his head. "We've sent fireballs at the dragon till we were all overheated and drained, but it had little effect on the dragon."

Fergus nodded. "And standing here out in the open is going to get us roasted. The Library guard and the Waatch guard have defenses set up at the Library north gate. I suggest we think of ways to defeat the dragon on our way there."

Remus nuzzled Ryn's hand. She looked down at him, and quickly away from Schiz's body in the background behind him. "Let's get going."

Ryn set off at a run, but everyone quickly outpaced her. She ran faster to keep up.

"Ryn!"

Ryn turned to see Regg running up to her, his hands dark with dried blood.

She frowned. "What are you doing here?"

"I saw the dragon chasing an eagle with the same markings as Yll. Where is she?" Regg asked.

Ryn waved her hand in the air toward the direction the dragon had flown. "My best friend is out there drawing the dragon after her."

All the color drained from Regg's face. "*What?*"

"Don't worry, my father's with her," Ryn said, but her voice was flat. She didn't really believe that the fact that they were both out there was going to make them any safer.

"*What?*" Regg said again. "Where's my brother?"

"Healing Nix," Fergus said.

"*Defenses*—who's in charge here?" Lar's words were short and clipped.

Library guards Bart and Ed were outside the Library gate directing the citizens of Waatch to find cover.

"Bart!" Fergus yelled. "How did the wolves get on the Library grounds?"

Bart threw his arms wide. "Everywhere, pick a spot."

"How do we defend the wall from a dragon that can just fly over us?" Fergus said.

"We need to draw the dragon and the wolves out of town," Ryn said.

"Bait," Tertius said.

"What kind of bait?" Lar snarled.

"I'm way ahead of you." Ryn's smile was more of a grimace. "Tertius, please stay here and help defend the Library. Lar, protect my mother. Regg, since you're here, keep an eye on Yll and the dragon."

"She sent me to protect you," Lar protested.

"The Library needs everyone it can get," Ryn shot back.

She turned and her gaze took in who was left. "Everyone else, come with me. I have something special for the dragon at Thax's."

Chapter Thirty-One

Though Praedo deflected the torrent of flame,
The roofs of the city were scorched and falling;
The heavens thundered, the crowds were calling—
They feared extinction and utter shame.

Gesta Praediana—Luc's Epic Poem

"I'm fine, grunt. We need to take care of that dragon." Nix swatted at Zo's hand.

Zo breathed a sigh of relief to see Nix sit up. The healing of artery and nerve damage he had to do was complex, and Zo had needed help from Praedo to fix it. He rubbed his hand across his forehead trying to reorient himself. He had been deep into Nix's body and the healing process.

He looked up at Ryette, who was in a heated discussion with Herb about guarding the door to the tree.

Zo's knees popped as he stood and took Ryette's elbow. "Where's Ryn?"

Ryette turned her anger-filled eyes to Zo. "She and Fergus took off after the wolves."

"Where did they go?" Zo asked Herb, who shrugged.

"Great." Zo turned, striding toward the Library entrance.

"Zo, we need to get back up on the roof. They are out of harpoons by now and fire is all we have," Nix called after him.

Zo was torn between his need to catch up with Ryn and the others, and helping with the Library's defense.

Iden came around the corner with the Library guards and Boiler Room workers who had left the roof when the wolves had entered the building.

"Dragon's back. Let's go hit him where it hurts," Iden said.

Zo took one last look in the direction of the Library's main entrance then sprinted toward the stairs after Iden and Nix.

* * *

Once on the roof, Zo went to the edge of the open panel to scan the skyline. There was nothing to the north, but to the south he could see smoke coming from a couple different spots in Waatch—one of which looked to be the Dining Room. Nix was standing next to Zo, his posture ridged, and his knuckles white on the railing.

"Incoming!" Someone shouted and Zo turned to see out the opposite panel where two tiny flying dots were being chased by an infuriated dragon.

Once the birds flew past, Iden sent a whirlwind of air shooting up at the dragon, causing its wings to falter and the dragon to spin around in the air. Iden sent another blast and the dragon plummeted toward the walls of Waatch. It disappeared out of sight behind the Waatch guard tower. Zo held his breath. He knew that wasn't the end, but his heart couldn't help hoping.

The dragon shot straight up, headfirst streaking high into the sky. When its eyes set on the Library, they almost seemed to bore straight into Zo.

"Ready the fireballs!" Nix shouted.

Zo began to form one in his hands, larger and more powerful than anything he'd created before.

"Into the catapult!" Nix called to Zo.

Zo looked at Nix. He had been thinking to just send it straight at the dragon himself, but he turned and set it into the iron cup that would send it with force.

Fire is the dragon's element, you must fight him with something more, Praedo voice came to Zo's mind as the launched fireball knocked the dragon to the side, but didn't stop him. That fireball had been the most powerful one Zo had ever created. How could he possibly stop the dragon?

Become a dragon, Praedo said.

"What? How?" Zo asked.

Iden cocked his head to the side and gave Zo a curious look as he used his air magic to give another fireball the extra force of a firestorm.

Like this. Praedo sent an image to Zo's mind—the details of how to shape shift into a dragon.

"Did you do this with the other dragon?" Zo asked.

It might have led to my fatal wound, but I'm sure you can do better, Praedo said.

Zo swore, pounded his knuckles on his thigh, then grabbed Iden and kissed him with all the love and passion he could put into something so rushed.

"You're about to do something stupid, aren't you?" Iden said when Zo broke off the kiss.

Zo shrugged. "Oh well."

Then Zo launched himself over the side of the Library roof into the air. As he fell through the air his arms became wings, his head grew, and from his backside grew a long scaly tail. Whereas Zmej as a dragon was black as night, Zo was a cool blue that blended into the sky. He found himself plummeting toward the ground till he spread his wings and beat at the air.

The black dragon roared and dove at Zo, who frantically beat his wings to get out of the way of the dragon's dive.

As Zo fought to gain control of his flying, he found himself over the north gate to the Library. He caught a glimpse of Ryn, Regg, and Fergus. Everyone was ducking for cover, but Ryn's eyes held his.

Zo, what are you doing? Ryn asked.

Praedo is having me try something that didn't work last time, Zo sent to her.

By all the stupid ancestors...I have a plan, can you get him out of Waatch?

Zo flapped his wings but barely cleared the Regent's building. *I'll try, but I'm not great at being a dragon.*

We'll meet you in the grassy field where they held the Ghost Festival by the bay, Ryn sent to him.

Zo swallowed the fire he almost breathed out on a group of Waatch residents pointing shovels and pikes at him. He beat his wings furiously to gain height. He managed to get high enough to turn toward the water and the Waatch docks. The beach looked so inviting. All he wanted was to put his toes in the sand and watch the waves roll in. He sighed and flames erupted from his throat, flashing out over the walls of Waatch. The people below him were running and screaming.

As he flew toward the water, he noticed boats anchored at the edge of the bay, protecting Waatch. Banners for House Mare and House Venti flapped proudly in the breeze. Having water and wind at his back was comforting. Zo flew out over the water to greet them, then realized they wouldn't know which dragon was bad or good, so he arced on the wind back toward Waatch, and right into the path of the incoming black dragon.

* * *

Ryn burst through the door into Thax's shop.

"Is it ready?" she called to Brynd.

"Almost. Thax had to put a few artistic flourishes on your creation," Brynd said.

"We don't have time for artistic. Thax!" Ryn yelled.

"It's done, it's done! We just need to load it on the cart." Thax came out of the back room.

Ryn turned to Fergus. "Let's get it loaded. We don't have time."

She felt a burning in her stomach that rose to her heart. Every moment they delayed, Zo, Yll, and Ryn's father were in danger from harassing the dragon and keeping him away from the Library.

Once the bait was loaded, they hurried Thax's horse and cart through streets of panicked people erratically looking for shelter. Someone yelled that there was a fire near the north wall. Ryn took a deep breath hoping they could still get out the north gate.

Fergus was beside her helping to push the cart forward. "Ryn, I want to try to take out the dragon with the sword. I think the idea of killing it from the inside will work."

Ryn's legs turned to mush beneath her. "No. Absolutely not. My plan will work."

"You're going to need time to set it up. At least let me try while you're getting the bait into place." Fergus frowned, the look on his face told her he was going to try it whether she liked it or not.

Ryn swallowed hard. "Please don't."

"I'm sworn to protect the Library." Fergus puffed up his chest.

Ryn knew it wasn't just the Library. Part of her plan was for her to attract the dragon's attention to the bait. He was stupidly going to get himself killed the same way Praedo had.

She took a deep breath and fought down the tears that threatened to rise up from her hurting chest. She didn't trust her voice to say anything, she just pushed on the cart as hard as she could, which wasn't much.

* * *

Zo swore, and it became fire shooting out of his mouth toward Zmej the dragon. Zo the dragon realized he was trapped between Zmej and the Ancestral ships. He would have started sweating if dragons sweated. The black dragon gained height on him and dove toward him. Zo blasted him with fire, but Zmej dragon dodged it easily. Zo flew back toward the shore, but people dressed in Ancestral house colors were pouring out Waatch's gates onto the grassy field. Zo tried to turn, but flew over the walls of Waatch. People were running in the streets. He hoped they would find shelter before Zmej followed him back into the skies over Waatch. Zo tried to bank hard to the right, but someone with Wind magic blew his wings, flipping him upside down. With his belly exposed, Zo saw the black dragon hovering over him, ready to pounce.

Upside down, he also saw a tiny figure that looked like Ryn, and Thax's horse pulling a cart. Zo struggled to flip himself over, only managing to do so just before the black dragon took a chunk out of him with his razor-sharp teeth.

A fireball zipped past Zo's head, singeing his scaly eyebrow. It hit the black dragon square in the face. Zo used the moment of distraction to flap his wings hard to back away. The black dragon opened his mouth and breathed fire on the houses below them. People screamed and flames crackled.

Zo! Get him back out over the water! Ryn sent to him.

I'm trying! He sent back.

Two eagles fluttered in between Zo and Zmej. They were soaring and diving like they were harassing a seagull. Zmej swatted at them, but his moment of distraction was enough for Zo to make a beeline for the bay.

Zmej roared, taking out more buildings, then chased after Zo.

Zo turned when he got to the line of ships. Water magic combined with Wind magic to create a waterspout chased after Zo, pulling at his tail, almost sucking him inside.

The black dragon killed the spout with one burst of blue flame. Zo turned just as the dragon bore down on him. Zmej's dragon jaws grabbed Zo by the throat, and they spiraled out of control toward the water.

Zo reached a dragon claw and grabbed the black dragon's throat. Even as a dragon he felt the old stirring of that temptation—the need to kill with Healing magic. It was shocking to realize that even though the Healing magic was restored, the ugly, dark temptation still lingered. His heart sank at the thought that he would carry it with him the rest of his life, and in this moment the temptation was overwhelming. He could end it all right now. One use of the Healing magic shot inside the dragon would stop its heart along with the death and destruction. It would save the Library and the Heart Tree. It would protect everyone in Waatch and especially his family and those he cared for. One touch and he could end it all…

But even with all the magics at his command, Healing was the one magic he could no longer live without.

Zo grit his dragon teeth and rolled to the side so Zmej was below him. The black dragon's wings hit the water, jarring the dragon's jaw loose from Zo's neck. Zo kicked Zmej hard in the chest and launched himself into the air. He beat his wings to gain altitude, narrowly missing a harpoon shot at him from one of the Ancestral ships. He turned to flee as Zmej came back at him for another round. This time the black dragon engulfed Zo in its wings and the two plummeted into the ocean.

Chapter Thirty-Two

We know not whether by will or design,
By vow fulfilled or errant spell,
But with the beast, through flame and knell,
His faithful twelve crossed fate's red line.

Gesta Praediana—Luc's Epic Poem

Just as Ryn reached the beach, she watched Zmej as the black dragon wrap himself around the blue dragon that was Zo and dive into the water. The font of water that erupted from the impact sent waves across the bay, making the sentry boats tilt and bob. Ryn stood in the seat of Thax's wagon. She watched the water anxiously waiting for the blue dragon to emerge, but the water settled to nothing. Ryn swallowed back her fear. Zo had all the magics now. He was going to be alright. He had to be alright.

A hand on Ryn's arm made her jump. It was Brynd, her white-blond hair bright in the sunshine, and her lips pressed together.

"Fergus is almost ready," Brynd said with a sad, lopsided smile.

"What's that?" Ryn pointed to the padded suit in Brynd's hand.

"Fire-proof suit." Brynd handed a jacket to Fergus and he slipped it on.

Despite being quilted, it seemed too supple to be effective against fire.

"You had that ready?" She glared at Brynd and Fergus. "Are you sure this will protect him?" Ryn asked as Fergus pulled the pants on over what he was wearing.

Brynd shrugged. "They use suits like this to fight fires."

Fergus nodded. "They have a suit like this in the Boiler Room for when the fires are too hot and they need access to the boilers."

Ryn's heart raced. "I still don't like it. Dragon fire is hotter than the Boiler Room."

Fergus finished tying on the pants and he leaned down to kiss her on the cheek. "With a little luck, I won't even need it." He pulled the fireproof hood down onto his head.

"I still think my plan is better," Ryn grumbled.

Fergus gave her a lopsided smile before hugging her. "We'll see. If this method doesn't work, we'll use yours."

Ryn turned away. She couldn't watch Fergus get eaten by a dragon.

Fergus stepped around in front of her, lifting her chin to kiss her quickly, then he hefted the sword and took off down the beach toward the water.

Yll landed next to Ryn and returned to human form. Regg jogged up beside her.

The black dragon shot out of the water sending sea spray everywhere, but the blue dragon didn't follow.

Ryn ran to the water's edge, searching the surface for any sign of the blue dragon.

"Come on Zo, where are you?" Ryn whispered.

Fergus ran up beside her holding the sword of Praedo. He started side stepping to the right as he tracked the black dragon. Ryn didn't want to watch Fergus' plan, and kept her gaze fixed on the water. Fergus would need Zo's help.

The sound of coughing and sputtering came from the shore off to her left. She turned to see Zo, in human form, crawling up onto the beach. She ran to him. He collapsed on the sand and rolled to his back, still coughing.

Ryn put a hand on his wet shirt. "Are you alright?"

He nodded, rolling to the side and coughing up water.

Sand kicked up as Regg and Yll ran up to join them.

Regg automatically put a hand to Zo's throat. For once Zo didn't object. He lay back down and inhaled deeply as Regg's eyes got wide.

"Zo, your body it's...different inside," Regg said.

Zo's eyes opened and were a startling sky blue, the color of the dragon, then they faded to his normal brown.

"I think that bead has changed many things," Zo said, taking a deep breath and sitting up. "Sorry everyone. I had him in my grip and I could have taken him out with Killing magic, but I couldn't go there again."

Ryn brushed the water-soaked hair out of his eyes. "I would never ask that of you. We will get him."

"What in the name of the Ancestors I hate does Fergus think he's doing?" Zo asked, eyes locked on the shoreline to the right.

"Slaying the dragon," Ryn said without turning around.

Zo flopped back onto the sand with a groan just as Iden came rushing up, engulfing Zo in hugs and kisses till Zo rolled him over, straddled him, and pinned his hands to the sand.

"Later," Zo said with a smirk, then let go of Iden and headed down the beach.

Ryn fast walked after him to keep up. "What do you think you're doing?"

"Keeping your boyfriend from getting killed," Zo said.

Ryn grabbed Zo's arm. "Wait, I need to tell you the plan..."

* * *

Zo watched as Thax uncovered Ryn's fake cow in the cart, while Fergus tried to entice the dragon to engage him in battle. He dodged dragon fire while trying to keep him close, but the dragon kept swinging back toward the Ancestral ships. Zmej had already burned two ships to the waterline.

Regg stepped up next to Zo. "That's never going to work—he needs a boost up there."

Zo turned to Regg then looked behind where they were setting up the cow on the cart. Ryn was hoping the dragon would be hungry enough to eat it. Zo wasn't sure—he hadn't been hungry as a dragon, but Zo wasn't really a dragon, he had just shapeshifted into one. Thax was messing with the cow.

Iden, Zo called with his mind.

Coming love, was Iden's reply.

Iden slipped his arm around Zo's waist. "What's up?"

"Can you boost Fergus up to the dragon with air?"

"Hmmmmm. Maybe, but it would be more stable with more than one stream of air to hold him." Iden rubbed his chin.

Zo glanced behind him to see Ryn waving her arms at Thax.

Ryn, Zo called.

She glanced over at him, waved her hand one more time, then headed toward Zo.

"Do we have anyone else with Air magic?" Zo asked her as she approached.

"Yes." she nodded.

Zo looked around. "Who? We need to lift Fergus, and I think a triangle of three streams of air would be secure."

"Me." She gave him a lopsided smile.

Zo rocked back. "How? Did you take one of the beads?"

"No," she said, and air began to swirl around her feet.

And in that moment Zo recalled many times when Ryn was upset and the air around her had swirled to match her mood.

"When..." He started, then caught the look on her face. "Never mind, let's get Fergus within striking distance."

Iden, Ryn, and Zo pulled on the air around them and sent it toward Fergus. He startled, then held the sword tight with both hands as the air lifted him up at the incoming dragon. The dragon tried to dodge Fergus, but the airstream deposited him on the neck of the dragon. He clung to the ridge of scales down the dragon's back as the dragon dove toward the water, then shot toward the sky trying to dislodge Fergus. Somehow, Fergus managed to not only cling to the dragon, but climb his way to the dragon's head.

The dragon turned toward the shore.

Next to Zo, Ryn gasped and put her hands to her mouth.

Fergus held Praedo's sword up so it glinted in the sunlight, then he thrust it deep into the dragon's skull.

The dragon roared, and shook his head, sending Fergus plummeting to the water.

Ryn screamed.

Zo and Iden pushed air to slow Fergus's fall.

Someone in a small boat near the docks rowed out into the bay toward where Fergus had fallen.

The dragon reached up with a claw and pulled the sword out of its head, dropping it into the water.

"That's it." Ryn said. "Plan B."

"And what is Plan B exactly?"

"We trick the dragon into eating sulfur."

"So what—it poisons him?" Zo asked.

Iden shook his head. "Boom!" His hands splayed out like an explosion.

"It does that?" Zo frowned.

"With a little heat. Come on!" Ryn took off toward the wagon full of cows.

Zo inhaled deeply. Turned and gave Iden what he hoped was not their last kiss, and he took off after Ryn.

* * *

Ryn's hands were shaking. This was her last hope to defeat the dragon. If this didn't work, she was out of ideas.

"Where did you get this irrational idea?" Zo asked.

"A book on how to kill a dragon." Ryn pulled a paper from her skirts and handed it to him.

Zo skimmed the suggestions, and pointed to the one where someone put themselves in a trunk, let the dragon swallow them, and then burst out and kill the dragon from the inside.

"This is what Fergus wanted to do isn't it?"

Ryn rolled her eyes. "Maybe."

"Dragon's burning another boat to the waterline," Thax said.

Ryn swore. Zo stared at her, slack jawed.

"Let's make this fast!" She yelled

"How are we going to get the dragon to eat the cow?" Zo asked.

"Bait," she answered.

"Isn't the cow bait?"

"Nope."

Ryn climbed up into the wagon. "It's good enough, Thax. Take Brynd and Regg and get away from here."

Thax was smoothing the cowhide on the fake cow. "Such a beautiful cut. I was so looking forward to the dress I was going to make out of it. Plus, all of my sulfur stores for dying fabric. This better work." Thax gave Ryn a sharp look.

"I'm sorry. We'll find you more of everything," Zo said, helping Brynd down from the cart.

Ryn watched the dragon soar over the water heading for Waatch and the Library. He was apparently done with burning boats.

"How do we get his attention?" Zo asked.

"Like this—you create an image of the Heart Tree next to the wagon, and I'll do the rest," she said.

"Illusion. Right. I haven't tried that one yet," Zo said, then his eyes went distant like he was listening to instruction.

When the tree appeared, Ryn used the air to project her voice up to the dragon. "Zmej! Here I am! I am the branch of the tree!"

The dragon ignored her, heading straight for the Library.

"Come on!" Ryn yelled.

Zmej flew past her.

Ryn felt someone join her in the cart. She turned to find Clayr, Jayne, Ryette, and Eladorys climbing up next to her.

Maybe the dragon wasn't interested in her, but he was certainly interested in all of them together.

"Come at get us, you miserable fiend. I stole your precious egg!" Eladorys's voice wasn't loud, but it traveled.

The dragon stopped and flapped its wings. When its head turned, the fire-red eyes locked on Ryn and the others.

She swallowed hard. "That's right! We're here, and you can't kill the tree with a piece of it here." Ryn's voice shook.

"Is that true?" Zo whispered.

"I don't know."

The dragon dove toward them and at the last minute, Zo wrapped his arms around Ryn and the others and Travel magicked them to the docks.

The dragon chomped down on the wagon and its fake cow, crunching it up.

"That's right, that's right, now swallow," Ryn whispered.

The dragon turned to see where they went and started toward the docks.

"How do we ignite the sulfur?" Zo asked.

"He has to breathe fire," Ryn shouted.

"If he breathes fire on the docks they'll go up in flames."

"We take to the air," Ryn reached out a hand.

Zo's brow furrowed, but he took her hand and together they used Air magic to lift them up and to soar over the water.

Flying gave Ryn butterflies in her stomach, but soaring over the water almost made Ryn forget what she was doing. She let the air take them one way, then another. The sight of people from the Ancestral Houses pouring onto the docks made her feel like they were tiny, and she was far away from everything. This had to work, or the dragon's devastation would be worse than before. She turned to find the dragon bearing down on them. That snapped her back.

The dragon opened its mouth and breathed fire at them.

They pulled on the water below and shielded themselves with it.

"It didn't explode," Zo said.

"The sulfur must not be hot enough."

The dragon turned toward the docks as a huge spout of water sprung up from that direction and washed over the dragon, as well as Ryn and Zo. They rode the wave of water as it pulled them out of the air and washed them up onto the shore. The water spun Ryn around and around till she came to a stop covered in wet sand, her hair dripping in her face.

Zo coughed next to her. "This is the second time now, this has to stop." He spat sand out of his mouth.

"House Mare is in full force here," Ryn coughed.

Her sandy hands parted her curtain of hair in time to see the dragon fly off over the Waatch wall toward the Library.

"Zo..." Ryn started.

"I see it." Zo jumped up into the air and transformed back into the blue dragon. He took off after the black dragon.

Just turn him around and make him come back. Fighting him over the water will be better than over the town. Ryn sent to Zo.

* * *

I'll do my best, he's slipperier than an eel. Zo pumped his wings harder to catch up with Zmej. Zo hoped he could think of a way to turn him around and get him to chase him back over the water.

Zmej approached the outer wall of the Library grounds—and stopped like he ran into something solid. Zo pulled his head back and flapped his wings to stop his forward momentum. He looked down at the barrier defenses and saw Tertius with his arms held high, forming an ice wall in front of the dragon. Zmej roared flames, but the ice held.

"Zo!" Lar called to him, waving their arms from outside the barricade, and wall of ice.

Zo flew down, changing back to himself as Zmej breathed more fire on the ice wall.

"What?" Zo asked.

"Take this, son." Lar pressed the Wild magic stone into Zo's hand. How had he gotten it?

The dragon gave up blasting through and decided to go up and fly over the ice wall.

Zo nodded, pocketed the stone, and flew away as a dragon.

Zmej was almost over the ice wall when Zo chomped down on his leg and pulled him backward. Zmej turned eyes of golden fire on Zo, who let go and turned tail toward the bay. One glance behind him saw Zmej was following.

Incoming! Zo called out to Ryn.

Perfect, Ryn thought back.

When he flew over the Waatch wall, Zo almost dropped out of the sky. Ships flying flags of all the House colors blocked the exit of the bay, with Ancestors on the docks and lining the shores. Out of the north gate of Waatch poured the sprites, the Waatch guard, Library workers, and Ordinary townspeople carrying anything that could possibly be used as a weapon.

Zo soared off toward Ryn, who was hanging in the air at the center of the bay. He changed back from a dragon into himself...and almost fell out of the air. Ryn grabbed his hand.

"What are you doing? You should stay a dragon," Ryn said as Zo got his air magic under him.

"I needed to give you this." Zo pulled the stone out of his pocket.

"The stone?" Ryn's brow furrowed.

Her eyes shut as she closed her fingers around it. "This is the key. The Wild magic couldn't defeat the first dragon so Praedo came. He defeated the dragon, but lost his life. This is what Luc was trying to tell us—we need to work together. Both magics to defeat the one."

Ryn put the stone back in Zo's hand. "When he opens his mouth, throw it in."

Zo swallowed hard. "He'll be getting ready to roast us when he opens his mouth."

Ryn nodded, then looked up to see Zmej being harassed by Yll and Moult as birds. Zmej took a deep breath and spewed fire at them. Both birds fell from the sky.

"No!" Ryn screamed.

Zmej turned and came straight at them.

"Take my hand!" Ryn yelled.

Zmej opened his mouth, Zo pitched the stone in as hard as he could, then quickly grabbed Ryn's hand.

Together they swirled their hands to create a huge firestream straight at the dragon's mouth. The dragon opened to return with its own fire. The two fires collided.

A fireball as large as a house came from a ship flying House Ingis colors, hurtling right down the dragon's throat.

A stream of fire magic came from the sprites.

Ryn and Zo pressed their fire after it. Zmej inhaled to breathe more fire...then stopped.

The dragon's throat glowed red all the way down to its chest.

And then he exploded.

Ryn and Zo ducked superheated chunks of dragon.

They dodged to the right and a dragon spine hit them, crashing them into the bay.

Ryn's dress dragged her down. She was paddling frantically.

Zo's head broke the water. "Third time today."

"Help, I don't swim well in deep water!" Ryn's eyes were panicked.

"Relax. Reach for your magic. Let the water lift you up." Zo's voice worked to calm her.

She tried, but her wildly beating heart was keeping her from reaching for the magic.

Just when her head slipped under the water, a hand reached down and pulled her up by her collar.

She was hauled into a boat. She turned to find Fergus grabbing her and enveloping her in a tight, wet hug.

"I thought I'd lost you," they both said at the same time.

"As Regg would say—jinx." Zo laughed, as he flopped into the boat.

Ryn turned and pulled Zo close to her into the hug.

"Who'd a thought a couple Ordinaries and a guy with a broken magic could defeat a dragon?" Fergus said.

Zo's eyes fixed on Ryn. "Who indeed? You've got some explaining to do, missy."

"I'll explain it when I know myself."

Ryn pulled both boys in for another hug.

Epilogue

Zo sat clapping to the music as his dad and Ryette twirled around the dance floor. He'd never seen his father look so happy. The torchlight was enchanting in the summer twilight. Flower strewn arches were everywhere around the grassy meadow next to Crystal Lake. The wedding decorations rivaled, if not surpassed, those from Prym's Debut party. It was almost a year ago, yet it seemed like longer. So much has happened in the last year. He remembered the day he met Ryn and Ryette, and now he was watching his father dance Ryette around the dancefloor as his bride, both of them laughing as he spun her and dipped her for a kiss.

The band invited more couples to join in the dance.

Fergus, in formal dress uniform, bowed then escorted Ryn. Nix and Wilmar were slow dancing cheek to cheek despite the upbeat tempo of the music.

With a formal flare of his arm and a sly smile, Errol invited Clayr to dance.

Regg took the glass of punch from Yll's hand, gave Zo a pointed look, and pulled her out onto the floor.

That was Zo's signal.

Zo smiled as he headed for the rope swing tree. Regg had a special surprise for Yll, and Zo was helping out.

Once Zo was in place, he whistled. Regg danced Yll out of the crowd and under the tree. Zo used his illusion magic to create a curtain of flowering vines. He snapped his fingers and the lanterns in the tree glowed a warm yellow.

Regg stopped dancing and got down on one knee, pulling out a long thin box.

"Yes!" Yll yelled, and Regg stood to kiss her, before taking the necklace from the box and placing it around her neck.

Zo smiled and slipped out between the vines to leave them to themselves. Regg finally found the time to give Yll the surprise he had been wanting to give her for moons, but he didn't want to take away from Lar and Ryette's day, so they came up with the vine illusion.

Hands in his pockets, Zo walked back to the table. It had been an interesting few months. He had turned down a lot of offers, but chose to run Wilmar's physician practice for now so Wilmar and Nix could retire, and Zo could train a new physician. He wasn't certain which direction he should take. He'd been offered everything from Administrator of Waatch, to Head of the Board of Regents, to some new position they wanted to invent which would make him Head Patriarch of all the Ancestral Houses. Having Praedo's magic somehow made him the most sought-after man in all the islands as well as on the mainland. He shouldn't have been surprised. It was one thing to seek after power, but holding it and dealing with the consequences was something he hadn't considered. He had been too caught up in the moment. He still loved Healing, but holding all the magics meant he could do so much more. He decided to first be a humble physician, then explore where his powers led him.

Remus cut in between Fergus and Ryn, and Ryn took Remus's paws and swung them back and forth to dance with him.

Zo laughed. Since Schiz's death, Remus had become Ryn's shadow. She was rarely without him unless she was working in the Library, and even then Remus was not far away, usually in the guard house being spoiled by the Library guards. It had taken Abby, Ryn's cat, time to get used to him, but she eventually accepted the newcomer at the foot of Ryn's bed.

A warm hand slid across Zo's back, and Zo leaned into Iden. Zo had felt him coming. Their connection, now that they both had Mind magic, was almost as if they were one person living in two bodies. They knew each other's thoughts, moods, and desires. The inner workings of Iden's mind were more fascinating than Zo could imagine. Iden was planning a spring wedding, even though Zo thought they should get married in the fall. Zo wanted to take advantage of the goodwill he'd been shown with his new powers. The more time went by without Zo displaying said powers, the more likely people would forget and possibly change their attitude. Zo's mother was insufferable, vying for Head of the Healing Council based on the fact that her son was the most powerful man in the Ancestor world. He hated it. Zo wanted a quick wedding, before his mother got any ideas about inviting every Matriarch and Patriarch of all the Houses. She probably already had. Zo sighed. All he needed to do was have Thax get Iden excited about some fall-colored suits.

"Dance with me," Iden whispered in his ear.

Zo flashed him his toothiest grin.

* * *

The next day Zo stood before Ryn. She had a large pack on her back and Remus at her side.

"Are you sure you'll be safe on your own, all the way to your dad's cave? Clayr gave him leave to go with you," Zo said.

Ryn looked incredibly small with the large pack on her back.

"The dragon may be gone, but his wolves are still out there," he added.

Ryn's hand dropped to Remus's head. "We'll be alright. I need some time to clear my head. The walk will be good for that."

Zo frowned. "Send me a message if you run into trouble. I'll come right away."

Ryn nodded, and Zo bent to kiss her on the cheek.

"I'll stop at Brynd's parent's house on the way to Dad's. After I see my dad, I'm planning on visiting the hot springs. I don't know how long I'll be gone, so don't worry about me," Ryn said, wrapping her arms around him and squeezing him tight.

"I can't wait till you get back. Thax wants to take us singing at his favorite tavern."

"Oh boy." Ryn's voice didn't sound excited.

"But don't let that keep you away." Zo held her at arm's length.

She nodded.

"We're family now. You can't get rid of me." Zo gave her his toothiest grin.

"I love you!" Ryn hugged him again.

Zo watched her walk away down the street past the Healing House headed for Waatch's south gate. He took a deep breath. If he had more time he would go with her, but Wilmar was spending his days filling Zo's head with as much information about his patients and the practice as he could. It was a bit overwhelming, and he knew Wilmar was anxious to be done and leave for his and Nix's cabin in the woods and their much-deserved retirement.

* * *

Ryn walked with Remus at her side through the gates of Waatch. The foot traffic parted around them, and the sideways looks she and Remus got were indicative of the impact Zmej's wolves had upon the people of Waatch. Despite all of that, no one said a word. They were still in awe of the Ordinary, who wasn't very ordinary, and her gentle wolf companion. She was sure it was going to be difficult for them to get used to. Maybe they wouldn't get used to it at all.

Once they started off west down the road toward the peninsula, someone with a cloaked hood over their head stepped out of the woods. Ryn jumped, but Remus only whined.

"Mother, shouldn't you be on your honeymoon?" Ryn asked, trying to get control of her fast-thumping heart.

"I am, but I thought I'd travel down this road a ways with you. Lar and I are leaving later today." Her mother smiled.

"Um—sure." Ryn gave a half smile, only partially covering her disappointment that she wouldn't be alone right away.

"If that's alright with you," her mother added.

"It's a long trip, so I can share it for a while."

Ryn and her mother walked the road in silence until the Waatch traffic began to thin.

"We didn't have much time to talk after the dragon. I admit I was surprised when you came out of the Heart Tree room fighting with magic. I suppose I should have seen it in you earlier, but I was living in fear of anything that might draw attention to us. My family is so wrapped up in their power."

"It's alright Mother, I can see why you were hiding from your family—plus if you hadn't been so protective, the dragon might have manipulated us sooner. If he had known I was the branch and key to the Heart Tree before I was old enough to be smart about dealing with him it would have been bad."

Ryn's dust-covered boot kicked a rock into the bushes, sending a rabbit bouncing away. It reminded her of that first day when she met Zo and Regg and he had kicked a rock, scaring a rabbit. Remus had been in the bushes following her, though she only saw glimpses of him at the time.

"You just spent time with your father fighting a dragon. I'm not sure why you need to visit him."

Ryn sighed inwardly. "I haven't spent much time with him the past few years. I want to make up for that, at least in a small way," Ryn said.

The real reason was her father said he had something to show her. He admitted he should have shown her when she was there, but didn't want to do it in front of all her friends. He also admitted seeing her in person, after so long being apart, made him scared to share what he had planned to show her. He told her before he left to return to his caves that he was ready to share something important with her, and asked her to come as soon as she was able to get away. She waited till after her mother's wedding. Clayr had given her a leave of absence from the Library. Ryn was so glad the board had been furious with Jeris's administration of the Library, and had reinstated Clayr, who had immediately brought back all the Ordinaries who had been fired. Jeris was allowed to keep his Regent position, and Prym was demoted back to her original assistant researcher job. Everything had been set right—except, as she put her hand down to pat Remus's head, she could almost see Schiz there beside them, fingers tapping at his temple as he fought to find the words he wanted to say.

Ryn's mother stopped and placed her hands on Ryn's shoulders. "I just want you to know that I'm proud of you. I'm proud of the grown woman you've become. I know it's been rough this year, but you've come through it all the best way possible."

Her mother pulled Ryn into a crushing hug. "Don't be gone too long, and I want to hear all about it when you get back."

"I'll try, Mother."

"That's my girl. Now I'm off to Saarimuto. The Mind magic island is supposed to be quite peaceful and beautiful." Her mother sighed. "On our way home, your grandmother wants me to stop at House Viator." Ryette sighed. "I think she just wants to talk me into taking my place as Matriarch in Waiting."

"You should consider it. I think Lar will be fine living on Viatoro." Ryn suppressed a smile. Through the attack of the dragon her grandmother had been supportive. She still tended to have machinations for control and power, but Ryn thought her mother as Matriarch would take House Viator in different directions than it had been going for decades, maybe even the last century. It was a good move in Ryn's mind.

"I'll consider it," her mother said.

"Good." Ryn gave her one more hug, then Ryn shielded her eyes as Ryette's travel magic kicked up dust and small pebbles on the road as it spun around her.

When the dust settled, Ryn took a deep breath, then set her sights on the open road.

* * *

After a brief stop at Brynd's parents to give them news of Waatch and their daughter, and after many hugs, tears, and praises of what a great job Ryn had done from Xylia, Ryn was on the road again. Even if her newfound magic could use Travel magic, which it couldn't, she was enjoying the walk down the warm summer, tree lined road. She inhaled deeply the scent of dust and cedar.

She and Remus reached her father's doorstep quicker than she thought they would. It had felt like such a long way the first time there, but this time it felt easy.

When Moult opened his heavy, wooden, partially repaired door to Ryn, his smile was broad. He took her in his arms, but one of his arms didn't quite make it all the way around Ryn.

"That arm still bothering you? You should have let Zo heal it before you left," Ryn said.

Her father chuckled. "I thought that dragon had me for sure. The wing hasn't been the same since, but there were so many people needing healing, I didn't want to bother anyone. Unfortunately, I was remembering a younger time when I actually healed from injuries."

Moult gestured to the table. There were two bowls of hot fish soup waiting for them.

"I heard you coming in my mind, so I went ahead and made us something to eat. Are you hungry?" Her father asked.

"Starving!"

While they ate, Ryn caught her father up on all the news from the Library. He was pleased they had restored Clayr and that they had finally awarded Ryn a researcher position.

"Not that I've been doing a lot of research lately. Clayr wants me to study the Heart Tree and give a full report on what I find. So little is known about it, and it's an important part of the Library."

Her father took a bite of soup and nodded. She wasn't sure if he was agreeing with her or enjoying the soup.

When dinner was through, and they had cleaned their dishes, Ryn went to sit by the fire. Even at the end of summer, the cave was cold. Remus licked the bowl of food Moult had given him then padded over to sit next to Ryn's chair.

Her father paced and fidgeted a bit. Remus's eyes followed him expectantly.

Remus whined.

Moult stopped. His eyes connected with Remus. Then he went to the dresser at the end of the cave and came back with a thin book.

"This is for you. Someone gave it to me at the Orphanage where I got you. I happened to stop in there about a year after we adopted you. It was cold, and rainy, and I was wet. They had asked me to update them sometime with how you were adjusting, so I took the opportunity to get warm and give them a report."

Ryn took the book into her hands. She ran her fingers across the soft leather cover, then opened the book.

Your Story was on the title page.

Ryn turned the page to find bright watercolor illustrations. The artistry was vivid and whimsical. It had an artist's rendering of Remus on the page. He looked serious. The background full of bright shining flowers was in stark contrast to his mood.

Before you were born, there was a handsome wolf named Remus. He was full of mischief and often upset his father and brothers. He would be gone for days, and would shirk the responsibilities his father gave him. Truth be told, Remus didn't like the things his father asked him to do. He felt they were wrong. So off into the woods he would go, until whatever his father wanted him to do was passed and done.

Ryn turned the page.

One day Remus was in the woods hiding from his father, when he happened upon a hot spring. Thinking that a dip in the hot water sounded like the perfect kind of bath, Remus jumped in, swimming and splashing around.

The picture was of Remus in the hot spring, steam rising as he chased a dragonfly across the water.
She turned the page.

Through the mists on the water came the most beautiful woman Remus had ever seen. Remus, being part human, fell instantly in love with the woman. She must have taken a liking to him, because she pushed him under the water, and when she let him surface, he was no longer a wolf, but a man, lean like a wolf, but muscular like an athlete. His white hair glowed in the sunlight. He held his human hands in front of him, examining them this way and that. He turned his wide eyes to the woman.
"How?" He startled himself with the sound of his human voice, but she just put a finger to his lips.

The picture on the page made Ryn's jaw drop. It was the man she'd seen in her dream. The white-haired man wearing a cloak with bare legs and feet, leaving a baby at the orphanage's doorstep.

They spent the afternoon swimming and playing in the water. Remus never got tired, nor did his human skin wrinkle in the water. It remained smooth and supple. The woman's name was Airlya. She was a water sprite.

The picture had several vignettes of the two of them, splashing each other, racing each other, and tangled up with each other like they were dancing.
Ryn turned to the next page.

As the sun set and the moon rose, Airlya took Remus into her grotto. Their passionate lovemaking filled the night air, causing the deer to pause, and the stars to twinkle with delight.

The picture was of Airlya holding Remus by his hand and swimming him into a cave shrouded in overhanging vines. Ryn felt herself blushing.

The next morning the sun came up, and Remus woke as a wolf again, lying on a carpet of pine needles in the forest. The grotto, and the hot spring were gone—and so was Airlya.

Remus whined as if he knew what page Ryn was reading.

Remus wandered the area for over a moon, but never found the hot spring again. Heartbroken, he found his way back to his father and his brothers.

The picture was of Remus the wolf leaving the forest, head hanging low and tail between his legs. The artistry was so remarkable Ryn could feel the sadness, and see the tears in his eyes.

As the moons went by, Remus often returned to those woods in hopes of finding the spring again. One day, several moons later, Remus, tired and disheartened, emerged from the dense trees to find the spring before him. He barked in joy and ran into the water, sending it splashing. He swam across the spring to where the grotto should be, but stopped when a different water sprite appeared before him. This one felt ancient, but didn't look much older than Airlya.
"You have been summoned here to help," the sprite said.
She turned and Remus followed her, and as he did, he changed into a human again. Remus was delighted.

His heart swelled with the hope that he would see Airlya.

The sprite pulled back the vines to the grotto to reveal Airlya, very pregnant and clearly in the process of giving birth. She reached out her hand to him.

The picture was of a sprite who resembled Eladorys, holding back the vines to reveal a sprite with a pained look on her face, reaching forward, almost like she was reaching for the reader off the page.

Remus was confused and concerned, but he had seen many different kinds of animals giving birth, so he felt he knew what to expect. When Airlya's pain became intense, he helped move her into the spring. A baby girl was born into the waters of the hot spring to two loving parents who were overjoyed to see her curling dark hair, and tiny toes.

As Airlya rested in the grotto, Remus held the baby girl, certain he could never be happier.

The picture was of Remus holding a sweet-faced baby, while Airlya rested in the background.

"You can't keep her," the old sprite said.

Remus frowned and clutched the child to his chest.

"The child is not a full sprite, so she will not be nourished by the land the way our people are, and you will return to the form of a wolf when the sun rises."

Remus looked down into the face of the sleeping baby. She inhaled deeply, causing her tiny hands to open, then she exhaled to settle down to sleep deeper.

"No. There has to be a way. Can't you take her? There has to be someone who can help us so we don't have to give her away."

Remus thought of his best friend Schiz. Before his magical accident he could have taken the baby, but he knew Schiz was no longer stable.

The old sprite shook her head slowly. "If she stays here, she will not survive. Go quickly before the sun rises and you resume your wolf form."

The picture was of the white-haired Remus holding a baby in his arms, tears flowing down his cheeks.

Ryn looked up from the page to see tears falling from wolf eyes. She's never seen anyone look so sad before. She wasn't sure how to comfort him. Patting him on the head seemed too condescending.

She turned the page.

Remus ran all night through the woods. Tears blurring his vision. When at last he found himself on the road through a village, it was nearing dawn. The sky was lightening, and he knew his time was almost gone. He passed a window with a light on inside. A couple were there tending to a baby. Remus thought perhaps this was the right family. They had a baby and would be able to feed and take care of his little one.

He knocked on the door, but the sight of him without clothes, holding a newborn child drained all the color from the husband's face. When asked if they could take the girl, the man shook his head and told Remus they had too many mouths to feed already. The man gave him an old, tattered cloak to wear, telling him there was an orphanage on the edge of the village he could take the child to, then the man sent him on his way.

The picture was of Remus, head bowed, holding the baby while the man at the door handed him a cloak.

A little farther down the road, Remus found a large building with a small fence around it, and a tree with a swing in the yard. He opened the gate and knocked on the door. When the kindly orphanage director finally opened the door, Remus held the child and sobbed. Eventually, he inhaled the courage to let go of the baby, then he turned and ran off into the sunrise, changing back into a wolf as the first sun rays shot up over the top of Dragon Mountain.

He was never human again.

Ryn's eyes filled with tears which slid down her cheeks and her nose. She wiped them away before they could drop onto the picture of Remus the wolf running off into the sunrise.

Once her eyes were clear enough to see she looked over at Remus with his head buried between his paws.

There was silence in the cave for a long time.

Moult was in a chair by the fire, his elbows on the armrests, his fingers steepled in thought as he stared into the fire.

"How come you've never shown me this before?" Ryn asked.

Moult glanced over at her. "I never told your mother I had the book. It seemed like a fantastical tale, and I wasn't sure if it was true. It wasn't until I saw Remus, and Schiz, then I knew. I knew it was all true."

"But who wrote the book?"

Remus whined and looked into her eyes with his sad tearful ones.

"It was Schiz, wasn't it? But how did he manage to draw and write like this when he could barely speak?" Ryn asked.

Moult shrugged. "Could be the magic affected many parts of his brain, but not his creative side. Perhaps being straightforward was difficult for him. Telling a tale with whimsy was easier."

Ryn ran her fingers lightly over the picture of the sunrise. "Schiz had Water magic, and this is watercolor. Perhaps that helped."

Moult nodded. "Perhaps."

Ryn shifted to look Remus in the eyes. "You're my father."

Remus nodded his wolf head.

Ryn stood and knelt in front of Remus. She put her arms around his neck and held him while they both cried. Remus put a paw on her arm.

When she finally pulled away from the hug she had a thought. "Wait—does that mean I am Zmej's granddaughter?"

Remus nodded.

"And your mother—she was from one of the Ancestral Houses."

Another nod.

"So I am part water sprite, part dragon, and part Ancestor descendant." She rocked back and sat hard on her bottom. "I have all the magics."

Remus grinned.

"How is it that I can't touch Ancestor beads?"

"That I can't answer," Moult said.

* * *

Ryn stayed with her father for a few more days, helping him cook and healing his arm. When she began to feel anxious to get to the last part of her journey, she reluctantly packed her bag.

Ryn's brow furrowed.

"You should return to Waatch. We could use your expertise at the Library. I could ask Clayr if you could help me with the tree," she said, standing in the doorway with her bag packed.

Moult nodded. "I have been here a long time. The solitude has been healing, but I think you're right. I think it's time to return. I want to make one more search of the caves here to make sure we didn't miss any beads and then I'll make my way back."

Ryn hugged him, inhaling his smell of dust and books. "I will miss you. I'll see you there. Don't let everyone worry about me if I'm delayed in returning."

"Will do." Moult kissed the top of her head.

Then her and Remus headed back down the peninsula road. Back to the entrance to the hot springs.

* * *

This time the crack in the wall opened to a forest instead of the narrow canyon. Ryn stepped back through the door to check and make sure she'd entered the right gateway. It was the same gate she'd entered before with Zo and Fergus. Remus led the way. He made a straight beeline for the hot spring. When they got there, he splashed into the water, just like the picture in the book. As he did so, he changed into a human. Rising from the misty waters was a woman who embraced him. Remus let out a bark of a laugh, then they kissed. They turned with smiling faces toward Ryn. They came to the hot spring's edge and beaconed her in.

Ryn hesitated. Her heart was pounding, and her stomach fluttered. She was here at last. Finally, she knew who her family was, but she didn't *know* them. They were her blood, and she was so happy they were excited to find her and meet her, but she felt closer to Yll whom she grew up with. All of this was unfamiliar. It wasn't the instant feeling of belonging she'd hoped for. She looked back toward the gateway and Waatch somewhere in the distance. Her family there was familiar, but not her blood. Would she ever feel she fit in?

She looked back at her parents, waiting for her. She supposed it didn't matter. For now, she had this moment.

"Daughter." There were tears in Airlya's eyes. "Come. I have waited so long to hold you in my arms."

She dropped her pack and flung herself into the water and their arms. There were hugs and tears and laughter.

"Oh! How I didn't want to give you up! I have ached every year on the summer solstice, the day of your birth," Airlya sobbed into Ryn's shoulder.

"My sweet Ryn, to have you in my arms at last. My wolf arms have craved for it." Remus held her.

When her parents released her, Eladorys was standing in the misty pool.

"Our Cya, you are of age and have a choice. You can return to your life at the Library as you are, or you can spend time learning the ways of the sprites. I must warn you, if you choose the way of the sprites, it may alter you permanently. It's possible you may never return to the Heart Tree."

Ryn frowned.

Airlya smiled at her. "Or you may become the Heart Tree's caretaker. It will all be determined by your life among us."

Ryn thought of her parents, Yll and Brynd, Zo and Fergus. She loved them dearly, but she needed time to get to know this family. She needed time to find out who she was, and to properly learn the ways of the Wild magic.

Ryn nodded. "I want to learn the ways of my bloodline."

She thrilled at the sound of those words. She never thought she would be able to say them.

Eladorys held her arms outstretched. "Welcome, granddaughter. We've been waiting for you for a long time."

And Ryn walked into her embrace, shedding the Ordinary girl she once was, and becoming something new.

Appendix I: The Ancestral Houses

House Terr
Earth Magic. House seat located on Daoterr

House Mare
Water Magic. House seat located on Shimamare

House Venti
Air Magic. House seat located on Kohventi

House Ignis
Fire Magic. House seat located on Ignisapan

House Lux
Lightning Magic. House Lux is located on Luxpulau

House Viator
Travel Magic. House Viator is located on Viatoro

House Dico
Mind Magic. House Dico is located on Oydico

House Muto
Shape shifting Magic. House Muto is located on Saarimuto

House Sano
Healing Magic. House Sano is located on Eileansano

House Pentral
Spirit Magic. House Pentral is located on Inispentral

House Vivus
Animation Magic. House Vivus in located on Ynysvivus

House Illusio
Illusion magic. House Illusio is located on Iegillusio

Appendix II: Luc's Poem as recorded in *On the Legend of Luc, Praedo's Scribe*

In shadows deep, where ancient echoes sing,
Shores were cursed by the serpent's wing.
Where the beastly dragon ruled the land,
The most majestic mountains stand.

Citizens cowered, afraid for their life,
When Praedo came to end the strife.
Holding great power he set on the quest,
To conquer the dragon, to vanquish the test.

With twelve companions to fight at his side,
The dragon had nowhere safe to hide.
His fierce evil eyes glowed of embering flame,
Praedo outsmarted the dragon with magical game.

Flashes of lightning and roaring thunder,
The earth moved and rocked asunder.
The dragon fell and crashed in the deep,
Where the waters devoured and his corpse sleeps.

Injured our hero fell to the ground,
To aid his needs his friends gathered round.
Alas it was late, as his dying breath whispered,
They drew near to him to help and they heard.

Take ye my bones and turn them to beads,
My magic will guide and protect your needs.
As long as it's used for the good of the land,
Ye shall hold great power within your hand.

The Healer's Magic

Pass this gift down through each family line,
To guard this place throughout all of time.
So they crafted beads from his magical bones,
And wore them round necks like tiny white stones.

What's left must stay safe and must be hidden,
To fall in the wrong hands is forbidden.
From the start where the mountains rise,
The treasure was hidden neath azure skies.

Seek the glade where whispers of pines,
Guard the secret that time defines.
By rivers winding through emerald lands,
Where the eagle soars, the seeker stands.
Follow the call of the owl at night,
To a secret passage where ye will find light.

Appendix III: Gesta Praediana

Invocation
In the verdant fronds of my solitudes,
My verses flourished with a mountain voice.
I sang the archaic echoes of the earth,
In the growing poppies, and the grassy herbs.
In the streamy waters, I sipped the sweet truths,
That the mountain gives to those who love them.

My lyre was foraging for the perfect cadence,
In the vitreous rhythms of a full, cold rain,
And under the moonlight, between sea and sand,
I searched the sonorous accents of the waves.

But alas! My verses turned into a lament,
Under the bright flashes of the traveling star,
Who would have thought that a radiant sky,
Omen would be of such pain and despair?

Sweet melodic accents dying in the ash,
Great agrestal anthems profaned in the flames,
Fire in the forest, trees becoming blaze,
And a solemn requiem left in the night air.

When the somber fumes invaded the skies,
They spread in fields, through cities and towns,
Becoming the voice, the herald, and sign,
Of pain and calamities, misery, and mourn.

But what was the cause of so much commotion?
What turned all my odes into burial hymns?
What tinted the lights of the day with black shadows?
The old vicious dragon and his conquest thirst.

The burdens of servitude fall on our backs,
Where freedom existed, bondage came to be,
Where joyfulness flourished, bitterness remained,
Where beauty and grace blossomed, only rot was seen.

334 The Healer's Magic

What will bring joy back to the chants?
Who will deliver from the iron yoke?
What will scourge the draconic lord?
The strong arm of Praedo, his power and sword.

I
Canticum Terrae

When our strongholds fell and our banners burned,
We fought without mercy, with steel and with flame.
The bravest of heroes first perished in fame,
And left all the people to sorrow returned.

Long months passed away with no cry of glory,
Till even the poet took sword in his hand;
And each grim assault laid waste to the land,
As traitors arose to rewrite our story.

The faithful withdrew to the forest's shade,
In the northwestern realm, between the two seas;
Two thousand at most, yet with courage and peace,
We gathered and counsel and comfort we made.

No fear of the grave in our hearts remained,
We rode to the plain for the last contention;
The host of the dragon came forth with intention—
To die in that battle was honor attained.

When both mighty armies at last converged,
A silence profound filled the trembling plain,
And ere the war-trumpet resounded again,
From heaven a star on the field emerged.

Astonishment seized both foe and friend,
For out of the light rose a gallant form:
A man clad in armor of emerald storm,
Whose voice like a clarion the heavens rent.

Then magic primeval was spoken aloud,
The vast plain trembled, the soil was riven,
The level was raised by the might of heaven,
And mountains eternal arose from the cloud.

The hosts were divided on either side,
The bloodshed halted, the slaughter ceased;
The noble defender our lives released,
And hope in our hearts once more did abide.

Never we learned of his homeland or kin,
Nor sought to uncover his birth or name;
He came from the sky with no wealth or fame,
But valor his banner, his sword, and his will.

II
Canticum Aquae

When the hero had risen and fashioned the hills,
He lifted his voice with a grave lamentation:
"Fly to the forests, depart these plains still,
For soon shall the dragon bring devastation."

Most of the people obeyed his command,
But I would not flee nor abandon the fight;
"This battle is ours, this land is our right,"
I cried to the heavens with sword in hand.

Then seven remained on that perilous ground—
Four noble women of spirit unbending,
Two valiant men to the last defending,
And I, the bard, by courage bound.

The hero beheld us, and kindly he spoke:
"My name is Praedo, remember it well.
The beast I shall face till its power is quelled,
For such is the vow my heart awoke."

Scarce had he finished his noble appeal,
When suddenly thunder rolled through the plain;
A shadow arose from the eastern domain—
The dread of the ages, the dragon revealed.

The furious monster breathed fire and storm,
Its blaze nearly burned us with merciless flame;
But Praedo ascended, his strength untamed,
And gathered the clouds in a wrathful swarm.

336 *The Healer's Magic*

Then from the heavens he wrung the clouds dry,
The torrents descended in roaring cascade;
The fires were quenched, the meadows remade,
And in the wide field a lake came to lie.

The beast in its anger commanded the wave,
From the newborn waters drew lances of ice;
He hurled them at Praedo with lethal device,
Yet Praedo made snow of the weapons he gave.

The waters, the vapors, the frost and the flame—
A battle unholy the world had not known;
Till shrieking in terror the dragon had flown,
And silence triumphant through heaven came.

From the snows that covered the mountain's height,
New springs awakened and murmured below;
They wandered as rivers in crystalline flow,
And still they are seen in this world of light.

III
Canticum Venti

The first great battle at last was done,
And Praedo descended in glory and grace;
Yet peace unfulfilled still shadowed his face,
For westward the wounded beast had run.

He told us the monster was hurt yet alive,
In need of refuge, of hunger and rest;
He asked if we knew, by sign or by quest,
Where such a vile creature might yet survive.

We spoke of the coast where the waters bend,
Of villages humble, of ports in chain,
Of fisherfolk bound by the dragon's reign—
And Praedo resolved their grief to end.

Then magic of air was at once revealed,
For Praedo invoked the spirits of wind;
We rose to the sky, to the clouds we thinned,
And swiftly the miles before us healed.

A fog dense and bitter enclosed the shore,
A darkness of salt, of shadow, of grief;
No light could pierce through its ghostly relief,
Nor sight could avail us a step or more.

But Praedo commanded the winds to divide,
The mist was sundered, the path made clear;
We came to a tavern to rest and hear,
What sorrow or secret the town might hide.

Yet no man spoke and no woman replied,
They turned from our question, from word and glance;
So I took my lyre and sang by chance,
The deeds of the hero we held in pride.

The son of the innkeeper, young and grave,
With hope in his eyes and with trembling hand,
Proclaimed that the fog was the dragon's command,
A spell of enslavement to the people he gave.

He told how the beast had conquered the coast,
How those who would flee were trapped in despair;
The dragon had called the black fog from the air,
To bind the free souls that had suffered most.

Then Praedo looked skyward, his gaze aflame,
He summoned the zephyr in solemn tone;
The dark mist scattered, the curse was undone,
And sunlight eternal upon them came.

IV
Canticum Illusionis

When once more the sun shone bright in the sky,
The villagers came, with joy in their eyes;
They offered us food and shelter likewise,
And we with their aid pressed onward, nearby.

The innkeeper's son, brave and steadfast of heart,
Joined our noble company on the way;
Through islands and villages he showed the way,
Revealing the homes where the dragon had part.

The Healer's Magic

For many long months we searched without rest,
Yet our labor was noble, our purpose true;
Through villages freed from the shadow's cruel hue,
We struck at the curse that oppressed the oppressed.

At last we arrived at a port high and grand,
Yet no soul was stirring on beaches or quay;
No answer was found, no light on the bay,
And terror grew swiftly as we scanned the land.

A shadow immense then fell on the plain,
Our hearts froze with fear at the dreadful sight;
Three monstrous dragons eclipsed the sunlight,
Their roars shook the heavens, their power profane.

So frozen with awe we could barely move,
When two young men, alike in form and hair,
Called to us loudly with voices of care,
Summoning courage the fear could not prove.

They bade us to run, to take shelter with haste,
But we, the brave, would not yield to their call;
For to fight without pause was our mission all,
And we would confront the illusions they faced.

The twins, inspired, ceased their urgent cries,
With bow in their hands they approached with a grin;
They spoke of the honor in battle to win,
And pledged to die with us under the skies.

Then Praedo appeared, laughing from nowhere,
With calmness and gesture of finger snapped;
The beasts simply vanished, the illusions collapsed,
All was revealed as a cunning snare.

V
Canticum Mutiationis

Our laughter rang loud through the clear, open air,
And with our delight, the people arose;
They laughed and they wept, struck foreheads in awe,
Rejoicing to see what had happened there.

Then we learned how a year past, the beast had come,
Shattered and weary in human guise;
He demanded at once that bread be supplied,
And protection from men lest his need become.

The people, though fearful, sought to assist,
Yet soon had the thought to oppose the foul fiend;
To strike while its strength from injury weaned,
And not leave the beast to continue its tryst.

The strongest among them, still left of the men,
Took weapons at dawn and prepared for the fray;
With them the twin brothers also came that day,
And soon the red clash of the battle began.

The cruel dragon returned to its form of flame,
Yet the brothers loosed arrows with unerring aim;
They struck with such valor that honor and fame,
Were theirs on that field, the beast pierced and maimed.

The dragon took flight to the high, empty sky,
Calling to kin with a roar full of dread;
Two more dragons arose, terror widespread,
Later, Praedo discerned the illusion nearby.

For all had appeared as true in that hour,
Yet none could distinguish the false from the real;
Praedo revealed what deception could steal,
And unmasked the spell with his limitless power.

After the tale, doubts arose in our minds:
Where had the beast fled, and could it be found?
Months of pursuit left no trace on the ground,
The task seemed as endless as winds and the tides.

So few were we left, only nine souls remained,
The world vast and time too fleeting to waste;
To find the foul creature we could not postpace,
Before it had healed, regained strength unchained.

To save us from months of fruitless pursuit,
Praedo unleashed all his powers at once;
With a calm gesture and serene salute,
He turned our own bodies into birds in flight.

VI
Canticum Cogitationis

With wings bestowed by the magic of Praedo,
We roamed through the islands, through caverns and caves,
Through mountains, through valleys, by air and by land—
Yet no trace nor shadow the beast ever gave.

Through journeys uncounted, through lands without end,
We found ourselves lacking for council or meeting;
Our voices grew faint, our plans retreating—
We needed a bond our thoughts could send.

Then Praedo, as ever, had wisdom prepared,
For every burden that darkened our way;
The sixth of his magics was shown that day—
A web of the mind that our spirits shared.

Though far were the roads and distant the towns,
His voice would resound within thought's domain;
The messages reached us swifter than rain,
And all our tidings together were bound.

It was in those travels the twins declared,
Grim news that chilled our hearts with dread:
That in southern bays an army was spread,
An empire's fleet by the foe prepared.

Then the hero spoke within our minds—
To me, the bard, and to my ten peers;
He bade us fly, to be witness and seers,
To seek those ships the rumor defined.

Below, where the bays like bright mirrors shone,
The band of Praedo was joined once more;
Their joy was plain, as in days of yore,
With smiles and hearts that beat as one.

Praedo with reverence met his dear friends,
And each he embraced with a heartfelt grace;
For friendship alone our bonds could trace—
No purer devotion the heavens send.

Yet joy was broken, and silence grew grim,
When the twins, with faces solemn and drawn,
Led forth two maidens into the dawn,
To tell the tale of a secret dim.

Some doubted the words the young ones bore,
Whether their hearts were faithful or feigned;
But Praedo, with magic his truth maintained,
Read through their souls—and trusted them more.

VII
Canticum Animationis

The noble maidens their story told—
They had been reared by the sounding shore;
Their father, a smith, was alive no more,
Fallen in battle, valiant and bold.

Their town had become, by the foe's design,
A fortress strong for the dark invasion;
There ships were forged for domination—
Swift were their keels and cruel their line.

They spoke of a plan, most grimly conceived,
To seize again all the northern lands,
To shatter the peace by Praedo's hands,
So long preserved, so long believed.

But only three days were left, they said,
Before the fleet would depart for war;
No time for counsel, no aid from afar—
We stood alone with our hearts of dread.

Praedo, unmoved, with a steadfast gaze,
Assured us that help would soon appear;
The seventh magic he made clear,
And calm returned to crown his face.

The night before the dreadful day,
Guided by maidens through shadowed halls,
We crept in silence to the armory's walls,
Where Praedo his wonder would soon display.

With voice resounding, he spoke unafraid:
"Awake, ye weapons of mortal making!"
At once they stirred, to awareness waking—
Each sword and shield in order arrayed.

Spears, helms, and armor obeyed his call,
Each metal heart by spirit ignited;
Their clangor rose, in glory united,
Awaiting command from one and all.

Then onward we marched to the barracks near,
Where soldiers slept in their nightly guard;
Between sea and steel we struck them hard—
Yet took the stronghold without a tear.

But when we turned toward the horizon's glow,
We saw what folly our joy had been:
A fleet already had left the scene,
And sailed to fulfill its mission below.

Praedo then thundered, his voice aflame,
And called to the cliffs of the shadowed land;
The blackened rocks obeyed his command,
And giants of stone blocked the sea way.

They rose from the waters, grim and vast,
And barred the fleet with walls unbroken;
The dragon's servants were left unspoken,
Their voyage ended, their doom steadfast.

VIII
Canticum Viatoris

The ships and captains we seized in the fight,
And joy arose at our swift salvation;
But fleeting was that exaltation—
A darker herald came with the night.

A haughty man, the fleet's commander,
Laughed with scorn at our victory's cheer:
"You win but a moment—your end is near,
For the Master marches with wrathful grandeur."

The tidings struck our hearts with dread;
A host unending the beast commanded,
To claim the north where peace had landed,
And drown the free in chains instead.

Then Praedo spoke through the silent air,
To allies distant, his words conveying;
He offered counsel, his will unswaying,
And bade us ready for war's despair.

Yet wings of magic could not avail,
For distance mocked our mortal speed;
Then came the eighth gift, born of need—
And space itself began to pale.

We knew not how, but in one breath,
From southern dock to northern shore,
Our band was carried—time no more—
From perilous life to defiance of death.

As spies we sent disguised as birds,
Who brought us news from the eastern plain:
The armies advanced with fire and chain,
Yet the dragon was not seen or heard.

Praedo, steadfast, devised a wall,
And with his power the mountains rose;
They sealed the path of the marching foes,
And bought us hours before the fall.

Our ranks were formed, our banners flown,
The villages sent their bravest kin;
Yet fear still whispered deep within—
Where lay the beast, and where its throne?

At last came word by dawn's faint fire:
The hosts had crossed the mountain's shade;
Our hearts stood firm, and Praedo prayed,
That all of us could have long lives.

IX
Canticum Spiritus

The foe drew near through the shivering plain,
The wind was bitter, the night unmoving;
Praedo stood silent, his soul reproving,
For sorrow had bound his heart with pain.

He summoned his comrades, the steadfast thirteen,
"Guard well my body," he softly pled;
"For I must speak with the ancient dead,
To seek the light their spirits have seen."

For such was the ninth and perilous art—
To pierce the veil where shadows sleep,
To call from silence the wisdom deep,
And bring their counsel to mortal heart.

The noble souls he thus implored,
Bestowed two magics, fierce and bright:
One blazed like fire, a spear of light,
The other renewed what time had scored.

They whispered too of a sacred way,
By which his gifts might yet endure;
He listened, though the words obscure
Soon faded into the coming day.

Then from without came the trumpet's cry,
Within, the bells of warning pealed;
The hosts of evil approached the field,
And dawn was lost to the shadowed sky.

Praedo then raised his hand to call—
And under the moon, in spectral gleam,
Ten thousand spirits began to stream,
Arrayed for battle beside the wall.

Those ghostly warriors, pale and pure,
Defended our ranks through the weary night;
But suddenly broke that fragile fight—
A roar from the depths none could endure.

The ground was shaken, the stones undone,
From beneath the fortress the Dragon came;
Its breath was terror, its eyes were flame—
And all our hopes were overrun.

How blind we had been to the beast below,
That slept in silence beneath our doors;
We searched through lands and distant shores,
While here it waited, our hidden foe.

X
Canticum Ignis

At last had come the hour of dread,
The long-feared battle would soon begin;
Never again would such strife be seen—
The hero and dragon in fury wed.

The sun ascended the flaming tide,
Staining with fire the shore and the sea;
Yet brighter still, unceasingly,
The dragon's wrath against us cried.

Though Praedo deflected the torrent of flame,
The roofs of the city were scorched and falling;
The heavens thundered, the crowds were calling—
They feared extinction and utter shame.

Before the gates the legions came,
Assaulting the walls with violent might;
Yet still our fortress endured the fight,
The portcullis held, the wall the same.

Then to the gate the dragon flew,
Its breath of fire the iron melted;
Through the great breach the foe exulted—
But Praedo rose, their fury he slew.

Master of flame and the earth's deep core,
He summoned fire from beneath the ground;
Then thrust the harbor, vast and profound,
Into the sea, and an island was born.

346 *The Healer's Magic*

Waters boiled between isle and coast,
The enemy halted in awe and dread;
But the dragon, raging, lifted its head—
And called down fire from heaven's host.

Praedo dispelled what flames he could,
Yet sparks fell burning upon the plain;
Explosions thundered, cries of pain—
The blaze consumed where once we stood.

Seeing the peril, Praedo sought peace,
To lead the battle from mortal lands;
He raised once more his radiant hands,
And transported the beast far away with ease.

We know not whether by will or design,
By vow fulfilled or errant spell,
But with the beast, through flame and knell,
His faithful twelve crossed fate's red line.

XI
Canticum Fulgur

The place where we stood, the seven of old,
Seemed strangely known to our wearied eyes—
The field where once, from heavenly skies,
The hero descended in past time told.

But little we lingered in sacred thought,
For a thunderous clamor split the air;
The hero and dragon were battling there,
With lightning and flame their fury wrought.

Yet here below, there were perils near—
Blood on the ground, and cries of pain;
The fire and arrows, a crimson rain,
Had wounded the friends whom Praedo drew near.

In haste we sought for a sheltered place,
For the war above grew fierce and dire;
The heavens resounded, the earth caught fire—
All light and order to chaos gave chase.

The waters, the tempests, the rocks, the flame,
All had become infernal spears;
No side could triumph—both knew their fears,
For neither would bow, yet both laid claim.

The dust and smoke in torrents rose,
Darkening even the noonday sun;
The breath of the world seemed nearly undone,
And heavy the air through which it flows.

The stormwinds howled, the embers flew,
They struck our ranks with brutal might;
We lived by mercy, not by right—
By fate's thin thread our spirits drew.

Then sudden stillness quelled the roar,
And through the haze of battle's crown,
We saw them standing, battered down,
The foes who would contend no more.

The dragon in wrath breathed flame anew,
And Praedo met fire with water's cry;
But deeper power he called from the sky,
And light from his hands in brilliance flew.

First came the bolts of azure hue,
Then came the thunder's vaulted scream;
From heaven descended a burning gleam—
Had the dragon met its doom at last too?

The beast was falling, fierce no more,
And with it fell through smoke and flame
Two silver tears, my eyes to claim—
The long oppression's weight was o'er.

Years of bondage, of wounds and fears,
Of futile seeking and bitter pain,
Were ended now—our hearts regained,
The peace long drowned in blood and tears.

XII
Canticum Sanationis

The Healer's Magic

There was perfect silence, all was calm, at rest,
No thunder, nor lightning, no loud fiery sound,
The clouds, humbly parted, made way all around,
For a pillar golden to descend from west.

And there, midst the column of glory and light,
With breastplate now shattered, his helm split apart,
His face bruised and dirtied, yet joy in his heart,
Praedo, smiling, joyful, came down from the sky.

It was all completed, we were fin'lly free,
The songs of great gladness returned to the soul,
Like waters soft flowing, the praises made whole,
Exalting brave Praedo, his courage and deeds.

But alas! The earth, the grove once divine,
The rivers, the meadows, all destroyed, decayed,
And there in the ruins, injured, almost dead,
The thirteen brave warriors whom Praedo assigned.

The hero himself was not free from pain,
His proud chest was bleeding, his strength nearly gone,
Yet weak as he faltered, his will carried on,
And showed the last magic we needed to learn.

He asked his companions to come, one by one,
And upon their heads his two hands he laid,
He murmured old verses in a distant tongue,
And with gentle power, he healed every face.

With what life remained in his dying frame,
He knelt on the soil, lifeless, torn, yet dear,
And thinking of us, with death drawing near,
He healed mighty rivers, the woods, and the plains.

The forests returned with their emerald hue,
The rivers shone clear like bright crystal streams,
The meadows adorned in gold, white, and green,
But Praedo's face paled as snow's icy blue.

With the breath so faint that still left his chest,
He called his friends close and gave them command:
"Carve beads from my bones, as fate may demand,
That I may yet teach you from my place of rest."

No more did he speak, as his eyes grew still,
His lips, softly smiling, lay calm as he passed,
His deeds may be finished, but echoes will last,
For his songs of valor the ages will fill.

Epilogue

Much have I spoken of Praedo the brave,
Yet little was told of the friend we knew well,
A brother, beloved, in kindness he dwelled,
A heart full of mercy, gentle, pure and grave.

Praedo's great power lay not in the blade,
Nor armor, nor magic, nor bone's sacred thread,
His strength was the truth that his spirit spread,
The faith and conviction he always displayed.

Twelve were his virtues, twelve powers he bore,
Twelve were the magics Praedo passed on,
All held in secret, though never quite gone,
Within the heart's depths forevermore.

The years have now passed, and in solitude,
I've sought my shelter, far from human crowds,
Among the high mountains and under the clouds,
Within the green woods Praedo once renewed.

And now, I've grown old, in a cavern I stay,
And search with my lyre for perfect refrain,
Till under the echoes of earth's arcane,
A deep song of bones calls my heart to play.

I carry the tale of Praedo with me,
His magic, his legacy, close to my breast,
His spirit I've guarded, his memory blessed,
And now I release it with this, my song, free.

Follow these verses to where they shall end,
Where both our stories shall join and resign,
And may his old bones your strength now refine,
When the dragon rises to battle again.

ACKNOWLEDGEMENTS

As this trilogy comes to an end, I am grateful to everyone who helped me over the past six years. It's difficult to put yourself and your art onto the page and send it out into the world. All of the love, advice, and encouragement kept me going. Thank you!

As always, much love and gratitude goes to the Potted Plant, my wonderful writing community. I'm here because of you. To Michael Roth for his fantastic plotting skills, I'm especially grateful because he generously gave of his time while working on his masters. I can't gush enough about my beta reading team: Laura Blegen and Kim Appersbach—you're the reason what I turn in is presentable. A special thank you to Marie Parks and Keith McCormick for understanding what I've been going through, encouraging me, and giving me love and hugs.

To my wonderful friends and family I grew up with, and whom I drew on for inspiration: Jyll Hambre, Lorenzo Frazier, Gregg Frazier, Jeanie (Brenda Jean) Robison, Noreen Harriette Hosack, John Moulton Hosack, Jeff Hosack (sorry about your character—it was Michael's idea!) Rindy (Clarinda) Zabkiewics, Larry Frazier Sr., Melissa Behar, Mike Pruett, Daniel George, and Jack and Victoria—sorry I don't recall your last names! Many on this list have passed, and I'm sad they didn't get to read my story.

To Lorenzo Frazier for making life fun, and inspiring me to want to write about it. Thank you for always having my back, and for plotting our book so I could know the ending of this one. Lastly, for giving me a safe space to finish this book—I am forever grateful.

To Space Wizard Science Fantasy—you're the best! To Courtney Brooks for editing my mess (I'm learning!), and to Katie Cordy for my wonderful covers. I absolutely love the cover for The Healer's Magic! Lastly to William C. Tracy for taking on my little adopted girl. I love working with your edits. I hope this story lives up to your fabulous catalog of stories.

One last giant thank you to Lehonti Perez Ovalle for his truly EPIC poem! It's a masterpiece and you're amazing!

ABOUT THE AUTHOR

CJ grew up in Southern California loving fantasy and science fiction. She has four children, and an ever-growing number of grandchildren. Adopted at eight months old, she recently found her birth parents. She has a Masters Degree in Public History from Southern New Hampshire University, and if she's not writing you can generally find her quilting, costuming, or traveling to spend time with those she loves. She's a wannabe dress historian, and has worked with museums on historical dress recreation. The Slayer's Magic and The Traveler's Magic are the first two books in The Beads of Bone series. You can find CJ at her website cjhosack.com and on Instagram @cj_hosack

Please take a moment to review this book at your favorite retailer's website, Goodreads, or simply tell your friends!

www.ingramcontent.com/pod-product-compliance
Lightning Source LLC
LaVergne TN
LVHW040133080526
838202LV00042B/2889